THE MIRACLE LIFE OF EDGAR MINT

Brady Udall, author of the highly praised *Letting Loose the Hounds*, teaches at Franklin Marshall University in Pennsylvania.

ALSO BY BRADY UDALL

Letting Loose the Hounds

THE
MIRACLE
LIFE

OF

Edgar Mint

A NOVEL

BRADY UDALL

JONATHAN CAPE
LONDON

Published by Jonathan Cape 2001

2 4 6 8 10 9 7 5 3

Copyright © Brady Udall 2001

First published in Great Britain in 2001 by
Jonathan Cape
Random House, 20 Vauxhall Bridge Road,
London SW1V 2SA

Random House Australia (Pty) Limited
20 Alfred Street, Milsons Point, Sydney,
New South Wales 2061, Australia

Random House New Zealand Limited
18 Poland Road, Glenfield,
Auckland 10, New Zealand

Random House (Pty) Limited
Endulini, 5A Jubilee Road, Parktown 2193, South Africa

The Random House Group Limited Reg. No. 954009
www.randomhouse.co.uk

A CIP catalogue record for this book
is available from the British Library

ISBN 0-224-05057-5

Papers used by The Random House Group Limited are natural, recy-
clable products made from wood grown in sustainable forests:
the manufacturing processes conform to the environmental
regulations of the country of origin

Printed and bound in Great Britain by
Biddles Ltd, Guildford & King's Lynn

for my parents,
Barry and Risa Udall,
who gave me everything

Acknowledgments

I'd like to offer my thanks to the National Endowment for the Arts for financial assistance and to the people of the Fort Apache Reservation for their many kindnesses. For their time, patience and expertise, thanks to Leon Metts, Edgar Perry, Canyon Quintero, Odette Fuller, Michael Lacapa, Dr. Ron Rudy and Father Tony Ugolnik. I owe a serious debt to Darrell Spencer and Peter Rudy for wading through this stack of pages and telling me where I went wrong. And my deepest gratitude goes to Carol Houck Smith and Nicole Aragi, who have done right by me every time.

Contents

SAINT DIVINE'S / 11

WILLIE SHERMAN / 97

RICHLAND / 237

STONY RUN / 389

SAINT

DIVINE'S

I F I COULD tell you only one thing about my life it would be this: when I was seven years old the mailman ran over my head. As formative events go, nothing else comes close; my careening, zigzag existence, my wounded brain and faith in God, my collisions with joy and affliction, all of it has come, in one way or another, out of that moment on a summer morning when the left rear tire of a United States postal jeep ground my tiny head into the hot gravel of the San Carlos Apache Indian Reservation.

It was a typical July day, ten o'clock and already pushing a hundred, the whole world lit with a painful white light. Our house was particularly vulnerable to the heat because, unlike the other HUD houses on the road, it was covered with black tar paper—the siding had never been put on—and there were no shade trees, not even a bush to block the sun. There was an old lightning-struck cottonwood in the front yard, a charred skeleton of a tree that offered no shade at all until my mother got into the habit of hanging beer cans from its charred branches with fishing line. The beer cans—there were hundreds of them, and more than a dozen new ones being added each day—would make a peaceful clanking when a breeze came up, but they never did much to keep the house cool.

When the mailman stopped in front of our house that day my mother was in the cave-like darkness of the kitchen polishing off breakfast (four Pabst Blue Ribbons and half a tray of ice cubes) and Grandma Paul was out back under the bear grass ramada in her traditional skirt and Mickey Mouse sweatshirt, grinding acorns and managing not to perspire. I was outside somewhere poking around in the weeds by the side of the road, or maybe wreaking havoc on a hill of fire ants—I guess it doesn't really matter where I was or what I was doing.

What matters is that the mailman, a small bird-boned man with sweaty orange hair that looked like the inside of a pumpkin, put his jeep into park and went to have a word with my mother. What matters is that during the time he was gone, something—God only knows what—compelled me to crawl under that jeep. Maybe I saw something intriguing under there—a page from a catalogue or a stray hubcap—or maybe the purple rectangle of shadow under the jeep seemed like a good place to cool off. I have to wonder: is it possible that seven-year-old Edgar, with his perpetually drunk and heartsick mother and his disappeared father—not to mention his crazy witch of a grandmother—might have considered suicide? Is it possible that Edgar, seven years old and tired of it all, simply laid down his head under the tire of that jeep and waited?

From the little I know of my life until then, it's not a possibility I could rule out entirely. Even with my less-than-ideal childhood, one of the small regrets I carry around with me is that huge parts of that boy are lost to me forever; I have a broken, leaking memory of him at best. I guess this wouldn't bother most people—who remembers what seven years old was like anyway?—but for me, obsessed with memory, with facts, with history on the smallest scale, obsessed not only with the whys but the simple whos and whats and wheres, it is a nagging absence, like the gap a knocked-out tooth leaves. I know more about total strangers than I do about seven-year-old Edgar; I'll never know what his favorite TV commercial was or where he hid all the worthless knickknacks he collected or what he feared most when he had to visit the shithouse in the middle of the night. I'll never know why he crawled under that jeep.

I do know, though, what happened when the bird-boned mailman

got back behind the steering wheel of his mail jeep, released the emergency brake and stepped on the accelerator. When he felt the jeep
labor against some resistance—maybe he thought it was a bump or a
rock in the road—he gave it a little more juice. The back end of the
jeep rose up sharply, dropped back down, and the engine died. The
mailman got out to investigate and when he saw my little body under
the bumper of the jeep, my face mashed into the gravel of the road,
blood already seeping among the shards of black rock as if welling up
from a place deep underground, he screamed so loud that the dogs in
the vicinity, most of them hairless renegades used to the worst and
loudest kinds of shouting and drunken argument, howled in terror.

Along the street only a few people came out of their houses, holding their arms against the sun. Grandma Paul took her time picking
her way around the woodpile and up to the road: she knew someone
was dead or dying, it was just a matter of finding out who. She saw
five or six people crowded around and a few more coming out of
their houses and she decided it had to be a pretty bloody disaster to
bring people out on a day like this. Even a couple of huge, roadkill-
fattened crows had landed in the beer-tree to see what was going on.

"Goddamn mail guy's run over somebody's kid," said big Emerson
Tuskogie to nobody in particular, sucking down the last of his Coke
through a straw. Emerson Tuskogie was well known on the reservation
as somebody who held the government responsible for everything.

By the time Grandma Paul had made it to the scene, ten or twelve
people were looking down at the sobbing mailman, who had rolled
me over onto my back and taken off his shirt, which he held around
my head in an attempt to stop the blood from seeping out of my ears.

When the mailman realized he couldn't stem the bleeding with only
his flimsy government-issue shirt, he took off his pants—an almost
impossible task the way his hands were shaking—and pressed them
around my head as if he might somehow keep the blood inside where
it belonged. Everyone stared at his fiery hair and mayonnaise-colored
skin, which seemed to be glowing, putting off a light of its own.

"Ambulance?!" he cried, looking around wildly. Old Oonie Neal had already sent her grandson off to call the tribal police, but nobody bothered to say a word.

The mailman put his ear to my chest, heard nothing, then looked into my eyes, the whites of which had turned a stark demon-red from the capillaries bursting under all that pressure. He looked up into the sun as if he might find some kind of answer there, but this seemed to disorient him even more. Finally, still holding my head in its bundle of clothes, he lowered his mouth over mine and began breathing into me, even though my lungs and respiratory system were fine—it was my head that was the problem.

"Ambulance'll be coming," someone said, but the mailman kept on, blowing into me with everything he had. Blood gargled up out of my throat, making it difficult to get any air into me at all.

Emerson Tuskogie politely tapped the nearly naked mailman on the shoulder and said, "Kid's dead."

Everybody pretty much agreed with Emerson on this point, even Grandma Paul; you don't run over some kid's head with a mail jeep and hope to keep him going with a little CPR.

The crows looked down and seemed to whisper between themselves, the sun burned and the poor mailman had nothing left to do but kneel on the sharp rocks in the incomplete shade of the beer-tree, half naked and shuddering, his face covered with tears and snot, his mouth rimmed with my blood, holding his clothes around my head, waiting for the ambulance to come and take me away.

THE RODEO

I DON'T BLAME my mother for not coming out of the house that day. When she heard the mailman scream she knew, just like Grandma Paul, that something terrible had happened and she didn't want anything to do with it. She stayed in her chair at the kitchen table and didn't move, didn't even stand up to stretch her legs until late that night when there was no longer anyone around who would fetch her a beer. From all that I know about her, my mother never was the kind of person who liked to confront things head-on; she was always standing back, protecting herself. It's one of the reasons she drank so much beer—if you drink enough of it, beer can protect you from anything.

Until she became pregnant with me my mother had never tasted beer or alcohol of any kind. Grandma Paul's father and brother and both her sons had all died as a result of alcohol in one way or another and she forbade Gloria, her last living child, to touch the stuff. My mother obeyed Grandma without question—never even had a drop—until she was eighteen years old. It would take becoming pregnant with me to turn her into the dedicated alcoholic she would be for the rest of her life.

"She was a good girl," Grandma Paul used to say, "and then she met the white guy."

The white guy was my father, Arnold Kessler Mint. Arnold Mint was a would-be cowboy, and fittingly enough, he met my mother at a rodeo. He was only a spectator at the rodeo, though he had aspirations of becoming a bronc-busting star, and my mother was selling cotton candy in the grandstands. This was up north in Holbrook, where my mother was living with her cousin Lily for the summer, trying to get away from Grandma Paul and the dusty desolation of San Carlos and hoping to make a little money in the meantime. She was eighteen and probably not prepared for someone as good-looking and charmingly dumb as Arnold Kessler Mint.

After seeing my mother, the first thing Arnold did was buy all the cotton candy she had in her tray. He had just finished a two-month stint on a sheep ranch in Luna, New Mexico, his wallet was fat with bills, and he was working on growing a respectable mustache. He gave my mother a ten-dollar bill, lifted all the cotton candy out of the tray, and squeezed it to his chest in a great bear hug. He looked around, unsure what to do next, then took a big chomp out of the mound in his arms—a long wisp sticking to his chin, making him look like Uncle Sam on the I WANT YOU FOR THE U.S. ARMY poster— and said to everybody around him, "Boy, I love cotton candy!" This was his way of trying to impress my mother. My mother handed Arnold Kessler Mint his change and went back to the concession stand to pick up more cotton candy. When she had a new supply she went to the far side of the grandstands, as far away from Arnold as she could get, but he spotted her and waved his money in the air like a hankie.

Arnold Mint was trying his best to be the big, brash, the-hell-with-the-rest-of-you cowboy he had always wanted to be. He was originally from Lebanon, Connecticut, about as far away from cowboy country as you can get. He had come out West two years before, thinking he could hitch on with some outfit and become a carefree whistling buckaroo in no time flat—he'd read the comic books and every Zane Grey novel he could get his hands on, signed up for the John Wayne fan club and watched all the shoot-em-ups on TV; he believed he was ready and qualified to start punching cattle. No, it didn't go the way he planned. He spent his first eighteen months in Arizona washing toilets and hauling horse carcasses for a dog food factory. There simply wasn't a pack of ranchers falling over each other to hire an Easterner with corduroy pants and a funny accent. Finally, two months before meeting my mother, Arnold, in spite of his corduroy pants, had got a shearing job with a desperate sheep rancher and now that the job was over, here he was at the Navajo County Rodeo, feeling pretty good about himself with money in his pockets (he had already spent thirteen dollars of it on a mouse-gray Stetson cowboy hat), an armful of cotton candy and designs on my mother.

If Arnold had been a true cowboy he probably wouldn't have looked twice at my mother. Among cowboys—white ones, any-way—you kept to your own kind. Hispanic or Asian girls were okay for a one-nighter, but Indian girls, or Big Reds as most cowboys called them, were pretty much out of the question. According to under-the-hat barstool cowboy lore, Indian women had the unholy power to get themselves impregnated with your sperm one hundred percent of the time, whether you wore a condom or not. This little bit of hoodoo-voodoo, more than anything else, is often what—at least in terms of romance—kept the cowboys away from the Indians.

But to Arnold Kessler Mint, who wasn't yet aware of these cowboy codes, an eighteen-year-old raven-haired Apache girl must have been the most exotic thing he could imagine. My mother marched up and down the steps trying to ignore Arnold, but the thick-necked guy in the new cowboy hat (there was still a tag hanging off the brim) would not give up. He waggled his money in the air, whistling and hollering for more cotton candy. By now he was so covered with the fluffy pink and blue stuff he looked like a huge baby bird just out of its shell.

Nobody had ever given my mother such attention, especially not in public and with two thousand people looking on. She didn't know what to do, so she wandered up and down the grandstand steps, trying to hide behind the remaining puffs in her tray.

Arnold bided his time until the call came over the loudspeakers for amateur bull riders. Anybody who had the desire could try their luck on an old worn-out bull named Wicked Joseph. A rider who could manage to stay on for the required ten seconds would win a fifty-dollar gift certificate from the B&B Williams Tack and Feed Store. Besides Arnold, the only other person who took the challenge was a fat teenage kid in a too-tight T-shirt who appeared to be drunk; he pumped his knees and shook his butt as he went down the steps, which made the considerable fat contained in his shirt jiggle and heave. Everybody in the stands clapped and hooted and agreed there's not much that can beat a fat drunk kid for entertainment. Not to be outdone, Arnold promenaded down the steps, kicking his heels and throwing his hips around like a belly dancer—but the drunk fat kid had been much funnier, so only one or two people bothered to give Arnold any encouragement.

The fat teenager went first and he fell off the bull—right into a

fresh puddle of cow shit—before he made it out of the chute.
Wicked Joseph never even got a chance to buck; the big gate swung
open and the kid slid right off the old bull as if it had been slathered
back to front with petroleum jelly. The kid picked himself off the
ground, half covered in green, pudding-like bull puckey, raised both
chubby fists in victory, and the crowd went crazy for him.

Undaunted that he was getting one-upped by a fat drunk kid,
Arnold got on Wicked Joseph. He stayed on the bull well over the
required ten seconds; he stayed on so well that once the horn had
sounded, he didn't really want or know how to get off. The old
Brahma kept bucking away, his gargantuan balls flailing like cathedral
bells between his legs, and Arnold, holding on with two hands now,
began to slip slowly off to the side, managing to hang on by wrapping both arms around the bull's neck and squeezing with such conviction that he looked like he was trying to strangle the thing.
Wicked Joseph, who was, I imagine, thoroughly annoyed with
Arnold's persistence, situated himself in a corner of the ring and
began ramming Arnold into a steel livestock gate, which made a
boom-boom-boom noise like somebody banging on a battleship with a
sledgehammer. Still Arnold hung on, his brand-new, jammed-on hat
getting loose from his head, quarters and nickels and dimes zinging
out of his pockets, his big round face still caught in that oblivious
grin. All around the arena cowboys were standing up on the fence,
cussing and shouting, "Let go you idiot!"

Finally Arnold was rammed into the gate with enough force that
his collarbone was broken and he had to relinquish his death grip on
poor old Wicked Joseph. Even with the broken bone he hopped
right up, looked around and yelled, "Where's my hat?" An exhausted
Wicked Joseph galloped a wide U-turn and made a halfhearted
attempt at goring Arnold in the back, but Arnold spotted him and
scrambled through the slats in the fence. This time the crowd was
duly appreciative; Arnold got a standing ovation.

After locating his hat, accepting his fifty-dollar certificate and having his shoulder inspected by the on-site doctor, who told him to get

his crazy ass to a hospital as soon as possible, Arnold tracked down my
mother near the concession stand. He stood next to her, his face still
flushed from his bull-riding triumph. She tried not to look at him
while she waited for the concessions manager to count out her pay;
she had seen him ride the bull and thought he was a lunatic.

He cleared his throat like he was preparing for a speech. "I'd—hah—
I'd like to ask you a favor, you know, help out a guy a little," he said.

Arnold took off his hat, which had been destroyed by one of
Wicked Joseph's hooves, peered at it for a second and put it back on
his head, where it clung like a clump of old moss. He pointed to his
broken right shoulder, which slumped a good two or three inches
below his left. "Looks like I broke my shoulder bone here and I was
wondering what would be the chances of you helping me out. My
rig's got a manual transmission and I need someone to help me shift
so's I can make it to the hospital. The doctor over there with the hair
sticking out his ears said I could do some damage to myself if I don't
get there this very instant."

Arnold was doing his very damnedest to sound like a cowboy.

This time my mother glared at him with her oily-black eyes, hoping to scare him off, but Arnold Kessler Mint was not the kind of person who knew how to take a hint. He pressed on: "Anyhow, I got this
gift certificate—it's worth fifty dollars and I'll give it to you if you'd
help me out." He paused, rubbing his bad shoulder. He couldn't stop
smiling. Finally, he said, "Fifty dollars is a lot of money."

My mother didn't take long to decide; even though she thought
Arnold was the strangest person she'd ever met, fifty dollars *was* a lot
of money, more than she would make in her three days at the rodeo.
She thought of the dresses she could buy, the nice shoes—she
thought about getting herself a pair of sunglasses like Marilyn
Monroe wore in *Some Like It Hot*. My poor mother wasn't aware that
the gift certificate was for a feed and tack store.

With his good arm, Arnold guided my mother out to the parking
lot, opened the door to his old, dented Ford, and helped her in.
Down the road they went: Arnold, my father, worked the pedals and

the steering wheel and Gloria, my mother, shifted. Exactly nine
months and two days later I was born.

THE AMBULANCE

A GLOWING-WHITE mailman weeping over a boy with a broken head
leaking blood and spinal fluid out of his ears, a throng of Apaches
standing back at a safe distance, an old grandmother off to the side in
the hackberry, already beginning her funeral wail, two fat crows in a
tree full of blue-and-white cans presiding over it all: this is the scene
Ed and Horace Natchez, twin brothers and tribal ambulance volunteers, came upon when they pulled up in the makeshift reservation
ambulance. Ed and Horace lived only a quarter of a mile from
Grandma Paul's house, and they were pissed off that there hadn't been
enough open road for them to really get that ambulance hauling ass.

It should be noted that what Ed and Horace were riding in was
not a true ambulance. It was actually a huge black Dodge van the
tribal police had recently confiscated from a group of German hippies who had been caught selling marijuana from the side of the
highway. Nobody had gotten around to painting it yet, and there was
no money in the budget to outfit it with modern emergency equipment. All it had was an oxygen tank, an emergency field kit no bigger than a bass fisherman's tackle box, and a World War II army
stretcher someone had found in the cellar of the elementary school.
It wasn't much, but as could be said about most things on the reservation, it was better than nothing.

Ed and Horace had only minimal training, so when they got their first
good look at me, they came to the same conclusion everybody else had:
the boy with the mailman's clothes wadded around his head was a goner.
They didn't even bother with any pulse-taking or pupil-checking, they

simply pried the mailman's hands away from the boy's shoulder and gently put the limp body on the stretcher, which, in its time, might have transported wounded boys on the battlefields of France or Okinawa.

"Hey, will you guys bring me back a pack of Pall Malls from Globe?" Emerson Tuskogie asked. Emerson had to shout to be heard over Grandma Paul's wailing.

"Don't got no money!" Ed shouted back.

Emerson began digging through his pockets for change while Ed and Horace got the stretcher situated in the back of the van.

Horace took the clothes from around the dead boy's head and handed the bloody clump to the mailman, who knelt in the gravel, his face gone blank.

"You don't want to get sunburned," Horace told him.

Ed shut the heavy rear door of the van and Emerson said, "Damn, I only got thirty-five cents."

Off in the mesquite bushes, Grandma Paul's praying got even louder. She prayed to Jesus, and to Yusen, god of all living things, and to the ghosts of the dead. She prayed not that I would survive, but that I would find my way through the perils of the afterlife, that I would be free from the wily clutches of the devil and make my way home to Jesus. Grandma Paul wailed and prayed and paused only for a second to watch as Ed and Horace got into their seats, slammed the van's big black doors and started out over the damaged reservation roads, carrying me away into a strange new life.

THE RESURRECTION OF EDGAR

FOR ME, IT'S a little hard to accept—my own death and I have no recollection of it. Like most of what occurred in the first seven years of my life, I'll have to take someone else's word that it ever happened.

All I can say for certain is that at some point between the time the tire flattened my head and I was wheeled into the tiny emergency room of St. Divine's Hospital in Globe, I stopped living. My ravaged brain threw in the towel and my other vital organs gave in shortly thereafter. My heart quivered to a stop, my lungs shut down and I became an inanimate object; just as alive or dead as a cereal bowl or a park bench.

It was a young, baby-faced doctor named Barry Pinkley who decided he was going to bring me back from the land of the dead. Any other doctor would have taken one look at me, recorded an approximate time of death and called the hospital chaplain. Not spitfire Barry Pinkley, a graduate of Johns Hopkins who had recently finished his residency at Hartfell Memorial in downtown New Orleans, where he saw enough grisliness and gore to make a combat surgeon shudder. It was only Barry's second day at St. Divine's and he was so thoroughly bored with the slow pace of everything that when a seven-year-old half-breed was brought in with a crushed head and no vital signs, he decided he was going to liven things up and perform a miracle.

Barry later said, with a touch of doctorly arrogance, that he was not about to see his first real patient head for the morgue instead of the ICU. (He had had two previous patients, who, in his mind, didn't count: a man with a fishhook in his eyelid and a two-year-old girl who had swallowed half a quart of motor oil.)

The first thing Barry did after checking little Edgar's vital signs was to start an IV and insert a tube down his throat. After half a minute when no pulse came, he took the next step: chest percussion. Instead of placing his palms on the boy's sternum and pumping, as you often see in the movies, Barry hammered on little Edgar's chest with the meaty part of his fist and he was not at all shy about it: he lifted his arm over his head as if the boy was a vampire and he was going to drive a stake into the heart of him. He pounded him with such force that the small body jumped a few inches off the gurney and the attending nurses gasped and backed away as if Barry might go after them next.

It took twelve solid hammerblows to the chest, he told me later, to persuade my heart to start pumping again. "Wherever you were, you must have liked it there," he said. "I had to beat the hell out of you just to get you to come back."

After that, Barry couldn't do much more than give me a shot of steroids in hopes of bringing the swelling around my brain down. Barry reluctantly allowed me to be rushed to Phoenix (in a real ambulance this time) where a neurosurgeon was waiting. Barry had brought me back, and like Dr. Frankenstein who gave the monster life, I think Barry felt a kind of ownership toward me, a responsibility. He didn't like it at all when he had to relinquish me to the care of a two-thousand-dollar-an-hour champion neuro-surgeon.

This neurosurgeon didn't do much more than give my head a few X rays, staple the jigsaw-puzzle pieces of my skull back in place, and drill a few burr-holes from which fluid and blood could be drained. After the three-hour operation he snapped off his gloves and told the attending nurses he'd buy them all dinner and drinks if I made it through the night.

I stayed in Phoenix less than a month. Everyone agreed that my survival was either an absolute miracle or a freak happenstance, how-ever you wanted to look at it, but there was also general agreement that simple survival was as far as the miracle would go: there was no chance on earth I was going to be anything but the mental and phys-ical equivalent of a turnip. Even though I was off the respirator with-in two weeks, even though my heart was strong, they simply couldn't believe that a brain which had received such trauma could ever work properly again. That is why they shipped me back to Globe. The offi-cial reason for sending me back was that I would be closer to my family. The real reason was that they wanted to fill my bed with somebody who actually had a chance.

EDGAR IN A COMA

SO FAR, EVERYTHING I've told you is secondhand, no more reliable than gossip in church. It is my story, but all I've related until now either happened out of my presence or while I was unconscious or dead. A small luxury, then, to be finally getting to a portion of my life I can actually remember.

After three months in a coma, I guess the only thing dramatic about little Edgar's return to consciousness was that nobody expected it. I had been shoved into a corner of a room which I shared with three men who were quite pleased to have a new roommate so quiet and unassuming, so perfectly well behaved.

Edgar lay in his bed completely still, like a fish on ice, the windows and doors of his brain nailed down tight. After a week or two they pretty much forgot about him—he was nothing more than a piece of unused furniture pushed into the corner of the room. He was especially easy to disregard because during those entire three months he never once had a visitor.

Not that I was completely ignored; each day doctors shone penlights into my eyes, raked their knuckles across my chest, dug their fingers into my eye sockets, pressed the point of a paper clip or a pencil into the beds of my fingernails, did whatever they could to get a response, any response at all. Orderlies massaged my muscles and worked my joints, nurses changed my IV bottles and bedpans, all of them thinking the same thing: *What an incredible waste of time.*

At some point toward the end of those three months, my brain began to make brief forays into consciousness. I can't say I was exactly *conscious* during those times; I did not think or want or feel pain. But some small part of my mind would whir to life temporarily, like a pump priming itself, and record what was going on around me. I know this because, even though I was in a coma, there are things I remember.

I remember those damn penlights. I remember the voice of the intercom in the hall, deep and disembodied like the voice of God, calling doctors here and there, making pronouncements. I remember snatches of conversations, the *clink-clink* of silverware on trays, the subterranean rumble of the mining machinery outside, the nurses' shoes busily beating the floors like rubber hammers. I remember, word for word, a conversation between two young men—they must have been orderlies—right above my bed:

Orderly one: "I don't know, man, it's like everyone on TV is *shouting* at me. It's scary. It's like every room I go into the TV is *yelling* at me."

Orderly two: "How much of that tab did you drop?"

Orderly one: "All of it."

Orderly two: "All of it! I told you to drop, what, half of it maybe?"

Orderly one: "You don't know what it's like to walk into a room and have Walter Cronkite start *screaming* at you. It's exactly the kind of thing that makes me nervous."

Orderly two: "The whole tab!"

Orderly one: "You should hear what he said to me."

Orderly two: "Who?"

Orderly one: "Walter Cronkite."

Orderly two: "Shit."

Orderly one: "He called me a *hairbag*."

Orderly two: "A what?"

Orderly one: "You heard me."

Orderly two: "Geez. Maybe you'll listen to me next time then."

Orderly one: "Well at least this kid is peaceful. He keeps his mouth shut. He's a nice kid as far as I'm concerned."

Orderly two: "It's the cops that ran him over. He's nice and peaceful because of the cops."

I remember some of the dreams I began to have, too: brief, claustrophobic hallucinations that only an eight-year-old boy (during my coma I'd had a birthday) in a semi-unconscious state could have:

flying hamburgers and cartoon pigs with fangs and malfunctioning robots throwing themselves out of trees on top of me. I remember doctors whispering to each other about their sexual fantasies involving a certain nurse, nurses bitching about the doctors and the ungrateful patients, patients complaining about the doctors, the nurses and the food.

And suddenly, as if a switch had turned on somewhere, I began to smell things. To this day the smell of ammonia cleaner, the kind they mop floors with, makes me physically sick. The way the nurses smelled, some like sweat, others like soap or perfume; the garlic breath of the doctors as they checked my pupils for the thousandth time; the smell of gauze soaked with mucus and needing to be changed—salty, fecund and dead. There was the chance whiff of flowers, the weak stench of my own shit, and the overpowering smell, almost a rival to the ammonia floor cleaner, of Art Crozier's cheap cologne.

Art was the patient in the bed next to mine. His face was the first thing, after three months in the dark, that I laid eyes on.

My coming out of my coma was a gradual thing; there was not a scene, like in movies and soap operas, where I suddenly sat up and asked for a hot fudge sundae and the *New York Times*. During the last weeks of my three months of coma, the doctors noticed that I was showing signs of life—I was beginning to react to some stimuli, I was moving my limbs during the night. Then one bright afternoon I opened my eyes and looked around. And there was Art, his small, terrifying face hanging over me. Luckily, my vision was screwed up by the utter whiteness of the place. Everything in hospitals is white—white walls, white floors, white sheets, white people walking around in white clothes. Why so much white? I have no idea. I only know that whiteness and all the ricocheting light it creates can be a shock to the retinas of somebody who's been living in a world of black for so long. So I really wasn't aware that the misshapen thing in front of me was actually a face.

"Lookit!" Art shouted through his reconstructed mouth, loud

enough to make my eardrums ring. His voice carried like a shout in a cave. "The kid's got his eyeballs open!"

It wasn't long before there was a crowd of doctors, nurses and other patients gathered around my bed. Someone would move and I could see an after-image of that person moving slowly behind, like a spirit too slow for its body. People were muttering, elbowing in, jockeying for position. I wanted nothing to do with any of it, with the light, with the roaring, obnoxious noise. I worked at my tongue, which felt like a hunk of old bread. There was one word in my head, and that word croaked out of my mouth, dusty and hoarse: "No."

That got a response. I had intended to shut everyone up but it only made things worse; the real griping and jostling started, the doctors giving out orders, the nurses calling for the orderlies to clear the room, the patients protesting and complaining. Over the din, in his booming voice, Art hollered, "Give the child some space, got-*dangit*!"

I shut my eyes tight, hoping to block it all out, but there was nothing I could do; for better or worse I was back in the world.

A RESERVATION ROMANCE

IF MY LIFE could be contained in a word it would be this one: accidents. Not only do I share in a notorious family history of calamity and accident, not only was I involved in a life-altering accident at age seven, not only would I be involved in a few more accidents in my time, I actually *was* an accident; as you might have imagined, my birth was not a planned one.

Two days after leaving the rodeo together my mother and Arnold Kessler Mint checked into the Wig Wam Motel on Highway 70 just west of Holbrook. At the Wig Wam tourists could pay for the privilege of spending a night in one of twenty-five thirty-foot-high pink or purple (your choice) cement teepees which were furnished with a bathroom, a TV and a vibrating bed. It was off-season, only a few Japanese tourists were about clutching rubber tomahawks and snapping pictures of everything in sight, so Arnold was able to convince the manager to give them a discount rate for the week.

I don't believe my mother ever really knew what she was getting into. In a family of drinkers and daredevils, my mother was the reserved one, the cherished and protected little girl who never had a drink until she became pregnant with me, who never had sex until, at age eighteen, she slept in a purple cement teepee with a white man named Arnold Kessler Mint.

During that week they had alone together, Arnold blew his whole savings, everything he had made shearing and tending sheep, on my mother. He treated her to huge pancake breakfasts, took her to the movies, bought her perfume and dresses and a pair of dark green alligator-hide pumps that she would cherish above all her other possessions. Arnold Kessler Mint was in love.

And what about my mother? I don't know if she was in love with Arnold then; to her, this week spent at the Wig Wam Motel might have been nothing more than her first fling in the big wide world, but the fact is, if she didn't love him then, my mother came to love Arnold in a way that would color the rest of her life. I like to think that at least she had that week of freedom and unrestraint, because things were going to turn sour very shortly.

First of all, there was Grandma Paul, waiting down in San Carlos. Grandma Paul was not known as a patient woman, or a forgiving one, or even a particularly nice one, and she was overprotective of her daughter. She had already lost her husband and two sons to early deaths and the world be damned if she was going to lose her last surviving child to a white man.

When my mother showed up in front of the little house sitting shotgun in Arnold's blue '56 Ford, Grandma Paul marched out across the weed-ridden front yard and yanked my mother out of Arnold's pickup as if she was pulling her from a house in flames. Grandma Paul was not a big woman, but she locked both hands around my mother's elbow and began towing her toward the house, my mother screaming protests, Grandma Paul cursing my mother in shrill, arm-shaking bursts, and Arnold Mint standing next to his truck, grinning and sweating like somebody was holding a gun to his head.

Grandma Paul wrestled her all the way to the front door before my mother was able to break free and sprint back to where Arnold was standing. She was able to tell him, in a whispered rush, that he should leave and come back tomorrow, that they could meet at noon out by the stop sign—and then Grandma Paul was on her again, pulling on her shirt and rearing back like a tiny, determined dog.

Arnold got into his pickup and rode away. He drove slowly down the cratered dirt road and waved to the people who had come out of their houses to see what Grandma Paul was up to now, but nobody waved back. Arnold didn't know what to do; he was nearly out of cash and he surmised, correctly, that spending the night alone on the reservation might not be the best idea. He ended up driving to Globe, where he bought a ten-cent hot dog for dinner and spent the night in the back of his pickup in the parking lot of the Safeway.

In the meantime, my mother did what she could to convince Grandma Paul that Arnold was nothing more than a stranger kind enough to give her a ride home from Holbrook, but Grandma Paul was sharper than that—she could see that my mother was not the same girl who had left for Holbrook three weeks before. She moved differently, she had a giddy, wild look in her eye, she even smelled different; Grandma Paul could smell the love on her as if she had rolled in a pile of compost.

Somehow, Arnold and my mother were able to find ways to meet. There wasn't much Grandma Paul could do; my mother had changed from a submissive, obedient girl to one who would suddenly charge out the front door and down the dirt road to a prearranged meeting place with Arnold, Grandma Paul trailing behind and shouting curses until her old lungs gave out. My mother would come home late at night or early the next morning, smelling of sex and cigarette smoke, and there was nothing Grandma Paul could do but hope that white guy would come around again so she could personally put the fear of Jesus in him.

THE ACCIDENTAL FOUR

SO THAT'S IT: little Edgar woke up from three months of coma and croaked, "No." Not as much drama as one might hope, but a miracle just the same. That word: miracle. Edgar heard it two dozen times a day at St. Divine's, heard it so much that the hard-syllabled sound of it made the pain in his head flare like a bad tooth. The nurses, the orderlies, even the doctors, uninclined to any word that smacked of the supernatural, could not help themselves: miracle, miracle, miracle. Edgar was the miracle-boy, a marvel, a saint, the luckiest child on earth. He even had the Mexican women who worked downstairs in the cafeteria coming into his curtained-off area as reverently as pilgrims, pressing their crucifixes to his lips, whispering their prayers.

And the doctors would not leave me alone either, though they did not come to pray. They came from all over to study me, to find out where the small miracle of my existence fit into their tables and statistics. During those first few months it seemed whenever I woke up there was a new doctor at the foot of my bed, looking over charts, asking impossible questions. Even though I could barely say a word or lift my hand to scratch my nose, they wouldn't stop with their questions and requests.

"Will you count to ten backwards for me?"

"Where am I pinching you?"

"What color is this pen I'm holding?"

"Can you roll your eyes in a counterclockwise fashion?"

"How do you feel?"

Let me answer that last one here and now: I felt like shit. My skin burned, my ragged nerves spit sparks, my eyeballs throbbed, and whenever I tried to focus on something—a doctor's bow tie or the face of a nurse—the colors and shapes would shift and melt together, transmuting themselves, until I would fall into such an intense nausea my bones felt like they were vibrating. I would lie with my eyes closed, concentrating on keeping perfectly still, breathing in, breathing out, in, out, slow, slow.

For much of the time I was awake, which was in those first months only two or three hours a day, I hallucinated. I saw ghosts floating above me, the spirits of dead people come to take me back where I belonged. My peripheral vision was tormented by murmuring phantoms. Sometimes at night I could feel them touching me, a hand placed lightly on mine, a kiss on the forehead, and I would struggle away in such a terror that I would pitch out of my bed, ripping out tubes, tangling the sheets, pulling the IV tree down on top of me.

After this happened two or three times they put restraints on me, binding me to the bed with canvas cuffs placed on my ankles and wrists, a leather strap across my chest.

"You bunch a blackhearted quacks!" Art hollered at them the first time the restraints were put on. "This here is a boy, not a got-danged criminal!" To me, it sounded like he was shouting from the bottom of a mine shaft. The orderlies and supervising doctor ignored him as usual. Later that night, Art, grunting and cussing the whole way, climbed down from his bed and came over to mine.

There were four of us in the room and Art was the only one not completely bedridden—one of his arms was in an industrial-size cast, the left side of his face was collapsed and most of his internal organs were in a state of constant breakdown. All in all, though, he was doing pretty well—he was the only one of us who could tiptoe to the toilet when he felt like it.

Five months before, he had rolled his Pontiac into a cement

drainage canal. He was ejected, thrown thirty feet before crash-landing
on the front steps of a farmhouse, shattering his arm, bursting his
spleen, breaking his leg, most all his ribs and a few vertebrae, and
pretty much destroying the bottom left half of his face on the
wrought-iron rail. As it turned out, he was the lucky one. His wife
and two teenage daughters were wearing their seat belts; all three
drowned upside down in fetid water laced with insecticides.

Despite his face, which seemed to have been put together with
wire and chewing gum, despite the fused vertebrae in his back and
his mangled arm and the highly unpredictable state of his lower
organs and his lungs, which constantly had to be drained of fluid,
Art, by most accounts, was nearly well healed enough to get his pink
slip. But every time someone would bring the subject up, he would
begin to complain about some new ailment, convincing the doctors
to let him stay a few more weeks.

That night, he painstakingly climbed down from his bed. I could
hear his joints grinding like rusted-out gears. "I'm not a going to let
them treat you like this, son," he said, his face an inch from mine. The
smell of his cologne made me so light-headed I felt like I might
faint. "We can't let any of 'em treat us this way."

He unbuckled the restraints—it took him awhile to figure them
out with only one good hand—then stole every extra pillow and
blanket he could find in the room and placed them around my bed,
creating a landing pad. That night I threw myself off the bed twice,
and both times Art was there to help me back up, make sure I didn't
have any lasting injuries, and to argue with the nurses when they
came in wanting to know why the restraints had been taken off.

"I don't care if he falls off that dad-crumbed bed every last hour of
the day, I don't care if he splits his head wide open again!" Art yelled
at them, crouching over me like a guard dog, the scarred portion of his
face glowing pink, the echoes of his words racing madly up and down
the halls. "This boy's been through enough. This boy is a miracle. I
don't think you people understand it. You don't tie a boy like this up."

My night episodes only lasted another couple of weeks, and Art fought with the nurses and doctors the whole time about it. "You put one hand on that boy," he'd growl at the poor orderlies when they came to put the restraints on, his gold tooth gleaming from the cavern of his mouth, "and I will put my hand on you."

When Art wasn't aggravating the hospital staff, he mostly lay propped against the pillows and looked out the only window in the room, usually half obscured with orange dust from the old Ildicott Mine, which had been bought by foreign money and put back into operation after twenty years of lying dormant. Dump trucks with wheels as big as hot tubs had begun to roll around, moving dirt and slag piles, licking up plumes of dust. All day long the screech and rattle of machinery rose from the old smelter, which was now being brought up to standard. Farther off, mountains of smelt curved and sloped like impossibly high sand dunes, and beyond them the strip mines like gargantuan whirlpools sucking down into the earth.

At night, when the trucks and bulldozers were quiet, Art would stare out at the steep hills of town, which were jeweled with the lights of shanties and mobile homes perched on limestone outcroppings. Only very late, with the swamp coolers off and most of the hospital sleeping, could we hear the faint silvery trills of Mexican radio trumpets floating across the vast, dark space.

Art did his damnedest to ignore Jeffrey, who had the bed directly across from mine. Jeffrey could not shut himself up if he wanted to; his mouth did not seem to be his to control. He spouted off about how the cooks were trying to poison us, how St. Divine's was really a government facility used for human testing, how one of the orderlies, a big swaybacked guy named Herb, had tried to molest him on several occasions and was always giving him meaningful looks.

Jeffrey also had a compulsion for sudden recitations of poetry and obscure quotations. He would raise his head off his pillow, hold one hand up to the heavens, and in a quavering British accent intone,

Every Night and every Morn
Some to Misery are Born;
Every Morn and every Night,
Some are born to Sweet Delight;
Some are born to Sweet Delight,
Some are born to Endless Night.

"*Ppfft,*" Art would always say.

"William Blake," Jeffrey would say. "That poor bastard."

Only one word could describe Jeffrey adequately: ill. He looked as ill as anybody I'd ever seen. His skin was waxy and yellow, his eyes gray and wrung out. He twitched and coughed and sneezed constantly—it appeared as if half a dozen diseases were having their way with him. He had a long, sparse Fu Manchu and a wispy tuft of hair that rose off his head like a flame.

Both of Jeffrey's legs were held together with metal pins and he wore a brace that kept the broken bones of his hips from coming apart. It took two orderlies to lift him out of bed and into a special wheelchair so he could get down to the room where they hooked up his distressed kidneys to a machine. A month before I had arrived at St. Divine's, Jeffrey fell off a three-story building. He had thrown a party on the roof of his apartment to celebrate his engagement to his girlfriend, who they had just discovered was pregnant. At some point during the party, Jeffrey, sky-high on a mixture of wine, marijuana and celebratory merriment, worked himself into an eastern-European-style jig, stomping his feet and clapping his hands over his head, guitars and tambourines pounding wildly, everybody whooping and whistling until Jeffrey jigged backwards right off the roof.

His fiancée stopped visiting him after only a few weeks. The last he had heard, she had gone to Mexico to get an abortion.

Had they not been severely disabled, I'm sure Art and Jeffrey would have gone at each other like two cats locked in a suitcase. Jeffrey would rant and rave and Art would say "*Ppfft,*" or occasionally, when he'd *really* had it, really couldn't take any more talk about the Kantian soul, or the puppet war being staged in Asia, or the fascist messages that Broadway plays were full of nowadays, he would blow up, his rumbling voice rising out of him like thunder, and he would shout with such quaking force that the whole hospital would quiet for a moment: "WOULD YOU SHUT YOUR TRAP FOR ONE LOUSY MINUTE YOU GOT-DANGED DING-A-LING!"

That Art, everyone agreed, had a powerful set of lungs.

Usually, Jeffrey would sulk for awhile, but he couldn't help himself; he'd start philosophizing about the possibility that the bedpans we used were made from radioactive scrap metal or that the nurses, who used secret signs and handshakes, were all Republicans, and the whole cycle would start itself over again.

"What about compassion?" Jeffrey always asked the doctors. "This place is crawling with bacteria and perverts and nobody seems to care."

The only thing that could stop Jeffrey's ranting was a hot look from Ismore, who had been in a car accident (in a hospital filled mostly with the diseased and cancer-ridden, we were known as the "accidental four") and was now a quadriplegic who breathed with the aid of a respirator. Ismore was a big Indian man with long hair who looked like he had been poured into the hollow indentations of his bed. The only part of him that looked alive at all were his eyes, which radiated a red snapping heat of anger that not even Jeffrey could tolerate for very long.

Mostly Jeffrey ignored me, preferring to spend his time nettling Art or begging nurses for tranquilizers, morphine, penicillin, Bayer tablets, anything they could spare. But one afternoon while Art was off having some X rays taken, Jeffrey sat up in bed and looked at me for a minute. It was sometime in late November—still hot outside—but for some reason the old baroque radiators had been cranked up and both Jeffrey and I were soaked through with sweat.

"You know you're a lucky kid, don't you?" he said, shivering so hard his teeth clacked together with the sound of ice rattling in a glass. A huge droplet of sweat hung trembling from the tip of his nose.

Jeffrey waited for an answer, but I didn't give him one: I knew I was a lucky kid. Every last person I met told me so.

"I mean, losing your memory, forgetting everything, what could be better? Think of it!" Jeffrey had a faraway look in his red-rimmed eyes, as if he might start crying with the joy this idea gave him. "All the terrible shit in your life, all the guilt, and regret, it would be gone, washed away. You take a little head trauma and—zap!—you're a new man."

He paused again, breathing deeply. "I'm telling you, there'd be nothing better," he panted. "We should all be so lucky."

MRS.   RODALE

FOR ME THERE is no such thing as forgetting, nothing is hazy or vague. I can remember it all: every name, every glance, every word, every throwaway scrap of a moment. The thing I fear most is forgetting, so I have become a hoarder, a pack rat—everything is significant, I throw nothing away.

In this catch-all memory of mine I can see that hospital room perfectly, the single window forever shrouded with orange dust from the mines, the faded checkerboard-tiled floors, the bare electrical wires, black and sinister, twining together in the corners of the ceiling, the polished stainless steel trays, the suspended IV bottles throwing sunlit, watery reflections on the walls. I can even step away for a moment and see little Edgar in his oversized bed, the scars from his surgery not yet hidden by his hair, trying to distinguish the various smells of the hospital—Vaseline, urine, lemon disinfectant, cafeteria grease—and listening to the hive-like drone of the place, the talking, moaning, screaming of the patients, radios crackling, toilets flushing, the beeps and clicks of medical machinery, fluorescent lights buzzing, the high hooting laughs of nurses in the rec room, the deep hum of gargantuan swamp coolers that perched on the roof and pumped the rooms and halls full of wet, boggy air.

Once a Catholic hospital full of somber statues, old oaken doors and stairways that led nowhere, St. Divine's had been taken over by the county and now it was the last refuge for the poor, the illegal, the dispossessed who came from all over the vast desert that stretched eastward toward the White Mountains and south to Mexico. In two years, St. Divine's would be shut down for good, condemned by the county that ran it and bought for a pittance by the mining company to be gutted out and used as a garage for their machinery and trucks.

Even though I can remember every last smell and sound and sight of that place, my memory begins to betray me when I try to conjure exactly what was going through the lumpy, ruined head of that boy for those first few months of his new life. Edgar, who were you? Besides pain and nausea and delirium, what did you feel?

I know that everything seemed like one big mystery to him, an ever-shifting puzzle. I know that his immediate concerns took up most of his time: dealing with his headaches, the constant testing by the doctors, trying not to wet his bed in fear when the ghosts came in the night.

But did he miss his mother? Did he cry for her before he went to sleep, like any kid would? I don't think he even remembered her then, not consciously—he didn't think about her. I'm sure he felt a certain longing, a loneliness, but no single twisting in his gut that said, *I want my mother. I want her arms around me.*

The first person to ever mention my mother was a state social worker, a black lady named Mrs. Rodale, who had an afro so large and unruly that it seemed to have a personality all its own. I had never seen hair like this, I don't think I even realized that it *was* hair, so she was having a hard time getting me to pay attention to what she was saying.

The nurses had pulled curtains around my bed so we could have some privacy, and Mrs. Rodale sat very close to me in her metal chair, her hair looming like a great thundercloud. She asked me if I was feeling all right, if the hospital staff had been treating me well, and I kept nodding my head, mesmerized.

She clutched a small stack of papers which she flipped through for a moment, the huge beaded bracelets on her wrists clacking like billiard balls. She looked exhausted; her eyes were bloodshot and she constantly battled yawns.

"I'm here to talk about some important things with you, Edgar, I hope that's alright," she said. "I know that you might have a hard time remembering, but I wanted to talk a little about your mother. Do you remember your mother?"

"Mother," I said, trying out the word, and suddenly I saw an image of her in my mind; her long, blue-black hair that crackled like a dark fire when she brushed it, her slim fingers covered with cheap silver rings. I could smell the waxy smell of the smoky pink lipstick she wore, I could hear her high squeaking laugh. It made me feel dizzy.

"We asked the staff here not to talk to you about your mother until we could locate her, but we haven't been able to," Mrs. Rodale said. "From what we've been able to gather, she's in California, but that's all we know. Your grandma is in a hospital down in Tucson, she's a little sick, just like you. If she gets better, maybe she can come for a visit."

"California," I said. I knew about California—it was some kind of island with palm trees—I'd seen it on the TV. I could understand why my mother might want to go there.

Mrs. Rodale sighed. "We're going to do all we can to contact your mother. And we're trying to find any other family you might have. In the meantime, we want you to get all better. The doctors tell me great things about you. Are you happy here?"

Happy? Nobody had ever asked me that. I nodded, which seemed to please Mrs. Rodale. She smiled at me and said, "Want to touch my hair?" She bent her head close to me, and instead of just running my hand along the surface of her afro, I plunged my hand deep inside it, hoping to find something, I don't know what, maybe something that would clear everything up, answer all the questions, but there was nothing there, just a fluffy, coarse cloud of hair.

After Mrs. Rodale had gone and a nurse had pushed back the curtains, Art sat up in bed and said, "That woman certainly had a hairdo."

I laid my head on my pillow, pulled my knees up to my chest. Art looked over at me, then out the window, where a windstorm was going on: sand blowing by in sheets, a muffled howl. He started talking about bat shit. He said, "Did you know bat shit—ah, guano, bat guano—is something of a valuable product?"

He told me how, when he was growing up in New Mexico, his family made a living by digging bat guano out of caves and turning it into fertilizer. "My brothers and me, we spent most of our childhood years knee-deep in it, like shoveling cold gray pudding all day in the pitch dark. You couldn't get away from it, see. Everything smelled like bat guano: house, car, dog. Bat guano don't smell all that great, if you weren't aware. When we'd go to church people would clear out of the benches front and behind. Even our cat was treated bad by the other cats in town. Maybe if my mama hadn't a died a way back when—we sure coulda used her. No woman around to get the right kind of soap or to make us take showers every day, it was difficult. What I'm saying is you've got a mama, she might not be right here right now, but she's around and she loves you, that I can tell you for sure. Mothers love their children. That's God's rule, the only one you can count on."

I didn't say anything, didn't look at Art. I closed my eyes, listening to the swirling grit outside blast and scour the window, and tried to go to sleep.

THE DUNGEON

WHAT IS THE difference between an accident and a miracle? Most people would try to tell you the distinction is clear, but I'm not so certain—my life has been so rife with both I couldn't tell the differ-

ence. My early days at St. Divine's, though, were full of what most anybody would call miracles. With me, it was one miracle after another.

First, I had survived a mail jeep running over my head. Then, after
three months in a coma, I had simply awakened, almost without
warning, and with only minimal brain damage. According to science
and simple common sense, I should have been a vegetable, lucky to
spend the rest of my days diapered and spoon-fed, my skull full of
jelly. But I was progressing so well the doctors didn't know what to
make of me; they'd shake their heads, muttering under their breaths,
checking and rechecking their charts, utterly perplexed, as if my
continuing miracle was causing them to lose faith in the things
they'd held most sacred all along.

The miracles continued: two months out of my coma I could sit
up in bed and feed myself; by Christmas I was able to start physical
therapy; by Easter I could walk to the bathroom on my own. Just like
a baby figuring out the fundamentals, I was complimented on my
bowel movements, my appetite, and anything, no matter how incoherent, that came out of my mouth. In no time I was learning to
read, passing all the coordination tests without much effort. In a hospital full of mostly cranky old people waiting to die in some unpleas-
ant way, I was the man of the hour, the star of the show. When the
Mexican women from the cafeteria would come up to the room to
touch their crucifixes to my forehead, Jeffrey would call out in a
mocking falsetto, "All hail, Saint Edgar, blessed coma-boy!"

Of course, I was not getting off scot-free. There was the distant
throbbing in my head that would occasionally intensify and turn
into a pain so furious and insistent I would curl up around myself
and hope for the simple miracle of death. Most of the time the world
seemed to smolder around its edges, sometimes shriveling and
bunching like burning plastic. There were the ghosts I saw, too, figures outlined in white and yellow light, disappearing and reappear-
ing again, their voices like warped, underwater sounds in my head.
And then my spells started up—because the doctors didn't really
know what they were, they called them "non-epileptic mini-

seizures." My head would fill with sizzling bursts of light and I would
black out for a second, go completely unconscious, and instead of
thrashing about like your run-of-the-mill epileptic, I would, in Art's
words, "vibrate like a Buick with shot bearings," my eyeballs popping
out of my irregular head.

The first time I had one of my non-epileptic mini-seizures was
down in the Dungeon, the huge, low-ceilinged basement room
where all the physical and occupational therapy was conducted—a
place where I would spend a lot of time during the rest of my stay at
St. Divine's.

Except for a few quick junkets to the radiology center, I had not
left my room in five months, and I was giddy with excitement just to
be going somewhere. By the time we made it down to the Dungeon
by way of an ancient, creaking elevator, I wasn't so sure. I sat in my
oversized wheelchair, a tiny king in his makeshift throne, and tried to
take it in. They'd been doing therapy in the Dungeon since the early
fifties and it was still filled with dusty, little-used contraptions, relics
made of leather straps and pulleys and buckles—instruments of torture, if you didn't know any better. The room, so enormous and
shadowed that the snapping fluorescent light overhead didn't seem to
have any effect, was filled with all kinds of odds and ends: a small,
algaed water-therapy tank, two or three easels, a slumping Ping-Pong
table, a set of drums, an old-fashioned loom, a bandsaw, a battle-worn
dinosaur of a piano, long splintery tables covered with paints, scissors,
newsprint, wooden blocks, clay, half-made baskets, kitchen utensils.

On the far wall hung a huge, crumpled banner made of butcher
paper that said, in dripping red paint, I WANT TO I CAN DO IT WHY
DON'T I? The banner still bore the ochre stains from when a former
patient lurched out of his wheelchair, tore the banner down in a fit
of rage and urinated all over it.

It wasn't the size of the room, or the contents of it, but the chaos
going on inside it that was unsettling. It was a Tuesday morning,
the day outpatients came from all around to get their government-
subsidized therapy. The room was packed, sick and broken people

everywhere: a teenage boy with a mangled hand pounding nails into a board, a bandaged burn victim throwing darts, an enormous woman with bedsores peppered across her back splashing hip-deep in the aqua-tank, a young girl yelping out in pain on a manual treadmill, a man with no legs hefting barbells from his wheelchair, a palsied old couple—a husband and wife who could not remember each other's names—rooted to their spots on the floor, expertly swatting birdies over a woman receiving a slap-massage at the hands of a small muscled black man. Sue Kay, the head therapist who had hair so red it stood out like an emergency signal, would float around the room, completely unfazed by the hubbub, like the gracious hostess of a wild party, offering encouragement, making notes in her book, giving orders to her assistants and any of the volunteers who might have been there for the day.

Sue Kay got me situated in the corner at a small table with some Play-Doh and a bedpan full of crayon nubs. "I want you to make something nice for me, pumpkin," she said. Sue Kay was from the South and called everybody honey or sweetheart or pumpkin. "I'll come around to check on you every so often."

I barely touched the clay or crayons; I couldn't take my eyes off the circus around me. About thirty feet away, a thin man who swayed like an underwater plant did his best to place a couple of metal rings onto a wooden peg, but it appeared his hands were not his to control. Time and time again he would miss, dropping the rings, and each time he would cry in a desperate voice, "This is not fair, this is not fair."

Under the big banner a tiny dark woman sat alone in a chair, singing. The woman had a thick bandage taped over one of her eyes and she seemed to be missing her nose and she sang beautifully and with great feeling, *We will be buried in the stream in Jesus' blessed name, oh rise, rise, rise, out of the water.*

Off to my left, a fierce hopscotch match was going on between a man with a plastic leg and one of the orderlies, a Mexican kid named

Pito. They would hop around for a minute, then the one-legged man would call out, "You cheated! Right there, you missed a square!" and Pito would get right in the guy's face, like a baseball manager arguing a call with an umpire, and shout, "Me cheating? *Me?* You falling down all the time, missing the squares everywhere, and you say that? I kicking you ass you one-leg motherfucker and you say *cheating?*"

I hummed and scratched myself and nibbled at my Play-Doh. It had a nice consistency but was much too salty for my taste. I tried the crayons, which crumbled easily and didn't have much flavor.

Through all the moving bodies I finally located Art, who was working on his bad arm with a contraption that consisted of a series of ropes and pulleys attached to a bag of sand. He sweated and huffed and grimaced and cursed with that voice of his that carried over everything. Once in awhile he would disengage himself from the machine and stand up to peer across the room at me.

At some point I decided I needed a drink of water; the Play-Doh had made me thirsty. The fountain was no more than fifteen feet from where I was sitting and I thought I could make it without the wheelchair. Already, with a nurse's help, I had taken a few mincing steps around my bed—I was certain I could walk anywhere I needed to. Just getting to my feet made me dizzy, but I took two or three small steps, my legs stiff as chopsticks, got some confidence, took a couple more. It was when I got to the fountain, feeling exhausted and weak, that an electrical current traveled up my legs like a lit fuse and set my whole body trembling, flashbulbs popping off behind my eyes.

I don't remember blacking out, only waking up to find a frail, walleyed woman smiling over me like a deformed angel. She put a gnarled finger to my head which came away with blood on it. She said, "Boo-boo."

It took a minute for anybody to notice me wedged in the corner against the water fountain. Pito arrived, then a couple of others, and I could hear Art shout from across the room, "Doctor! Nurse! Shit!"

Apparently I had hit my head on a pipe that fed the water fountain—
a small gash that would need five or six stitches. In a hospital, you
wouldn't have thought the sight of blood could cause such an
uproar—people began shouting and crowding around, their distressed
faces pressing in: Edgar the miracle-boy was wounded and down.

Later that day up in my room, after they had strapped me on a
gurney and carted me up to the same emergency room where I had
temporarily died eight months before, after they had shaved away a
patch of my hair and sewed me up, Art asked me a question I would
be asking myself for the rest of my life.

"Boy," he said, "why can't you keep your head out of trouble?"

The next morning a nurse came to check the stitches and to wash
what was left of my hair. She was busy massaging my scalp when
something dislodged from my head and fell into my lap. I picked it
up and looked at it: a small shard of black rock, about as big as a
nickel and crusted with blood and flakes of dead skin.

"My God," said the nurse, "where'd that come from?"

"My head," I said.

"Can I see it?"

"No," I said and held it tightly in my fist.

She ran off and grabbed Dr. Waters, a balding man with a round,
coarse face like a pomegranate. They came back together, with the
nurse explaining to the doctor how something had fallen *out of my
head*.

"It fell right *out of his head,*" she kept saying, her eyes wide.

Dr. Waters wanted to see the rock, too, but I wasn't having any of
it. It was my rock. I didn't own a thing in the world except a hospital shift and a stuffed animal, a furry carrot with eyes that one of the
nurses had given me.

Finally, we settled on a compromise; I could keep the rock if I
would just open up my hand so Dr. Waters could see what it was.

"I won't even touch it," Dr. Waters said.

I opened my hand and let Dr. Waters, with his arms behind his

back, have a look at it. He peered at it for a minute and then inspected my head.

"Came out right here," he said, touching a place just above my
right ear. "Would you look at that? Must have been in there since the
accident. I've seen little pieces of glass work their way out months
after an accident, but never a rock."

He gave my head a thorough inspection but was unable to turn up
any more rocks. "Just a few lumps," he said. "You're going to have to
take things a little easier for awhile, Edgar. No walking. You want to
go anywhere, make sure it's in a wheelchair."

I was thrilled with that rock. I felt I had accomplished something
by keeping it in my head for so long without anyone finding out
about it. I would get under my covers and study it in the dim light
for a moment, then jam it under my mattress in case anyone might
be watching. It was like owning an important clue; this rock had
been a part of the accident that I couldn't remember, the accident
which had sent my mother away and put me in this hospital.

The rock turned out to be the first in my secret collection of odds
and ends. During the rest of my stay at St. Divine's, I began collecting things. I became a connoisseur of whatnots and knickknacks. I
had no inclination to keep or collect things that were given to me; I
only kept things which I could take, things I wasn't necessarily supposed to have. I filched a deodorizing puck from a urinal in the
bathroom, a chess piece from a set in the Dungeon, a penlight from
the pocket of a doctor's smock hanging on a chair, a crucifix with a
little bloody Christ I had found behind one of the radiators. I kept
these things in an empty Kleenex box and when everybody was
asleep or doing something else, I would pull the box out from under
the bed and arrange the objects between my legs, turning them over
and imagining what they meant, what purposes they had once filled,
what histories they contained. It seemed to me that they were pieces
of some vast, complicated puzzle, and if I kept up my collecting I
would finally understand it all.

COWBOYS AND INDIANS

WHEN ARNOLD MINT hooked up with my mother he had no idea
what he was getting into; being from Connecticut, he simply didn't
realize the dangers involved with keeping the company of an Indian
woman. It took a bunch of backward, greasy ranch hands to explain
it to him.

Because Arnold had blown every hard-earned dollar on impress-
ing my mother, he couldn't spend all his time hanging out on the
reservation, trying to look inconspicuous, waiting for the hour of
rendezvous when they would make love in the back of the pickup
down by the river for an hour or two before she had to go home.

Arnold needed a job. He spent a week checking in at the employment agency in Globe, scouring the want ads he fished out of
garbage cans and siphoning gas from old ladies' Cadillacs in the parking lot of the Safeway. There were all kinds of listings for fix-it men
and secretaries and temporary track layers, but Arnold didn't bother
calling on any of these—he had his pride. He had come to Arizona
to ride fences, to punch cattle, not to fix water heaters.

When he finally found work it was with an old leathery whip of a
guy who ran a calf and heifer outfit just outside a little town called
Hope. The man needed an extra body for the summer and was willing to pay Arnold minimum wage to do the grunt work around the
place.

For two weeks Arnold cheerfully worked his ass off, building
fence, shoveling out corrals, clearing ditches, hoping all the time that
at some point he might get to sit on a horse. When he got his day off
he drove up to San Carlos, picked up my mother and took her back
to the ranch. He wanted to show her the cattle guards he'd dug out

and the barbed wire he'd strung. The other hands were polite when he introduced her as his fiancée, but once she was gone, they got all over him. What did he think he was doing with a squaw? And an Apache squaw, the very worst kind. He was from back East and obviously didn't know his own asshole from the bathtub drain, so they filled him in on everything: squaws are full of diseases, they have sex with their own fathers, and no matter what, even if you wore a condom, even if you wore *five* condoms, they always got pregnant, no matter what, it's this power they have. They want you to get them pregnant so you will take them away from the reservation and their daughter-buggering fathers. It's a goddamned fact.

Arnold tried to protest, saying he'd had quite a bit of sex with this particular Indian girl and he was pretty sure she wasn't pregnant. Also, his pecker was in good shape, as far as he could tell.

You just wait! they all shouted at him. *You stupid son of a bitch! Just wait and see!*

For the next two weeks Arnold worked and worried, and did his best to endure the taunts and jokes. They started calling him "chief" and "Geronimo" and every day they asked him if his pecker had fallen off yet. Each morning when he woke up Arnold checked on his pecker and every day he was relieved to find that it hadn't suffered any noticeable alterations.

It was a confused, miserable Arnold Mint who drove up to San Carlos to see my mother that Sunday. He waited around in the white rippling heat at their prearranged meeting place, a small, faded billboard by the side of Highway 60 that said ASK JESUS under which somebody had scrawled *don't bother*. When she didn't show up after half an hour, he drove over to the house. Nobody appeared to be home—the front door was closed, which was unusual, and everything was perfectly quiet. After waiting for fifteen minutes in the cab of his pickup, he got out, cautiously hopped the little ragged fence which was laced with all manner of windblown trash, and peered into the dust-caked windows, hoping to spot my mother. He was just rounding the back of the house when Grandma Paul ambushed him, began beating him about the shoulders and head with some kind of thick bone—the femur of a long-dead deer or cow—that she gripped with both hands like a baseball bat.

Arnold smiled—it's what he did in any stressful situation—and tried to keep things cordial by asking questions: "I was wondering—*twop*—do you think you could tell—*twop*—ow! All right then—*twop twop*—I was hoping you could tell me—*twop*—where—*twop*—Gloria might be?"

Arnold didn't have much choice but to quit with the polite questions and get the hell out of the way. He ducked past Grandma Paul, his arms shielding his head, and went into the backyard, where he saw my mother, laid out on an old mattress under the shade of the beargrass ramada. Gloria didn't look well at all; her face and arms were polished with sweat and even in the open air the sharp smell of vomit lingered.

"Huh," Arnold said.

My mother propped herself on her elbows. She had the distracted, frantic look of somebody who is going to puke any second. "Arnold, I'm sick," my mother said. "I think I've got a baby."

Arnold felt his knees go loose. Welts were rising up all over his neck and arms and he began to feel sick himself. Just then Grandma Paul came up behind him and gave him a shot in the right kidney that buckled him in half.

Straightening up and clutching his side in pain, Arnold wheezed, "Pardon me," and yanked the bone away from Grandma. He tossed it on the roof of the house, where it clattered loudly on the tin until it came to rest against a rusted TV antenna.

Arnold turned toward my mother and watched her dry-heave into an old coffee can by her head. He started toward her, holding out his hand, then backed away. He yanked at his chin in desperation. He said, "How . . . ?"

Grandma Paul grabbed an old shovel resting against the house, which got Arnold's immediate attention, but she did not go after him with it. Instead, she went over by the bean patch where the dirt was soft and dug a small hole, no more than a foot deep. She dropped the shovel, walked up to Arnold and snatched his beloved Stetson, still showing the effects of Wicked Joseph, off his head. She had to make a little jump to reach it, but once she had it she crammed it into the hole and began saying Apache words over it, looking up at Arnold occasionally and making tiny circular gestures with her hands. Gloria yelled out for her mother to stop, but Grandma Paul kept it up until she had covered the hat with dirt and stomped on it.

Arnold was rooted to his spot, the sun beating down on his white, thinning scalp. At that moment Arnold wished he was back in Connecticut, where things were easy, where everybody knew what was expected, where things made *sense*.

He couldn't look at my mother. He looked anywhere else, up at the ramada that shaded her, as if trying to figure out how it had been constructed, down at his boots, over at a couple of ragged donkeys munching knapweed in a vacant lot.

"I'm sorry," he said.

Grandma Paul shouted something in Apache, picked up a softball-sized dirt clod and hurled it at him, just missing his head.

Arnold glanced at the final resting place of his hat, wiped his forehead with his hand, then turned—dirt clods zinging past him on both sides—and sprinted across the street to where his Ford waited for him, motor running.

HERMES JUBILEE

DESPITE A BAD FIRST DAY, I grew to enjoy my time in the Dungeon. In the hopes of preventing further injury they got me a special helmet, a padded leather thing with straps and buckles. The helmet was old and ravaged, like something used in the National Football League before plastic and face masks.

Everywhere else, I had to be pushed around in a wheelchair, but in the Dungeon Sue Kay allowed me a little freedom. Once I had finished with my blocks and clay and puzzles, I was allowed to roam the room, retrieving things for Sue Kay or her assistants, playing checkers with somebody who needed an opponent, helping a senile patient relearn how to use fingernail clippers. Sometimes Art would take me in my wheelchair outside to the ruined courtyard, where the dry heat would hit us like a slap and we would watch men with plastic legs and hooks for hands hitting a volleyball over a rope stretched between two crumbling statues. Once or twice a month Sue Kay allowed me to swim in the aqua-tank. I remember splashing around, gulping copper-tasting water, happy to be alive, while next to me a man hung suspended from the ceiling in a harness, like a beached whale about to be returned to the wild, kicking his legs in the water and groaning with a deep, unfathomable suffering.

I wasn't really sure what was going on in that room; to me it mostly seemed like a bunch of people trying to have a good time and not really succeeding. There was a hopefulness that verged on desperation: we were broken and afflicted and maybe if we played enough badminton, painted enough pictures, weaved enough baskets, we could make ourselves whole again.

I got bored pretty quickly with the clay and the Lincoln Logs and the puzzles. Sue Kay started me on a reading program; even though I had been well past the age at the time of my accident, I had never been to school. I caught on quickly, though; it wasn't long before I was wearing out the few children's books they had on hand and I eventually moved on to the pulp novels that filled the Dungeon's library, which was actually a pile of two hundred or so molding, falling-apart books that had been donated by past patients, mounded together behind the piano. Not exactly a lot of great literature in that pile—a couple Dickens, an untouched Jane Austen, a ragged copy of

Huckleberry Finn. Mostly, they were books with titles like *Widows Won't Wait, Cold Night, Hot Stranger, The Groom Lay Dead* and *A Corpse for Christmas*—books with lurid covers—women sporting cleavage, mustachioed men on horseback, shadowy figures in alleyways—that you could read almost without looking at the words.

If I wasn't sleeping, eating, or down in the Dungeon I was probably reading one of those books. I liked the Westerns best. They were the most straightforward, the easiest to understand. A man kills your brother? Hunt the son of a bitch down and shoot him through the heart. Somebody steals your horse? Hang him from a bridge. There was something beautiful and simple about the way things worked in these books, something the romances couldn't claim.

When I didn't understand a certain word, I'd usually ask Jeffrey. Though he was a complete mess, he had a vocabulary. I could wake Jeffrey out of a dead sleep, ask him what "sarcophagus" meant, and he'd say, "Huh? Oh, ah, sarcophagus—uh, big stone coffin favored by mummies," and be right back to sleep.

Art, on the other hand, had more of a difficult time with my questions. The better I felt, the more energy I had and the more thinking I was able to do: little Edgar had a lot of questions. And Art was the only one around with the time or the patience to deal with them all, though sometimes even he would get fed up with me.

One morning I noticed one of my bottom teeth was loose. Though my life was full of much more serious complications, I had never had a loose tooth before—it concerned me. I asked Art what I should do about the tooth while we were eating breakfast in our beds: powdered eggs, Spam, and a biscuit you could hurt somebody with.

"It's going to fall out on you, no way around it," he said. "But the good thing is you can put it under your pillow and the tooth fairy will leave you a dime or a quarter, something like that."

"Tooth fairy?"

"You don't know about the tooth fairy," he said, shooting me the skeptical eye. "All right," he sighed, "the tooth fairy. This is the fairy that lifts up your pillow in the middle of the night and takes your tooth. She collects teeth, you know, for some reason. She's a teeth collector. She leaves a quarter under your pillow for your trouble."

"What's a fairy?"

"It's like this little old lady with wings who flies around."

"The lady has wings?"

"Well, she's not exactly real, like me or you, she just floats. I think."

"Like a ghost?" I didn't want to have anything to do with a ghost who floated around lifting up pillows.

Art struggled to keep his voice down. "She's not a ghost. She's nice, dangit. She's a fairy."

Art taught me all kind of things but there was one thing he certainly learned from me: patience. He was tired and bitter, a wreck of a man, but he took the time to make sure I understood how things worked; he would field my questions, asked at all hours of the day and night, until he looked like his face might explode. He did his best to keep me informed, but the one thing I am most grateful to him for is the little idea he had just after breakfast down in the Dungeon. "Why don't we just get the boy a damn typewriter?" he said to Sue Kay that morning.

For a few weeks the doctors had been working on a solution for one of the lingering effects of my brain damage: Edgar could not write. He could read like a champ, could recognize shapes and letters without any problem, but for some reason when he put pen to paper to make the letter A or T or L, no matter how much he concentrated and sweated and willed his hand to do it right, it always came out looking like scribbled knot, a complicated hieroglyph. He could not make so much as a circle or a simple straight line.

As with everything else about him, the doctors were dumbfounded; they had never seen anything like this. "Dysgraphia" was the word they were finally able to attach to my condition, a word that means, simply "the inability to write." "You have *dysgraphia*," they told me, relieved, as if this diagnosis were a solution to something.

More than my fits or headaches or the ghosts in the night, this *dysgraphia* (a word I would chant over and over again, hoping to lessen its power over me) tormented me. The doctors believed that with enough therapy this was something I could overcome. I spent an hour or two every day gritting my teeth, trying to make the most rudimentary of shapes—a cross, a square, a circle—but I could never get it right. Instead of jaunting about the Dungeon as before, I spent my time at my little desk trying to copy shapes and letters into old elementary primers, grinding my crayons into the paper until I cried. I would bite my hands, punishing them for not obeying my will, but it was my brain, my own mashed-up brain, that was the real traitor. Some tiny part of it was ruined beyond repair, as useless as spoiled hamburger, and so I could not perform the fundamental act of writing my own name.

So it was Art who came up with the solution. *Get the boy a damn typewriter.*

I have to say it was not love at first sight for Edgar and the Hermes Jubilee 2000. Sue Kay carried it into the room one day after therapy, holding it out in front of her with a formal stiffness, as if it was a velvet pillow with the crown of England on top. She had just stopped by Art's empty house, according to his instructions, located the thing somewhere in his garage, and rushed it over like an organ that needed transplanting.

"This is for you, sweetheart," Sue Kay beamed, setting it on my bed. "It was Art's idea."

The machine was shiny black and sinister-looking, something made to cause pain. After being in a hospital all this time, especially one with a Dungeon, I was certain that there was no such thing as a machine that could do anything besides draw blood or clean out kidneys or make X rays, a machine that could actually offer some kind of pleasure. I slid my legs away from it and looked up at Sue Kay.

"Ooo look," Jeffrey said, pulling his pillow over his head, "we're going to turn the miracle-boy into a secretary."

Art grabbed the rails of his bed and swung his legs to the side, grunting and wheezing like a worn-out accordion. He shuffled over to us, his face alive like I hadn't seen it before. "This is a machine right here. Built like a Panzer. Drop it off a skyscraper one minute and you're typing up a love poem for your sweetheart the next. Hoo-boy."

"Oh fuck," came Jeffrey's muffled voice from beneath the pillow.

"It's a *typewriter,* pumpkin," Sue Kay said to me, in the same slow way she talked to the senile or retarded people down in the Dungeon. "We think this will help you. You can write all you want and forget about that bad old pencil and those primers."

"Lookit," Art said, ripping one of my progress sheets from the clipboard at the end of my bed and spooling it into the machine using only his good hand. "You feed paper in it like this here, see, and then you can type up words, however you want. Watch this." He stabbed at one of the keys with his finger and the ratcheting thump the hammer made striking the paper made me flinch as if a gun had gone off.

"See that? Hit the button with the K on it and there you've got a K on the paper." Jabbing at the keys with one finger, Art typed out, "T-y-p-i-n-g i-s a h-o-o-t."

Sue Kay picked the machine up and put it on my bed table. "Maybe he can try it out tomorrow."

"Let him give it a try right now!" Art protested.

Sue Kay stood in front of him and guided him back to his bed. She said under her breath, "Come on, honey, let's give him some *time.*"

I had felt Art's impatience with me, sometimes even his indifference, but never in the time I knew him had I ever felt disappointment. For two days, he hardly spoke to me or looked my way. And the Hermes Jubilee squatted on my table like an evil presence, untouched.

The next morning over the din of the Dungeon I heard him say to Sue Kay, "He's afraid of a *typewriter?*"

The whole thing made me feel horrible. Art was disappointed in me, I was a victim of dysgraphia, I was afraid of a typewriter. It could get no worse than this.

It took me a few days, but I got up the courage to have a go at the typewriter. Art's disappointment in me was too much; I would have dived headfirst out of our third-story window to win back his acceptance, to get things back to the way they had been.

One morning when everyone but Ismore was gone down to the Dungeon, I got out of bed and retrieved the typewriter from the table. It was even heavier than it looked; it was like trying to heave an anchor onto my bed. I sat cross-legged, playing absently with my loose tooth, and regarded it for awhile. With its strange shape and exposed mechanical guts, I half expected it to try to scuttle away, but it stayed where it was, giving off its oily machine-smell. I read over and over the sentence Art had typed a few days before: "Typing is a hoot."

"Typing is a hoot," I said out loud, hoping it would make me feel encouraged.

I reached out and put my fingertip lightly on the E, then the D. The keys were lacquered and smooth and as big as pennies and I rubbed my fingers along all of them, listening to them click and settle against the slightest pressure—I could feel a power in them, a quiet, mechanical volatility. I jabbed my finger at the E key. I jumped when the hammer struck the paper, lightning fast, I almost couldn't see it, but nothing worse than that happened, nothing blew up or reached out and bit me. Nothing happened except that there was an E on the paper where there hadn't been one before.

It had spooked me when Art had done it, but now that I was the one hitting the keys it felt like magic. An E where there was not an E before, in the blink of an eye. I was so delighted I cackled.

I hit the D and the G and then gave up immediately trying to write my name—what was the use of that?—and began hitting the keys helter-skelter, drumming up a good rolling rhythm until the letters ran off the page. It took a minute or two of panic before I figured

out how to return the carriage so that I could continue my key-
striking. There was something so satisfying about hitting those
keys—the slight resistance at first, then the key finally giving way, like
pulling the trigger of a pistol.

By the time Art and Jeffrey had returned from therapy I had torn
off and pretty much blacked out everyone's progress sheets.

"Look," I said when a nurse wheeled Art into the room, "I have
decided to type."

Art took one of the typed-over progress sheets and inspected it.
"I'll be a redheaded chinaman," he said, looking it over as if inspect-
ing it for errors. "Yessir. Hmm. I see. Real good, Edgar. I believe you
got it nailed."

From that day on I have been a typing fool. I cannot think of a day
since that February morning that I have not spent at least an hour
together with my little typewriter, getting things down on paper, trying to make sense of them, or simply striking the keys without regard
to sense or meaning, like a drummer lost in the beat, pounding away,
losing myself in the letters and words mounting up on the page.

Having the Hermes Jubilee seemed to complete something about
my stay at St. Divine's; I was beginning to settle in. My health was
nearing a hundred percent. I loved going to the Dungeon, loved my
typewriter, loved the time I got to spend with Art, even enjoyed listening to Jeffrey and his theories. As Sue Kay put it, I was beginning
to be a "full-fledged member of the hospital community."

Because I had no visitors, nobody from the outside to bring
flowers or balloons like most of the other patients, Sue Kay, with the
blessing of the staff, had begun a campaign to get people to come
talk to me during visiting hours—she cornered just about everyone
in the hospital and made them promise to pay me a visit. Most likely, she thought few of them would actually come, but was she
wrong. I practically had to make appointments there were so many
people stopping by: patients, nurses and staff from the south wing,
secretaries from downstairs, relatives of other patients I had never
met before.

The nurses would pull the curtain around my bed, place a chair next to it, and I would be ready to accept visitors. A few of them came only once, but many kept coming back. There was a housewife with a stomach virus, a teenage boy named Moony who'd lost most of his foot to a lawn mower, a sad old mechanic who talked with a buzzing microphone held to his throat, a hydrocephalic young woman, a downtrodden marine with a botched buzz cut who raked his groin with a letter opener shaped like a sword.

"Sorry," he would apologize. "My privates tend to itch."

Edgar lay in his bed, still as a lizard on a rock, and listened to people talk about themselves. What is it about a child that makes an adult want to open up and share his secrets, his darkest sins? Maybe it was the cramped atmosphere of the curtain room, just like a confessional, and me, the miracle-boy, lying in the bed like a tiny, benevolent priest. Most of the people, like Art, began by telling me about how things were when they were kids, or telling me about their own kids—they just wanted to relate, I guess—and then, often, they'd wind their way into deeper, darker territory; their teenage screwups, their misunderstanding parents or ungrateful children, their business failings, their worst moments, their doubts about God, their misdeeds and regrets, their broken hearts.

I heard just about everything you can imagine, and though I didn't understand all of it—didn't understand most of it, actually—I enjoyed it just the same. My fingers would be itching to type as they talked, wanting to get it all down. There is truly something satisfying, maybe even entertaining, about people you barely know sitting at the side of your bed, divulging all the gritty details.

Often during the course of these visits Art would peek through the crack in the curtain, making sure everything was all right. Sometimes when somebody took an extra-long time, had a long list of grievances or sins to tell, Art would yell out, "Okay, wrap it up, the boy needs his shut-eye!"

As I continued to get better, it became very hard to stay put in my bed. Often I would get up and wander the halls in my sweat-stained leather helmet, just for something to do. I'd walk with my back straight as a board—Jeffrey told me once that I should try to stay upright because the screws the doctors had put in my skull might come loose and if I were to bend over the top of my head might come off, allowing my brain to roll onto the floor. So I walked the halls with exquisite posture, my spine ramrod straight, making sure my brain stayed in my head where it belonged.

Just to have an excuse to get out of bed and walk the halls, to get out among the people, most of whom knew me and would call out "Edgar!" and pat me on the helmet, I was always claiming I had to pee. I could spend fifteen or twenty minutes sitting in one of the bathroom stalls, reading the graffiti. In fact, I became obsessed with the graffiti. Who were all these messages to? I wondered. What did *Reggie is a cocksucker* mean exactly? And who was Reggie? And why hadn't he come to visit me?

Every time I used the bathroom I chose a different stall—sometimes even snuck down to the second floor—and memorized as much of the graffiti as I could. I would then race back to my Hermes Jubilee and add to my already long list:

> *Liquor in the front Poker in the rear*
> *PLEASE PLEASE LET ME DIE*
> *Cunnilingus is next to Godliness*
> *genitals prefer blondes*
> *God bless the farmacy*
> *has anyone besides me checked out nurse falinski's ass??*
> *I feel better now*
> *Eat shit, Marty!!!*

I would secretly pore over these lists, until I had them all memorized. I had certain favorites: *Eat shit, Marty!!!* seemed particularly hilarious to me and I would giggle to myself under my covers, imagining Marty eating shit, until my sides ached and a nurse would come in to see if I was all right. My only regret was that I could not, however much I wanted to, scribble on one of those stall walls my name or a message of my own.

But I began to feel something—Mrs. Rodale, the social services lady, had asked me that day if I was happy, and I was pretty sure that was what, despite everything, I was beginning to feel: happiness. I was starting to feel comfortable with the place, coming to believe that St. Divine's would be a good place for me to stay, when Dr. Barry Pinkley, the man who had saved my life, crawled through the window one night and threw everything out of whack.

FIRST BEER

FOR THE SEVEN years my mother and I were together, I was nothing but an inconvenience to her, a burden, a source of pain, and her pregnancy with me was no exception. Once Arnold's sperm had penetrated one of her eggs to create a single cell that would eventually become little Edgar, everything went to hell; she fell violently ill, puking every other hour, unable to do much more than lie on the old mattress and get some sleep between attacks of nausea.

During the two weeks after Arnold had run off into the street my mother held out hope that he hadn't really left her; maybe the sight of her pregnant had spooked him, maybe Grandma Paul had scared him off, but she knew the hard truth: he was never coming back.

My mother didn't know why her being pregnant could have frightened him away. On a few of those sweet nights in the back of Arnold's pickup after making love, the moon out and the river rustling the dry stalks, they had talked about having children. Arnold said that he wanted to have a family, wanted to buy some land far away from Grandma Paul and the reservation, maybe raise a few horses and cows along with a handful of kids.

The only real reason my mother could come up with was this: Arnold was a white man. If nothing else, Grandma Paul had taught her that white men are strange, white men make no sense, and always, without fail, white men will tell you one thing and do another. Grandma Paul said she knew of only one trustworthy white person in all of human history and that was Jesus Christ Himself. Grandma believed that even the pastor of her Pentecostal church, Reverend Bernadine, was a fraud.

On a Sunday morning my mother woke up to find an envelope pushed through a tear in the screen sometime in the night. She knew immediately who it was from, and for awhile she did nothing but stare at it, imagining Arnold standing at her window in the silver moonlight, looking in on her while she slept.

The envelope contained a two-page letter and eighty-five dollars and thirty-five cents, Arnold's entire pay for the previous two weeks. Arnold began his letter like this: *Dear Gloria, I am SORRY, I am SORRY, I AM SORRY.* He went on to tell that he was leaving that very day for Rock Springs, Wyoming, where he and one of his new buddies from the Hope ranch were going to get on with a real cowboy outfit. Arnold was still hoping for his chance to ride a horse.

He went on to say in his convoluted and overly polite way that because he was from Connecticut he hadn't understood that white folks and Indians were never meant to be together. *I AM SORRY,* he wrote. *I just wish somebody would have told me about this·sooner! Please take this money and buy some nice things with it. Give my best to Grandma Paul. Good luck! Your friend, Arnold*

My mother tucked the letter back into the envelope next to the money and put it on the floor where she'd found it, hoping that if she left the room for a minute, it might disappear. She went outside under the ramada and knelt next to the slop bucket, desperately wanting to vomit but unable to. Looking down into that bucket she was reminded of how her father, Grandpa Lonny, used to sit out under the ramada and drink all day until he puked into the very same bucket. She remembered how serene he always looked, how particularly unworried and careless, sipping at his Pabst Blue Ribbons, sometimes chasing the beer with a swig of homemade bathtub gin. Even when he puked everything inside him into that bucket, puked so hard his jaw came unhinged, he would keep that perfectly calm expression, as if the cycle of drinking and puking were a meditation.

My mother stood up, went back into the bedroom and picked the envelope off the floor. She took out two bills—a one and a five—and held them up to her nose, hoping to find some trace of Arnold on them, but to her the money smelled like just what it was: betrayal, loneliness, other terrible things she now knew had been chasing her all her life.

She went out into the front yard and called for Nola Herrera, the little mestizo girl who lived across the street. She told Nola that she'd give her a dollar bill to take the five over to Arliss Sloan's house (Arliss was widely known as a prepared drunk; he always had his refrigerator well stocked with beer and homemade pickles) and exchange it for a couple of six-packs, Pabst Blue Ribbons if he had them.

When my mother got the beer she went out back under the ramada and sat in Grandpa Lonny's old chair next to the slop bucket and popped open the first beer of her life. She drank and drank, and during the entire rest of her pregnancy never vomited again.

GHOST IN THE NIGHT

IT WAS IN the middle of a hot March night that Edgar woke from a dead sleep knowing a ghost was coming for him. For two weeks now he had been using his urinal puck to ward off the ghosts who came in the early morning hours and until now it had seemed to work: as long as he slept with the puck under his pillow, the ghosts hadn't shown themselves.

There was a muffled clanging that seemed to vibrate through the floor, converging toward me. I sat up in bed, instantly wide awake. I took the puck from under my pillow and rubbed at it fiercely, its sharp, disinfectant smell burning my nostrils. The clanging stopped and a figure appeared in the window, a black cutout without face or depth, backlit by the lights of Globe and a sky glittering with stars.

For a long time the figure stayed motionless, as if trying to survey the room through the darkness. I did not blink or swallow. There was a tapping noise and the window opened an inch, then another, shrieking with each pull. The figure, a man, swore under his breath and yanked at the window, but he couldn't seem to make it budge any more. This was definitely not like any other ghost who had come before.

Art continued to snore like he was sleeping submerged in a bathtub and Jeffrey made little yipping sounds and whistled delicately through his nose.

The figure stuck his head through the window, looked around, pulled his arms inside, and just about had his torso in when he slipped forward, his weight dragging him down and pulling his legs through the opening, so that he was dumped all at once on the tiled floor.

Art turned over in his bed and bellowed, "What in Judas—" and the figure scrambled on his knees over to Art's bed and whispered fiercely through his teeth, "Mr. Crozier, it's me, Dr. Pinkley! Please keep it down."

Art reached out with his good hand and grabbed a handful of Dr. Pinkley's shirt and pulled him nearly onto the bed. "Who is this?"

"Please!" Barry Pinkley almost screeched, "you've got to whisper! I'm Dr. Pinkley. I used to come by here on rounds a few months back. I'm a doctor."

Art scrutinized Barry's face for a second, then let go of his shirt so that Barry had to grab the bedcovers to keep from sliding onto the floor. Jeffrey kept up his nose-whistling and through the open window came the smell of dust and fumes and the faint barking of coyotes. It was the first time the window had been open since I had been there, and those smells and sounds—the *chuff-chuff-chuff* of sprinklers, the dry, sagey heat of the desert you could taste on your tongue—were as much a shock to my senses as this ghost crawling into our room in the middle of the night.

"Jesus, Art," said Barry, pulling himself to his feet and clamping his hand over his face. "You still wearing that cologne? I think my nose hairs just fell out."

He moved to the foot of Art's bed and stood in a narrow band of light coming from a streetlamp in the parking lot. To me, Barry looked like a baby, a six-foot-tall baby. His face was round and soft and he had pink cheeks and fleshy lips and fine, curly hair that was damp around his ears. His skin had a milky white cast that allowed the branching blue veins of his temples to show through. Even the long threadbare trench coat he wore could not hide the way his belly protruded and his chest seemed to suck in with each breath. He was sweating so much that his face sparkled in the dark room.

Art groaned, twisted himself into an upright position. "It's got to be three in the got-danged morning."

Dr. Pinkley squinted and scanned the room but it was dark except for the light he was standing in. "Just came by for a visit, see how things are going."

"It's three in the morning and you just crawled through the window."

"I truly apologize, but I didn't have a choice. The bastards here won't let me through the front door. They've barred me from the place altogether, if you can believe that. You call that America, somebody barred from visiting his former place of employment? It's fucked up, Art, that's why I'm crawling through the window this time of night."

"I don't know what the hell you're talking about."

"It doesn't matter. Is he here?"

"Who?"

"Edgar Mint. I got word he was still in this room."

Art leaned forward, tried to grab Dr. Pinkley by the arm. "Now don't go waking the boy."

Barry pulled a penlight out of his pocket and waved the beam across the room until it rested on me. I kept quiet, squinting into the light.

Barry knelt next to me, his face very close to mine, and switched the light off. I could see that he was smiling at me, his teeth tiny and square and evenly spaced—the teeth of a baby. Barry might have looked like a baby but he did not smell like one; the stench of cigarettes and gasoline came off him in waves.

"God, Edgar," he said, putting his hand on my shoulder. His eyes were lit with a keen, fevered light. "I've wanted so much to stop in and see how you're doing. I've been hearing great things about you. How are you feeling?"

I about gave in and said "Fine" but I kept my mouth shut. Just when I thought I was pretty much free of the medical profession, here came another doctor, through the window in the middle of the night no less, with his penlight, his tie, his "How are you feeling?"

"He's peachy," Art said. "Now why don't you git."

"Why don't I *git*?" Barry spun to face Art. "I'm not going to *git* because there has to be somebody to look out for this boy's welfare. His parents are gone, he's trying to recover from head trauma the likes of which I've never seen, and they've got him here in this piece-of-shit hospital with the likes of *you*. You might have forgotten, but I saved this child's life and it seems I'm the only one who gives a damn about him."

"That's it," Art said. "I'm calling in the cavalry." He reached out to **hit the call** button next to his bed, and knocked a steel medication **tray to the** ground, causing a tremendous clatter. Jeffrey shot up clutching the air and shouted, "Please, not my fingers!"

Barry Pinkley sighed. "Look, I'm not here to cause problems." He shined his penlight at his watch. "Nurse Lovett is on rounds down in the second wing, will be for twenty more minutes, so you don't need to bother with the call button. You're not dealing with an idiot here."

"And who is this?" Jeffrey wanted to know. Barry shined his light on Jeffrey, whose eyes throbbed and hair swayed back and forth on top of his head like seaweed.

Barry went to the window and pulled something off the fire escape: an old-fashioned leather doctor's bag with a silver clasp. From it he took out a six-pack of beer and handed it to Art, the gold cans dully glinting. He then took the paper sack the beer had been in and pulled it over the lamp next to Art's bed. When he turned the lamp on it gave off an orange, smoky glow, just enough to see everyone by.

"I remember you saying this is what you missed most about being in here," Barry said, gesturing to the beer, which Art held out in front of him like a bomb. "I even brought something for Jeffrey."

"And who are you again?" said Jeffrey.

Barry produced a brown pill bottle from his pocket and when Jeffrey saw what it was, and what was written on it, he forgot all about Barry's identity and went to work trying to get the cap off.

Barry checked my pupils, had me squeeze one of his pudgy fingers, asked me to follow his penlight as he waved it in front of my eyes. Then he put his hands into my hair, pressing lightly on my skull with his fingertips in different places, like somebody worrying over a cantaloupe at the supermarket. "A little lumpy, but not bad."

Barry threw his hands in the air. He seemed exasperated in a happy sort of way. "Well, this is quite extraordinary, isn't it? I really thought they had to be pulling my leg. Skull fracture, three months in a coma, and here he is looking ready to join the Marines. This just doesn't happen, no it doesn't. There's something special about you, Edgar, you've got some kind of destiny to fulfill. That's the only explanation."

"Destiny!" cried Jeffrey, who had wrestled open the bottle, sucked down a couple of pills and was now propped up against his pillow, a look of transcendence on his face. It was much too soon for the pills to have begun working but it appeared that just the possibility, the expectation of a high was enough for Jeffrey. He looked like a man who was about to find the answers to everything.

Art said to Barry, "What I want to know is, as long as you're here, whatever happened to the policeman that ran over him? I don't know how no policeman can run over no little kid and not have to spend a day in jail."

"Policeman?"

"The policeman that ran over him."

"There wasn't any policeman. It was a mailman. Some mailman in a mail jeep."

"*Ppfft,*" Art said. "This is how it is in here. The boy nearly dies, and we can't get the correct information on it. If we didn't have this radio they could tell us the moon fell out of the sky and killed every last person in Kansas and we wouldn't be any the wiser."

Barry looked at all of us. "You mean you really don't know what happened?"

"We don't know a thing!" Jeffrey beamed.

Art was starting to get himself worked up. "I mean, here is a boy, all alone in here, don't know what's going on, and they won't explain what's happened. He asks me about it, asks me about his mama and everything else and what am I supposed to tell him? Why won't they give us the information?"

"They're fuckers, is why," Barry said. "This place is full of know-it-all fuckers who don't give a shit about anything but their own reputations."

"Watch your mouth in front of the kid," said Art.

"Fuckers!" Jeffrey cried jubilantly.

"Christ in the early morning," Art said.

Barry apologized to me for swearing—said he wouldn't let it happen again—and then told the story, in full and painful detail, of my accident. He didn't leave out a thing; he told about the makeshift ambulance and the way Grandma Paul wailed and the way the mailman had taken off his pants and wrapped them around my head. He told us of how he had pounded the life back into me with his fists and the newspapers had given credit to the neurosurgeon who had done nothing more than put my skull back together, which any imbecile with a drill and some wire could do.

"I guess that mailman got all tore up over it," Barry said, smiling and shaking his head. "He thought he'd killed you. Everybody was sure you were dead! Everybody. How could a kid survive a mail jeep on his head? In the end that mailman tried to commit suicide."

"Suicide?" I said.

"Hey, suicide," said Jeffrey, "all right!"

Barry shot Jeffrey a dirty look. "He tried to kill himself. Stabbed himself in the neck with an ice pick, if you can believe that. Everybody assumed you were dead and nobody bothered to tell him differently. I sewed him up, right in the emergency room here. He was blubbering incoherent jibber-jabber, and his wife only told me he stabbed himself, didn't tell me he was actually the guy who'd run over Edgar. So I put a few stitches in him, referred him to the staff psychiatrist and sent him on his way. Next thing I hear he and the wife have disappeared, skipped town."

Jeffrey clucked his tongue. "Tragic," he said. "Tragic, tragic, tragic."

Barry knelt down next to me again, put his face close to mine. "I don't want you to worry about any of this," he said. "I'm going to make sure you're taken care of. I don't want you to be afraid."

He took a small toy—a red cast-iron tractor—out of his pocket and handed it to me. "I used to play with this when I was a kid. It was my favorite. I want you to have it."

Far off down the hall, we could hear Night Nurse's shoes squeaking toward us. Barry switched off the lamp, grabbed his bag and dove through the narrow opening onto the fire escape, his boots clattering against the window frame.

"Hey, you're coming back aren't you?" Jeffrey eyeballed the bottle in his hand. "There aren't that many pills in here. If it's money you need, I can get that. Money is no object."

"I'll be back, don't worry," Barry whispered from outside. He shut the window and was gone.

THE GOOD DOCTOR

IT WASN'T UNTIL later that we found out why Barry had to crawl through the window that night instead of dropping by during visiting hours like a normal person. Barry had been fired from St. Divine's a month after he saved my life. Even though he had done an extraordinary job of reviving me, he had not followed standard procedure in my resuscitation, and the head nurse, who had already developed an extreme dislike for Barry in the two days she had known him, filed a report. The medical board sent Barry a politely worded reprimand, which would have been the end of it, but Barry could not let it lie. He had saved the life of an innocent child and he was being *reprimanded* for it? He simply couldn't live with that; his pride wouldn't allow it. He wrote letters to every member of the board, telephoned the state medical examiner in the middle of the night, sent long angry missives to all the area newspapers and waged such a campaign against the hospital that the board asked him to accept a transfer. When Barry refused they fired him.

During the days between his first visit and second, Jeffrey and Art argued constantly about Barry. Art didn't want Barry sneaking in at night. *If he comes again,* Art said, *I'm going to sic Night Nurse on him, I'll tie a knot in him myself if I got to.* Jeffrey was wholly and passionately on Barry's side. Barry was an angel, Jeffrey argued, a man who looked on human suffering with a little compassion, unlike the vampires in white coats walking around St. Divine's. Within a couple of days, the doctors and nurses began to remark on how pink and healthy Jeffrey was beginning to look, how calm and composed. Every night Jeffrey would stay up, tucked under his covers, watching the window like an orphan on Christmas Eve. By the weekend,

Jeffrey had run out of pills. By Monday, he was looking yellow and sickly and desperate.

When Barry showed Tuesday night, Jeffrey nearly fell out of his bed with joy. Barry wrenched open the window and toppled into the room.

"Goddamn window!" he whispered, picking himself from the floor and grabbing his knee. Art gurgled and farted but did not wake up.

Barry went through the same ritual as before: closed the door to the hall, put the paper bag over the lamp and distributed his gifts. When Barry delivered a new bottle of pills to Jeffrey, he got the kind of heartfelt hug usually reserved for men coming home from war. When Barry went to give Art a pint of Jack Daniel's, Jeffrey, in the middle of gulping down a couple of pills, raised his voice, "Ah, let's not bother the gentleman. He gets a little violent when he's awakened. We'll make sure he gets his liquor."

Barry put the bottle down on the bed table and came over to me. "Edgar," he said, and pulled up a chair next to my bed. Tonight he was wearing a dirty overcoat, a white oxford and a tie that looked like it had been used to wipe up a spill. His breath was full of cigarettes.

He pulled a stethoscope out of his pocket and listened to my heart. He seemed to calm down almost immediately—his twitching went away, his eyes quit darting and his breathing slowed.

"That's one strong heart. A real pure-D thumper."

"Pure-D," I said.

"Do you like that tractor I brought you?"

"No," I said. "How come you didn't bring something for Ismore?"

Barry looked surprised, as if he didn't know who I was talking about, then he turned to look at Ismore. Ismore stared back from inside that dead body of his and Barry turned quickly away—nobody, not even nurses, could lock eyes with Ismore for very long.

"I forgot about him. You're right, I should bring him something. Where are my manners."

"You know," said Jeffrey, who already had that lost, beatific look on his face, "we should probably go ahead and kill Ismore. That could be his gift. I'm sure that's what he wants. What do you think?

Brady Udall

A hypodermic full of insulin into his IV tube and that would be the end of it. Then he wouldn't have to be so pissed anymore."

"I've been doing some checking around," Barry said to me, glancing at Jeffrey from time to time. "I found out where your grandma is. She's in a place for sick old people. I was thinking, if you want, I could go see her myself, see how she is, tell her I've seen you."

"What about the mailman?" I said.

Barry raised his eyebrows.

"The mailman in the accident," I said. "Where's he?"

"He must be . . . look, Edgar, I don't think the mailman is the important thing in all of this."

"Can you find him?"

"Hey Doctor?" Jeffrey said. "I wanted to ask you something. Why is it that we wash our hands *after* we go to the bathroom and not before? I mean, shouldn't I be a little more concerned about getting certain germs on a certain part of my body than on my hands?"

"Would you shut up?" Barry said.

"Yes," said Jeffrey.

Barry pulled his chair closer to me and said over his shoulder to Jeffrey, "I'd like to talk to Edgar here without any interruptions. Do you think that would be all right with you?"

"No interruptions," Jeffrey said, waving his hands. "I cease to interfere."

Barry turned back to me and went through the standard battery of doctor-questions, beginning with the well-worn opener, "How are you feeling?" I gave all my standard answers until Barry got to a question I'd never heard before.

"Are you homesick?"

"Homesick?"

"Do you want to go back home?"

"No."

"Well, I don't blame you. From what I saw it's not much of a place. A shack is what it is. Do you miss your mother?"

I thought about it for a minute.

"Yes," I said.

"Yes, yes you do. What about your grandma, do you want to see her?"

"I don't know."

Jeffrey began to whistle a peppy rendition of "I've Been Working on the Railroad." Barry snapped his fingers, which silenced Jeffrey instantly.

"Are you lonely?" Barry said. "Do you feel sad sometimes?"

"I don't know."

"Yes, it's difficult, no way around it. I don't want you to worry. I'm going to take care of things."

Barry got up and opened the door a crack, peeked out into the hall. "I better get going," he said, doing a pantomime of a tiptoeing burglar. "These bastards would have me shot if they knew I was in here."

"Not to interrupt, but I'm getting some money so I can pay you," Jeffrey said to Barry. "I told my mother to take my turntable to the pawnshop."

"I don't want any money," Barry said. "Just make sure that Art gets his whiskey. And be good to Edgar. He doesn't have anybody."

Jeffrey held up his new bottle full of pills as if it was a glass of champagne and he was making a toast. "You, sir, are a saint," he called.

Before Barry slithered back out the window, he came over to my bed, bent down and left a light, dry kiss on my forehead, right between the eyes.

BIRTH OF A HALF-BREED

THE DAY EDGAR was born it snowed in the desert. A freak thunder- and snowstorm had rumbled through and dropped an inch of dry snow-pebbles that instantly froze together and formed a grainy crust—the first snow to hit the ground in San Carlos in four years. My mother woke up just after midnight with her first contractions and after two or three hours could not lie quiet in the bed anymore. She got up, threw her blanket around her shoulders and walked out into a star-bright night, down the hill to the river, to get some beer.

My mother kept her beer in the river because Grandma Paul didn't want it in the house and she liked her beer ice-cold. On the way down the hill another contraction stopped her in her tracks, nearly dropped her to her knees; little Edgar was clamoring to get out.

My mother hardly noticed the snow. She walked barefoot across the dry, buckling crust of ice, holding her belly with both arms, and without so much as a flinch waded out into the freezing river, casting about with her feet in the shallows for the two six-packs which were kept tied to a tree root like a bunch of trout. When she couldn't feel the cluster of cans right off she panicked, bending awkwardly to search the shallows with her hands, splashing and groaning, nearly losing her balance. Just as her hand found one of those Pabst Blue Ribbons another contraction hit—the worst yet—but in the midst of it she was still able to pull the tab off the can and pour the beer past her clenched teeth. The bitter taste, the feeling of it foaming down her throat immediately calmed her and she stood in that river, her feet numb, and had three more beers, calmly sucking them down, until her water broke and the warm, soupy fluid which had surrounded and cushioned and contained little Edgar for the whole of his existence ran down her legs and mixed with the freezing waters of the San Carlos River on its way to the muddy ponds and cement irrigation canals of the Sonoran Desert.

My mother dropped her beer and cried out. The pain of the contractions had been one thing, but this, the sudden gush between her legs, the fluid draining out with the warmth and consistency of blood—nobody had prepared her for anything like this. She thought about sitting down in the river and letting it all go, giving in completely, but something made her pull herself out of the river and start up the hill toward the house on numb, ice-crusted legs, dragging her precious beers behind her at the end of a mossy length of twine.

Grandma Paul was already outside, building a fire in the pit next to the ramada and situating my mother's mattress next to it. Grandma Paul had the power of premonition; she could not foretell the weather, or see the future, but she had an uncanny sense about tragedy and pain. She could feel them coming like a wind.

My mother's labor lasted all day and into the next evening. She lay propped up on the mattress, heaving and crying out and swigging Pabst Blue Ribbons in between. During her entire pregnancy she had only had three or four beers a day, not enough to get her truly drunk, but sufficient to keep the nausea down, to help her forget about Arnold and where he might be, to help her forget about the baby inside her. Now she was truly tanked, obliterated. In between contractions she shouted at the turkey buzzards orbiting like dark planets in the blank white sky, kicked at Grandma Paul when she tried to take away an empty can collapsed in her fist, laughing until she began to choke.

Bright-eyed and furious, Grandma Paul commanded my mother to be quiet, to have some dignity, but my mother did not care. She chugged her beer, laughed at the sun and shouted until she was hoarse, "Arnold!" She giggled until she choked, as if the name itself were the funniest thing she could imagine. "Arnold! Arnold! *Ar*-nold!"

Out in the street a few kids were attempting to sled down the street in cardboard boxes but the snow was now just loose slush and their boxes soon melted away into a heavy, fibrous mess. As the day wore on and the autumn sun consumed the snow completely, more of the neighbors stopped at the fence, peering through the rickweed to see what all the racket was about. Folks were starting to get annoyed with the incessant noise, but nobody complained. The closer I got to making my appearance, the more people showed up to watch. The birth of a half-breed was not a common occurrence on the reservation; people wanted to see if I would come out with some kind of freak characteristic, like pink albino eyes or, better yet, a long hooked tail.

It was dusk when my mother stopped babbling and really began to scream, a high wordless wail. Most of the onlookers had gone home to cook up their beans and fry bread, watch TV and drink their own beer, so they did not get to see my grand entrance (or exit). I came out bloody and squinting and did not cry even when Grandma Paul grabbed me by the neck and shook me like a doll. I gasped and gulped in silence like a dying fish and the last few spectators were left to straggle home disappointed: I was not strange or different in any way, just another black-haired, red-skinned baby born on the reservation.

A JAR OF DIRT

SOON BARRY PINKLEY became a regular part of the routine at St. Divine's: every Wednesday around 1 A.M. his dark outline would block the lights of town and he would clamber through the window like some low-rent incarnation of Santa Claus, clutching his doctor's bag full of liquor, cigarettes and drugs.

It took awhile, but Barry and Jeffrey were finally able to ascertain what it was that would make Ismore happy: porno magazines. Every week Barry would show up with a couple of well-thumbed issues of *Gent* or *Dude* which he placed in front of Ismore on a scarred, graffiti-spangled music stand which he had paid one of the orderlies to swipe from the local high school.

"Just keep those things away from the boy," Art would say every time.

After my checkup, Barry would usually stay about half an hour or so. He could go on at length about all the hospital gossip coming down through the grapevine, which nurse was sleeping with which doctor, which orderly had been caught filching morphine from the narcotics cabinet. He would walk up and down the aisle between the beds as he ranted about the bastards on the medical board doing their best to destroy the practice of medicine as we know it, pausing every so often to turn the page of Ismore's magazine.

One night, after Art had dozed off and Jeffrey was absorbed with his pills, Barry sat on my bed and said, "I'm glad all of this has happened, Eddie."

"Edgar," I said.

He chuckled and shook his head with false amusement. "You wouldn't think your getting run over and me getting fired would be good for either of us, but look at us now! If I was still a doctor here, I'd never get to talk to you like this man to man, it would all be, 'How are you feeling, what color is your urine these days?' There's no such thing as *feelings* when you're a doctor. Everything's quantifiable, no such thing as mystery. That's why the brain is the most interesting of all the organs, the most *mysterious*." Here he touched my head with his fingertips, felt around a little and sighed with satisfaction. "People would try to tell you it's the heart, but the heart is just a pump, no more complicated than a lawn mower engine. It's our brains that make us who we are. Our hearts don't have anything to do with it."

Barry patted my cheek, smiled down at me, and I said, "I don't know whether to shit or go blind." This was something I'd heard Art say a few times and I liked the sound of it.

Often I would type while Barry talked, *tak-tak-tak*ing away like a courtroom stenographer, which, I could see very clearly, aggravated him to no end. His shoulders would creep up toward his ears and a muscle in his jaw would start to quiver. The more agitated he became, the harder I typed. He would try to talk above my typing, giving me nervous glances and finally he would stop, go completely rigid and shout, "Christ! Would you put that thing away for a minute?"

Even though Art, I'm sure, was just as agitated by my typing, he always told Barry to watch his mouth. But whenever Art stood up for me like that, I began to detect a weakness in his voice, a kind of resignation, that I'm sure Barry picked up on as well, because he began to ignore Art, began to realize the power he had over the sorry-sack lot of us: a quadriplegic, a drug-crazed crony, a grief-stricken drunk and a head-injured boy.

It was with the intuition of a child that I knew the arrival of Barry spelled the end of my short-lived happiness at St. Divine's. I had found a small oasis of contentment; I was relatively pain-free, I had a friend and protector in Art, and I felt like I was part of something. I believed that my life had been spared by some miracle so I could stay and live out my days in this run-down, foul-smelling hospital. Most important to me, I had come to believe that if I were to leave someone might actually miss me.

Barry made me feel uneasy and sometimes half-panicked, but his visits seemed to affect Art worse than anyone. Art, never a talkative man, became even more closemouthed, going days on end without saying a word to anyone, except for calling the nurses "sour-faced old heifers" under his breath or the orderlies "wisenheimers of the first degree." He even stopped wearing his cologne, which allowed the smell of alcohol on him to become noticeable for the first time. He grew increasingly impatient with my questions and my typing, and once, after I followed him around in the Dungeon wanting to know what the word "bungholer" meant (I had heard an old man with a botched cleft palate use it on one of the new orderlies), Art turned to me and growled, "No more questions, please, could you keep quiet for a single minute?"

He might as well have kicked me in the stomach. I backed away from him and sat down at my little desk, my eyes stinging, and pounded my Play-Doh into one colorless lump.

Back in our room that night, Art kept the curtain pulled around his bed, something he had never done before except for a few times during Barry's visits, his mouth set hard as a doorknob. Once the lights were out I could hear him swallowing his whiskey at even intervals, the quiet pop of suction when he pulled the bottle from his mouth. I was finally able to sleep but woke up in the dark morning hours when I heard Art moving around. He shuffled along the floor in his slippers, clicked on the lamp next to his bed and opened the drawer of the Formica-topped nightstand on which the lamp sat. He grunted, climbed back onto his bed and was quiet for a moment before a whining hiss came from the other side of that curtain, a sound like air escaping from a break in a hose.

I climbed down from my bed and padded around the curtain until I could see through a gap in the cloth about six inches wide. Art sat in his bed in the small rectangle of yellow light, weeping. Not loud boo-hooing, but more like humming at a pitch so low you could barely hear it, his face red and shining with the effort of trying to hold it in. He had a number of objects laid out on his bed: some photographs I could only see the edges of, a battered old book, a bottle of Wild Turkey with a couple inches of whiskey still left and a Mason jar filled with dirt. I knew what the Mason jar was; a few months before, not long after I'd come out of my coma, a wiry man in a dark wool suit—probably a pastor or maybe the funeral home director—brought the jar one day during visiting hours, handed it to Art and told him it was dirt from the graves of his wife and daughters. In a low monotone the man said that since Art had not been able to attend the funeral, he thought he might want a memento of it.

The man tried to go on, to offer Art his condolences, but Art told him that he didn't ever want to see him again, that he better get out of the room now while he still could. The man stood up, his eyes wide and his head moving back and forth with alarm, and backed out of our room as if Art had a gun leveled at him.

I never saw that Mason jar after that, but here it was now, on Art's lap as he shook and clutched at his face as if he were trying to fight back something inside that was trying to make its way out. From where I stood I could smell the whiskey, sour and sharp. Weeping harder now, Art picked up the jar, fought to wrench open the lid with his good hand while gripping the jar between his thighs. Grief and anger had twisted his face into something desperate and horrible and I was terrified by it. Once he got the jar open he lifted out some

of the dirt with his fingers, calming just a little as he watched it spill
into his lap. He dug out more dirt and this time looked at it for only
a second before scooping it into his mouth, poking with his thick
fingers to make sure it stayed in. He shoveled in more, trying hard to
swallow, his teeth making gritty crunching noises as they came
together, until black, oozing mud began to seep from the corner of
his lips and down the hollow of his neck. He sobbed harder, almost
noiselessly, his blackened teeth and tongue standing out against his
pale, stricken face.

"Goddamn," he said, his voice thick with mud. "God*damn*."

I thought about yelling at the top of my lungs, anything to make
him stop, but my chest felt like it was wrapped in cables pulled tight
with a ratchet. I watched until I couldn't stand it anymore. I backed
away, looked over at Ismore, who was awake and glaring at me like
the devil himself, and stumbled to my bed and lay there until the
weeping stopped, rubbing my urinal puck on my cheek until I slept.

THE LIGHT OF DAY

THE NEXT DAY, Edgar was taking his morning stroll down the Ward
B hallway, greeting and glad-handing the sick and infirm, when
Delancey, one of the orderlies, walked up behind him, took his hand
and said, staring straight ahead, "Edgar, my man, walk with a nigger
for a minute."

Delancey was big, still a teenager, and his hand was like a huge
hairless spider locked onto mine. We took the elevator to the first
floor and walked down a little-used corridor past doors marked
MAINTENANCE and SUPPLIES. Delancey stopped at a door without
any markings, knocked twice, took a quick look each way to make
sure nobody was around, and pulled me inside. The room smelled
like old oil and was filled with a dusty, dim light provided by a single
window half hidden behind a stack of boxes. Besides the boxes, the

room was filled with broken or unused machinery: several old wheelchairs, a massive dialysis machine, rusted parts strewn across a desktop, a couple of floor buffers hunched in a corner.

"Hey," Delancey whispered into the empty air. "I got the kid here."

As if it were a trick of light, Dr. Pinkley appeared from behind the dialysis machine. Delancey jumped like he was being jerked off his feet by wires and said, "Fuck, man!"

Barry folded his arms and smiled grimly. He wore a white doctor's smock and, instead of four or five days' worth of beard, was clean-shaven and had a pink, just-scrubbed look about him. To me, Barry had always been just another ghost in the night, so seeing him like this, with a new buzz cut and smelling of Listermint, real and substantial in the hard light of day, made the hairs on my arms stand up.

Delancey was still trying to get over the fright Barry had given him—swearing under his breath and stomping his feet—when Barry Pinkley told him to be back in exactly three minutes to pick me up and take me back upstairs. "And if anybody asks you what you're up to you tell them the boy got lost and you're taking him back where he belongs." Delancey went out the door mumbling to himself, "Damn, did that fucker scare me."

Barry grabbed me under the arms and hoisted me up so I could sit on the desk next to him. "Look at this helmet they've got on you," he said, shaking his head. "The third world."

He took the stethoscope from around his neck and handed it to me to play with. This must have been some kind of ploy he had learned in medical school; I knew I was supposed to treat it like a toy, put it in my ears like a real doctor, be amused and comforted by it, but I held it away from my body as if it were a dead snake. "You scared me, too," I said, looking down at my lap.

"I didn't mean to scare anyone, but I have to be careful in here. If they knew I was in here they'd have me in the slammer before you could say boo."

I thought about yelling "Boo!" at the top of my lungs, loud enough to be heard down the hall.

"We don't have much time so I want you to listen," Barry said.

"They're going to take you away from here. They've decided your mother is a lost cause so they've found a legal guardian for you, put you with some long-lost relative you've never met before. Do you hear what I'm saying, Edgar?"

I stared at the stethoscope in my hands. Barry took my chin between his finger and thumb and turned my head so I was looking him in the eye. "Do you understand what I'm saying? They're going to send you away, get rid of you. They don't want to deal with you anymore. So they found the easiest way out."

He put his face closer to mine and I could see the packed, feathery folds of his irises. "I'm going to take you away from here. There's nobody here that cares about you, nobody anywhere. Your mother abandoned you, Edgar, left you for dead. Two different times the Indian Health Service had to take care of you while your mother was in the hospital for alcohol poisoning. Once, when your grandma was in New Mexico visiting relatives, the social worker stopped by and found you sleeping in the crawl space under the house with the family dog, your mother nowhere to be found. I know you don't like to hear that, but it's the simple truth and it's something you've got to understand. They don't care. The doctors, the nurses? Just looking for a paycheck. You might think Art is your friend, but he's just a sick old man who needs somebody to talk to. And now they're trying to pawn you off on some seventy-five-year-old janitor who's never even met you. I'm not going to let them do this to you, Edgar. I'm going to take care of you."

"Eat shit, Marty," I whispered.

"What?" Barry said.

"Eat shit," I said, this time without any whisper at all.

I saw the muscles in Barry's jaw spasm, but then his face softened. He put his hand on my shoulder then took it off quickly. He couldn't seem to decide if he was angry or sad. "I think . . ." he said, stopping short, gathering himself, then bent down so we were face to face again. He locked eyes with me, his antiseptic breath puffing into my face.

"I know maybe you're a little afraid of me. I know Art says bad things about me and the hospital thinks I'm a blackhearted criminal, but I'm trying to help you, I really am. This is not a trick, I don't want anything from you. But I know what it's like to be alone, to not have anybody. I've dealt with it my whole life. It's terrible, Edgar, the worst thing in the world. You need someone who'll take care of you. That's why I'm here now. Thursday night I'm coming to get you. I've made my decision. I've got it all set up and I want you to be ready. I'm going to take you away from this place and give you whatever you want. You'll be happy, I promise you. I'll take care of you."

For a few moments we stayed like that, eye to eye, and it was very clear to me that Barry meant what he said, that he believed it.

He took the stethoscope from me. "Is that okay with you?"

I waited for a few beats and then said it: "Okay."

Barry gave me an awkward half-hug and just then Delancey slipped through the door, bouncing on the balls of his feet, nervous as a rabbit. Barry helped me off the desk and slipped some money into one of Delancey's big hands.

"Be ready," Barry whispered to me as Delancey led me out into the hall. "And not a word to anybody."

THE SMELTER

ART WAS HAVING a hard time keeping his arm down. A few minutes before, they had cut off his cast, and now he was sitting on his bed, his big feet with their horny nails sticking out, looking at his arm, which was angled out from his body like a chicken wing.

"Won't that beat everything," he said. He pushed his floating arm down with his good hand and watched it come right back up. "It won't stay down for nothing."

Art's newly liberated arm was as pale and limp as a noodle, covered with pink scar tissue where the flesh had been scraped away, but it didn't seem to bother him much. I pulled back the curtain so

Ismore could see and we all watched Art's arm float up like a thing with a mind of its own.

"Entertainment for all," Jeffrey said. "Too bad they're finally kicking you out of here. What *will* we do for our amusement?"

Art's arm suddenly stopped its levitating act. He glared hotly at Jeffrey and turned away from both of us.

Earlier that day, one of the doctors had come in and, loud enough for us to hear, informed Art that everything looked good for him to go home once and for all. They'd send a therapist to work with him there until he was well enough to make weekly trips to the Dungeon.

Yesterday I'd had similar news: Mrs. Rodale stopped by to confirm what Barry, in his spooklike way, had already found out. Uncle Julius, Grandma Paul's half brother, was going to take over my care and upbringing. Uncle Julius, Mrs. Rodale informed me, was a janitor at the Willie Sherman School, a BIA boarding school for Indian kids. It was a perfect situation in many ways, she told me, sticking a pencil into her hair so that it disappeared from view. Not only would I be with a member of my family, but I would be living right there in the dormitories with the other students, learning and playing sports and participating in all manner of social activities. She made it sound like I was going to live in a carefree place of sunshine and happiness, a place like California. All they needed, she said, was to put the paperwork in order, get the clearance from the doctors and I would be on my way to Fort Apache.

I had planned to tell Art all about my talk with Barry, but now I wasn't so sure. I didn't want to go with Barry, but neither did I want to live in a school with a man named Uncle Julius who I had never met before. I thought maybe Art could help me come up with a way for me to stay at St. Divine's—he had done pretty well keeping himself in the hospital against all odds—but now he was going home and I didn't particularly want to spend my days with only Jeffrey and Ismore to talk to.

For the next two days, Art seemed to get back to his old self. He told me I was spending way too much time henpecking on that typewriter of mine, so he accompanied me down the hallways on my walks and even took me outside to the courtyard, where we played a little game of trying to kick a half-inflated volleyball into the fouled fountain. In the middle of the fountain was the crumbling, ochre-stained statue of some cowled female saint. When I was able to get the ball in the fountain, Art clambered over the edge, grabbing his gimpy leg with both hands and hauling it up like it was a piece of luggage. He stood on his tiptoes in a puddle of green mosquito water, put his arm around the statue, his hands on her buttocks, and kissed her right on her stony lips. I laughed like I never had before, fell on my back and howled like a lunatic until a voice came from one of the second-floor windows, "Would somebody shut that boy up?"

On Wednesday evening, the day before Barry was to come in the middle of the night and steal me away, Art took me up on the roof to watch his smelter. "I think they're going to start her up tonight," he said, nodding seriously. "Got a feeling. Been trucking that ore in two days straight now. I was hoping maybe we might catch them pouring off the slag. Oh, it's something to see in the dark."

We were supposed to be in the cafeteria eating our dinner, but instead Art grabbed some Saltines, a couple of mealy apples and a bottle of dairy creamer, stuffed it all in the pockets of his bathrobe and took me up a flight of stairs that led out onto the flat roof of the administration wing. The sun had just gone down and the sky was pink at its edges, the moon faint and indistinct like a patch of frost on a window. Across a flat expanse of scrubland were the hills of Globe, where heat-buckled asphalt streets zagged and switchbacked between shanties and mobile homes perched on the slightest outcropping. Down below a thin line of smoke drifted out of the smelter's single enormous smokestack.

I shoved crackers into my mouth and sipped at the dairy creamer while Art took out his little telescope and looked the whole operation over. The tar paper we were sitting on was still warm and I felt like leaning back and falling asleep.

Art lost himself in a brutal coughing fit for at least a full minute.

"Ah," he said when it was all over, "I got about as much strength as a squashed cat." He was silent for awhile, spying at the smelter through the glass. Then he pointed to the flat expanse of desert between the smelter and the hill on which St. Divine's had been built.

"You see that hole in the ground right there, surrounded by a fence? That's called Bob's Drop. It's a old mine shaft. Ever since the mine played out, they been dropping dead folks down that hole. A half mile deep, and they won't close it off because they think there's more silver to be had. I think everybody's forgot about it by now, but it used to be the most popular place around to make a corpse disappear. I've thought maybe I'd go down there sometime and take a leap, spare somebody else the trouble."

I looked up at Art and he laughed and patted me on the back. "I'm only thinking out loud, Edgar, don't worry. I couldn't jump into a hole if I wanted to. Heights scare the billy heck out a me."

He turned the glass toward the glowing lights of town. "That's my house, right over there, the little green one under the water tower. I'm going to burn it down, I think, just to see the flames, and then I'm going to find a motel to live in. I don't even know how to make my own bed, you know. It'd be a disaster for me to live in any place except a motel."

Art removed a quart whiskey bottle from the pocket of his robe and took three large swallows, his Adam's apple moving like a piston. He shook his head, not bothering to wipe away the whiskey that had run out of the damaged side of his mouth and down his neck. "Now that you're going off, seems like I should give you some advice, words to live by, you know, but I ain't got nothing. Be polite, that's about as far as I'll go. Anything more and it's likely to backfire on you."

"Backfire," I said. "Okay."

"Do you know your right from your wrong?"

"No."

"Well, okay then. Stay away from girls, but you probably already heard that one. Women'll betray you every time. Don't take crap from nobody, eat your got-danged vegetables, I don't know." Art's words were beginning to slur. "I'm a wreck. Any questions you wanted to ask me? I'm as useless a friend as you could likely find."

"Is tomorrow Thursday?" I said, after some consideration.

"I believe it is, yes. You're making it easy on me."

"And today's Wednesday?"

Art nearly choked on another swallow of whiskey. "Well, I guess it is. I don't believe there's any doubt that it's Wednesday."

From somewhere far away came the sound of voices, a man and woman arguing in Spanish, the woman suddenly screeching as if in pain. We listened for a moment and Art sighed like he was trying to get every bit of air out of his lungs. "Lord help us this world is a horrible place."

It fell dark around us. We didn't say a word for a long time, just watched as lights blinked on around the smelter, but not much else happened. The humps of slag rose up dark and foreboding against the starblown sky. Art sipped his whiskey and I worked at the crud in my belly button. Suddenly there was a swish around our heads, a disturbance of air, a strange high squealing like BBs whizzing past and Art began waving his hand around and calling out in a slurred staccato, "Jumping Jesus Christ!" And then, "It's just bats. Whole tribe of 'em out looking for skeeters."

I watched the swarm of bats move through the yellow lights of the parking lot, clearing out the moths and gnats in a matter of seconds, and I thought about Art and what he told me about his days shoveling bat guano from caves, and the way he and his brothers stunk like pigs and how his wife and daughters were dead forever and not coming back. I thought about my father, Arnold Mint, who was also never coming back, and my mother in California and Grandma Paul sick in a hospital not too far from here and the red-haired mailman who had run over my head, living out there somewhere in the dark thinking he'd killed a boy. I thought instead of going with Barry Pinkley or with Uncle Julius off to the boarding school, maybe I should take off by myself, go find some of these people, search them out on my own to tell them that I was fine, I was going to be all right, there was no need to worry.

We waited in the dark for something to happen down at the smelter, for it to miraculously bloom into a beautiful nighttime spectacle, but it just sat there, the warning light on its smokestack blinking red in the dark. The woman screamed once or twice more, but that was it for excitement.

"False alarm," Art said finally, and we descended together into the swampy air of St. Divine's.

THE FIRES OF HELL

A HOT THURSDAY night in April, and Ismore and Edgar were the only ones awake. On Barry's regular visiting night Jeffrey was usually bright-eyed and fidgety, his face putting off a low-wattage glow of expectation, but tonight he was twittering peacefully, absolutely nightmare-free.

I rubbed my urinal puck between my palms and occasionally looked over at Ismore, who was glaring at the ceiling like he was willing it to fall in on him. After awhile, I noticed an orange flicker lighting up the window and climbed off my bed to have a look. Across the dark plain the smelter was pulsing with bursts of light and what looked like magma ran down the black heaps in thick, slow-moving rivulets. Through one of the large open doors I could see sparks flying and a sudden orange flare like fireworks going off, and here came more molten slag, farther along the line, snaking down the piles. The sight made a thrill run through me, but I couldn't bring myself to wake Art; he was sleeping just as peacefully as Jeffrey, his lungs creaking like an old screen door.

Instead of getting back into bed, I paced the tiled floor of the room, my guts roiling. Occasionally I peeked out the door to see if

Night Nurse was at her station, but the hall was dark and silent, the whole hospital unnaturally quiet.

"Eat shit," I said to myself as I paced, "eat shit, eat shit, eat shit."

I ran my fingers along the keys of the Hermes Jubilee, held the urinal puck cool against my face.

"That's good, that's real, real nice," Jeffrey croaked in his sleep.

Five seconds before I felt the vibration of Barry coming up the fire escape, I knew he was there. Unlike the other times he had come up, there was no *clang clang clang,* only the slightest trembling—the fire escape would make more noise than that in a light spring wind.

I stood frozen at the window for a minute, then turned and hunched over so my face was right next to Art's. "Wake up," I said, waving the urinal puck directly under his nose the way I'd seen the nurses use smelling salts on fainters in the Dungeon. Art stirred a little and I put my hand on his scarred jaw, moved it around until his head popped up. He seemed to struggle with all the muscles in his face to open his eyes.

"Edgar?" he said, his bloodshot eyeballs rolling in their sockets, trying to focus.

"Barry's coming up right now," I told him, my voice a hiss. "He told me he's going to take me away. He said he's coming to get me."

Art seemed to see me for the first time. He said, "Go, get in your bed. Hurry now."

I was pulling my covers up when Barry's form appeared on the fire escape. He slid the window open as far as it would go and gingerly stepped in, as graceful as a cat. He had an army rucksack slung over one shoulder, a yellow flashlight in his hand.

He looked around the room, sidled over and sat on the edge of my bed, started pulling things out of the rucksack. "Ready to go?" he said brightly, not bothering to whisper.

I looked at Art, who hadn't moved.

"Don't worry about them," Barry said, grinning. "Look at 'em sawing logs. I made sure a couple of sleeping pills got into their after-dinner meds. Here, put on these clothes I got for you. Are you ready to hit the wide-open highways? Man, this is exciting!" Barry was wearing a silk jacket with a dragon stitched in gold thread on the back. When he turned the dragon writhed and coiled in the indefinite light.

Busy pulling socks and pants and bright new hightops from his bag, he didn't notice Art slide off his bed and stand up as straight as he could manage, his back to the window, his small, bent form lit by the flickering orange glow.

"Get away from the boy," Art said.

Barry didn't even turn around, just sighed and leaned with both arms against my bed, shaking his head, as if this was something he had been expecting all along. "Art, this is none of your business. Go back to sleep and we won't have any problems."

"You get away from that boy now." Art took a step closer.

"We don't have time for this," Barry said, stuffing the clothes back into the bag. When he began to slide his hands underneath me to lift me up, Art was on him, clamping onto him from behind, both arms locked around his waist, dragging him to the floor. Barry pitched to the left, arms flailing, trying to twist away until both he and Art crashed together into the foot rail of Jeffrey's bed, pulling down Jeffrey's IV bottle, which bounced once on the mattress and crashed onto the floor, its clear liquid spreading out into a thin puddle that reflected the murky shapes in the room like a mirror.

Barry was the first to his feet. He had two fistfuls of Art's gown and with a great groan he swung him around and let go, heaving Art into the wall. There was a moment of silence—Art didn't move and Barry bent over, his chest heaving—and then Art was up again, bull-rushing Barry with his head down, his arms held wide.

What a strange sight to see Barry, a giant, oversized baby, battling Art, an old child-sized man, as they slipped and clutched at each other between the beds. Edgar, filled with the rare adrenaline of violence and fear, clapped his helmet on his head and began winging whatever he could get his hands on—urinal puck, crayons, bedpan— and slinging them into the middle of the melee.

Barry and Art went to the floor again—the broken glass cracking and grinding underneath their knees and elbows—and now Barry had a solid advantage, straddling Art's torso and twisting his bad arm until Art roared like an animal, his oiled hair breaking loose and flapping over his face. Once I was all out of small objects to throw I didn't even think about it. I lifted the Hermes Jubilee off my night table, positioned myself at the bottom of my bed and heaved it over the edge. One corner of it clipped the edge of my mattress, which altered its trajectory so that it caught Barry square in the small of the back, making a horrible ringing noise as it rolled onto the floor, a noise that left me with a pang of instant regret.

Barry arched his spine, yelping in pain, which gave Art the opportunity to turn and deliver a forearm shot to Barry's throat that made him go to the floor face-first, slumping in on himself like a man made entirely of rubber. Art then proceeded to deliver a series of short, vicious rabbit punches to the side of Barry's head, the bones of his fist making a hollow popping noise against Barry's skull. I could see that all the hurt and anger was coming out with those punches, and he delivered them with a satisfied ferocity, with a zealous light in his eyes, like a preacher pounding the pulpit. He didn't seem to tire, showed no signs of stopping, until Night Nurse, scolding and piping wildly about patients needing their rest, burst through the door, slid a foot or two in the IV fluid and landed on her ass.

There were a few seconds of silence before Jeffrey turned over in his bed, yanked his blanket up around his chin and groaned, "Jesus it's hard to sleep around here."

I was amazed to see Barry, after lying as still as a corpse, push Art away, stand up and make a barking series of coughs, trying to get air in and out through his damaged windpipe. As he stumbled for the window, he looked over at me for a moment and I could see pieces of glass stuck in his chin and cheekbone, the dozens of tiny cuts inflicted by Art's knuckles. His ear—swollen and raw as a fresh pork cutlet—was bleeding two thick lines of blood down his neck.

Barry didn't bother trying to climb through the window, just dove through it headfirst, his pants catching and ripping on the latch, his feet clattering against the sill as he pulled himself through. There was the wild clanging of the fire escape as he bounded down it and the squeal of tires as he sped off into the flat darkness, heading, it seemed, straight for the smelter, where lava flowed and burned in the darkness like the fires of hell.

"Don't you ever come back here!" Art roared out the window, his face the twisted, flickering orange of a devil's. "You come around this boy again and I will kill you dead!"

LEAVING ST. DIVINE'S

MY GOING-AWAY party, though sparsely attended and about as festive as a funeral wake, was the only going-away party for a patient anyone at St. Divine's could remember. "God help us with all the hubbub you've caused around here," said Nurse Lovett, who had red valentine lips painted over her regular lips, "but it looks like we're going to miss you."

Along with a few other nurses and some orderlies looking for free cookies and punch, Sue Kay was there, as was Mrs. Rodale and Jeffrey, who was sweating and suffering as usual in his wheelchair. The cafeteria ladies had made a cake for me on which was written ¡VAYA CON DIOS EDGAR! in mangled pink icing and there were a couple of bowls of pastel butter mints that were so hardened and chalk-like the partygoers had no choice but to spit them into napkins or directly into the empty aluminum garbage can, which every so often rang out with a hollow, ricocheting *ga-gong*. The party was held in the old chapel (now used for staff meetings), which was a spacious, high-ceilinged room with a crucifix so far up the wall that in all these years since the government had taken over for the Catholic church, nobody had the ambition or daring to climb up there and pull it down. So while we drank watery punch and picked the slabs of hardened icing off our pieces of cake, a bloody, battered Jesus looked down on us in pity from His cross.

In the week since Barry and Art had brawled in our hospital room, a week full of visits by the police asking questions about Barry's nocturnal visits and tittering gossip among the nurses and the patients in the Dungeon, a week in which Art, despite his newly bruised ribs and dislocated shoulder, had disregarded the doctor's advice, packed up his things and gone home to his empty house in the hills, Edgar had lost one of his front teeth. Nearly overwhelmed with nervousness and dread, he grinned as broadly as he could, showing off the new gap in his smile. In one hour a government van would come to pick him up and fetch him to the William Tecumseh Sherman School, where he would stay into some indefinite future.

The party didn't last fifteen minutes before the chitchat died down and the nurses began scattering to their rounds. This is when Art, dressed in a natty dark blue suit like an ink stain in the white of the hospital, showed up in the doorway lugging an enormous green suitcase on wheels, the scarred mess of his face a glowing pink, his hair slicked back over his scalp. In his baggy civilian clothes, Art looked so tiny and pathetic I hardly recognized him.

"Lookit," he said. "My friend lost a tooth."

Jeffrey scowled and nobody said hello to Art except for Sue Kay, who called him sweetie pie and told him he better come get some cake before Delancey got off his morning shift and ate everything in sight.

Now the room emptied quickly: Jeffrey banging around in his wheelchair and knocking his cast against the doorjamb on the way out, Sue Kay giving me an armful of school supplies from the Dungeon and hugging me so hard my ribs creaked, Nurse Lovett handing me a stack of postcards and making me promise to write. Soon it was me, Mrs. Rodale, and Art, who kept forgetting how bad the mints were and now had three or four of them clicking around in his mouth, too polite to spit them out.

We went back up to the room. Ismore kept his withering stare locked on all of us while Mrs. Rodale helped me out of my gown and into a stiff new pair of jeans and a store-smelling T-shirt and showed me how to put on and tie the laces of some outsize brogans she had taken from the Lost and Found over at the YMCA. She chattered the whole time, telling me that she and the rest of the agency had checked out everything thoroughly, that Uncle Julius was a good, caring man even though he couldn't come down to the hospital because he didn't own a car, didn't know how to drive, and refused to ride in any motor vehicle whatsoever.

"They'll take good care of you up at Fort Apache," she said, while I loaded my urinal puck, my stacks of paper and my other odds and ends into the duffel bag (another item from the YMCA). "Those are your people, you know."

After walking down the halls for the last time, the nurses scurrying over to kiss me on the forehead and pat me on the helmet, everything moving by in a haze, we emerged into the blank white light of the out-of-doors. It was only April, but a hot breath of wind hit us full in the face, sucking at our clothes, lifting up a plume of dust around us and sending it out into the vast, corroded expanse of hills and water-cut arroyos. I felt so light, so unmoored, that if I dropped my duffel bag and kicked off these shoes that felt like mailboxes on my feet, the wind could easily have lifted me away.

Art asked Mrs. Rodale if he might have a moment alone with me. I followed him around to the other side of an old saguaro growing in a patch of white gravel and he opened up the suitcase, which he had been pulling behind him like a dog on a leash, and showed me what I had dared not ask about, my Hermes Jubilee. He had taken it home with him and retooled the whole thing entirely, replaced its bent arms, fixed the platen which had come loose, and written my name on its side with a metal engraver: *Property of Edgar P. Mint.* Also in the suitcase were some folded clothes—T-shirts and jeans his daughters had once worn—a large tea jar full of hard candy—"a fella's got to have his sweets now and again"—and a pile of *National Geographics* to look at if I ever got bored.

"I got two things else I want to give you," he said, squatting down next to me. He pulled out his wallet, out of which he removed a roll of bills. "Tooth fairy asked me to give this to you. She knew you was a little nervous around fairies so she asked me to pass it along."

I took the money and stuffed it into my underwear; it had been quite awhile since I had worn pants and I guess the whole concept of pockets was something I hadn't yet locked onto.

Art looked at me, scratched the stubble on his throat, and then took a long, pearl-handled jackknife out of his boot. He opened the blade, which together with the handle made the knife nine or ten inches long. He turned it over in his hands, the pearl handle giving off different colors, the nicked and oiled blade catching the sun. "My granddaddy give me this knife when I was baptized. I'd like to give it to you, but I want you to promise me something first."

I nodded and Art looked me in the eyes, held out the knife in the space between us.

"If that Dr. Pinkley ever gets near you again I want you to stick him with this, right in the ribs." He pointed a blunt finger a few inches below his heart to illustrate the spot I should aim for if the time came. "No need to be shy about it, neither. Stick it in there hard as you can, maybe give it a twist if you feel like it."

He folded the blade back into the handle and then passed it over to me. It felt as heavy as a tire iron and the rainbow hue of its pearl handle looked to me like the sky of a small and distant world. Following Art's lead, I lifted up my pant leg and slid the knife into my sock so that it settled all the way into my shoe.

Now I had my Hermes Jubilee, some money in my underwear and a knife in my sock. I felt better. But I had nothing to give Art in return. Not my urinal puck, I decided, I couldn't let go of that. I opened the bag Mrs. Rodale had given me and rifled through my clothes until I found it: my tooth. From what Art had told me, and from the wad of money I could feel settling in nicely under my scrotum, I understood that a tooth could be worth a lot of money.

Art took the tooth, rolled it between his fingertip and thumb. After staring at it for a long time he tucked it into his shirt pocket. "Thank you, Edgar," he said in a voice thick and hoarse. "You're a good boy."

He held out his hand, with its purpled scars and craggy, uneven knuckles, and we shook. His grip was so tight it hurt, and I felt like the small pain of it might make me cry. I didn't understand what it was that made my eyes burn, except that his hand was so strong and insistent, squeezing mine. A blast of wind hit us, lifting up the hair on our heads, making me look away. Art pumped my arm a couple of times, like a man drawing water from a well, and then he slowly limped off toward the parking lot, dragging his bad leg behind.

WILLIE

SHERMAN

I T W A S S T I L L early in the morning but the sun was bearing down on Edgar like a weight; he sweated and blinked and held his arms up against it until a large Indian woman with a face like a ham stepped out from a side door and barked, "Line up, hey! Lines!"

In the space of five seconds the jostling knot of kids in which I was tangled fell into two lines, boys on one side, girls on the other, and I was left to shuffle in near the back. Every two or three minutes the same meaty woman would stick her head out and yell "Girl!" or "Boy!" and a student would pass through the door—to where I had no idea.

My first day of school at Willie Sherman and I was about to realize that I was no longer Saint Edgar the miracle-boy, hospital sweetheart, beloved by all, but a walking target, a chicken among the foxes. Not only was I the new kid, so nervous that I bit at the knuckles of both hands until they bled; not only was I a crossbreed, obvious to all not because my hair or skin or eyes were necessarily lighter or differently colored than anyone else's, but because I had a few traitorous freckles scattered across my nose. I also sported various gaps in my quailing smile—I was now losing teeth at an alarming rate—and a sweat-stained leather helmet clamped securely on my head.

Any idiot could see that little Edgar had not yet learned the art of blending in.

Though this was in fact my first day of school, I had been living at Fort Apache for over four months, but that did nothing to lessen my anxiety. When I arrived in April, it was decided that instead of attending classes for only a few weeks, I would wait for the next school year to begin. My Uncle Julius, an ancient, wrinkled man with skin the color and same oily texture of a Tootsie Roll, lived down in the boiler room in the basement of the boys' dorm. For those first months that is where I stayed, sleeping on a cot and taking my meals—when they came—sitting on a milk crate. It was often like a sauna down in that room, and while I would sweat until I began to drip from my elbows and the ends of my fingers, you could not have found a drop of moisture anywhere on Uncle Julius' person, even though he wore the same flannel shirt every day, buttoned up to his chin.

"Indi'ns don't sweat," he advised me once. "Try to be more like a Indi'n."

During those last weeks of school while the students were on recess or free time between the end of classes and dinner, Uncle Julius kept me close by, handing him pliers while he fixed a broken faucet, sorting out nails and screws in the maintenance hut, helping him locate the rats that were forever crawling into the farthest reaches of the heating ducts to die. I can tell you that I didn't need any encouragement to stay away from the other kids—they frightened me. I had been an only child, shunned by other children my whole life, and had spent the last eight months in a hospital full of adults—to me children of every kind seemed as alien and unpredictable as insects.

When the spring semester finished and most of the students left to go home for the summer, a few were left behind, a couple of girls, four or five boys, who, like me, had lost their parents through death or abandonment and had nowhere else to go. "Permanents" we were called. Though there were no more classes, there was still something of a regimen that I was left out of. They ate two meals a day in the cafeteria, worked in the morning pulling weeds on the parade grounds or picking up trash along the fences and roadway, were sometimes bused to Show Low or Globe to see a movie. I was told to keep away from them, act as if they didn't exist. "You ain't a student here yet," Uncle Julius told me in his breathy, almost inaudible voice. "Them's bad kids."

So you might imagine how I felt standing outside the infirmary on the first morning of school in my best school clothes (shoes two sizes too big, Toughskin jeans, lime-green sweater which had belonged to one of Art's dead daughters) with nearly two hundred other kids shouting, squealing, jostling, hooting, living out their last moments of freedom. I gulped air and kept a hand locked tightly on my groin; it was all I could do to keep from wetting my pants.

There were titters and girls whispering behind their hands and all I could think to do was smile like I did when I sashayed down the halls of St. Divine's, brightening up everybody's day. It wasn't long before we had the interval timed pretty well—a student would pass through the door and there would be a sudden rush of wild activity, pushing and shouting and mock karate-fighting, and then, as if by collective intuition, things would calm down the second before the woman opened the door, gave everyone a meaningful stare, and let another student through.

When there were only twenty or thirty of us left clustered outside the door, I felt a thump on top of my helmet and turned to find a skinny, bandy-legged kid in a red windbreaker grinning at me with a mouthful of rotten teeth. He had a few long whiskers poking out of his chin and his matted hair looked like something pulled from a bathtub drain.

"You got something on your head, heh, heh?" he said, and gave me another swat, windmilling his arm and driving the palm of his hand into the top of my helmet, as if I were a tent stake and he was going to hammer me into the ground.

I staggered backwards, trying not to fall down. From all around

came giggles and enthusiastic shouts. Somebody from behind gave
me a shot that made everything go liquid for a moment. I turned
and tried to smile—I wanted to be liked—but a girl wearing glasses
with smoked lenses rushed in and delivered an overhand slap that
made my neck compress and little green zags of lightning appear in
my vision and then there were four or five boys surrounding me,
gleefully whacking me on the top of my head, as if for the simple joy
of hearing the sharp slap of flesh striking leather. Next thing I knew
I was kneeling in the dirt, my hands on the ground in front of me,
drooling a small dark spot in the dust. My eyeballs felt dislodged
from their sockets and my head had become so heavy and unwieldy
that I could not raise it up to look around.

Everything went suddenly quiet and the door opened. I heard
the woman's footsteps before I saw her chalky, sandaled feet appear
next to me. She helped me to my feet and surveyed the crowd until
Rotten Teeth piped up. "I think that kid's sick or something!"
Everybody laughed and someone near the back of the line howled
like a wolf.

The woman helped me into a musty, windowless room where
another woman, this one anglo and bony and wearing a white polyester dress and white thick-soled shoes, sat at a desk sorting syringes.
A nurse! I thought to myself with a small surge of joy that turned
quickly to homesickness. In my woozy state I walked up to her,
yearning for something I couldn't really name, and said, "Nurse."

She looked me up and down and narrowed her eyes. "What's you
wearing?"

"Helmet," I said.

She raised her eyebrows. "Well what's you wearing it for?"

Was this some kind of trick question? Even though my head still
felt like a bowling ball attached to a broomstick and had already
taken a pretty good beating, I ended up giving myself a pretty solid
slap on the head to indicate the way my helmet was supposed to
shield my damaged head from the kind of violence I had just been
the target of.

The big one sighed. "Maybe we should make 'em all wear helmets."

She helped me undo the buckles and, once the helmet was off, took an aluminum canister with holes punched in the top and doused my head and the inside of the helmet with a white powder that made my scalp burn and my eyes tear up and my throat constrict with hot, acrid fumes. I coughed and gagged while the nurse, hoping to catch me by surprise, came up behind me and speared a needle into the back of my arm. I hardly flinched—shots were something I knew all about; the pain was even comforting in its way—and then I was once again subjected to the famous doctor's routine: eyes, ears, heart, throat, lungs, reflexes. Just when I was beginning to feel really at home I was released, hustled out another door and into the pounding sun.

By lunch, I was starving and faint. I stood at the back of another very long line—now the teachers and staff were mixed in with the students—and tried to be vigilant about anybody sneaking behind me and smacking me on the head. Lucky for me, everybody was as starved as I was and seemed to have lost interest in further violence. I took my tray of food—corn dog, mashed potatoes, crusted chocolate pudding—and sat down at the table next to the row of battered steel barrels which served as garbage cans. In an attempt to establish a routine, to find a place for myself, I would sit at the same spot at the same table for the rest of the school year, alternately wanting only to be left alone and hoping that someone might find it in their heart to take a seat next to me.

At recess I didn't know what to do with myself; it was all I could do to keep from tearing off for the hills or leaping down the stairs of the boiler room, three at a time, and hiding under my cot for the rest of the day. The parade ground was a wide expanse of weeds and clump grass with basketball hoops on one end, where a group of older boys played vicious games filled with swearing and the sounds of slapping flesh. On the other side, a bunch of smaller boys played a mad game of keep-away with a dimpled rubber ball, and in the far corner of the field some girls bumped a volleyball back and forth. But overall, recess seemed to be nothing but unmitigated chaos, a lot of running around and talking behind hands and shouting for no reason. I had nothing to do but stand in the middle of it, lost.

I wasn't surprised at how quickly Rotten Teeth found me. There were two other boys with him and they sauntered up, smiling like we were all the best of friends. I was glad to see that, like me, they still had the white lice powder trapped in their ears.

"Hey, are you sick?" Rotten Teeth said. His two buddies guffawed and looked around nervously. One of them, a potbellied little guy with stubby arms and a face like a rat, put his hands down his pants and slipped his finger through his open fly, waving it around.

It seemed like a pretty good joke to me, but nobody else noticed.

"What you laughing at?" said Rotten Teeth.

I pointed. "The kid with his finger."

"I think maybe you're a faggot."

"I'm not," I said, though I had no idea what a faggot might be.

"I think maybe your mama is a nigger then."

"No."

"Then I guess you're an asshole, right?"

I shook my head, but I thought I was beginning to get the hang of this conversation. I looked Rotten Teeth right in the eye and said, "Eat shit, Marty."

This seemed to have an effect on all of them. They stopped their snickering and stared at me. Rotten Teeth seemed particularly surprised; he stood there, dumbstruck, before a look of pure pleasure and anticipation crept over his face. He stepped forward, and instead of giving me a solid one on the head, as I expected, he put his arm around my neck and led me off toward the back of the boys' dorms where a row of outhouses stood.

William Tecumseh Sherman had indoor plumbing, but the sewer system was so outdated and prone to backing up that these two-seaters—left over from the old days—were always kept in use. While his buddies made sure I didn't run off, Rotten Teeth took his time finding a rusted tin can, punching a hole in it and tying to it a length of blue thread he painstakingly coaxed from the hem of his pants. Then he disappeared into the shithouse and whistled cheerfully for two or three minutes.

When finally he came out, beaming triumphantly, holding the can in front of him, only then did I think to run. I made it a good ten feet before they tackled me from behind. The two boys pinned my shoulders while Rotten Teeth stood over me, waving the can around like a decanter of incense.

"Look at this fish I caught," he said. "A big one! And this kid here is gonna eat it for us."

I determined right then that there was no way I was going to allow him to put that turd into my mouth. I set my teeth so hard that my head began to ache, but Rotten Teeth lingered over me with the patience of a monk, grinning and humming, until he decided time was up and reached over and pinched my nostrils together with two callused fingers. I held out for a good ten seconds until I was forced to open up to take a breath and like it was something he had been practicing for years, he deftly slipped the turd into my mouth so that I sucked it in along with a mouthful of air.

I kicked and thrashed and spit and gagged and whatever I was able to get out Rotten Teeth smashed and rubbed into my face and eyes with the rusty can, the other boys cackling like a couple of old women. Before they ran off to tell everyone what they'd done, Rotten Teeth theatrically waved his hand in front of his face and said, "Whew! Somebody's got bad breath!"

The recess bell clanged three times. Edgar, splayed on the ground, could feel the vibrations made by hundreds of feet stampeding toward the classroom building. Still he lay there, listening to the hoppers clattering in the weeds and staring up into a blank white sky. When he finally got up he didn't go to class, or to the rest room to wash up, but descended into the boiler room, where he sat down in front of his Hermes Jubilee and typed himself a little reminder: *Dont tell anybody eat shit again.*

CONTRABAND

I HAD SLEPT the entire trip from St. Divine's to Fort Apache, so I never got to see the changing of landscape, the bone-colored out-croppings and desert scrub of Globe gradually giving way to cedar and juniper and finally to thick stands of ponderosa pine and Douglas fir of the White Mountain Reservation. I went to sleep watching a dust storm fan out across a vast expanse of sandy hills and woke up to the smell of sap, the thin air of the mountains.

My Uncle Julius was there at the cattle guard to meet me. He signed a paper the driver gave him with a meticulously drawn X and, without a word, picked up my suitcase and headed for the main build-ing, a white-stuccoed edifice with the words WILLIAM TECUMSEH SHERMAN SCHOOL stenciled in red letters above the two main doors.

The school was actually a converted army fort, Fort Apache itself, back from the days when General Crook was chasing Geronimo into retirement. Once the Apaches were under control, there wasn't much point in having a fort anymore. They kept the fort operational for a few years, just in case the unpredictable savages caused more trouble, but eventually they shut it down and converted it into a school. It seemed reasonable enough: Fort Apache had been instrumental in beating the Indians into submission, why couldn't it be helpful in educating them?

So the main building went up, along with a cafeteria and two mon-strous three-storied dormitories (for several years the students had been housed in the old cavalry barracks) built of great coffin-sized sandstone blocks and positioned on each end of the old parade ground, flanked on one side by the main building and cafeteria and on the other by a row of elegant stone houses—the old officers' quarters—which were fronted by a narrow lane shadowed by towering elms. For a small rent the teachers lived in the old officers' homes. The commanding officer's quarters, a three-tiered stone house with ornate, painted eaves and French windows and forty-foot-high lookout tower, was reserved for the principal.

Compared to cramped and ramshackle St. Divine's the place seemed spacious, enormous, too much to take in at once; along with the dormitories and school buildings and houses, there were the old falling-apart barracks, a stone commissary building, guardhouse, magazine and across the highway the cavalry stables, storehouse and granary.

I had arrived in the middle of the afternoon—the students were all in class—so the place was quiet except for a faint *chop-chop-chop* from the kitchen. I stood next to the cattle guard and looked around dumbly until I saw that Uncle Julius had already made it to the front doors and was waiting for me there.

While I sat in a reception room overseen by a young Indian woman bending paper clips at a desk, Uncle Julius went in to see the principal—Principal Whipple, from the name on the door. Apparently, my arrival was a surprise to Principal Whipple, because even though I could not see him, I could hear him yelling at Uncle Julius. *Where's his certificate of Indian blood? Is this all the paperwork? What about parental consent forms? Does he even have a goddamn Social Security number? The last thing I need right now is another goddamn orphan without any paperwork.*

Orphan, I thought, and felt a jolt of recognition, like spotting some old acquaintance in a crowd. I don't believe I'd ever heard the word spoken before, but I knew exactly what it meant and that it applied to me. That's it, that's who I was, a *goddamn orphan.* It comforted me to understand my place in the world, to put a name to it.

The secretary told me I could go in now and I stood in the doorway, unsure of what to do next. Principal Whipple was half hidden behind an avalanche of papers and old coffee cups and Uncle Julius sat just on the other side of the desk, his hat in his lap, as stiff and wooden as the chair he sat in.

Principal Whipple took one look at me and said, "God help us."

The principal had thinning, silvery hair and a dark and bushy rust-colored mustache which was almost enough to draw your attention from the mole on top of his left ear which looked as hairy and alive as a bumblebee. He wore industrial black-framed glasses with magnifying-glass lenses that made his eyes seem to hover a few inches in front of his face. He spoke with an air of insincerity that reminded me of the doctors from St. Divine's.

"Sit down," he said. "How old are you anyway?"

I looked at Uncle Julius, who looked at Principal Whipple, who tore through a stack of papers like he was trying to dig his way out of the mess around him. He pressed the button on an intercom box on his desk.

"Maria, where's this kid's file?"

"What?" the intercom squawked.

"Where is this kid's file?"

Now the box only made a loud buzzing noise.

Principal Whipple stood up and roared, "WILL YOU BRING ME THE KID'S FUCKING FILE!"

Maria was there immediately with a manila folder. When the principal had the paper he was looking for he said, "This kid's not nine years old. What's he doing here? Ten and up, that's our policy, isn't it? Can he even speak English, has he ever been to school before?" Purple veins were beginning to stand out on his flat stump of a nose. He turned to me. "Can you speak a word of English?"

Again, I looked at Uncle Julius, whose hands were shaking badly beneath his hat. "The woman told me he can read books."

Principal Whipple exhaled out of his nose, which produced a thin whistling noise like a badly played flute. He nodded, grabbed some kind of pamphlet and held it out across the desk. "Son, why don't you step over here and read this for us, just a couple of sentences."

I didn't need to get any closer; I could read it from where I stood. Up in the left-hand corner it said STAFF HANDBOOK and the first paragraph mentioned student discipline and how the teachers and staff were responsible for maintaining a consistent approach in terms of punishment and correction. I was starting to read the second paragraph to myself when Principal Whipple tore the pamphlet away and tossed it over his shoulder, so that it fluttered in the air for a moment, like a shot-gunned duck, and landed with a slap on top of a filing cabinet.

"I wonder if he's even *seen* a book before," Principal Whipple said.

"He don't got anyplace else to go," Uncle Julius whispered into his lap.

Principal Whipple pushed back from his desk so that he rolled a little ways on the wheels of his chair. He put his hands in the air and said, "That seems to be the standard line, doesn't it? No place else to go. Nobody else will take 'em. Last stop along the line. Well, send 'em over to us, then! Sure, you bet, we'll take 'em! Send us whatever you got."

The trembling in Uncle Julius' hands had moved up into his arms and it seemed that he, like me, wanted nothing more than to get out of that office. But there was one more thing. Principal Whipple opened one of the drawers of his desk and pulled out a large canvas sack on which was written, in stenciled block letters: CONTRABAND. I would learn later that Principal Whipple liked to show this bag and its contents to everyone who visited his office for the first time, no matter if it was a new student, a new dorm aide, a parent, a paint salesman, a representative from the BIA.

"Even if you don't speak the language, son, I think you'll be able to understand what I'm saying here," he said as he carefully cleared a space next to his coffee mug. One by one, he took each object out of the bag and placed it delicately on the desk, as if he was handling relics of great value: a bowie knife, a straight razor, a Mexican bull-whip, a slingshot, a baggie of rolled joints and multicolored pills and loose marijuana, a sharpened butter knife, a stainless steel whiskey flask, a pair of homemade brass knuckles, a wire garrote, a small pistol with its chamber removed.

"These are just a few of the things we've confiscated in the two years I've been here, a small sampling," he said, a little wistfully. "I want you to know that if you've brought anything with you that resembles one of these items and you fail to give it up now, it will be confiscated from you—we will find it—and you will be punished. So if you have a weapon of any kind, drugs, cigarettes, alcohol, do yourself a favor and drop it right here in this bag, right now."

He held the bag out to me and waited, smiling, a patient trick-or-treater. The knife in my sock felt like it was scorching my ankle and I had to resist the urge to reach down and touch it. I stared at Principal Whipple and he stared back, those eyes of his floating in the space between us. The hospital bracelet I still wore began to itch. Finally, he placed each item of contraband in the sack with the same care he had removed it, put the bag back in its drawer. Then he turned to Uncle Julius and said, "I'll be in Show Low tomorrow for meetings. Why don't you come in here and see if you can get that air conditioner up and running again."

Uncle Julius rose from his chair, put his hat on his head and shuffled out of the room, me following behind. I paused in the doorway for a second, turned around and recited as loudly as I could, "Discipline is of the utmost concern here at WTSS. The atmosphere in your classroom and in the dorms will be determined by your expectations and your efforts to let the students know what their behavioral limits are. Staff must exercise strong authority and always strive for control, discrimination and consistency . . ." but the principal had already turned away and was now laughing in his girl-like way at what someone was telling him on the phone.

THE MOTHER LODE

AT FIRST, I was glad to move out of Uncle Julius' basement room and up to the second floor, where I shared a room with sixteen of Willie Sherman's newest recruits. In the dark, listening to the breathing, the choked noises of someone in the midst of a nightmare, the soft padding of a dorm aide come to check on us in the middle of the night—it all comforted me. Even the weeping, the homesick sobbing those first few nights, made me feel less lonely myself. In the four years I lived at Willie Sherman I never saw anyone cry in the light of day, but doing it in the darkness, anonymously, seemed to be acceptable. There were eight pine bunk beds crammed into that room and it seemed, sometimes, with all the creaking wood and sleeping noises, that we were packed into the hull of some great ship at sea.

The first time I peed the bed, Raymond, our dorm aide, didn't get all that mad. It was early in the morning and the smell of it was strong in the room. The other boys made their beds and put on their clothes, sniggering among themselves, highly satisfied that somebody else was the bed-wetting fool.

Raymond, a short, stocky Apache man who, for some reason, spoke with a Spanish accent, came in the room, and before he could belt out his one and only wake-up call—*Feet on the floor! Feet on the floor!*—took one whiff and said, "Man, that's some bad-smelling pee!" Raymond said it with such cheerfulness that I was happy to take full credit for what I had done. After all, I had often wet my hospital bed and nobody ever got upset about it; the nurses would chirp and scold and the orderlies would mumble under their breaths while they yanked the sheets free from the mattress, but it was all standard; pretty much everybody wet the bed at St. Divine's.

Apparently, bed-wetting wasn't so well tolerated at Willie Sherman. The third or fourth time I wet the bed Raymond did not even have to step foot in the room. From out in the hall he yelled in that funny accent of his, "God, Ed-gar, not again? What, we going to have to get you, son kind of big diaper or son-thing, son kind of rubber sheets?"

I had already stripped my bed, but my undershirt and briefs were soaked—they were all I had until laundry day. Raymond grabbed me by the neck and marched me into the bathroom. While the other

boys watched from under the spray of the gang showers, I stood
naked over a sink, rubbing my sheets and underwear with a pink
brick of Primo soap, my testicles shriveling up into nothing.
Raymond stood by the entire time but never offered to help; he was
determined to teach me a lesson. So when I had rinsed and wrung
out everything as best I could, I put the sodden sheets back on my
bed, dressed in dripping wet underclothes, and spent the entire day
in soggy Fruit of the Looms and that night in sheets so dank they
began to turn black with mildew.

My bed-wetting episodes did nothing to enhance my social status
at Willie Sherman, but I was beginning to learn how to make things
a little easier on myself. My first stroke of genius: dropping my helmet down the same shithouse hole Rotten Teeth had fished the turd
out of. I would miss that helmet—it was one of my few possessions,
and the *plurt* it made in that shadowy muck made me wince with
remorse—but I understood that, in the end, it was doing me more
harm than good. My second modification was more subtle but just as
important: I began to develop a knack for anonymity. In class, I said
absolutely nothing. When asked a question, I gave only blank stares.
When the students passed their assignments to the front of the class,
I handed forward a blank piece of paper. The teachers seemed to
approve of me and my approach. Occasionally they patted me affec-
tionately on the shoulder the way you would a blind person or a
very old dog.

I was so quiet and well behaved I was often asked to lead the
Pledge of Allegiance, which we all jabbered incoherently, as if we had
come up with a whole new language to express our boredom and
disregard.

The playground was a little more difficult to figure out. For a
week or two, my main concern was avoiding Rotten Teeth, which
involved camouflaging myself as best I could, becoming invisible. To
do this, I had to find a way to join one of the groups which had
formed on the playground as naturally and quickly as oil beading up
on a rain-slick road. Though Willie Sherman was on the Fort Apache

Reservation, the students came from various tribes (there were, in fact, very few Apache): Pima, Papago, Yavapai, Maricopa, Havasupai, Hopi. WS had become a dumping ground for the schools in the BIA system, the last stop along the line for the troublemakers, castoffs, delinquents, strays, head cases and orphans like me. We were all Indian in some form or another, but that is pretty much where the similarities ended—we spoke different languages, some of us came from big cities like Phoenix or Albuquerque, some of us from places in the desert where electricity and running water were only a rumor; except for our black hair and our various shades of brown skin, the only thing we had in common was that we were here because nobody else would take us.

It is true that the playground clans formed themselves along tribal lines, but there were also alliances of other kinds. One group, which consisted of five or six young boys who were new to WS and fell in with each other because not even their own brothers or cousins or fellow tribesmen would have them, seemed to be my best bet. During recess and free time after dinner I shadowed them, hoping to be included by virtue of proximity alone, but they scowled at me, turned their backs, and acted as if I did not exist. I was a bed-wetting, brain-injured crossbreed and they knew I drew exactly the kind of attention they were trying hardest to avoid.

I was persistent, though. While the other boys played furious games of pickup basketball or sent mysterious sign-language messages across to the other side of the parade ground where the girls played, my little group shot marbles in a wide patch of dirt over in the shadow of the old cavalry bell. Their pockets were always bulging with marbles—agates, cat-eyes, steelies—which they traded back and forth and used as viable currency for goods and services of all kinds. The games they played were various and complicated and almost impossible for me, the freckle-nosed dummy, to understand.

I would like to get me some Marbles, Edgar typed, as if his typewriter might have the power to grant wishes. *Blue ones and Green ones and the Clear kind with the Ribbon in the middle. I LOVE MARBLES!*

How much did Edgar lust after those marbles? He would have gladly eaten another turd, even two, just to have a single cat-eye for his own.

The game I liked best—one of the few I could make sense of— was called "pit." It was a simple game of winner-take-all: a small hole was dug and each player placed three or four marbles in the hole to start. From a distance of about twenty feet they would each roll a marble, tossed underhand like a bowling ball, trying to get it into the pit. If they missed, their marble would be added to the pot; if they made it, they won it all—the jackpot.

The pit games were always the most hotly contested; the players were jittery and tense, biting their lips and slapping their pants, shouting and pulling at their hair when their marbles barely missed, gloating and greedily digging the marbles out of the dust when they prevailed.

One Thursday afternoon after daily duty, which had me scrubbing the stains out of cooks' aprons, an epic game of pit was underway. The players were having a hard time getting the marbles into the hole, so it began to fill up, and it wasn't long before everybody was beginning to run out of marbles; whoever won this one would be taking home a pile of marbles so large kids were coming from all over the parade ground to watch.

"The fucking mother lode!" a kid named Delvis kept shouting, as if in great pain. Every time another player's marble missed, he would throw himself on the ground in relief, kicking his legs and rubbing his nose in the dirt like a pig.

I got so caught up in the game, so delirious at the thought of somebody winning all those gorgeous marbles, that during a pause when the players were jawing at each other about somebody fudging over the line, I stepped up and tossed the only thing I owned that might roll well enough to have any chance of going into that hole: my urinal puck. Right off, it started wide left, bumping along the uneven ground, the sun glinting off its milky, ice-white surface, but as it got closer to the hole it careened off a small clump of weeds, wobbled lazily, and miraculously veered into the hole, making a nice *click-click* as it landed on the pile of marbles.

No, Edgar wasn't any stranger to miracles.

I hollered and jumped while the other players looked at me, their mouths hanging open. I headed for the pit to ascertain that my puck had actually gone in the hole and the other boys were on me in a second; they thought I was going to take off with their marbles. One grabbed me by the arm and another had a handful of my shirt and they were doing a little tug of war with me while I struggled toward the pit, twisting and throwing elbows; I wanted to get my puck back. I heard somebody say "Get away" and they let go of me so suddenly I pitched forward into the red dirt and landed right on my face.

I was lifted up off the ground and turned to find myself looking up into the enormous smiling face of Nelson Norman. I had seen Nelson around and heard his name; Nelson was impossible to miss. For one thing, Nelson was *old;* though he was in the sixth grade, Nelson was fifteen—an adult, any way you cut it. His real distinguishing feature, however, was his size; he weighed easily over three hundred pounds and was as wide as a love seat. Nelson was a Pima, and though most Pima are hefty, Nelson was in another category entirely; his head was like half of a watermelon sitting on his shoulders, his fingers as thick and blunted as saltshakers, his feet so wide there wasn't a pair of shoes made that would fit him; even in the midst of the coldest winter months, in ice and snow and mud, he wore flip-flops.

And Nelson was merry. He had the look of a person prepared and willing to laugh at anything, and when he smiled his eyes would disappear into the creases of his face and his cheekbones would stand out like those on a drugstore Santa Claus.

Nelson laughed at me so cheerfully I couldn't help but grin up at him. He said, "I been watching and I guess you won some marbles." He went over to the pit and with a great, ponderous effort, went down on one knee. He picked up my puck, turned it over in his hands, shrugged, tossed it to me. Then he lifted up a handful of marbles and let them fall through his thick fingers. "You better come over here and get all these marbles you won. Whole big pile a marbles."

I filled my pockets, front and back, until the seams of my pants began to come apart. When I had found a place on my person for every last marble—I had to put some in my sock and a couple in the band of my underwear—I looked up to see Delvis and the others standing back at a safe distance, their faces confused between anger and fear. I immediately began trying to dump the marbles back into the hole—the last thing I wanted was to have those boys mad at me—but Nelson grabbed my arm and said, "Those are your marbles. You keep 'em. Come on over here with me."

I followed Nelson over to the old guardhouse, a stone building now in ruins, way over on the side of the school grounds behind the girls' dormitory. There was an imaginary line halfway between the boys' and girls' dormitories, a line we were forbidden to cross; who knew what might happen if Indian boys and girls were allowed to mingle? But Nelson plodded right across, without even looking for the teacher on playground duty or at any of the girls who stopped jumping rope or gossiping in huddles to stare. I followed at his heels like a humble squire, clicking and clacking as I went.

The old guardhouse was dark and musty inside, its dirt floor covered with cigarette butts, pieces of rotting mattress and the bleached pages of a Sears catalogue. The whole structure leaned to one side and there were holes in the wall where large, round river stones had fallen out, loosened from the mortar by rain and frost.

"You're Edgar," Nelson said, and I nodded, hitching up my pants, which now weighed about fifteen pounds and threatened to pull themselves down around my shins.

"You got something wrong in your head?"

I nodded again.

"What's wrong with it?"

I put my finger just above my left ear, where I could feel the narrow metal plate, cold and rigid, that helped keep the pieces of my skull together. "Mailman ran over it."

Nelson laughed. The jolly, high-pitched sound of it echoed off the stone walls and rang loudly in my ears. He slapped his huge thigh, which quivered alarmingly. "So you're retarded then, hey? Some kind of idiot?"

I yanked at my pants again and said, "I'm a goddamn orphan."

Nelson peered out through one of the breaches in the wall, scanning the playground, a huge smile still pressed into his face. "Okay then, Lone Ranger," he said. "I was thinking you could help me out. I think you're probably a smart guy. That's what I think."

This was as close to an offer of friendship as I had ever heard. I carefully inserted one finger in my pocket (one finger was all that would fit) and fished out a marble, a gorgeous clear-blue one with a swirl of red in the middle. I handed it to Nelson and he looked at me for a second, then took it out of my hand, put it into his mouth and swallowed it like an aspirin. He said, "That's what we'll do then, hey? We'll help each other."

KING KONG NIGHT

IT DIDN'T take long for Nelson to find a way for me to help him. Two days later, after dinner, we all gathered in the gymnasium for one of the few treats that Willie Sherman had to offer: movie night. Boys on one side, girls on the other, we'd sit in creaking metal chairs and watch Jimmy Stewart talking to an angel, John Wayne swaggering up the bloody sands of Iwo Jima, Audrey Hepburn dancing with some rich guy on a tennis court—all projected twice as big as life against a chipped and cracking cement wall. (Movie night had been a tradition here way back to the days of old Fort

Apache. One particular night in the winter of 1898, one of the officers of the post invited a number of Apaches to come see the "moving pictures" in the post amusement hall, where a Projectoscope was
set up on one end and a sheet hung up on the other. The hall was
packed and everything went just fine until a scene showing a steam
fire engine drawn by three enormous horses at full gallop was
shown. As the horses barreled toward the camera, growing larger and
larger, the officer alternately banged on a gong and blew a whistle
for added effect. It was all too much for the assembled Apaches, who
clambered out of the assembly hall and gathered outside in the snow
where they whooped and brandished knives in a riot of protest until
well after midnight.)

That night the movie was a Willie Sherman favorite, one that was
shown over and over again, often twice in one semester: *King Kong*.
King Kong was a real favorite, partly because most of the other
movies Mrs. Theodore had in the film closet were boring romances
involving old guys like Cary Grant or Montgomery Clift, but mostly because of a little tradition that had started years back; the first
time King Kong the great beast of the jungle showed himself on
screen, someone—the person must have been chosen beforehand—
would yell out with feigned terror, "Oh no! It's a big monkey!" and
everyone would fall apart laughing, egging each other on, until the
movie would have to be stopped, the lights turned on and order
restored.

It all happened according to plan that night, and though the eruption of chaos, the raucous hooting and foot-stomping panicked me
for a moment, I was soon laughing with everybody else in the dark
until I felt a hand on my arm. It was Nelson, laughing so hard he was
starting to choke. "Come on!" he said, gulping air. "Before the lights
come on."

Nobody noticed us as we made our way to the rear door and
emerged into a clear, cool night, full of crickets chirping and
nighthawks diving and chittering. There was still a strip of pink just
over the mesas to the west and stars were beginning to pop out

overhead. I followed Nelson, who kept sighing and shaking his head, around the building to the front, where another Pima boy, this one smaller and younger than Nelson, was sitting on the steps. From here we could still hear the laughter in the gymnasium crackling like static.

When the boy saw us, he heaved himself to his feet and said, "Oh man, are we missing King Kong night?"

"Glen, you shithead," Nelson said. "That's why we're doing it tonight. Everybody's at the movie."

"*Damn,*" he said with an air of pointed regret. "I *love* that King Kong." Glen shrugged, peered at me. He had a faint, homemade tattoo, three letters that ran down the middle finger of his left hand:

S

E

X

He said, "This kid don't look white."

"He's only part, I guess. He says it's a mailman ran over his head. He's pretty funny."

In the deepening evening, I walked across the parade grounds with my new friends, Nelson and Glen, and did my best to keep my marbles from making too much noise; I had brought them with me to dinner, intending to give them (except for a couple I had stashed in my pillowcase) back to the boys, but they had stared across the tables at me with such hate that I had been unable to approach them at all.

Halfway across, a cloudy-eyed reservation dog slinked up to us, looking for handouts, and Nelson gave him such a ferocious kick that he rolled three times in the dust before he was able to right himself and limp away, glancing back and crying in pain. I stopped to watch the dog go, but Nelson grabbed my sleeve and pulled me along. We crept along the row of houses, all built with large river stones hauled up from the canyon by Apache prisoners of war. A couple had lights on, but the last three, close together under the night shadows of one massive elm, were dark. We went around to the far side of the last one and stood in the tall weeds under a small round window about six feet off the ground.

"This is the one window they never lock," Nelson whispered. He explained what my part was in this fun we were having. They were going to boost me up so I could get through the window and into the bathroom. From there, I was to go into the kitchen, locate the refrigerator and take as much Budweiser as I could carry. If there was any money lying around, or candy bars, or rubbers, I should take those too. Then I was to go out the front door, making sure to lock it behind me again. For their part of the job, Nelson and Glen were going to wait in the old guardhouse for me to bring them their beer.

"Budweiser?" I said.

"*Beer,*" Glen said, "don't you know what beer is? Fuck, man!"

"White cans with red letters," Nelson said.

I decided not to ask about the rubbers.

Glen helped me onto Nelson's shoulders, lifted me like I was no more than a toddler, and they both helped shove me, headfirst, through the tiny porthole of a window. Once my eyes had adjusted to the darkness I saw that I was indeed in a bathroom; there was a claw-foot tub in the corner and a chipped porcelain sink with its stainless steel pipes exposed, glinting in the darkness. It occurred to me that there was going to be no good way to get to the floor without slithering through the window and landing headfirst on the toilet below.

I heard a noise, a faint *nuh nuh nuh,* and saw through the bathroom doorway that it was coming from the bedroom just across the hall. It was brighter in that room, probably the glow from the porch light coming through the window. I could see the corner of a bed and, on top of the bed, two pairs of legs, one on top of the other, two feet pointed at the ceiling and two at the floor. The legs writhed and almost seemed to be battling each other and the sound from the bedroom came a little clearer now: *nuh nuh, ah ah, nunnh, nunnh.*

I then heard, unmistakably, a man's voice say, "Almost there, sister."

It sounded to me like somebody was in pain.

I cupped my hand over my mouth and hissed, "There's somebody in here!"

"In the bathroom?"

"In the house! I heard somebody say 'sister'!"

"Fuck, there's nobody in there," I heard Nelson say. "Mrs. Thomas is at the movies. Now get on in there and meet us at the guard-house."

They took their hands from my ankles, which upset my center of gravity and made me pitch forward a little, so that I had to brace my arms against the tiled wall to keep from sliding through. I heard them crash away through the tall weeds and then the faint *flap flap flap* of Nelson's sandals.

I wished fervently that I was back in the gymnasium with everybody else, laughing in the dark, waiting to see what the big monkey would do. Here and now, it seemed I had two choices, neither worth much consideration: falling a good four feet headfirst onto the toilet or backing out of the window and having to face Nelson and Glen, beerless and without excuses. While I tried to come up with some alternative, I hung there, the window sill digging into my belly, the marbles in my pockets cutting off the circulation in my thighs, and watched the legs in the bedroom, listening to the low moaning and the squeak of the mattress. It was when the moaning began to change, turned into something that sounded like a yip of pain—*ai! ai! ai!*—that I felt the vibration in my legs that meant a fit coming on.

I only had a second or two before I blacked out, and in that moment I did not try to figure out the best way to fall forward or try to scramble out backwards, I simply hung there, doomed, and thought longingly about my helmet, lost forever under the muck of shithouse number two.

A GLOWING WIRE

THE INFIRMARY AT WS was nothing more than a large closet with an
army surplus cot, a dented swivel stool for the nurse to sit on, and a
cabinet on wheels that held bandages and other supplies, but it was
more than enough for me to feel like I was back at St. Divine's, being
attended to, my needs taken care of. Here, I figured, I could pee all
over the place and there'd be nobody to complain about it.

Hollow-faced Nurse DuCharme (who doubled as a cafeteria
worker) was the same one who had poured lice powder on my head
the first day of school. She scowled a lot, filled the tiny room with
her cigarette smoke, sang Johnny Cash songs to herself in a husky
monotone and disregarded Edgar entirely. He secretly pined for any
of the nurses from St. Divine's—big Nurse George with her behind
like a bag full of wet clothes, Nurse Lovett and her red lips, Nurse
Sweet and her black licorice breath—but decided, under the circumstances, that he should be happy with what he could get.

I don't believe I belonged in the infirmary at all; I had only a small
goose egg on my forehead from falling on the toilet tank—no con-
cussion, no broken bones, not even a cut—but somebody had decided that with my history, it was better safe than sorry. And it turned
out I was not the only casualty from the night before. Mr. Thomas,
husband to Mrs. Thomas the librarian, who worked construction in
Phoenix and stayed at Willie Sherman only on weekends, had rushed
in from what occupied him in the bedroom to see what all the racket was about and ended up dislocating his elbow after slipping on the
marbles scattered all over the bathroom floor.

I was unconscious for only a few seconds—from my seizure, not
from the blow to my head—and when I woke up I saw Mr. Thomas,

buck naked and baffled, holding his wrist and skating wildly on the ricocheting marbles. He went down hard on the tile floor and I could not take my eyes from his pecker—it was enormous and purple and had a slick sheen to it which made it glisten in the dim light. What's more, it was erect, but quickly wilting, shrugging in on itself, as if it was more embarrassed by this whole situation than anybody. Although Principal Whipple had talked to me briefly that night about what had happened, he came in this morning with a yellow tablet, which he scribbled in as I spoke, propped up on a pillow that smelled like a cat had peed on it some years before. In the end, I told him everything, except the part about Mr. Thomas being naked, and how his penis had looked. These didn't seem to be the kind of details that could help anybody.

At first, I tried to obscure the fact that Nelson had been involved, but Principal Whipple kept asking questions and I kept giving answers until I had offered up everything. Principal Whipple didn't seem particularly angry with me—he was mostly tired and distracted—until I told him about the people I had seen and heard in Mrs. Thomas' house.

"People?" he had said. "You mean Mr. Thomas?"

"I don't know," I told him. "I saw two people on the bed. I saw their legs. They were making noises." I thought about it for a second and then did my best to mimic the grunts and gasps and yipping and yapping from the night before. Apparently, I did quite a good job of it, too, because the principal looked like somebody had swatted him across the face with a newspaper. He yanked off his glasses, pressed his lips together and proceeded to whistle a little tune of anger through his nose. "Two people you say? Who was it? Did you see their faces?"

I tried to tell him that I didn't see any faces, only legs, but he waved his hand in my face, stopping me.

"So you didn't see them, but you saw their feet, correct?"

I nodded. I had seen their feet very clearly.

"I want you to tell me one thing," he said. Without the glasses, his eyes looked like tiny puckered holes with nothing in them. "Did any of those feet have their *toenails* painted?"

"Pink," I said, and Principal Whipple was out the door before I could say another word, leaving his notebook on the floor.

I stayed in the infirmary for two days, eating my meals in bed, listening to the radio that Nurse had brought in, reigning supreme in my own little private kingdom, but it wouldn't last long. On Tuesday, I was sent back to class, and when morning recess came, Miss Clemente, my homeroom teacher, put a hand on my shoulder and told me I would be under detention for the next two weeks; no recess, no free-time activities, no going along on field trips if any were planned (none ever were). Also, for the next two weeks I would be on breakfast duty in the cafeteria, washing trays, swabbing floors, scrubbing the burnt oatmeal out of the bottoms of pots the size of garbage cans.

"You're lucky they didn't bring the tribal police in on this one," she said. "Usually they catch somebody breaking into one of the staff houses and here come the flashing lights, out come the handcuffs. A big show for everybody."

But Miss Clemente didn't say this with any meanness. I could tell she liked me: I didn't cause her any trouble, and that's just about the best thing a teacher could say about a student at Willie Sherman.

My detention might have actually been a blessing in disguise, a two-week reprieve before Nelson could get his hands on me, but Nelson was much better than that; if he couldn't get me during recess or after class, he would figure out another way. I understood this and accepted it; there really was no way out. Even though the teachers and staff knew how dangerous Nelson was, what he was capable of, they couldn't watch him all the time; they had two hundred other budding criminals to worry about.

It was two nights after they let me out of the infirmary that I woke up to find Nelson's round face hovering over me like a rising yellow moon. "Hi Nelson," I said, and immediately he smothered my mouth with one enormous soft hand like a catcher's mitt.

"We're going out to the guardhouse now," he said into my ear. "You want to come?"

Even in the shadows of a dark room at midnight, his face showed not a hint of menace; he had that smile of his going full blast.

In only my underclothes and tennis shoes, I walked out into the cool night with Nelson. It was the middle of September and already the mountain air was turning cold enough at night to leave a crust of frost on the grass. Tonight, there was a skinny moon out and the faint shrieking of coyotes echoed up and down the canyon. By the time we made it to the guardhouse, I was shivering so hard I could barely walk.

Inside the building, three boys were gathered around a squat candle which threw odd, warping shadows against the stone walls. Wrong-eyed and slack-faced, they passed around a paper bag, sucking on the fumes of model airplane glue. One of the boys, skinny, with long hair and a bandanna, I didn't recognize; but the other two I knew. One was Glen, chewing on a cigarette burned down to its filter, the other Rotten Teeth.

"Hey, it's Edgar!" he called out. Without looking up, Glen head-slapped Rotten Teeth with an open palm and said around the nub of his cigarette, "Keep it down, cocksucker."

Nelson found an old paint can for me to sit on and took his place on the mattress next to Glen. "You remember when I brought you in here the last time?" he said to me.

I nodded.

"What did I say?"

"You said I was a smart guy."

Rotten Teeth guffawed and got another head-slap from Glen.

"I also said we were going to help each other, right? But you know what? You didn't help me at all. You *told* on me. You told 'em it was me and Glen who helped you get into that house. You get off easy because you're just a little kid, you know, and a retard, but me and Glen, we got three days' suspension, weekend cafeteria duty for a month. And you didn't even get us our beer."

Nelson got up from the mattress and kicked around in the debris until he found a rusted coat hanger still bearing a paper covering advertising *Red Rocket Dry Cleaning*. Meticulous as a surgeon, he tore off the paper and straightened each bend in the wire until he had a long, copper-colored wand. We all watched, rapt, as he held the end of the wire over the candle flame until it began to glow, first a dull red that quickly turned into a yellow the same color as the flame.

Glen rubbed his hands together and said, "Roasting wieners," which made Rotten Teeth let out a cackling hoot. He looked grateful when nobody tried to hit him.

When Nelson lifted the wire away, the other boys grabbed me, wrestling me easily to the ground and holding my arms and legs. With his free hand, Nelson yanked my underwear down around my thighs and knelt down at my side. He held the glowing tip of the wire up to his face, the light of which reflected off the fine hairs inside his nose.

"We can still be buddies," he said. "But you're not ever going to tell on any of us guys again, are you?"

I shook my head and let out a laugh that was pure terror. Rotten Teeth had his leering face in mine and his breath smelled like burnt rubber. Squinting, he said, "My pecker's a lot bigger than this kid's."

Nelson let the glowing wire drift slowly down, like a snake blindly searching for a meal, until it was only a few inches from my crotch. I squirmed and pumped my legs but couldn't get enough air from my lungs to make more than a hoarse croak.

"We're being nice to him, right?" Glen said. "He's lucky he's not getting it right in the eyeball."

Nelson laughed and lowered the wire. The instant the tip touched the side of my penis, my bladder loosened like a deflating balloon. Because of my bed-wetting problems, Raymond reminded me every night to use the bathroom before bed, and often watched over me as I did so, but tonight I had fallen asleep early and I guess he didn't have the heart to wake me up. So my little bladder was full to bursting, and had I not been out here in the old guardhouse being tortured with a red-hot coat hanger I would have soaked my bed for sure.

It was this smaller-than-normal bladder that saved Edgar from a lot of undue suffering that night. I let go a tight, laserlike stream of piss that shot out over Nelson's head and arced down across his pie plate of a face, nailing him right in the eye and getting into his opened mouth. He bellowed and lurched away, whipping the coat hanger sideways, lodging the glowing tip in the outer curve of Rotten Teeth's ear. In the midst of his howling, Rotten Teeth stood up, did a little foot-stomping jig of pain, and kicked over the candle, instantly casting everything into darkness.

I was kicked in the head and stepped on, but without much trouble I was able to turn over and scuttle out the door on my hands and knees. I started to run, but my underwear, already around my knees, fell down about my ankles and sent me sprawling into the frosty grass of the parade grounds. I got up, and as I pulled my underwear up enough to free my legs, I looked back at the guardhouse, but no one had emerged yet; they were still busy spitting and cussing and yelling at each other. I set off again and ran right past the boys' dormitory, crossed the road and dove into a thicket of mesquite, where I stayed the rest of the night, shivering and cupping my groin with both hands until just before dawn, when I crept back into the building and slipped into bed five minutes before Raymond burst into the room like a drill sergeant, heartily booming his wake-up call.

SYLVIA ORTIZ

FOR LITTLE EDGAR, it was plain as anything: the miracles were over, the luck run dry.

It seemed the best and only option was to make a break for it—but here is where I always got stuck. If I ran away, where would I go? I thought of going to California to find my mother, but California, wherever it was, seemed as distant and unreachable as the moon. The place I really wanted to escape to was St. Divine's. I dreamed of arriving there, dragging my suitcase behind me, to a grand welcome by the nurses, by Sue Kay, by all the patients in the Dungeon: Edgar and his triumphant return. I imagined Art would be there in his old bed, grimacing with that old face like a mess of roadkill, the sharp scent of his cologne hanging in the air like a haze of insecticide, and my bed would be empty, the blanket turned back. I could get rid of my heavy clodhoppers, jump into a hospital shift, lie back in bed and not have to worry anymore.

For most of October, I devised ways to get myself back to the hospital. First, I tried squeezing through the steel bars and jumping from my second-story window. I had to do it twice before I was able to sprain my ankle well enough to limp over to the cafeteria and present my swelling foot to Nurse DuCharme, who was busy feeding fatty scraps of beef into a meat grinder. She glanced at my foot and told me that there was a bunch of old crutches stacked up with the banquet tables under the stage; if I wanted to, I could go find a pair that would fit me.

I limped around for a few days feeling sorry for myself before I decided I was going to have to work at this. My head had gotten me to St. Divine's in the first place and I decided it had to be the best way to get me back. Whenever I got the chance, I would grit my teeth and ram my head into the hardest thing I could find: a wall, a desk, a flagpole, once even the cavalry bell, which made its low, liquid *oooowng* and had everybody doing a double take, thinking it was time for dinner. I even tried throwing an old brick in the air and standing under it, but I would always flinch at the last second and end up with a bruised collarbone or scraped ear. I managed to give myself headaches, make myself dizzy, even make my head bleed a little, but my head had survived a half-ton mail jeep—it could certainly withstand my pitiful assaults.

The other students did not have to hit themselves with bricks or jump out of windows to escape Willie Sherman—they simply ran. They had homes, families and friends, places and people they could run to. And did they run. For the first few weeks of school, someone would make a break for it nearly every day. Usually it was the newest ones, the ones who had never been away from home or family, who did not speak English well, who had never sat at a desk, who had never slept on a bed, they were the ones who took off and never looked back. But others ran for different reasons. Some ran to be with a boyfriend or girlfriend, some ran out of simple homesickness. Some ran, I think, just to hear the wind in their ears.

The school had what they called a "Search and Rescue Plan." Because a student could disappear at any time during the day or night, roll was called every morning and night, at the beginning of each class and at every meal. Sometimes in the middle of the night, the whistle above the boiler room would blast three times and we would straggle out onto the parade grounds, wrapped in our army surplus blankets, and line up according to height so that roll call could be taken. They told us these middle-of-the-night roll calls were fire drills, but we knew better. They wanted to keep us off guard, to know that we were always being watched and checked up on—if we tried anything in the middle of the night they would be after us.

When a student did go missing, a search of the grounds would be conducted, an AWOL report sent to the tribal police, the parents notified, and the real search would begin. If a student was gone for more than twenty-four hours, their name would be written in red ink on the AWOL list outside Principal Whipple's office and within five minutes everybody would know that one of our own had a chance.

I remember one evening, just after dinner, when a tribal police car pulled up and two deputies with beer bellies dragged a skinny Chiricahua girl named Sylvia Ortiz out of the backseat. Sylvia had been missing for five days and it looked like she had spent all of them out in the mountains; her long hair was matted and full of debris, her clothes crusted with mud, her lips so badly sun- and windburned they were peppered with black scabs. She tried her best to kick and bite the deputies, and though her hands were cuffed behind her back it was clear those two big men with pistols and billy clubs were afraid of her.

To keep Sylvia from running again, she had to be strapped onto her bed at night and handcuffed to her desk during class, her table during mealtimes. During recess, they handcuffed her to a pole outside the administration building where she doggedly yanked and rattled the short length of chain until her wrist bled.

This went on for three or four days until one morning we heard a commotion outside and went to the windows to see Sylvia Ortiz running across the parade ground, stark naked and handcuffed to a metal chair which she dragged behind her. Mrs. Theodore had handcuffed her to the chair so that Sylvia could take a shower by herself without supervision —Mrs. Theodore had other things to do besides guard the door while one of her girls took a shower. But once Mrs. Theodore was out of the bathroom, Sylvia made a break for it, hefting the heavy metal chair over her head and creeping down the stairs.

It was Principal Whipple himself who saw her tiptoeing behind one of the school vans. He chased her twice around the dorm building and then she struck out across the parade grounds. She gave up trying to carry the chair on her head and let it drag behind her, clattering and kicking up dust. Behind her, Principal Whipple seemed to be running in slow motion, his heavy glasses threatening to rattle off his nose, his long wing tips clapping through the weeds like clown shoes.

"Somebody grab that girl!" he cried, waving his arms like he was trying to bring a plane in for landing.

Nobody made a move to join in the pursuit. All of us, the students, the dorm aides, the cafeteria workers, the secretaries, watched from our various places to see how the chase would unfold. Eventually Sylvia began to tire. The chair, which seemed to be yanking on her arm, rearing back like an animal on a leash, was having an effect on her. She was slowing up, occasionally looking back to see if Principal Whipple was gaining any ground. It was on the gravel road by the cafeteria that he finally caught up to her. He could have simply grabbed her—she was not a big girl—but he tackled her, knocked her down from behind, and they both sprawled out together in the middle of the road, kicking up a great cloud of dust.

Principal Whipple, whose glasses were now misted opaque, put all his weight on top of her, pressing her into the ground. Sylvia, chalky with dust and covered with bright red scrapes, clawed and kicked and screeched "Fuck! You fucker!" until finally she gave up, and lay there scraped and bloody and naked, the spirit gone out of her.

Eventually, they let Sylvia go home to her grandmother and grandfather, who lived in a shantytown on the outskirts of Nogales. What else could they do, what else could be done with a girl like Sylvia Ortiz? They took her away, and even though we never saw her again, never spoke her name, to me and every other student at Willie Sherman, Sylvia Ortiz was a hero.

A CARD IN THE MAIL

IT WAS A LONESOME little Edgar who wandered through the rest of his first year at Willie Sherman, hiding in the weeds during recess, steering clear of trouble, dodging the crab apples that came from the old gnarled tree near the water tank. That fall the students would fill their pockets with the hard, bitter apples and zing them at each other when the playground monitor looked the other way. Because I was as defenseless as could be, walking by myself, I was a favorite target for everyone, even the girls, who could chuck those apples as hard and low as any boy. I never ducked or jumped out of the way—that would only draw attention and invite more throwers to try their luck. I would take an apple square in the small of the back or on the side of the neck and it was all I could do to stand up straight and keep walking, to not let them know how much it stung.

Dashkin! ("White boy" in Apache), they shouted at me. *Hey Freckles! Retard! Whitey-ho, whitey-hey!*

Mrs. Rodale had told me I was coming to Fort Apache to be among my own kind. If I was sure of anything, it was that these kids, these teachers, were *not* my own kind.

I'm the only one, Edgar typed on his Hermes Jubilee. *I'm all there is.*

When I got a postcard from Art, this kind of thinking vanished like smoke. The picture on the card was of a donkey wearing a straw hat and suspenders and on the back Art had written, in a quivering seismic scrawl that was barely inside the margins of human communication:

Dear Edgar,

Meaning to come see you, but they wont let me drive, my legs is bad. Its tipical. Please type me up a note on your typewriter. They say Ismore is dead. Fell out of bed, unhooked all the machines. Doctors say its impossible to happen, but it happened, just like everything else. How is your new tooth coming along?

Your friend, Art

I read the card hundreds of times during the next week, wanting to make sure I hadn't missed anything. Then I began my letter. What was a letter supposed to contain? I wasn't sure, so I included every-thing: I told Art how I came to Willie Sherman, about the cold nights and my bed-wetting. I told him about Nelson Norman and Rotten Teeth and my shit-eating episode. I told him about falling onto the toilet and how now I had not only a wounded brain but a wounded penis as well, with a little red scar like a question mark. I told him that I still had the money he had given me, I hadn't spent a cent of it, and I still had the knife. I asked what might happen if I found my way back to Globe one day. Could I stay with him? Would he recognize me without my helmet?

When I finally typed *From, Edgar,* I had thirteen pages of extended, meandering paragraphs, all single-spaced. I carefully made an envelope out of two sheets of paper, addressed it on my Hermes Jubilee and took it over to the secretary's office. Maria was there, working on her nails with a filing stick. She had long, blue-black hair and hoop earrings big enough for a small rabbit to jump through.

I announced that I wanted to send a letter.

She took the letter from me, looked it over. "This don't got no stamp. You got to have stamps on it or it won't go nowhere."

I could only stare at her. She smelled sweet and clean, like cinnamon candy and what else? Rain, maybe. Or new grass. She smelled even better than a nurse.

She looked at me and sighed, which made the hoops in her ears swing and jangle. "All right, I'll get some stamps for you, but next time you're going to have to pay, little man." She took two stamps from one of the drawers, licked them with a pointy, pink tongue and slapped them on the envelope. "There it is, all ready to go."

She put the letter in the mailbag and looked up, surprised that I was still there. "You can get on out a here now."

I didn't budge. I cupped my groin, staring at her with a strained smile, unable to move.

"Shoo fly!" she cried, waving her hands at me and laughing. "I got work to do!"

In my dorm room I lay on my bunk and tried to preserve in my leaky head exactly the way Maria had smelled so I could call it up whenever I needed to. I thought about going down to my typewriter and somehow getting her smell down on paper, but I knew even then that there are some things words just can't do. Instead, I imagined where she might go when she was done working each night, the kind of house she lived in, the things she did there. I wondered if she lived alone, or if she shared that house with a man, or her grandparents, or a daughter, or maybe a son.

THE JUMPING PLACE

LUNCHTIME ON A windy spring day and I was lurking around behind the old log ruins of the officers' quarters, doing my best not to be noticed. From where I stood I could see Principal Whipple up in the lookout tower above his house, scanning the hills with a pair of army recon binoculars. The slim turret, which jutted twenty feet above the house like a chimney gone haywire, had been used during the Apache Wars as a meteorological station and observation tower, but now the principal would spend an hour or two up there each day, with his binoculars and maybe a lemonade or a soda, and do his best to keep tabs on his maroon-haired wife, Mrs. Whipple.

Mrs. Whipple, a woman whose perpetually erect nipples never failed to catch the immediate attention of every boy in school when she sauntered across the grounds to her husband's office to take him lunch, liked to go for long walks in the hills or take drives out into the narrow dirt roads of the reservation backcountry. I was completely out of the rumor and gossip circuit at WS so I was left to decipher odd references. I heard some of the boys call her "Mama Beaver." I heard something being said about her "headlights." In shithouse number three, there was a prominent piece of graffiti carved out next to the seat that said *I want to suck on Mrs. Nipples.* The boys, especially the older ones, would grab their crotches and grin at each other when she worked outside in her garden or sat on the porch of that big stone house sipping whiskeys brought to her by her little humpbacked maid, Aurelia.

I heard a metallic jangling sound and looked down the slope to see Sterling Yakezevitch, partially obscured by underbrush, stomping

around near the edge of the canyon, those steel and leather leg braces
of his creaking and jingling. What kind of Indian could be named
Sterling Yakezevitch? It was a mystery to everyone. Sterling was the
only one besides me who stayed away from the parade grounds at
recess, the only one who wasn't part of any playground tribe. I don't
believe his name had anything to do with it. His hair was braided
into one thick rope and the bowlegged way he walked with the sad-
dle-and-spurs sounds of his brace made me think of the cowboys—
Tom Mix, John Wayne, James Coburn—that we sometimes saw on
movie night.

I looked up at Principal Whipple, who was engrossed in his spying, and then I crawled down the slope, creeping under overhanging
branches of gambel oak and paloverde, but didn't get too close. A
few months before, back when I still believed I could find somebody
to be my friend, I had tried to sit next to Sterling on the steps of the
classroom building during recess and he gave me such a vicious
elbow to the ribs that for a week afterward even the most shallow
breath was a painful enterprise. Sterling Yakezevitch was a loner like I
was, and a cripple, but nobody ever bothered him. Nobody threw
apples at him, nobody taunted him and teased him in the showers,
nobody ever pushed him to the back of the lunch line. I wanted to
know what his secret was.

He stood at the edge of the cliff, looking down into the canyon at
something I couldn't see from my place behind a bush. The canyon
was called East Fork and it was one of the reasons Fort Apache had
been built in this particular location; more than sixty feet deep in
places, with a fast-running river at its bottom, and over a mile long, it
was a perfect defense against an army of Indians coming down out of
the hills from the north.

It wasn't long before Sterling noticed me watching him. He glared
up at me and I considered making a break for it, but after awhile he
yelled up at me, "Hey! What's you looking?"

I shrugged, did my best to act like I was minding my business, half concealed in a bush as I was, Sterling looked around to make sure no one could see us and waved me down. I came the rest of the way down the slope but stayed a good ten feet away from him—I hadn't forgotten that elbow, and I now knew enough to be wary of any gesture of goodwill, no matter who it came from.

"Look down there," Sterling said, pointing at the canyon floor, which was about fifty feet below us. "You see them rocks down there?"

The canyon floor was scattered with rocks. I could see a lot of smooth, gray and white river rocks, which were now mostly covered with the flooding White River, and the giant black boulders of pitted volcanic rock which had, over thousands of years, slowly cracked and broken away from the canyon cliffs.

Sterling was pointing almost directly below us. "Them red ones."

They were hard to see, jumbled in among the river rocks as they were, but there was no doubt they had been brought from somewhere else, five or six shards of red sandstone, each more or less the size of a dinner plate, embedded in the dirt like stepping stones in a garden.

"If you jumped from here, you think you could make it to 'em?" Sterling asked me in a whisper.

I backed right away from that edge. I wasn't jumping anywhere.

Sterling regarded me with his hot, dark eyes. There was something in them that reminded me very much of Ismore. "You're scared, eh? You ain't a brave little anglo?"

"What are those rocks?"

"Them's what you jump for. When it's time, you go for them rocks. Only one boy ever made it to that farthest one, that's why they marked it there. Anybody ever gets it past that one, they get their own marker." Sterling let out a high wail of a war whoop that echoed off the canyon walls and shot up in the sky, loud enough to get Principal Whipple to turn his binoculars on us for just a moment before he resumed his spying.

I stepped forward to take another look at the rocks. They looked impossibly far from where we stood. If somebody was crazy enough to jump, he would have to take a full running start to land anywhere near them.

"You don't tell nothing to the teachers, or nobody. I know you's anglo, but you's Indi'n too, so you should know about it."

"About what?"

Sterling shook his head in the same way my teachers did when they looked at the blank pages I turned in: a gesture of utter pity. "This is the jumping place, *right here*. Shit, man! This is it. And you don't tell nobody I told you. These days, you know, some'll eat a bunch of pills or shoot theirself in the head with a pistol, but this is the way here, this is *it*." Sterling took a couple of steps forward—the squeaking of his brace almost an animal sound—and stood so that both of his scuffed boots hung over the edge a couple of inches. "Been guys jumping off here since this school started, probably before. Hundred fucking years and only one guy made it that far. That fucker could just about fly, I bet. Some got close, them's marked by the rocks behind that farthest one. Some never got close, didn't even get a rock, which is the worst thing you can do. Every one of their blood is down there, all mixed together."

Sterling was so intent on the rocks below that I was able to back away, slowly, carefully, without him noticing. As I edged back up the slope, I realized I was following a faint path through the weeds and bushes that bore down in a perfectly straight line to the spot where Sterling stood, considering distances, dreaming about death. It was like a narrow runway, a little overgrown but still perfectly useful.

Faster now, I began to clamber up the incline. Sterling started after me, grunting and throwing his legs forward with a violent twisting of his hips, but there wasn't any way a cripple like him could catch up with me.

"Don't tell anybody, fuckhead!" he shouted up after me. "Or I will throw you off a here myself!"

THE GAUNTLET

THE REST OF that spring and summer I dreamed about sprinting down the runway, launching myself off the corroded cliffs, wind-milling my arms and legs like a long jumper, yearning for those blood-red rocks fifty feet below. The whole idea terrified me, gave me a hard jolt of adrenaline each time I thought about it. From then on, I did everything I could to keep away from Sterling, whose legs each day seemed to become more twisted and uncontrollable, like two wild animals trying to bust out of the braces that held them.

I continued putting a lot of my energy into avoiding Nelson, too, but slowly he began to reel me back in. He did a few favors for me: pulled off a couple of bigger girls who were trying to steal a carton of juice I'd saved from breakfast, found me an extra pair of sheets I could make a quick change with when I peed the bed, had Glen and Rotten Teeth beat up a kid named Frankie who had jumped me one Sunday morning when no one was around and kicked and punched me senseless, seemingly just for the sheer entertainment of it. Before I knew it, I was doing him favors in return. It started with the sim-plest of things: swiping a bathroom pass off Mrs. Theodore's desk, for instance. But it wasn't long before I was breaking into the cafeteria kitchen at night to steal cans of syrup and yeast to make home brew, bags of white sugar that Rotten Teeth liked to keep under his bunk and eat at his leisure. Soon, I was slipping into the teachers' lounge in the middle of the day to take beer out of the refrigerator or siphon-ing gas out of the school vehicles so Nelson and his buddies could snort the fumes until their eyes spun in their heads.

For Nelson's purposes, I was perfect. Unlike most of the others, I was small enough to slip through the window bars. I knew every inch of the school grounds, had the duct systems memorized and had access to Uncle Julius' tools whenever I needed them. And I was a natural burglar: thorough, cautious and patient as a statue. But more importantly, I was a brain-injured retard who didn't have the good sense to dodge an apple when it was thrown at him—I was never suspected of anything.

In return for my services, I was kept under Nelson's protection—in a sense, I now had a tribe of my own. Though I didn't really understand how it had come about, this is the pact we had made. I would do his dirty work, and Nelson let everyone know that he owned me and I was not to be messed with or used by anyone else. Of course, this only made people like Glen and Rotten Teeth resent me all the more. While nobody threw anything at me on the parade grounds or towel-whipped me in the showers, every so often I'd get a surreptitious punch to the gut in lunch line, or a homemade dart stuck in my back during class.

It was an enormous relief when May rolled around and everyone, except five or six of us permanents, went home for the summer. What a luxury it was to be able to spend three or four hours a day pounding on my Hermes Jubilee, getting it all down. I typed because it felt good, because I had nothing else to do, because I thought by getting it on paper, by turning the nameless into words, I might understand things a little better. I made up stories about my mother in California, how she lived on a beach with palm trees and every day wrote letters to the police trying to find out where I was; about Art, discovering that it was all a mistake, his wife and daughters were not dead at all but had been living in a castle with a bunch of nuns; about the mailman who had run over me, who every day took letters and packages to people and told them, "I am a bad man, I killed a boy." I typed because typing, for me, was as good as having a conversation. I typed because I had to. I typed because I was afraid I might disappear.

I helped Uncle Julius with his maintenance work, snooped around the teachers' houses, tried to spy on Mrs. Whipple whenever I could. Every once in awhile, a tourist or two, usually foreigners—Danes and Swedes and Germans who idolized the noble red man and his spiritual worldview—would come to look at the old historic buildings, to see the place where the last remnants of the wild, rampaging Apache had been hounded into submission. The tribe had put up a few markers indicating anything of historical significance, and even started a tiny gift shop out of the old post office, but Fort Apache was so far out of the way that we could go a whole week without seeing a stranger.

The first tourist I ever talked to was an enormous hippie pushing around all his belongings in a shopping cart. He wore only a pair of grime-stiffened shorts and leather sandals and he strolled around the grounds, maneuvering his cart through gravel and weeds like the happiest of shoppers.

When he saw me watching him, he came over and looked down at me through the matted bramble of his hair. Then he opened his arms wide, gesturing at the officers' quarters, the old barracks, the cavalry stables up on the hill, the mountains in the distance.

"Wild," he said slowly, drawing the word out. "It's all wild."

He stayed like that, swaying just a little bit, then turned his attention back to me. "Can you say something, you know, in your native tongue?"

"Cunnilingus," I said.

He squinted at me for a moment. "Wild," he said.

By the time August came to an end, I was so shot through with boredom I couldn't help but be happy at the thought of school starting, of having something to do. The first day of school I managed to remain invisible until lunch recess started and I saw the older boys rounding up the new ones, herding them into the center of the parade grounds like wayward cattle. I was startled when Rotten Teeth came up behind my hiding place under the bleachers, grabbed the short hairs of my neck and yanked me toward the scrum of terrified boys. I tried to protest, reminding him that Nelson and I were on good terms, but he yanked harder.

"This is for all the new kids, don't matter who," he said.

"But I'm not new!"

"You're new enough."

Scotty Pena, a slope-chinned Papago, was the master of cere-monies. He indicated how the other older boys should make two parallel lines about three feet apart, and then grabbed the first new kid he saw, a chubby yellow-skinned guy. The older boys pulled off their belts or searched the ground for sticks. I could see Sterling, way down at the end, slicing the air with his new arm crutches, which he could no longer get around without. "This is how the old Indi'ns used to do it!" Scotty called out gleefully, to nobody in particular. "I saw it on TV!"

The yellow-skinned boy was already blubbering before he took the first hit, and as he bounced his way through the gauntlet, he cried out mournfully with each kick, punch and swat of the belt. The worst of his beating came when he fell down and was crowded around by a knot of older boys, laughing and gritting their teeth while they stomped him and swung their belts in short vicious arcs. Once he emerged from the other end he collapsed on his belly and puffed like a fish heaving onto the banks of a river.

I watched three or four boys go through, little *poofs* of lice powder rising each time they took a shot to the head, and I came to this sim-ple conclusion: run fast and, no matter what, keep your feet.

When it was my turn, I did not hesitate, did not give the tiring gauntleteers a chance to gather themselves from the last beating. I covered my head with my arms as best I could and ducked forward like somebody stepping out into a hailstorm. I veered crazily, bump-ing into knees and stomachs, taking a few good shots here and there but keeping my feet under me and eventually emerging at the end, feeling like I had accomplished something; I had managed, for once, not to get too badly hurt. Despite a split lip and a stinging scrape on the back of my neck, I felt strong, full of juice. I thought I might be

142   *Brady Udall*

getting the hang of things after all. That's when Rotten Teeth came up behind me, and with a doubled length of rusted baling wire whipped me across the lower back so hard that it felt like I was cut in half. I let out a high yelp, like a dog, which gave everyone a good laugh.

The two playground monitors that day, Mr. Stevens and Miss Oliver, sat at one of the outside tables two hundred yards away, their backs to us, eating their lunch and chatting about their carefree adult lives. From the other side of the grounds, the girls had gathered to watch and pretty soon they were rounding up the new ones and organizing a gauntlet of their own.

At lunch, the new boys, cut up, bruised and hangdog, commiserated silently at one table, shoveling food into their mouths while keeping an eye out for any sign of further danger. I wanted to shout at them—*This isn't the worst! If you only knew!*—but I passed on by. I could have joined them and nobody would have complained, I might even have been welcomed, but a certain pride rose in me—I was not a new boy, I had *experience,* I was a *sixth grader.* Despite being only ten years old and never turning in a single assignment or saying a word in class except to ask about using the bathroom, I had passed the fifth grade.

At the far end of the seething lunchroom I saw someone sitting alone in my space under the basketball hoop. There was no mistaking it was another new boy: purpling welt at the side of his eye, dusty clothes, blood-crusted nostrils. I placed my tray on the table just across from him and began to eat. He sat stock-still and looked at his food as if he didn't know what it was. He had a flat, padded face, a thin gash of a mouth and perfectly bowl-cropped hair that was as black and shiny as crude oil. Except for his rough flannel shirt and jeans, he looked exactly like one of the Winomami—mostly naked Amazon aborigines I had read about in the *National Geographic*s Art had given me. Could he have really come all that way to live at Willie Sherman? I knew that some of the kids came from places far away, but the Amazon was a *jungle.*

I caught his eye and said, "Winomami?"

He met my gaze but said nothing.

I tried another of the jungle tribes I remembered reading about: "Kayapo?"

He might have raised his shoulder ever so slightly—a shrug—but that was it. If he was an Amazon tribesman, I guess he didn't feel like discussing it.

We kept silent for the rest of lunch, occasionally sneaking looks at one another. He didn't touch his food and when he stood up to go, he held out his unopened carton of chocolate milk. I took it and drank it down, keeping my eyes on him, and was almost sure I saw the barest hint of a smile. We were both bruised and bloody and white on the edges with lice powder. His name was Cecil and he would become the best friend I'd ever have.

REUNION AT THE CATTLE GUARD

IT WAS THE very day I met Cecil, just before dinner bell, when William Dye came into the kitchen where I was standing in a garbage-can-sized aluminum pot trying to scrape the burnt oatmeal off the bottom with a small collapsible army shovel.

"Some guys out there who want to talk to you!" he yelled over the grinding roar of the automatic dishwasher. William was kind of the school clown, a sore-eyed kid who made cat noises in class and could fart on cue.

"Guys?" I yelled back.

"Two guys over by the cattle guard," William said, hauling me up out of the pot. "They gave me a buck to find you. If they give you any money, you're giving it to me, right?" William dug his fingers into my arm. "Okay?"

I crossed the gravel road, still wearing my stained, oversized apron, squinting to see through the dust to the cattle guard, where I could make out two men leaning against a car in the shade of the old scarred elm. A little twitch in his brain, a nervous shudder, something like instinct told Edgar to turn and run like hell, but he walked slowly closer, circling around the car, keeping his distance. Both men were young, thin and wearing sunglasses, but that was it with similarities. One was clean-cut and verging on dapper, dressed in a blinding white shirt and pressed slacks, while the other, with wild hair and a patchy beard, wore a tight, striped T-shirt and plaid bell-bottoms which bloomed out over a pair of pointy-toed cowboy boots.

The neat one smiled when he saw me, held his arms out as if in welcome, while the other, now splayed out on the hood, seemed to be asleep in spite of the wild guitar music vibrating out of the car's stereo. The neat one said something to me but I couldn't hear it over the jungle thump of bass. He looked around, motioned me over, and after a second of hesitation, I entered the ring of shade under the elm.

The neat one squatted down in front of me and shouted, "Edgar!"

I looked at him, dumbfounded. His face was angular, sheened with sweat, and he was close enough to me that I could see two, bloated, upside-down versions of myself in his mirrored sunglasses. Again, he said something that got lost in the music, then cupped his hands over his mouth, turning back, and hollered, "Turn that down!"

The guy on the car's hood startled, throwing out his elbows and sliding sideways off the fender before scrambling through the open window to get to the stereo. There was a moment of profound silence before the man in front of me pulled me awkwardly to him. It was not until I felt his hands on my shoulders and smelled his antiseptic breath that I was jarred into recognition: I was hugging Dr. Pinkley.

I must have stiffened because Barry pulled back, looking hurt.

"It's me," he said in a strange, raspy voice, like paper tearing. He unhooked the glasses from his ears. "You really don't recognize me?" It was Dr. Pinkley, no doubt about it, but somehow he had transformed from a soft-shouldered ghost in the night with a pad of fat under his chin and the rosy cheeks of a baby to this lank wedge of man made of nothing but angles. His dark hair spiked off his head like the spines of a cocklebur. Even his voice had changed, the result of Art's forearm shiver that April night a lifetime ago.

The bearded one was now standing next to me and he gave me a light slap on the back. "Hey, it's Edgar the miracle-boy!" he said.

Dr. Pinkley's jaw tensed and he turned his head. "Jeffrey, would you *shut up*?"

I stood there in the shady dust, looking at both of them, feeling like I had stepped out of the sunlight of Willie Sherman into a shadier, alternate world. Since leaving St. Divine's I had come to believe that once a person disappeared out of my life—my mother and father, Grandma Paul, Sue Kay and Art—I would never see them again, that I was forever cut off. And yet here were Barry Pinkley and Jeffrey—or incarnations of them, at least—with me under a big elm tree on the grounds of Fort Apache, both of them grinning like conspirators. I laughed because I didn't know what else to do.

Barry grabbed my hand and said, "You probably thought I gave up on you, didn't you? No, Edgar, no way. It's just that I've had to be careful. People have been looking for me. They still are."

"A wanted man," Jeffrey said, flicking ants off his boots with his middle finger.

"Are you ghosts?" I asked them.

"Ha!" Jeffrey slapped his knee. "Ghosts! Ha!"

"I've been here a few times before, to check up on you," Barry said. "But I had to be careful. It's dangerous just to be talking to you like this."

I squinted at Barry, trying to reconcile the sleek man with the sandpaper voice who sat next to me now and the lumpy, buttery-voiced guy who had trouble getting through the window at St. Divine's. "What happened to you?"

"Me?" he said. "You mean what I look like? Yeah, I guess I've lost some weight, people have told me that. Things are working out quite well for me these days, but I really came to find out how you are, what I can do for you."

Barry asked how I was feeling—Were there any more seizures? Headaches? Did the school have adequate medical facilities?—and when I didn't answer he dragged out his medical bag, which was now stuffed full with bottles and baggies and syringes, and began thumping my belly, squeezing my head, working my joints, investigating my ears. "What's this white stuff all over you?"

"Bug powder," I said.

"Jesus," Barry said.

"Are you all right in this place, is it horrible?"

I shrugged. "I'm fine."

"Well good, that's good, we can talk about all of this later, but I came mostly because I have some wonderful news for you. I've found your mother."

Barry waited for me to react but I could only stare back at him, numb. At that point, I would not have been surprised if my mother had leaped out of the trunk of the Cadillac wearing a bikini and holding a birthday cake.

"She wants to see you, Edgar, I'm going to arrange it, don't worry. You don't know how much work it took, but I found her and she's not very far away from here. You're going to see your mother."

Just then the dinner bell rang and a clamor like a gathering riot rose up as everyone converged on the cafeteria doors. I tried to pull away from Barry, but he held tightly on to my hand.

"Keep quiet about this and everything will be fine," Barry said. "Things are looking up for all of us."

I yanked my hand out of his and headed for the cafeteria, crashing through the bushes and weeds like a spooked deer. Just as I jumped the cattle guard I heard Jeffrey call out behind me, "Run, coma-boy! Run like the wind!"

EDGAR AND CECIL

SO I SHOWED Cecil around the place. I showed him the maintenance hut where I helped Uncle Julius in the summer, the old cavalry stables still filled with ancient horse apples and molding tack, the boiler room where I typed every day, the secret pathways of ducts and crawl spaces I used to creep around in, the cliffs Sterling had shown me and the red markers below. "When it's time, this is where you jump," I told him. "Those rocks are red because people bled all over 'em." He nodded solemnly, seemed to understand completely, no need for further explanation.

Everywhere we went, Cecil would pick up trash—orange juice cartons, cigarette butts, old math assignments—and would stash it in his pockets. He would meticulously pick bits of papers caught in the thorns of prickly pear or ocotillo and would go ten feet out of the way to retrieve a bottle cap. I didn't ask him what he was doing. As long as we were walking around, I thought, why *not* try to clean things up a little?

Another of Cecil's more interesting habits was his addiction to Dum Dums. He had the amazing ability to nurse one of those tiny lollipops for three or four hours before sucking it down to the stick. He never once offered a Dum Dum to me, and whenever he opened a new one he would carefully fold up the wax wrapper with an air of solemn ritual, like a Marine retiring the flag. Then he would tuck the wrapper into his pocket for eventual transfer to the nearest trash receptacle.

Cecil and I did not talk much. Cecil's English was pretty bad, and I was not what you would call a conversationalist. We walked around, mostly in silence, sat together in the cafeteria and ate our food. Who needed talking? I just wanted someone to *be* with.

It took some effort, but I finally learned that Cecil was not an Amazonian aborigine at all, but a Havasupai, a tribe that lived on a reservation at the bottom of the Grand Canyon. He explained this using an old travel brochure he carried around in the pocket of his shirt. I had never heard of the Grand Canyon before, but Cecil assured me that it was still a good place, even though the hikers and fat-ass donkey riders were filling it with garbage. All the English he had ever learned, he told me, was from park rangers and backpackers who he sold ice-cold well water to for a nickel a cup. This was the first time he had ever been to the United States of America, as he put it, the first time he had ever been to school. Because both parents had died when he was a boy, he had been living with his uncle's family until a few months ago when the uncle had lost his job with the Forest Service for drinking on the job. So he sent Cecil off to school and allowed him to return only for the summers, when he could earn his keep selling water.

"You like it here?" I asked him once while we waited in line to get our polio shots.

Cecil looked slowly around with those soft eyes of his. He made a low whistle and said, "Little bit shabby."

The novelty of hanging around with Cecil, of having somebody to be with, was almost enough to keep my mind off Dr. Pinkley and what he had told me about my mother. In bed at night I would try to convince myself that I really hadn't seen Barry and Jeffrey at all, that I imagined them, or they were ghosts from my life at St. Divine's, just like the ghosts who'd come to persecute me for not dying as I should have. And my mother—she truly *was* a ghost, in my mind. She was nothing more than a fleeting whiff of perfume to me, a hazy, decomposing image in my memory, a few seconds of ringing laughter. The ghosts who plagued me at St. Divine's were much more real to me than she was.

It had been over a week since school started and still Nelson had not come to me with an assignment to steal, spy or sabotage. I almost wished he would: it would give me something to do at night other than lying there, my eyes cranked wide, wondering when I would hear from Barry again. What's more, I was beginning to worry that Nelson might not need me anymore, maybe he had found some new boy to do his work for him, and I would be thrown to the wolves once again.

It was almost a relief when, just before class one morning, Nelson cornered me near the rear stairs of the dormitory.

"Good summer, eh?" he said, steering me into the shadows. It was early in the morning but already the air was a stifling blanket of heat that made it difficult to breathe.

I tried to assume the expression I had been working on for a few months now, a look of utter blankness that betrayed nothing.

"What, you don't talk no more? Remember, you ain't no silent Indi'n. You're a anglo, and anglos *love* to talk, that's all they do, talk, talk, jabber, jabber, yah, yah, yah. See? So why don't you talk to me about this little headhunter you're walking around with."

"Cecil," I said.

Nelson tried to stomp on a yellow grasshopper, missed. "I just got done talking with him in the bathroom. I don't think he's the kind of kid you should be walking around with. I tried to make friends with him, but he wasn't so nice about it."

"You hurt him?"

Nelson, big as Humpty Dumpty, smiled broadly. "Hurt? Nah. A little."

"You going to hurt me?"

With a quick snap of his arm Nelson reached out and grabbed my crotch, digging his fingers in hard. I tried to pull away but he began to squeeze until he had my genitals in a thumb-and-forefinger grip, like a farmer milking a cow.

"This hurt?" he said.

I immediately went to my only emergency plan, which involved pissing my pants. But he had everything clamped shut—I couldn't get a drop out.

"And what about these two white guys the other day? Now you got all kinds of friends, hey? Who are them two guys? They FBI guys? You in the FBI now? They want you to do things for them?"

I was happy to explain everything, but it was as if Nelson was wringing my windpipe along with my balls; I could only make a popping sound with my lips.

He took out a neatly folded piece of paper and shoved it into my shirt pocket. "That's a note from your FBI friends. It's for you, but it got to me first. You might want to tell 'em you're busy, you know, you got other things to do. I think maybe that's what you should do."

He laughed, let go of me, and walked away. I sat down in the dirt long enough to recover, to get myself breathing again, and then was off looking for Cecil. I found him in his dormitory room, across the hall from mine. He sat on his bunk, his hair wet and twisted up on his head like somebody had wrung it out by hand.

I said, "Nelson get you?"

Cecil explained what had happened, pantomiming most of it. They had rammed his head in the toilet and flushed several times, in the process chipping one of his teeth on the porcelain bowl. Then they had pulled off his pants and towel-whipped him until he was able to make a break for it and hide in the utility closet.

"You ran from them?" I said. Even though that's exactly what I did the first time Nelson got me, it seemed like pure foolishness to me now.

Cecil nodded. "They hitting me *Pop! Pop! Pop! Pop!* I run away fast."

He ran his thumb along the nick in his front tooth and began to idly pick his nose. He pulled a pineapple Dum Dum from a hole in his mattress and went through his little wrapper ritual. He gave the yellow sucker a good once-over, held it up to the light as if checking for flaws, and placed it solemnly on his tongue.

I was confused. Nobody made him eat shit? Nobody put a hot wire on his pecker? Head in the toilet, a little towel-popping—that was *something*—but it seemed like maybe Cecil had gotten off easy, which had never once, as far as I knew, ever happened to me.

Cecil rolled the Dum Dum around in his mouth and began combing his hair down in a straight line above his eyebrows, the way he preferred it. No doubt about it: I was jealous.

I remembered the note in my pocket. It was written on a pink prescription slip, with the words *Dr. Barry Terrence Pinkley, M.D.* printed in the upper left-hand corner. It said:

> Edgar,
>   I'll pick you up tonight 11:00 at the gate. Don't tell anybody. I have a big surprise for you!
>
> > See you soon,
> > Barry

EDGAR'S MOTHER

THE HOUSE SAT back from the road under the spreading limbs of a thick-trunked poplar. Covered with a shaggy coat of white stucco, it had lounge chairs and card tables and dented aluminum kegs scattered all over its flat roof and a couple of woolly dogs chewing on a bicycle tire on the hard-packed dirt of the front yard. Every window was lit up with yellow electric light and I could hear the garbled hum of voices, the low rumble of drums. Overhead, a full moon shone over everything like a spotlight.

"Is this your house?" I asked Barry, who had just turned off the engine of his Cadillac. Earlier tonight, I had snuck out of the dorms and met him at the gate, and we had driven for nearly an hour, Barry quizzing me on everything from the conditions at Willie Sherman, to the nutritional quality of what I was eating, to what I was learning in class. When I asked him if my mother was going to take me home he only waved his hand and said something about putting the carriage before the horse. He continually checked the rearview mirror and fiddled with the sunglasses he wore even in the dark.

"A friend's," Barry said. "Don't worry about those dogs. They only bite the police."

The dogs didn't even look at us as we walked to the door. Inside the house, which was filled with a low pall of smoke as if a round of firecrackers had just gone off, people were everywhere, slumped on couches, leaning against the walls, drinking and smoking and talking in low tones. In a far corner, a woman with an eye patch was slapping a pair of large African drums.

Holding my hand, Barry led me through the house, greeting people, shaking hands, laughing and winking, stopping every couple of feet to have brief whispered conversations. We stepped over a man facedown in the aqua shag carpet before coming to a door at the end of a narrow hallway.

"She's in here," Barry said. "She may be a little tired, but you can talk to her for awhile."

My mother sat at a Formica-topped table in a small, brightly lit kitchen. Her hair was short now, badly cut, and there wasn't a single ring on any one of her thin brown fingers. I had come here telling myself that it would probably not be my mother at all, but some other person, an impostor, or even the ghost who lived in my head, certainly not the flesh-and-blood person who had given birth to me. I felt something move in my chest like a stone rolling over in a riverbed.

"Gloria," Barry said in his phony, doctorly way. "This is your son Edgar. He's waited a long time to see you."

My mother looked everywhere in the room but at me. "Got any more?" she said to Barry in a light, airy voice that made my insides clench and hold.

Barry sighed, yanked open the fridge and pulled out a can of beer. "This is the last one. We'll have to get more later." He set it on the table in front of my mother and gave her chair a gentle shake. "Gloria, it's your boy. Here he is."

My mother pulled off the tab and drank half the beer before she looked at me. She seemed to be seeing me from a great distance. Her eyes were bloodshot and clouded and her face twitched. "He's so big," she said. She held her hand over her mouth and began to cry.

Barry had me sit in a chair across from her and set a warm can of Pepsi in front of me. "You two go ahead and talk," he said. "I'll come get Edgar in a few minutes."

My mother wept noiselessly, one hand trembling wildly in front of her face, the other locked around her beer as if it might get away. I watched her and said nothing. She took two deep breaths, gathering herself, and drained what was left in the can. "You're getting a lot bigger," she said, nodding, tilting her head and wiping her mouth with her wrist.

"*Ppfft,*" I said, just to hear myself make a noise, to make sure I was really there.

My mother looked up at me, surprised. Her face tensed and it looked like she might start to cry again, but she relaxed, picked up the saltshaker, put it back in its place. She shrugged and said, "We all thought you were dead."

Out in the other room somebody said, "A one . . . a two . . . a one-two-three," and a chorus of voices began to sing "I'm All Shook Up." There were whoops and shouts and clapping and somebody hollered, "You're killing me!"

My mother picked up my can of Pepsi, inspected it for a moment, then pushed it slowly back across the table. I watched her fingers vibrating against the tabletop, her lost, hungover eyes searching the room for her next drink, and I knew without a doubt that it was I who had done this to her.

We listened to somebody on the other side of the door go to town on the drums, thumping out a rhythm that made the windows shake. When the cheering and hooting quieted down I said, "I lost some teeth." Though I had pretty much lost all the teeth I was going to lose, there were a couple that hadn't completely come back in yet and I made an exaggerated smile to show these off. My mother reached out and ran her finger into the narrow crevices. I wanted to bite down, draw blood, but I kept my mouth open until my jaw burned.

For the rest of the time until Barry came back, trailing smoke and the pungent incense, my mother I stared at each other, two strangers in a room, passing the time. I stopped at the door to tell her good-bye but she had already turned her back and was ransacking the drawers and cupboards of the kitchen for something, anything, to drink.

BUZZARD-BAITING

WHEN WE COULD, Cecil and I walked in the hills. Evenings, in the couple of hours after classes let out and before dinner, we would hike up past the cedars and alligator juniper to the foot of the mesa where thick-barked ponderosas shaded everything. Cecil showed me a cave he had found in the red cliffs and we would hole up in the stale, dusty dimness and do nothing but sit in the absolute silence of the place, the security of it. Sometimes, on weekends, we would venture farther out, walking along dirt roads and game tracks under the shadows of the pines. We saw coyotes and mule deer and enormous, snorting elk crashing through the brush on the slopes above us. At dusk we would watch quietly as the trees were taken, one by one, into the great wash of dark.

Cecil showed me how to follow butterflies to find home brew buried like treasure around the outskirts of Willie Sherman. Malt, yeast, maple syrup, potatoes, corn flakes—home brew could be made

with just about anything a student could get his hands on. I had
stolen the ingredients for it many times, but never got to see it made.
I only knew that it was usually done in the middle of the night and
the ingredients, according to some arcane recipe, were poured into a
bucket or a barrel or a wooden box made watertight with kerosene
and tar. Buried and left to ferment into a vile concoction, it could
get you drunk so long as you could keep from vomiting it back up.

Whenever we found a new batch—there was always a swarm of
yellow and orange butterflies careening madly above it—Cecil
would claw away the dirt with his hands, pull off the lid and scoop
out some of the noxious, foaming brew with a cupped hand.
Everybody made their home brew differently, and every batch had
its own unique bouquet. Sometimes it smelled like gasoline, sometimes like bile, often like a rotting fruit. Cecil would always offer
some to me first and I would always refuse. He would take only the
tiniest little sip, which would throw him into convulsions of disgust,
his face contorting, his eyeballs popping. He would clutch his throat
with both hands and gasp, "Bad! Ach! Oh bad! Wow!"

We would watch the butterflies cluster around the edges of the
hole and get drunk until they couldn't fly anymore, only flop and
flutter helplessly like paper confetti caught in a breeze. This was good
entertainment as far as we were concerned.

Another thing Cecil showed me was buzzard-baiting. While I hid
under a tree, he would find a nice open spot to lie down and wait
until a buzzard spotted him—it usually didn't take more than fifteen
or twenty minutes to have half a dozen birds funneling in the drafts
directly above us. Slowly they would descend like great black shadows, banking as they turned, their wing feathers splayed like out-
stretched fingers. I don't know how he was able to do it, but Cecil
could lie perfectly still without even the slightest rise or fall of his
chest, without the tiniest twitch. And here those buzzards would
come, lower, lower, craning their big pink turkey-heads for any sign
of movement, for that telltale whiff of death, and when the first one
was so low to the ground that you could hear the soft *shoosh* of it

bearing down through the thick air, Cecil would leap to his feet, wave his arms and cry, "Dirty-fucker buzzard! Watch out! Ha-ha!"

The poor buzzards would nearly drop out of the air with astonishment. They'd jerk back and flap like crazy, trying to scratch out some altitude with those big clumsy wings made for gliding, and off they'd go, looking back at us under their wings, embarrassed as it is possible for a buzzard to be.

One November afternoon after a satisfying round of buzzard-baiting, we heard voices in the trees below us. Immediately, we scrambled for cover; we both understood what would happen if Nelson or some of the others caught us together. On the playground, in the dorms and cafeteria, we now had to ignore each other; Cecil was being routinely persecuted for refusing to join Nelson's tribe and it would only get worse—for both of us—it they knew we were together at all.

We slunk around a couple of cedars until we could see a black Dodge pickup with two people in the back. The man, an Indian, sat up against the cab. As for the other person—a woman it looked like—we could only see her maroon hair bobbing up and down in the man's lap. The man, for his part, seemed very happy, and once in awhile he'd pick up a small pair of binoculars and look off in the direction of Willie Sherman.

The woman stopped bobbing and we heard her say, "Is he up there?"

"Nah," the man said, "he's off paddling girls on the butt or something."

The woman rose up and kissed the man, a low moaning rising out of her like the purring of a cat. She began to make a yipping noise—*ai, ai, ai*—and the blouse she wore billowed out for a second to reveal a pair of dark nipples, like two mysterious eyes. It hit me at once that not only was this woman Mrs. Whipple, but she was also the person I heard yipping that night in the Thomas house, the owner of those pink toenails. We watched and listened and my throat began to tighten and my heart beat against my ribs with an audible *thup-thup*.

"What are they doing?" I managed to whisper to Cecil.

"Ficky-fick," Cecil said.

"Ficky-fick," I said.

"Oh mama," Cecil said.

It was only a couple of days before that Principal Whipple had stood on the stage of the auditorium and told us, with a righteous thunder in his voice, that it was time to pay the piper. He had been distracted by other things, he told us all at the special assembly, he had let things get too lax. There had a been a rash of robberies, personal items taken from the dorms, certain papers from the administration offices, tools from the maintenance hut, food from the kitchen, the American flag right off the pole. There were fights nearly every day on the parade grounds, vandalism all over the school grounds, drunkenness at school functions, abuse of the teachers and staff. A student had been cut with a razor in his sleep, another dragged into the woods and tied to a fence post. As he went down the list, barking out the various offenses, his steamy glasses inched slowly down his nose and white specks of saliva sailed out of his mouth, arcing like tiny comets into the bright stage lights and disappearing into the darkness over our heads.

Where are your *morals*? he asked us, slapping the podium so that the mike whined with feedback. Did we know what *decency* was? Were we savages? What would it take for us to act like moral, upright, civilized human beings?

Out in the darkness somebody—probably William Dye—let fly a loud, wet fart. Oh, we laughed, the tee-heeing and ha-haing drowning out the teachers trying to shush us up. Principal Whipple slumped a little, shaking his head, then stepped to the side of the podium, straightened up and seemed to glare at us individually in a way that said: *I will not be defeated by a fart.*

"Until discipline is restored," he declared, "until we find out who is responsible for these acts, everyone is going to suffer. No more morning recess—you will sit at your desks and do homework during this time. No more Saturday night movie privileges, no more bimonthly dances. Every student, I don't care who you are, gets Saturday morning work detail. Standard detention times will be doubled. When will you get your privileges back? When you earn them."

Right now, instead of watching Mrs. Whipple ficky-ficking with an Indian guy in the back of a truck, we were supposed to be scrubbing mildew off the walls of the dorm bathrooms with five or six other boys: part of our new work detail. But we had walked off the job risking an entire month of detention time and kitchen detail. We had made a good gamble, it turned out. Not only were we able to witness a full session of ficky-fick in the broad light of day, but we caught a brief glimpse of Mrs. Whipple's famed and completely uncovered nipples.

Before they got in the cab and drove off, Mrs. Whipple and the man she was with yipped and yowled so loud a flock of small brown birds startled out of a wild oak and zoomed off in alarm.

On our way back I tried to ask Cecil why he wouldn't join Nelson's tribe, do him a few favors—steal a few things, maybe light something on fire—it really wasn't all that hard. Then we could be together in the dorms or on the playground and there would be nothing to worry about. Cecil didn't seem to be listening; he was watching a fat little horned toad sitting in the bowl of a rusted hubcap, huffing tranquilly in a warm patch of sun. He snatched it up easily and turned it over, stroking its shiny belly until it closed its eyes and went still, its miniature alligator arms twitching. Cecil took out a steel box cutter he kept hidden behind his belt and with the tip of the razor blade, neatly sliced open the toad's broad belly, making two rectangular flaps that could be pulled back to reveal the glistening, multicolored innards, like jewels packed in oil. The toad never struggled or fought, just seemed to smile with a dazed, bleary-eyed contentment.

Cecil pointed to himself, then to the toad. "I'm Nelson and this you. See?"

I looked at the toad. "This is me?"

Cecil nodded. "And I'm Nelson. See? Okay?" He puffed out his

cheeks to add to the effect. These kinds of charades, full of gesticula-
tions and props, were how Cecil liked to make his points. I nodded
to show Cecil I understood: he was Nelson and I was the toad.

Cecil took the box cutter and, with the delicate care of someone
removing a pearl from an oyster, lifted out the tiny, still-beating
heart. The toad did not seem to miss it at all. Cecil turned to me
grinning widely, showing all his teeth—a perfect imitation of
Nelson—and held the twitching heart up to his mouth for a
moment before sliding it past his lips and biting into it, filling his
smile with blood.

WILLIE SHERMAN CHRISTMAS

CHRISTMAS AT WILLIE SHERMAN was just one more punishment. Everyone
escaped for the two-week break except for a few permanents and a
couple of staff to watch over us. Raymond, who was as much a permanent at the school as I was, always tried to make things cheery for
us. He'd lead us up the mountain to find a Christmas tree, slogging
through the wet snow in our inadequate loafers, sawing down a too-
big tree and covering ourselves with sap and scratches as we heaved it
down the mountain, groaning in sync like galley slaves, to the empty
gymnasium where we would decorate it with construction paper
cutouts and stale popcorn chains and never look at it again.

On Christmas Eve, members of the Ladies Aid Society of Show
Low would stop by with a home-cooked meal and a bag of presents
for us, all of which we had to earn by singing carols we didn't really
know the words to and present a Nativity scene, which mostly
entailed standing around with towels on our heads. The ladies—
broad-rumped old matrons toddling about in a cloud of perfume—
would clap politely and comment on what cute, brown-faced little

things we were. With the women watching over us but not joining in, we would wolf down the turkey and potatoes and cranberry and finally open the presents, which were always the same: a plastic bag full of ancient rock-hard candy, an assortment of trial products (shampoo, toothpaste, shaving cream, deodorant, mouthwash), a comb, a yo-yo, a set of colored pencils.

Under Raymond's supervision, we would thank the ladies profusely—*Thank you, ma'am, Merry Christmas, ma'am*—and once they had gone home feeling like good Christian women, we could hunker down and eat our Civil War–era candy until we were sick—one year I ate my entire tube of toothpaste and washed it down with a swallow of Listermint—and go to sleep with no visions, of sugarplums or Saint Nick or anything else, dancing in our heads.

That year, though, we had a surprise. We woke up and looked outside to see not one but two Santa Clauses, wandering across the parade grounds looking lost, dragging a couple of heavy, army-issue duffel bags through the snow and calling out, "Ho, ho, ho! It's Christmas! Ho, ho! Where the hell is everybody?"

Raymond, hungover in boxer shorts and clutching his hair with one hand, was the first to get to them. "Hey, what's this?" he yelled from the front door of the dormitory.

"Where are the kids?" one of the Santa Clauses hollered. "We got presents!"

I could recognize Jeffrey's high, reedy voice anywhere. He swung his duffel bag around a little too enthusiastically, which threw him off-balance. He ended up sprawled in the snow, his feet pedaling the air. "Fuck!" he cried. "I lost my beard!"

In the foyer of the boys' dorm they passed out presents. We gathered around, bedraggled and stupefied, while they handed out G.I. Joes, squirt guns, Barbies, cowboy pistols, water rockets, oranges and apples, matchbox cars, an avalanche of candy bars and bubble gum. They had obviously thought there would be more kids around, but it was only us: four boys, three girls and Raymond, all of us sleeping on one floor of the boys' dorm to save money on the heating bill.

Jeffrey was missing his beard, and both of them reeked of cigarettes and pine-scented car deodorizer, but they played their parts
with enthusiasm, slapping their pillow-bellies, and ho-hoing until
they were hoarse. It was the first time in my life, I think, that I had
ever experienced the joyful chaos of a true Christmas morning: there
was shouting and fighting over who got what and the wide-eyed
ecstasy of ripping open boxes. Raymond looked on in a foggy stupor. "Now who . . . what . . ." he said, turning around in place and
scratching his belly. Chester Holland, a little Pima boy with an enormous gob of bubble gum in his mouth, got so excited he dashed
around the room in his underwear, unable to stop long enough to
play with any of his toys.

One by one, Jeffrey took everybody on his knee, just like a depart-
ment-store Santa, and asked questions: "Have you been a good boy
this year?" or "Do you brush your teeth every night?"

When he got his chance, Barry pulled me aside, hooked his arm
around me and asked me if I was having a good Christmas. I was
clutching two G.I. Joes, a Lone Ranger doll and a fire engine; I wasn't
particularly interested in the toys myself but I knew, in the long run,
they would be worth something to somebody and it would be a
mistake to let the other kids take them all.

This was the first time I'd seen Barry since he'd taken me to see
my mother. A few weeks before, he'd sent a cryptic letter that said he
was very busy and that he would come and visit me when he
thought things were safe. He'd enclosed a twenty-dollar bill and
signed the letter *You know who.*

"Is my mother here?" I asked him. Maybe she was waiting out in
the car. Maybe she would show up in a Santa costume herself. With
Barry, it seemed, anything was possible.

"What do you think about these toys?" he said. Now he had me
up on his lap, just like Jeffrey with the other kids.

I asked again about my mother. Barry ho-ho-hoed and whispered
that we could talk about it later.

"You're such a serious little boy," he boomed in his fake Santa voice, which sounded more like a bad Count Dracula. "Try to have some fun!"

Eventually, Barry and Jeffrey were able to get away before Raymond could really start questioning them. From a clear patch in the fogged-up window, we watched them strike out across the parade grounds toward the road, swearing when they tripped on the hardened snowbanks, constantly losing the hats off their heads, the pillow under Jeffrey's coat tearing at the seams as it worked its way out, leaving a trail of swirling feathers. Standing behind us, Raymond said, "What in the name a goddamn hell." We tried our best to keep our eyes on them, but even in their bright red suits they grew smaller and less distinct, dissolving into the drab colors of the clouds and the trees, and then they were gone, vanishing as quickly as spirits or angels or beings from another world.

A HOLE IN THE GROUND

SNOW FELL IN heavy, wet flakes the day Principal Whipple took me out of my homeroom class. It was late February and he trod ahead of me through the dirty clumps of hardened slush and said nothing. I had been found out, I knew it. My stealing and spying and sneaking around had been found out and I was now being marched away to take my punishment. Edgar was so delirious with relief he almost collapsed into the snow at Principal Whipple's heels.

For months the entire school had done extra work detail, missed Friday night movies and special events and morning recess, suffering because of me, not only because I would not take responsibility for my crimes but because I continued to commit them. In spite of the principal's crackdown, Nelson never stopped coming up with projects for me: ice-picking a certain teacher's tires, sneaking into the girls' dorm in the middle of the night and pulling the fire alarm so we could see them in their underthings, running packets of pills or cigarettes or bottles of glue, stealing town passes off Maria's desk right from under her nose. I was not the only criminal at Willie Sherman, but I was becoming one of the more accomplished; I never got caught, never once was questioned.

A small woman wearing a gray dress suit and galoshes was waiting for us in the office. "This is Edgar," Principal Whipple announced and immediately disappeared out the door.

In a confidential tone, the woman explained that her name was Penny Miller and that she worked for the BIA and that she was sad to have to tell me that my mother had passed away.

I tried to understand. Was this the punishment I was supposed to receive?

"Your mother has passed away," Penny Miller said, enunciating each word clearly.

"Passed away," I said. "Did she go back to California?"

Penny Miller narrowed her eyes at me. She stood up, as if to call for help from the other office, but then sat back down with a sigh. She checked her watch.

"Listen to me. Your mother died. She's dead." Penny Miller ruffled through her papers. "You're Edgar Presley Mint?"

"I saw her awhile back," I said. My voice sounded far away to me and my vision seemed to be going dark at the edges. "We talked in a kitchen."

"Be that as it may," Penny Miller said.

I stared into my lap. At that instant I felt hate for this woman Penny Miller grow inside me like a black cloud. I thought about opening the drawer of Principal Whipple's desk and taking out the sack of CONTRABAND and stabbing, choking, shooting, torturing her with all the weapons and implements therein. I picked up a brass letter opener on the desk and thought about the different ways I could make her hurt. I thought about ripping out her hair with my hands. Then, as quickly as it had come, that feeling bottomed out and left me feeling lost again, everything before me gone fuzzy, out of focus.

"I think you know she hasn't been well for a very long time," she said, scanning one of her sheets. "It says here that she suffocated in her bedding, no doubt alcohol-related. We had some trouble locating next of kin. Things took awhile to make it through to our agency, but we've notified the grandmother and funeral arrangements are being made. Edgar, I'm very . . ." She put her hand to her nose and looked up at me. While she talked, I'd opened the floodgates; my piss was not only filling up the seat of my orange plastic chair but dripping out of the left cuff of my jeans, dribbling down my shoes and onto the floor.

"I'm sorry," I said, and this seemed to puzzle her because it's exactly the thing she had started to say to me. I wanted her to be angry with me, to hit or curse me, but she only looked irritated and confused.

"I'm sorry," I whispered.

Penny Miller peered at me and closed her file. She pursed her lips and said, "That's quite all right."

After Penny Miller hurried away, Maria came in to clean me up. She looked down at me with a sweet, sad face and said, "Oh, honey." She knelt to dab at my shoes with a tissue and I put my hand lightly on her shiny black hair and held it there.

Two days later, I was sitting in the cab of an old green GMC between Uncle Julius and Raymond, who was driving us down to San Carlos for the funeral. We slid down the icy mountain roads, the old truck's tires spinning and throwing slush, until we leveled out gradually as the snow and pine trees disappeared and were replaced by sage-covered hills and low, wind-twisted cedars. Uncle Julius gripped the dashboard with both arthritic hands, letting go only to take a pull on the flask of whiskey from his coat pocket. It was the first time he had been in a moving motor vehicle in fifteen years.

It turned out there was not really a funeral at all, but a brief graveside service in the San Carlos cemetery, which was full of sunken, unmarked graves and looked like a landfill with bleached plastic flowers scattered everywhere, shards of pottery and colored glass, small animal bones tied up in bundles, graves piled with rotting carnations and matted stuffed animals, a child's tiny shoes hanging by their laces from the arm of a wooden cross, layers of windblown trash snared by the rust-eaten wrought-iron fence. Except for the gravediggers and the fat preacher who sat in his Volkswagen Bug puffing on a hand-rolled cigarette, we were the first to arrive.

The rough pine coffin sat suspended on ropes above the black mouth of the grave.

"She's in there?" I asked Uncle Julius, but he only looked at me with those wooden eyes of his and said nothing. I wanted to know if I could open the box and have a look at her—I wanted to make sure it was really her, that some kind of trick wasn't being played on me.

We got out of the truck and walked over to the grave. Low gray clouds scudded across the mesas to the east and a cold wind rose up suddenly, yanking at our clothes, then sucked itself away, leaving us in a vacuum of utter stillness.

The preacher toddled up behind us. He was a flabby Indian man in a beige suit, with a coiffed hairdo that was having a hard time keeping itself together in all this wind. The preacher kept patting at it like a woman just back from the beauty parlor. "Is that all that's coming?" he called out cheerfully.

"Keep your trousers on," Raymond told him. The preacher smiled and nodded and reached out to rub his fat fingers along the edge of the coffin as if he was proud of it, as if he had constructed it himself. Behind us, the gravediggers—two men in orange jumpsuits with black serial numbers stenciled over their hearts—squatted next to a wild growth of prickly pear and drank from a bottle wrapped in a paper bag. I wanted to put my ear against the coffin, to find out what I might hear.

A green van rolled up and two orderlies in white uniforms opened the side door to let out Grandma Paul, already wailing like

a siren. The orderlies tried to help her down but she swatted at
them with the aluminum canes she carried in both hands like six-
shooters. She was a small woman, with eyes like buttons and stark-
white hair wrapped up in a bun at the back of her head. She wore
her Mickey Mouse sweatshirt, a yellow one so threadbare that it
was translucent in places, patched with multicolored thread and
pieces of a red handkerchief. That Mickey Mouse unlocked something inside me and I felt a pang of homesickness so sudden and
fierce that my knees felt like they might buckle. I choked to
breathe and moved closer until I could mash my face right into
Mickey Mouse's little red shorts. Grandma Paul's smell—a mixture
of sweat and woodsmoke and lavender skin cream mixed with the
sad, antiseptic smell of hospitals—made the pain in my chest even
worse. I held on to her shirt until I could feel my legs beneath me
again.

The orderlies went over to join the gravediggers and one of them
said, "That old squaw is nutty as they come."

Grandma planted both canes in the ground on either side of me
and continued her angry wail—a high, arching cry that sometimes
fell into a thrumming moan—while the preacher did his best to
carry on with some kind of ceremony. He read from his Bible and
yelled over the racket about the resurrection and how we will all rise
together on that great and glorious morn, God's children every one.
He pointed at the sky and hollered. He called on Jesus, oh Jesus
please, to heal us in our sorrow. Jesus, won't you take away our sins.
Jesus! Oh Jesus now! Cleanse us with your blood!

He never mentioned my mother's name, never said anything
about her.

When he was finished, he snapped his Bible shut and told the
gravediggers to stop swilling the devil's bathwater and get to work.
With a lot of grunting and cursing in Apache, they let out the ropes
and lowered the coffin into the hole until it settled with a rattling
thump. They picked up their shovels but Grandma beat them back
with both canes, spitting at them. She knelt in the yellow mound of

dirt and began pushing it into the grave with her twisted, bony hands. The first big clods made a reverberating *thonk thonk thonk* on the lid of the casket but it gradually became muffled until there was only the soft hiss of falling dirt.

Grandma Paul did not attack me with her canes when I climbed up on the mound next to her and began shoveling in dirt with my hands. She began her wail again, which became more of a song with high keening notes, an old Apache song that didn't have any words. Eventually someone came to take the gravediggers back to jail and the preacher putt-putted away in his little car. The orderlies smoked cigarettes and remarked to each other that at least they were away from the puke and shit and moaning for awhile. Raymond and Uncle Julius sat in the truck out of the wind and watched.

It took us more than an hour to get that hole filled. We worked at the dirt until our hands were raw and our fingers bled from underneath the nails. The gray, misting clouds were so low that occasionally one would tail down, dragging across the ground, and for a moment we would be lost in an obscuring whiteness. When we had finished, when we had finally humped all the loose earth into an oblong mound, I kept a last fistful of dirt to myself. Grandma Paul was quiet now and we stood together, looking at our handiwork, no sound but the wind like static in our ears.

On the way home, with Raymond listening to Roy Orbison on the radio and Uncle Julius dead drunk and snoozing against the window on the other side of me, I inspected the ball of dirt in the palm of my hand. I had meant to save it, keep it as a record, the only physical memento of my mother I had, but instead I put it all into my mouth, held it there until it dissolved into a gritty paste that began to seep past my lips. I worked at it, choking and gagging, but try as I might I couldn't swallow it down.

Back at Willie Sherman, instead of following Raymond into the dormitory I walked over to the administration building, where one light burned in a window. A heavy snow was falling and the light outside was a dark particled gray quickly falling into darkness. I tromped up the steps and entered the bright fluorescent buzz of Maria's office. She was behind her desk, already in her heavy coat and boots, singing to herself, looking at her eyelashes in a compact mirror. Her just-brushed hair hummed with static and the smell of nail polish was everywhere. When she noticed me standing in the doorway, melted snow dripping off the stalactites of my hair, she tilted her head slightly and put out her arms. I threw myself at her.

"Oh, honey," she said and gathered me in, pulling me up on her lap. She crossed her arms around me and I pressed the side of my face into the smooth brown skin of her neck. I held perfectly still, afraid that if I moved or spoke she might make me go away.

BED-WETTER

A FEW DAYS later I woke up before everybody else and wet the bed on purpose, soaked myself good. Raymond smelled it halfway through his wake-up call.

"Edgar?" he said, yanking back my covers, bewildered. It had been at least six months since my last accident and we all had come to assume that wetting the bed was one bad habit I had left behind.

Raymond threw up his hands. In his funny, clipped accent, he said, "You are ten years of age now? Eleven? Son-thing? What can we do?"

Before he had to ask I stripped off my pajamas, pulled the sheets away from the bed and marched with the entire wet, stinking bundle to the bathroom. Raymond walked behind me, and I knew without looking that he was shaking his head. Boys staggering out of their rooms, their faces and hair still pressed with sleep, paused long enough to snigger and snort as I went by.

When Raymond came back with the pink brick of soap, I said to him, "My mother's dead."

Raymond sighed, looked around. He spoke in a low voice. "I know that."

"Where is she now?"

"Who?" Raymond looked perplexed.

"My mother. Now she stays in the ground forever?"

"No, she ain't in the ground. It's . . . she's in heaven, you understand?"

"Heaven?"

"It's a nice place, where dead people go."

"Like California?"

Raymond paused to holler at two boys who were having a pissing contest in the showers. "Maybe it's like California. There's angels there, God's there, they got music there, I think. Pretty nice place, I guess."

"And the tooth fairy?"

"What?"

"Heaven's where the tooth fairy is?"

"Jesus, Edgar," Raymond said, taking the sodden sheet from my hand and twisting it until there was no water left. "Just don't wet your damn bed no more."

On my way back to my room little Walter Reed, a new boy with a birthmark like a red patch of mold on his forehead, leered sideways at me as I passed by and said, "Bed-wetter."

He didn't have time to think about running before I was on him. I grabbed him by the hair, jerked him backwards and swung him hard into the concrete-block wall. Laid out on the floor, he held up his arms to keep me off, but I stood over him, naked and wild, and punched at that birthmark like it was a bull's-eye. Little Walter whined helplessly and boys began sliding out of the shower to see what was going on.

Raymond lifted me up from behind, both arms around me. I was slick with water and soap and I held up my arms, arched my back and slipped out of his grasp like a sardine out of a fist. Little Walter was already picking himself up, smiling sheepishly, trying to regain his composure, when I started in on him again, giving him a shot to the kidney and grabbing for his ear in an effort to tear it off his head. This time Raymond tackled me, pressing me into the floor with the entire weight of his body. I struggled and gasped until I had nothing left in me.

Before Raymond let me up, he whispered to me, his breath hot on my cheek: "Don't go bad, Edgar, don't you fucking go bad."

LIGHTS OUT

PRINCIPAL WHIPPLE'S CRACKDOWN continued well into the spring and didn't solve anything, didn't stop the daily fights, the vandalizing, the midnight home-brew parties, the thieving, the sabotaging, the general violence and mischief, all of which I took part in some way or another. He had to figure out new ways of punishing us. One of his new favorites was the middle-of-the-night fire drill, which was not a fire drill at all, but an opportunity for the staff to search our belongings for contraband while we froze our asses off in the cold. For every item of contraband found—even if it was nothing more than a dirty comic book under somebody's pillow—we would spend an extra fifteen minutes in ranks, all of us, standing perfectly still until our feet went numb and we began to tip and totter like a regiment of Saturday night drunks. Another was smaller portions at meals: the dinner rolls shrank, milk was withheld, dessert went missing, all of which put the food I regularly stole from the storage rooms in higher demand.

For the worst of us, the principal came up with something he called personal detention. Instead of being forced to sit in the detention room with other students after class and during recess, you were locked in one of several empty, windowless supply closets, alone with nothing but a chair and a desk. You could spend anywhere from a few hours to an entire week in personal detention, taking meals there, doing schoolwork, let out only to use the bathroom and to go back to the dorms to sleep.

Eventually, Nelson landed in personal detention when he and Glen were caught trying to get drunk on a two-quart bottle of vanilla I had stolen for them. And not even Nelson could maintain his regular routine of delinquency locked away in the Closet, as it had come to be called.

The night of his first day in the Closet Nelson found me in the bathroom just before Lights Out, sitting on the pot at the end of the row, reading graffiti. There were no doors on the stalls, so Nelson simply appeared in front of me, darkening everything like an eclipse.

"You done in there?" he said.

I clamped my hand tightly over my genitals and glared at him. Even with him locked up all day, I couldn't seem to get away from him.

Nelson chuckled, as if at some private joke, and said, "Got a little favor I need." He took a homemade smoke bomb out of his pocket—a ball of tightly wound string soaked in kerosene—and handed it to me. "I don't like being inside all day," he said. "Us Indi'ns got to be out in sun, know what I mean?"

I knew exactly what he meant; over these two years Nelson and I had come to a way of understanding each other that didn't much involve words. My job was simple: I was to light the bomb, put it behind the grate near one of the intake fans and within a few minutes the whole building would be filled with smoke, which would allow Nelson to get outside and conduct whatever criminal business needed to be carried out on that particular day. I was relieved that it was nothing more complicated than that.

Nelson had started to say something else when Sterling Yakezevitch came into the bathroom, the rubber tires of his wheelchair squeaking on the damp floor. Over the past months Sterling's disease had progressed to the point where even his new arm crutches could not keep him on his feet. He started falling constantly, his

useless, rubbery legs bowing and buckling and splaying out underneath him. They sent him away to a hospital, which made me burn
with jealousy, and when he came back he was strapped in a wheelchair, his traitorous legs locked in place against two steel plates.

Bound to that chair, he had to maneuver over uneven ground full
of gopher holes and rocks and stickers—there was no such thing as a
sidewalk at Willie Sherman. Everywhere he went, people were
always sneaking up from behind, trying to push him, help him along,
maybe heft him up the steps, but he would always shout helplessly,
"Hey! No! Shit! Get the fuck away!" He swatted at us with a broken-off car radio antenna, tried throwing rocks at us, finally settled
on taping a hand-painted sign to the back of his wheelchair, spelled
out in bold red: DONT PUSH ME.

It was difficult, but we let him alone to fight his way through a
patch of soft clay or take ten minutes to undo the buckles and climb
out of his chair, scoot up the steps on his butt and pull the chair,
clanking and banging against the steel pipe banister, all the way up
after him.

Now, he had parked next to my stall and was in the process of
transferring himself from chair to toilet. He fell to the floor, yelled
"Fuck!" and I could see through the holes in the stall divider that he
was pulling himself up onto the toilet, hand over hand, like a man
scaling a precipice. He slipped again, whacking against the stall,
swearing and groaning and nearly yanking the commode off the
floor as he attempted once more to hoist himself upon it.

"Hey, doing alright in there?" Nelson called.

"Go fuck yourself, fat-ass!" Sterling hollered.

Nelson continued smiling at me like nothing had happened. I
swear I would have given just about anything to be Sterling
Yakezevitch, wheelchair or no.

I held up the smoke bomb. "You want this for tomorrow?"

"Yeah, but I don't want you to do it. Don't want you getting
caught. Give it to your friend Cecil. He'll do it, won't he? I know
you two—"

Next door, Sterling growled, "I'm trying to *shit,* goddamn," and Nelson continued, without missing a beat, "—are fairy-faggots, going off into the trees to beat each other off, hey? Right?" He laughed and slapped his belly. "You tell him all he has to do is a couple of things for me once in awhile and you two run off fagging each other all you want, fine with me. Tell him tomorrow just after third hour would be okay."

With that, he was gone, his sandals pop-popping down the hall, and my stall was once again flooded with light. Sterling flushed his toilet, grumbling as he lowered himself to the floor so he could crawl back to his chair, which, in the midst of the struggle, had rolled backwards a few feet. The call "Lights Out!" came echoing down the hall, which meant we had exactly one minute to be out of our clothes and in bed or it was early kitchen detail for the next three days.

I leapt off the toilet, skidding out of my stall, and I could see immediately that Sterling was not going to make it. He was on his belly, shirt and pants soaked from the water on the floor, belt unbuckled, one black shoe off, slipping and scrabbling on the wet tile like a newborn calf. I reached down to help him up—I had seen orderlies hoist people into wheelchairs hundreds of times—but before I could get my hands under his armpits he swung his elbow around, clipping me just under the ear, and I fell backwards against the tin urinal trough.

"You think I care about Lights Out?" he snarled at me, grabbing the armrests on his chair. "What can they do to me?"

Edgar rubbed his head where it had hit the drainpipe. This head injury business was beginning to get old.

The hard little muscles in Sterling's arms knotted as he pulled himself up. He situated his legs into place on the angled steel plates and looked down on me from the height of his chair.

"Remember," he said. "You're Indi'n, not white. White's not going to get you anywhere, you hear me? Even if you got just a couple a drops a Indi'n blood, that's all it takes, it's like a disease. People around here calling you white boy, they don't know shit. You're Indi'n. That's it. So you better get some balls."

I watched him roll on out of the bathroom and continued to sit under the trough like somebody taking cover in an air raid. The lights went out.

THE BUTT TORCH

THEY GOT CECIL under the gymnasium bleachers. First they hustled him off the playground and into the empty gym, where they kicked him around a little to get things started. Then they held him face-down, three or four sets of hands pressing on his head and back while somebody pulled off his pants.

This is about the time I was brought in, Rotten Teeth towing me along by the hair. The atmosphere in the gym was ancient and gray, like the dim light in a cathedral, and every sound echoed and ampli-fied, rebounding off the distant ceiling and the painted-over win-dows. Under the bleachers it was even darker, the metal supports crisscrossing above us, the floor underneath our feet thick with left-over syrup of spilled Coke and garbage from basketball games that had happened years ago.

Three days before, I had given the smoke bomb to Cecil, begged him to do what Nelson wanted, but he took out a match from his pocket, lit the short wick on the bomb. "Ka-boom!" he shouted, making me jump. We watched it smolder into nothing, the wind stealing most of the smoke away. When it had burned itself out, Cecil picked up the crumbling cinder, put it in his pocket so he could transfer it to a trash can later.

"You're gonna get it," I told him, even though he already knew.

Cecil only shrugged and picked half of a sun-bleached playing card out of a hackberry bush. Right then, I wanted nothing more than to smash that wide, implacable face of his.

It didn't take long at all for Cecil to get what was coming to him. Nelson was fresh out of personal detention, ready for a little barbarity to get back into the swing of things. Most of the teachers and staff were in their weekly meetings, so it was a perfect time to give Cecil his due.

When I saw that they had his pants down, I knew it would be bad. With your clothes on you can get beat up, cuffed around, kicked in the ribs and not have to feel too ashamed of yourself. But you know that when they get your pants off, you have to prepare.

In that thick, dusty darkness, Nelson cast around, searching for something in the accumulated bleacher-garbage: withered popcorn, plastic cups, beer cans, bright orange candy peanuts, dust bunnies that quivered and jumped with any movement of air. Eventually, he came up with an old newspaper and rolled it up until he had a tight, slim funnel.

"Get his ass up in the air," he said, and the boys pulled Cecil's knees up under him so he was kneeling almost in a fetal position, his face mashed into the clotted debris of the floor.

Nelson put the narrow end of the funnel into his mouth and lathered it up with spit. Cecil squirmed and grunted but they had him down good. He then delicately pulled Cecil's butt cheeks apart with a thumb and forefinger and slipped the end of the funnel into Cecil's anus. A nurse at St. Divine's could not have accomplished it with a more calm expertise.

With the flourish of a magician, Nelson took a shiny Zippo from his shirt pocket. Its flame threw long, wheeling shadows on the bleacher seats above us. Grinning like a jack-o'-lantern, Nelson handed the Zippo to me and said, "I think we oughta let Edgar do the butt torch."

Instead of taking the lighter from Nelson, I turned and slugged Rotten Teeth in the groin. I guess this was the point I had come to: I'd had enough. Rotten Teeth yowled and quickly let go of my hair

and I went at Nelson, punching with all I had. It was like attacking a
water bed; my fists landed against him but barely made a noise. He
slapped me across the ear so hard it was like an explosion at the side
of my head. Behind my eyes a red star flared and went out. I was only
on the ground for a second when Rotten Teeth recovered enough to
give me a kick in the mouth, which split the inside of my cheek so
that blood poured down my throat.

I did not see the paper light, but a burst of orange lit up everything for a moment and the boys oohed and applauded like the
crowd at a magic show. I got up on my knees to see the paper burn
down, everyone shouting and clapping, and once it got near Cecil's
butt and started to smolder and die out they all blew on it, their faces
pressing in, so that it glowed pink and hot. Cecil did not scream or
cry out, but I could see the muscles in his legs jerking like plucked
wires, his calves balled up tight. Smoke billowed up, stinging my
eyes, and the smell of burning flesh came over everything.

Once the fire was out, they gave me a few farewell kicks as they
filed past and ran out across the gymnasium floor, their footsteps
booming and echoing with the sound of distant artillery.

I crawled over to Cecil. He had pulled his pants up and his face
had the pale blankness of shock. I squatted next to him and told him
that first I would go kill Nelson, I had a big knife hidden away, and
then I would find Nurse DuCharme.

"Crisco," he said, propping himself up on his hip. He took a Dum
Dum out of his pocket—root beer flavored—and sucked on it as if it
was the one thing that might save him. "No nurse. Crisco."

I sprinted to the kitchen and barged in like I was on detail, ready
to work, and grabbed a ten-pound can sitting next to the stove. I
hugged it to my chest and, with Ernest the cook watching me the
whole way, walked right out.

I helped Cecil pull down his pants and slather Crisco all over his
ass, which was burned black. This seemed to give him a little relief;
his legs stopped shaking and he slumped back against the wall.

"You're not gonna die, right?" I asked him. From my hospital experience, I didn't think a burnt asshole could be fatal, but I couldn't be sure of anything.

Cecil kept his eyes closed, breathed through his nose. Outside, the dinner bell rang.

"You don't want a nurse?" I said. "You can sleep on the cot and they'll bring you food."

He blinked and let out a thin, ragged sigh.

"You can sleep all day and nobody says anything about it. You eat your food right in bed. Sometimes they'll rub you with a sponge."

Cecil told me to help him up. He took a couple of hesitant steps, trying not to wince. He leaned on my shoulder and we walked like that, out across the parade grounds to the dorms. We stopped for a moment in the middle of the field. We were all by ourselves: everyone was packed into the cafeteria, stuffing their faces with food that there never seemed to be enough of.

"I'm not doing anything for Nelson anymore," I told Cecil. "He's a fat-ass."

Even with a burnt asshole, Cecil couldn't help but smile.

THE CAVALRY STABLES

AWAKENED BY A chaos of voices in the darkness, I sat up in bed and looked across a room filled with boys scrambling into pants and shoes. I heard something about a dead body and police cars coming up the highway from Whiteriver. Gilbert Cooya, in only his threadbare undershorts, crept into the room and announced that Raymond and Mr. Fitzsimmons were nowhere to be seen, the coast was clear.

"Somebody's dead!" Willis Martinez, my bunkmate, hissed at me. He was so excited he had put his pants on backwards. "We're going to go see!"

I raced down the hall to Cecil's room to make sure he wasn't the dead one. He was in his bunk, alive, watching the last of the stragglers stumble out the door. It had been two weeks since they'd done the butt torch on him, but he still had to tiptoe around like a baby with the worst kind of diaper rash. The skin under his eyes had turned papery gray and his cheeks had begun to stick out like the blades of a hatchet.

I worried about him, worried that the fire had burned something important inside him, maybe boiled his intestines or scorched his lungs—something that was slowly taking its toll on him—and I pestered him all the time about going to see the nurse, but he wouldn't hear of it. He drank only water and ate only soup and Jell-O when they were offered because he was afraid of what taking a shit could do to an asshole such as his.

In seconds the room had been abandoned and was now so empty and quiet it hummed.

"Want me to stay here?" I asked him.

"Go," he said. "Tell me it after."

I flew down the stairs in my underwear; I didn't want to be left behind. It was a warm, muggy spring night and the newly thawed ground was spongy and slick. I had only made it around the corner of the dormitory building when I saw movement, off to my right. I could make out a pack of boys running across the parade grounds, crouching like soldiers under enemy fire, heading south toward the cavalry stables across the road, where suddenly red and blue police lights bloomed out of the darkness, pulsing against the trees and the cement grain silo which stood over everything like a solitary wizard's tower.

I sprinted to catch up, taking a shortcut behind the old quarter-master's building, and by the time I made it across the road I could see dozens and dozens of boys, some of them bare-chested, some of them, like me, in nothing but their Fruit of the Looms, slinking through the bushes and trees like the spirits of the dead. Ahead of us the cavalry stables were flanked by four tribal police cars and an ambulance. The stables, two enormous, elongated barns built to house the horses of the Sixth Cavalry, were surrounded by dense stands of cottonwood and willow trees, and we fanned out in them, each of us finding a nice shadowed spot to hunker down and watch.

At the north end of one of the stables there were no windows or doors, but we could see flashlight beams swing around, cutting through the gaps in the planks. Principal Whipple and Raymond and Mr. Fitzsimmons and a couple of other teachers stood near one of the old corrals with a deputy who held a flashlight in his mouth and scribbled on a notepad. The other policemen leaned against one of their cars, talking to each other conspiratorially and laughing. They all had buzz cuts and thick brown arms and their badges flashed when they moved. Pretty soon, out came two paramedics in orange shirts on either end of a gurney. On the gurney was a body covered by a blue sheet. As the gurney bounced across the uneven ground, a leg with a black, thick-soled boot slid off to the side and dangled limply, knocking against the aluminum bracings. It was Sterling's leg. We all knew it immediately.

"I've heard of 'em shooting theirselves in the head or taking a bunch a pills or jumping off into that damn canyon like a bunch a goats," I heard one of the deputies say. "But this is the first one to string himself up, I know of. Could be wrong, but I think it's the first."

On the other side of the clearing I could see other pairs of eyes like mine peering out from behind tree trunks and clumps of foxweed. One of the boys, just a shadow, was watching from the top rung of the grain silo, which was bleached ivory with moonlight. I pulled my knees up to my chest and locked my arms around my shins to keep from shivering. Off to my left, some smart-aleck blew into his cupped hands, doing a bad impression of a whippoorwill—*woo-woo-woooo*. The deputy with the flashlight in his mouth looked up for a second before going back to his scribbling.

A big Indian in a cowboy hat—the sheriff—emerged from the other end of the stables and told everybody to get this thing wrapped up, there was nothing left to do. The ambulance turned off its emergency lights and eased slowly down the road toward the highway, crunching gravel, and the rest of the police and the others got in their cars and drove away. Within twenty minutes they were all gone and there was no sound but the stirring of leaves and the occasional far-off complaint of a screech owl. Slowly, cautiously, we crept out into the open, converging on the wide stable doors where one of the deputies had stretched a length of yellow police tape.

Inside, the stable was black as a pit, and though it had not been used in fifty years, it still smelled of horse manure and rotted leather and hay. Narrow blades of moonlight knifed through the cracks and knotholes of the old wooden planks. Clumped together now we were quite a crowd—seventy or eighty boys—and we entered that dark space like pilgrims into a cathedral: shoulder to shoulder and so careful and quiet as to be reverent. The only sounds were our feet shuffling in the thick straw and the collective rasp of our breathing.

When Harris Neal struck a match we all flinched as if a grenade had gone off. He kicked apart a length of rotten board and lit one of the splinters, which had a thick knot at one end. The pitch in the knot sizzled and popped as the flame hissed brighter, enough to light this end of the stables with a pale orange glow. The rope from which Sterling had hung himself was frayed at the end where somebody had cut it, about seven feet above the ground. Directly underneath it, Sterling's overturned wheelchair glinted balefully in the low, shifting light.

DONT PUSH ME it said.

The rope went all the way up into the darkness of the rafters, tied to one of the rough-cut crossbeams. It swayed the tiniest bit, almost imperceptibly, its shadow snaking over our faces. It had been there as long as anyone could remember. All of us, even Sterling, had swung on it before, grabbed the knot and jumped from one of the supports above the door, holding tight against the pull of gravity, flying for a moment, arcing out toward the opposite wall and back again.

Until I left Willie Sherman, teachers and staff would occasionally bring up the possibility that Sterling Yakezevitch had been murdered,

that there was no way a person in his condition, crippled and bound
to a wheelchair, could have managed to wheel himself from one side
of the grounds to the other, across the highway, up the gravel road to
the cavalry stables and still have the strength and presence to climb
up on his armrests and hang himself with such flawlessness. But we
knew better: we knew that a kid like Sterling could do pretty much
anything except die in the way he saw fit.

A couple of boys touched shanks of wood to Harris' torch and
within a minute or so we all had a flame of some kind and the place
was lit up with the chaos of sputtering shadows. We spread out, kicking through the straw, searching for something else, something to
keep us from looking at the rope with the upended wheelchair
beneath it, but there was nothing new to see: only the beer bottles
and dead, garbage-cluttered fire pits and the broken-down stalls, each
marked with a metal plate giving the name of some long-dead horse
and the soldier who had been assigned to feed it, groom it and ride it
into battle:

LUCKY/ 871
Lt. GREENFIELD

BIG DAVE/ 445
Pvt. MOE

RED DEVIL/ 902
Sgt. BARKER

It was Ernest Snyder, one of the oldest boys in the school, who
stood under the rope for a moment, looking up, before reaching up
with a torch made of twisted cardboard and lighting its frayed end.
The rope caught uncertainly at first, the blue aura of flame guttering
slowly upward until it reached the rafter and spread itself like a large
orange hand grasping the entire beam.

The rest of us touched our torches to whatever we could—the
molding piles of straw, the wooden feed troughs worn glassy smooth

by the muzzles of horses, the planks and studs of the old barn itself.
Within seconds the entire space was lit up like a stage and the rising
huss of the flames was a great drawing in of breath that sucked away
the air and made our ears pop. We all stumbled back out into the cool
night, coughing and blinking and twisting our necks to see the finger-
jets of blue flame already hissing out of the nail holes in the corru-
gated tin roof.

Somebody let out a shrill war whoop which was answered half a
dozen times and we began to move around the stables, bouncing on
the balls of our feet, staring into the growing radiance of the blaze,
too full of adrenaline and heat to stand still. In no time the entire barn
was a single body of fire, the beams and joists glowing within like red-
hot bones, the ancient, dried-out pine boards dissolving in the flames
like curtains of gauze, spitting embers and cracking apart with the
sharp reports of gunfire. The roof came down with an eruption of
sparks and then the whole thing collapsed in on itself, sending up a
fireball that lit up the trees and the silo and the far-off mesas in a single white flash. I fell back, covering my face, a strange, prickling thrill
running through me like a current. I stood up and shouted with
everything I had, a soprano keening that tore my lungs raw, joining
the other boys as we spun and hollered at the edge of the firelight
under a shower of sparks. There were sirens and cars pulling up and
the policemen and teachers standing back in the darkness near the
road, but we kept it up, circling the blaze, bare-chested and heedless,
our eyes full of fire, stomping and howling like the savages we were.

NIGHT DRIVING

IT WAS THE summer after the fire that Barry started coming regularly to Willie Sherman, always in a different car, always with a different
place to go. He would take me along on his deliveries and pickups:

mysterious packages wrapped in black plastic or butcher paper or silver duct tape, sometimes twisted up in a paper bag. I stayed in the car
while he completed his transactions; it usually took no longer than a
minute or two and then we'd be off, back the way we came. We
drove to Superior, Gila, San Ramone. A couple of times we descended into the blinding sea of lights called Phoenix.

"I now have a few friends in the right places, Edgar," he told me
one night on the way back from a town called Snowflake where he
met a couple of small, dark-skinned men in the parking lot of a construction company. "I have worked long and hard and it's paying off.
I can now move around with some impunity."

In the summers, nobody missed me while I was out, sometimes
until dawn. Once in awhile Barry would bring Jeffrey, and the three
of us would take a ride up to Big Lake or Escudilla and we would sit
around a fire and listen to Jeffrey play his guitar badly. Barry sometimes brought women with him, a different woman each time, who
would fawn over me for five or ten minutes and ignore me for the
rest of the night. Despite myself, I began to look forward to Barry's
visits; they killed the crushing boredom of the empty summer, and
more importantly, Barry *told* me things. He was the only adult I had
ever met who did not seem to purposefully withhold everything.

One of those first nights I asked him to tell me again the story of
how I died and Barry beat me back to life with his fists. Barry
gripped the steering wheel and recited the whole thing, as if it was
an epic poem that he had written himself and memorized. On other
nights, Barry would tell everything else he knew about me, drama-
tizing quite artfully: how my father and mother met, my father's disappearance and my mother's drinking, the circumstances of my
birth, my life before the accident.

"Bet you didn't know all that, did you?" he said one July night on
the way to Superior. We were in a new beige Duster with dimpled
vinyl seats and the whole thing smelled overwhelmingly of plastic.
"The very moment you started breathing again, lying on that gurney, I knew there was something special about you. I knew right

then we'd always be connected in some way. So when I heard about everything, about your dad gone, your mom running off, your grandma in the hospital, I knew I had to be the one. I talked to your grandma, to all your old neighbors, to the guys who drove the ambulance, to everybody I could find. I turned into some kind of serious detective—I wanted to know everything. That's why I took a lot of time out of my work schedule to track down your mother. I've done all of this for you."

Once the stories about me began to peter out, Barry drifted easily into his own life story. He told me about his father, a surly offshore oilman who never called him by his real name, called him Lardass, Knucklehead, Chump; his mother who died when he was a baby; the foster homes he lived in after his father was killed working an oil rig in Venezuela.

"My last foster family, the Shapiros, decided to adopt me. They wanted me to go into law, become a politician, do away with taxes or some damn thing. The old man was the mayor of Ruttstown, Ohio, and thought he was the King of Siam. I told them I wanted to go to medical school and they went cold. Can you believe that, a family ashamed of a son who wanted to be a doctor, to help and heal people? They thought I owed them something. They said I wasn't 'respecting their wishes.' They didn't come to my graduation, didn't send a present. Two months afterwards I got a card from them. It said, 'Congratulations, Steven and Annie.' Not 'We love you, from Mom and Dad.' Not 'We're proud you're our son' but 'Congratulations, Steven and Annie.' Well, fuck them. You see what I mean? Fuck them."

I looked at him, the dull green glow of the instrument panel on his face, and was amazed to see his eyes filled with tears.

"I know what it's like. Do you see? I've been alone since the day I was born and nothing I do seems to help." He sniffed and wiped at his mouth, which was loose and wet. "I understand. I know it's not easy. That's why I'm here. You need anything, you have any kind of problem, you let me know. You tell me and I'll take care of it."

We wound our way down to the bottom of Salt River Canyon: hairpin curves and sheer drop-offs without guardrails. Below us, somewhere in the darkness, the Salt River was nothing more than a trickle among the rocks.

I wanted to unload it all on Barry, tell him everything. For the last two months of the sixth grade, before he went home for the summer, Cecil had been talking about killing Nelson. Even though Cecil's burned asshole saved him from getting punished for the stables fire—he didn't have to, like all the rest of us, spend two weeks emptying the outhouse pits with nothing but shovels and buckets—it didn't save him from further persecutions from Nelson and his tribe. No, Cecil's burned asshole didn't help either of us. Daily, we were ambushed, beat up, harried, threatened. We couldn't sit in the library or stand in line for lunch without at the very least taking a rabbit punch to the kidney or a quick, violent pinch at the back of the arm that could make your eyes flood instantly with tears. I stayed in the showers only with Raymond in sight; I peed into the mop bucket in the janitor's closet to avoid having to go into the bathroom; I stayed awake deep into the morning hours for fear of what might happen if I fell asleep. I would have gone back and done anything Nelson wanted of me if it wasn't for Cecil. He took it when Nelson's friends caught us walking out in the cedars, trailing butterflies or hoping to spot Mrs. Whipple again, and pummeled us, slapped us around or let us run while they fired rocks at us and then chased us down again, the way a pack of coyotes would toy with a wounded fawn. Like me, he began to take on a ragged, harried look, but he never complained. The only thing he ever said was this: "I think I'll kill Nelson."

And then there was the news of Grandma Paul's death. Uncle Julius found me typing in the basement one morning and told me that the hospital had called to say that Grandma had suffered a heart attack. There was going to be a funeral in a couple of days and Uncle Julius asked if I wanted to go. I turned in my chair, gripped with shame, and shook my head. I hated myself both because I didn't have the guts to face another funeral and because the news of Grandma's death had so little effect on me; I felt nothing but a vague sense of sadness at being abandoned once again, at becoming the lone survivor of a past I had lost all connection to.

As much as I wanted to tell Barry everything, I kept quiet, the car creaking and groaning as it barreled into the curves and out again. For so long, silence had been the only weapon I had with which to defend myself; saying anything, even just a few words, felt like I was giving something away.

After Barry had made his transaction that night—a small paper bag passed to a couple of women under the awning of a gas station—we stopped at an all-night truck stop and ate a pile of hotcakes with bacon and eggs. Barry, noticing my sunken face and pale skin, decided I wasn't being fed well, so after that he brought me bottles of vitamins and fish oil and whenever we took our drives he bought me milk shakes, hamburgers, banana splits, thick ceramic bowls full of truck-stop chili.

When he dropped me off at the cattle guard that morning the sky was smoldering at the edges and the birds were making a racket in the trees. I was comfortable in my seat and wasn't at all interested in getting out of the car to go live one more day of Willie Sherman life.

I had just opened the door when Barry said, "Do you want to come live with me, get away from this place?"

"I don't know," I said.

"Do you think I'm a bad person?"

I stepped out of the car, shut the door behind me. "I don't think you're bad."

"Then you'll think about coming to live with me?"

"Okay," I said.

"I'm working on it, Edgar, you can believe that. I'm not going to live this life forever. A little nest egg, the right woman, and I can settle down. Stability is what I'm talking about, security. It won't be long."

The rest of that day, just like every other summer day, I spent typing in the boiler room, wandering about the grounds, missing Cecil, sitting at the jumping place with my legs hanging over the edge, try-ing not to think too much about Grandma Paul, which in turn made me think of my mother in her coffin, the way it slid into the dark hole, the way I had helped to cover it up. I had fantasies about find-ing my way down to San Carlos, digging her up with my own hands, opening up the lid, and my mother sitting up, like she'd just had a long nap, saying, *Thank you, Edgar, thank you, I'll never drink another beer again.*

At night, this kind of thinking would always drive me into insom-nia and I would climb out my window and break into the kitchen to get a few things to eat, or creep around the grounds and spy on any of the teachers who had stayed on for the summer, sleeping peaceful-ly in their beds. I broke into the empty houses sometimes and snooped in closets and bathrooms, stealing only the things that nobody would miss. I lay for hours in the empty, stripped-down beds, imagining how it would be to have a mother or a father come in from the next room to bring me a glass of water and tell me good night. Often, I would crawl through the duct system that led to Maria's office to sit in her chair and smell her perfume.

When I got so bored that stealing or typing wouldn't satisfy me, I would lie on my bunk and look at the old medical books Barry had brought for me. He told me I might think about becoming a doctor someday, though he certainly did not want to pressure me into any-thing.

I was terrified by the ones with pictures in them. The gore both-ered me some—an eyeball hanging out of its socket, festering sores and wounds withering with gangrene, a pitted, tumorous growth clapped like a barnacle on somebody's throat, a bloody bone jutting from a thigh, an arm burned until it was blistered black, intestines slithering out of a wound—but it was the pictures of naked people, boldly lit in stark black and white, that bothered me the most. The men and their penises like clubs, the women and their dark-nippled breasts, the mysterious hairy absence between their legs.

Is this what it all comes to? I wondered. Is this how it is supposed
to turn out? You have your accidents, your broken bones and diseases,
and then there is a strange hairiness that overtakes you and pretty
soon you're dead, put in a wooden box and buried under a pile of
dirt?

The other permanents would sometimes get so bored themselves
that they would actually talk to me. A big Ute girl name Prissy liked
to sit next to me on the steps after kitchen detail and tell me stories
about her big brother, who was a criminal of the first degree. Even
during the summer, boys and girls were not supposed to socialize,
but that would have made things even more unbearable. Prissy told
me she got sick of the other two girl permanents and she had to talk
to somebody else, even if it was me. She told me proudly that her
brother had robbed grocery stores, stolen a zebra from a circus, burnt
down a restaurant (accidentally) and killed two old white women in
Texas who called him a nigger.

"You tell anybody about this, I kill *you*," she warned. "Warren's
escaped from prison and nobody knows where he's at. He might be
around here. He might come and get me. He knows I'm here, I've
wrote letters, and he wouldn't like it one bit. Warren hates school."

One morning she was explaining how Warren the criminal once
blew up a stray goat with a stick of dynamite, when two young
white men in white shirts came pedaling up the road on bicycles.
Even from a distance, we could see them smiling, their teeth bright
with the sun.

"Them guys are called the Elders," Prissy told me. "They talk to
you about Jesus Christ and all that."

"Jesus Christ," I said.

"And if you join up with them, join their church, they'll send you
to live with a rich anglo family somewhere. Utah, mostly. My cousin
Bertaline joined 'em and got sent to some place where everybody's
got this square patch of green grass in front of their house and all the
kids have red bicycles, new ones, and a truck drives around when it's
hot handing out ice cream. Bertaline told me all about it. The only

problem is it's you the Indian and everybody else anglos. They'll ask you stupid questions."

We watched the Elders coast around the far end of the parade grounds and stop in front of Mr. Hansen's house. I sometimes doubted what Prissy told me, but I knew she was telling me the truth about these two young men. They looked like they had just pedaled out of this world she had described, a world filled with green lawns and smiling people, shining with the kind of happiness that could only come from new bikes and free ice cream.

The Elders disappeared into the Hansen house and I planned to wait until they came out, maybe ask about the possibility of joining up, but a long blue convertible drove up with a woman in a scarf and a little boy next to her. This was a record day: four strangers and it wasn't even ten o'clock. The license plate on the car said CALIFORNIA and the mother held the boy's hand as they walked around the grounds pointing at the run-down houses in their crisp, new clothes, reading the misspelled markers. I followed them, hoping to hear what they were saying, to smell the woman's perfume. I tried to imagine the house they lived in—some big white thing next to the ocean with palm trees and acres of green grass—and I tried to figure out why they would want to come to a place like Willie Sherman.

They were looking at the cavalry bell when the boy turned and saw me. He had rust-colored hair and freckles that covered his face and arms like he'd been splashed with tomato juice. He came up to me and looked me over, put his face close to mine.

"These Indians stink," he said. His mother turned, took off her sunglasses and smiled at me. The boy smirked and pinched his nostrils, his pinkie finger sticking out.

Right then, I hated that boy a hundred times more than Nelson or Glen or Rotten Teeth. I took a few steps back, snatched a rock out of the dirt and drilled him in the belly with it. He made a tiny, surprised sound—*pooh!*—and the mother screamed, which brought Raymond running out of shithouse number one, where he liked to sit after breakfast reading dirty magazines. "He hurt my son!" the woman shrieked. She grabbed the blubbering boy by the arm and hauled him off toward the car.

Raymond whacked me over the head a few times with his magazine. "No Edgar! Bad! Very bad!"

Together, we watched the car swing around in the gravel and roar off in the direction of Whiteriver.

"What'd you hit him with?" Raymond asked me, once they were out of sight. I could see that Raymond's magazine was called *Big Mamas*.

"Rock," I said.

"You get him solid?"

"Pretty good in the stomach."

He patted me on the back. "That's the way."

THE SEVENTH GRADE

THE LAST FEW days before the start of the seventh grade, Edgar stood out by the cattle guard, waiting for his friend Cecil to arrive. The cars and pickups drove past, filled with families coming to drop off one or two of their own. A bunch of kids were brought in a battleship-gray bus, one girl even came riding up on a bicycle with a duffel bag slung over her back. It wasn't until late in the afternoon on Sunday that I spotted the black pickup that I knew would be carrying Cecil.

The big Ford rattled right on by me and stopped in front of the administration building. I jumped the cattle guard and sprinted across the dirt parking lot. Up ahead I could see Cecil standing next to the tailgate, lifting out his bags. He looked upset; his normally expressionless face was red and pinched and when he started to walk away he said something over his shoulder to his uncle, who was sipping on a beer in the cab. The uncle, who wore a striped conductor's hat, lurched out of the pickup and knocked Cecil to the ground with one blow to the back. He barked something in a language I couldn't understand and picked up one of the bags and emptied out the clothes all over Cecil's head. He tossed the bag away, shouted something at Raymond, who was watching from one of the dormitory windows, and drove off, knocking over a fence post as he went.

I helped Cecil pick up his clothes and take his things to his room. I sat on his bunk with him and said, "Your uncle."

Cecil nodded. "I kill Nelson, then I get him."

It turned out, though, that Cecil might not have to kill Nelson at all. Nelson did not show up for classes the first day, and each day thereafter was like a vacation for the both of us. We hardly knew what to do with ourselves; we played marbles with the fifth graders, tried to spy on the girls in the dormitory, walked the parade grounds feeling invincible. Once in awhile Glen would give us a flat-handed wallop or push us down in the showers, but his heart didn't seem to be in it without Nelson. At night, before bed, I showed Cecil how to slip through the bars and climb up onto the roof, where we sat, listening to the coyotes start up, and tossing paper airplanes across the road until the call for Lights Out came. Rumors circulated that Nelson had gone to prison for selling drugs, had killed his own cousin by sitting on him, had died of an attack from his own fat heart.

Then one day he showed up, sporting a few red blemishes from his bout with the measles, but not much the worse for wear. The good times were over. Within a few hours Nelson, Glen and a couple of new boys found me hiding in shithouse number three. Cecil and I figured it would be a good idea to split up, but who were we kidding? Nelson would get us no matter where we went.

They dragged me out, blinking in the stark light. Nelson smiled and Glen grabbed me by the neck and gave me a hearty, good-natured shake. He said, "Hi, retard!"

The new boys had a good laugh at that. They both looked terri-

fied; it was only their second week at Willie Sherman, and like most
new boys, they were so scared they laughed at everything.

"They tell me you're still running around with your fag-friend,
hey?" Nelson said. "Too bad his asshole don't work no more."

I glared at Nelson, then at Glen. I said, "Fuck off, fat-asses."

During the summer, with all that time to think, I had decided that
I could take over where Sterling had left off, that I could become
Sterling. I didn't ride around in a wheelchair but I did have a broken
head. Certainly it couldn't hurt to try.

Glen stepped forward and slugged me a good one, right on the
side of my broken head, and I have to say it hurt quite a bit.

Nelson told the new boys to finish me off. They came at me,
throwing haymakers. I rolled easily away and got to my feet. I was
not much of a fighter, but for the past two and a half years I had
taken so many punches and kicks that I knew how to spot them
coming and minimize the damage. Even with my ears buzzing from
the shot Glen gave me, I toyed with these boys, giving them a good
jab when they got too close; I was in seventh grade now and was not
about to let a couple of new boys work me over. Occasionally,
Nelson stepped in and gave me a cuff to speed things along, and
finally the new boys were able to get me down and punch away until
their arms got saggy and loose with the effort. I tucked my knees up
to my chin, covered my head, and let them have at it. When they
couldn't raise their fists anymore, I jumped to my feet to show them
they hadn't hurt me a bit. Nelson and Glen had already lost interest
and had gone over to send hand signals to some girls across the bor-
derline. The two new boys knelt in the dirt, exhausted, and I hit the
bigger one in the mouth as hard as I could, so hard that he fell onto
his back and began to spit blood.

The smaller one, kneeling, took one look at his friend, then at himself, scraped up and covered with dust, and wailed, "I hate this place."

That night, I snuck out and met Cecil in the boiler room. Uncle
Julius, who was going on eighty-five, was getting to be as deaf as a
stump. He had started to walk with a kind of sideways shuffle and his

arthritic hands had twisted up on themselves like old tubes of paint. Sometimes, he couldn't distinguish me from other boys.

Cecil and I could talk, roust around the room, bang on the old boiler with a shovel if we wanted to and he would never have known the difference. We stole a few pieces of butter toffee out of the front pocket of his overalls and hunkered down on a couple of crates to suck on them. Cecil had a pretty good scrape on his jaw and he told me he was tired of it all, he really was going to kill Nelson first chance he got.

"With what?" I asked. Even though I was terrified about what might happen if he actually went through with it, I was curious about how he planned to do it.

Cecil shrugged. "Get a gun, shoot 'im. Bow and arrows, maybe. Chop 'im with a machete." Cecil took out his box cutter and drew it across his throat. "Like this, and dead, *ploop,* right on the floor."

"You could hit him with a hammer when he's sleeping," I offered.

Cecil sighed. "Many ways. Many, many."

I showed Cecil the knife Art had given me. I kept it hidden inside my Hermes Jubilee, in the little recess behind the keys. When they conducted their searches, they went over every inch of the dorms, even Raymond's room, even Uncle Julius', but in all that time they never discovered the knife. Cecil turned it over in his hands, letting the light play on its mother-of-pearl handle, and I thought about the day Art had given it to me, what he had told me to do with it. I had long since stopped hoping for another letter from Art—he was just one more disappearance from my life—but seeing that knife made me miss him, even made me feel guilty: I had not, like I promised him, stuck Barry in the ribs with it first chance I got. Even though he was far away and I knew I'd probably never see him again, I felt like I'd let him down.

I told Cecil that if anyone was going to kill Nelson, it should be me. What could they do to me? I *was* just like Sterling Yakezevitch. I knew it, but nobody else seemed to.

Cecil laughed at me. "You kill Nelson? How?"

"That knife," I said. "You stick it right in the ribs, right here"—I gave Cecil a poke in the side—"and maybe give it a turn. That's how you kill somebody."

"You stick 'em right here?" Cecil said, jabbing me a good one in the ribs with his stubby finger, grinning. "Kill 'em like that?"

I jumped on him, got him in a headlock, and we wrestled around the room, laughing and howling, knocking over crates. We did karate chops, flying kicks, roundhouses, finger jabs to the eyes. We were cowboys shooting at each other, superheroes tossing bolts of lightning; for a couple of minutes we acted just like kids. I chased Cecil around the old rumbling boiler and he put his hands over his head, pantomiming great terror, "Oh no! Big killer boy going to kill me! Ah! Halp! Halp!"

Next thing I knew somebody had me by the ear. It was Uncle Julius, bedraggled and blinking with fury, yanking us up the stairs back to our rooms, not so deaf after all.

TRIBE OF TWO

CECIL SETTLED ON the bow and arrow. Every spare moment for three weeks he put all his energy into creating a weapon that could effectively kill Nelson. He had considered all the options and decided that the bow and arrow was the best way to get Nelson without putting himself in immediate danger. Using a knife like mine, he told me, would be like trying to kill a wild pig with a toothpick.

I offered to help but he shook his head and blew air through his nose, which meant he was busy and didn't want to be bothered. I watched anyway, watched him cut—with a butter knife he spent hours sharpening on a stone—a three-foot-long bow from a young, lightning-killed juniper, about as thick around as a broomstick. He smiled a crooked, faraway smile as he whittled and scraped, tapering and notching the ends, and when he was almost finished he rubbed the entire length with lard to keep it supple. Still, he worried over it, shaving off a bit near the hand grip or deepening the notch. Finally, when he had just the shape he wanted, he strung it with a tightly twisted double strand of some monofilament he had found tangled in a branch overhanging the river.

On our walks he studied the ground for old arrowheads he could use, searched under hawk nests for the best feathers for fletching. In a rare moment when he felt like talking he explained that his grandfather, now dead, had taught him how to make a bow and arrow, taught him how to hunt. He said he hunted rabbits mostly, but he didn't hit them very often. Rabbits, he said, could hear the arrow whistling through the air, could *feel* it bearing down on them and would dodge, always at the last second.

"You shoot arrow, hit rabbit?" he said. "Dumbass rabbit."

I tried to imagine Nelson dodging an arrow and decided he'd be lucky to dodge an apple thrown from all the way across the parade grounds.

"What about people?" I asked him.

"People?"

"Is it easy to shoot people?"

Cecil grinned. "People ain't rabbits."

All this time, I had been hoping that Nelson would eventually become bored with us, move on to some new project, but tormenting us seemed to become one of his favorite hobbies, along with selling the contraband that his lackeys stole for him and sniffing glue in the guardhouse. Besides the regular beatings we were used to taking on the playground, the towel attacks in the bathroom, the surreptitious knuckle-punches at roll call, the eraser-darts (a straight pin stuck through a pencil eraser and shot through a soda straw) in class when the teachers went outside to have a smoke and complain to each other, Nelson began to orchestrate newer, more creative ways to abuse us. The dead, maggot-ridden skunk stuffed into my pillowcase, the razor blade embedded in the seat of my desk, the cherry bomb thrown into shithouse number three while I sat reading about how somebody named Bardito was forever in love with somebody named Vicky. Or the time on the playground when a mob of new boys bushwhacked Cecil, stole his pants and underwear, and left him to shamble back to the dormitory with one shoe positioned over his privates and a hundred girls gawking and slapping their hands over their mouths.

I believe that for Nelson, this was no longer revenge or a display of power. He wanted to test our limits, to see how much we could take before we broke. For Nelson, this was entertainment.

We tried fighting back, a last resort. When somebody hit me I hit back, twice as hard if I could. Somebody got me with a dart in the arm during class? I'd hunt him down on the playground, and no matter if Nelson was nearby or Glen or Rotten Teeth or any of the others, I'd ambush him, inflict as much pain as I could before the rest of them got to me. I bit, I scratched, I howled, I swore. I even started packing my knife in my sock, slept with it gripped tightly in my fist. In the lunch line I let everyone know that the next person to touch me was going to get their scalp taken off, their eyeballs poked out. I felt so mean and terrified and exhausted I was close to tears all day long.

Cecil, for his part, seemed to recede. Not much of a talker to begin with, he could go days without saying anything. The skin around his eyes began to take on a drained, yellowish tint, and when we went up in the hills together we would sit, completely silent, and stare out into the wild colors of dusk, not a single thing to say.

It didn't take Cecil long to follow my lead: he began to carry rocks in his pockets to throw at anyone who got near him and would hunker down into a half-squat, ready to battle at the smallest provocation. Of course, fighting back only made things worse. When we fought back, we stopped being invisible. Instead of allowing ourselves to quietly get beat up, which the teachers and dorm aides generally allowed, we were raising a ruckus, causing problems for everyone. In the space of only a few weeks we had gone from being model Willie Sherman students, the kind who knew how to pass through their school years unnoticed, to the worst kind of troublemakers. Pretty soon we had more hours of kitchen and bathroom detail than anyone in school.

Cecil and I were a tribe of two and that, we quickly came to understand, would never be enough.

Cecil took two more weeks to finish making the arrows. He had found the perfect arrowheads, beautifully flaked and sharp as razors, hawk feathers for fletching, and thin shafts of willow that he hardened over a fire and straightened the crooks out of with an old bottle opener. He made four arrows in all and weighted each one on the tip of his stubby forefinger.

"Good arrows," he said one day, with the barest hint of a smile. "Not too shabby."

One December Sunday, Cecil took his bow and arrows out to look for rabbits. I started out after him but he stopped me, said he wanted to hunt alone because I made a lot of noise when I walked, like a bear walking on lightbulbs.

For the entire afternoon I waited and sulked. I couldn't help but show how pleased I was when he came back empty-handed, a consternated look on his face.

"Rabbits!" he cried.

After a few practice shots into a rotting bale of hay, Cecil hid his weapons under a pile of rusted roofing tin behind the old armory.

Nearly every day, I couldn't help myself, I would ask Cecil if he really intended to kill Nelson. Cecil would always stare at me, those eyes of his black and fathomless, and would raise his eyebrows just a little as if to say: Who knows what might happen?

I had come to the conclusion that assassinating Nelson with a bow and arrow in broad daylight wasn't a very good idea at all. Couldn't we, I wondered, find a better method, something quieter, sneakier, something we could *get away* with? I had worked for Nelson long enough to know the value of stealth, of slipperiness, of covering one's tracks, and I asked Cecil if maybe we should try one of the methods we talked about before: slitting Nelson's throat with a razor in the middle of the night. This, to me, seemed like the perfect plan.

The William Tecumseh Sherman School had its own secret lore: stories, told after Lights Out, about the spirit who inhabited the grain silo, about a witch doctor who lived in a wickiup far out in the hills and shambled around at night, hairy and deformed, gathering animal bones and casting spells, about the boys who jumped into the canyon and came this close to flying. There was a story I heard a couple of times about students—boys and girls both—waking up to find themselves murdered, their throats slit, their bunks covered with their blood. Over the years, this happened time and time again and nobody was ever caught. Some said it was the witch doctor, some a madman who slept under an abandoned house in Whiteriver, some the ghost of a cavalryman killed by Indians and out to take revenge.

We could slit Nelson's throat, I figured, just like the story, and we could blame the madman or the witch doctor or the ghost. Cecil wouldn't have to be sent away forever and I wouldn't have to stick it out alone at Willie Sherman. I couldn't lose Cecil, this I knew. As long as Cecil was around, I could stand the beatings, the torment, the boredom. Without him, I wouldn't last.

"No." Cecil shook his head. "Bow and arrow is far away, safe. You try to kill him close by, with a razor, maybe he kill you first." Cecil drew back on an imaginary bow, aimed at me, let the arrow fly. "*Shhhhhhhhh-zap!* See? No problem."

We looked at each other. I was not going to sway him. So I came up with another plan, one that I would have to execute on my own.

E D G A R ' S   P L A N

ON A FEBRUARY night with snow howling to the ground in funnels, I got out of bed, unlatched the window, slipped through the bars and climbed down the wall, feeling blind for the familiar hand- and toe-holds in the gaps of the great sandstone blocks, pressing myself flat as windblown snow hit me in waves. I marched right into the wind, leaning my way across the parade grounds, plumes of white rising hundreds of feet into the air, snow pellets like pinpricks on every inch of exposed flesh; I was wearing nothing but my underwear and a T-shirt. By the time I made it to the main building my skin felt like it had been rubbed briskly with rough-grade sandpaper and doused in alcohol.

I broke into Maria's office through the air exhaust vent: yanked off the steel grate, crawled through a narrow ventilation shaft, my breath like a roar in my ears, the tin under my knees buckling and popping, then pushing off the narrow rectangular vent inside and sliding down on top of Maria's desk, headfirst like a floundering snake. From there, it was only a matter of getting the key from the front drawer of her desk and opening the door to Principal Whipple's office, easy as you please.

The bag of CONTRABAND was right where it had always been, in the big lower left drawer. The principal kept none of his filing cabinets or desk drawers locked; who would be crazy enough to steal something from him?

I slung the bag over my shoulder and on my way out swiped half a dozen spools of typing ribbon from the supply closet. The bag was heavy and unwieldy, making the journey back much more difficult. Climbing through the vents and up the wall of the dormitory, I had to hold it clamped in my mouth until I was sure my teeth would be ripped out by the roots. Once I made it back up to my window, the snowstorm was petering out. I sat on the ledge—three stories up—and rested, catching my breath, looking out over the snow-clumped parade grounds to make sure I hadn't left any tracks.

Inside, I crept among the beds of sleeping boys, down the dark hallway to the big boys' room, where Nelson and seven of the oldest, and therefore most privileged, boys stayed. Someday, if I lasted long enough, I would sleep here too.

Nelson's bunk was in the corner and he lay on top of it, under a single green blanket, as big as a propane tank. I stood not two feet from him and looked down on his wide, yellow face, jolly even in sleep.

So easy, I thought.

I rummaged through the sack, came up with a beautiful, bone-handled bowie knife with a handguard made of nicked silver. I could stab him fifteen times, fill him full of holes, before he knew what had hit him. I pulled out an ice pick, imagined perforating him with it, and the way he might deflate, like a fat, gas-filled balloon, collapsing into nothing. I held the straight razor above his throat and thought of the single, easy stroke, like passing your hand through smoke.

I stood for a long time, shivering, the snow on my shoulders and hair turning to droplets of water that crawled slowly down my back. I put the razor to his throat, the sharp edge barely touching his skin, and held it there until my arm ached.

Do it, Edgar, I thought. *Easy, easy.*

On the other side of the room somebody called out something unintelligible and mournful, snorted and fell silent again.

Edgar couldn't do it. No, he wasn't strong or mean enough, not yet, and he was so disappointed in his own cowardice that for a second he considered using the straight razor on himself.

Nelson shifted in his bunk, which creaked under his weight. I decided to go with my original plan: I put the razor back into the bag and quietly, slowly, shoved it under Nelson's bunk, as far as it would go.

Halfway down the hall back to my room, I had an inspiration. I crept right back and retrieved the bag from under Nelson's bunk. I lifted the corner of his mattress and slipped the bowie knife and a few homemade Chinese stars between the lumpy cotton batting and the slab of plywood underneath. Next I went to Rotten Teeth's bunk, where I left a switchblade and a pair of brass knuckles, then to Glen, who got a crude shunt made out of a sharpened broomstick and the graceful Mexican bullwhip. I passed the contraband all around the room. The only person I spared was a buck-toothed Hulapai boy named Bruce who had once slipped me his box of raisins after Rotten Teeth knocked my tray of food all over the cafeteria floor.

The next morning, the sky had cleared and the snow melted quickly into silver puddles that reflected the dazzling light like a thousand scattered mirrors. I took my shower, brushed my teeth, ate my breakfast, and had to constantly remind myself to keep my breathing regular, to act normal. I had a hard time keeping my hand off my groin.

On my way to Principal Whipple's office I forgot to dodge the puddles and walked right through them.

Maria was at her desk, sipping at a mug of coffee. "Edgar?" she said.

"The principal here?"

"You want to talk to him? You sure?"

I nodded, looked up at the ceiling, thought I might faint.

Principal Whipple had one of his big orange feet up on the desk and was working at the nail of his big toe with what looked like a pair of tin cutters. Even though I had been in this very room only hours before, it looked entirely different illuminated with rippling webs of light.

"What?" he said.

I stood in the middle of the room, paralyzed, my shoes sopping.

"What is it?"

"Hah . . ." I said, having trouble getting my breath.

He put the tin cutters on the desk, took off his glasses to wipe them with a cloth. Without his glasses his eyes seemed to disappear right off his face. "Something you want to tell me?"

"Nelson," I breathed. I was relieved when he put his glasses back on.

"Nelson?"

I nodded fiercely. "It's Nelson."

"It's Nelson what?"

"It's Nelson got the contraband. Up under his bed. Contraband everywhere."

Principal Whipple wrenched open the drawer, which made a loud metal bark. His face went a shade dark and he looked up at me.

"How do you know this?"

"He wanted me to do it, I said no, so he did it himself." Like someone eavesdropping from another room, I heard my own voice saying these things.

Principal Whipple stood up to go, realized he had only one shoe and sock on, sat back down. He opened the drawer again. "Well, I'll be goddamned."

"I saw him do something else," I said. "Bad things with a lady."

I had decided to go all the way. I wanted to make sure Nelson would be sent far away and never come back. I couldn't take any chances.

"I saw him doing . . . ficky-fick."

Principal Whipple moved closer, cocked his head. "Ficky . . . ?"

"Ficky-fick," I said. "With Mrs. Whipple. Had her shirt open. They were making the noises." In a weak, airy voice I made the noises. A couple of *oh-ohs* and a few *ai-ai-ais*.

Principal Whipple seemed to melt in his chair. He grabbed his cheeks and pulled at them. He said, "*Nelson?*"

He staggered to his feet and pointed at me. "You stay here. Don't go anywhere." And clomped out of the room with only one shoe on. I went to the window and watched him make his way through a mass of kids heading toward the auditorium. Today was the big speaker the teachers had been telling us about for weeks. The great Native American poet Vincent DeLaine, some famous guy we'd never heard of. *Native American,* they said, like it meant something. I still wasn't sure what the difference was between a *Native American* and a regular Indian.

I lost sight of Principal Whipple for a moment and then he emerged from the crowd, holding Nelson by the biceps, as much of it as he could get in his hand. His face was a blaring red warning light and his sockless foot looked like it had been covered in chocolate. Some of the kids were whispering behind their hands and pointing; it wasn't every day Principal Whipple hauled Nelson into his office wearing only one shoe.

I ducked past Maria and fell in with the rest of the kids going into the auditorium. I wasn't about to face Nelson after what I'd done, even with the principal in the same room. I hoped that Principal Whipple would be angry enough with Nelson to forget about me.

We watched as a shiny metallic green Town Car *shished* through the mud and stopped near the big double doors. Out stepped a tall, regal Indian wearing braids and wire-rimmed glasses, and a short white woman holding a box with some papers on top. The woman leaned into the passenger-side window and said to the driver, "Make sure you lock the doors."

Inside, Mr. Hansen stood up and announced into the microphone that Principal Whipple had been detained momentarily and that he, Mr. Hansen, would be more than honored to introduce a Native American poet of great stature, author of five books at only thirty-three years of age, a voice of his generation, we're terribly lucky he'd take time out of his busy schedule and speak to us for such a small fee, a wonderful thing indeed, please help me welcome Mr. Vincent DeLaine.

Mr. Hansen paused and the only sound in the auditorium was the creak of chairs and some girls whispering in the back. "You can clap now," Mr. Hansen said into the microphone, and we clapped as hard as we could, really put up a roar until the Native American poet Vincent DeLaine shushed us down with his hands.

The first poem Vincent DeLaine read was something about stealing horses, and ponies neighing and the blood of the horses on the grass. Vincent DeLaine read his poem in a strange voice with an exaggerated singsong to it, the way white people talk when they want to make fun of Indians, the way we sometimes heard the cooks or the teachers imitating the students. Some of us laughed, but immediately quieted down when he looked up from his book and glared into the darkness. He wore a tomato-red shirt, a necklace with beads and animal claws, and braids that lay rigidly on his shoulders like brightly polished billy clubs. He was not, we finally understood, trying to be funny.

Vincent DeLaine read more poems in that singsong voice, poems about Indians getting butchered, about the sorrow of old women, about the coyote and the eagle and the crow and a bunch of other animals walking around talking to each other. Everybody around me seemed baffled or bored and I was glad to know I wasn't the only one who didn't know what he was talking about. Sometimes Vincent DeLaine raised up his arms and yelled some of his poems in a loud, angry voice; his mouth would twist up and his eyes shrink into the skin of his face and he would bark out the individual words with something like contempt. With his green Town Car and his own pretty lady friend and such nice clothes, I didn't see what he had to be mad about.

I sat up in my seat and looked over the expanse of black heads for Cecil. I wanted to tell him what I had done, that if everything went alright we wouldn't have to worry about Nelson. While Vincent DeLaine went on about the dancers and the feathers and the jingle-jingle of bells, I allowed myself to imagine how it would be without Nelson—negotiating the playground without fear, taking a shower without checking my back all the time, walking with Cecil without worry in the hills.

Near the end, Principal Whipple came in from the side of the stage. His face was still red and the cuffs of his pants were crusted with mud. One shoe was smeared brown while the other was as shiny as a bottle. He tried to screw his face into a smile but didn't seem to be having much luck.

For his last poem, Vincent DeLaine sang some old Indian song: *ey-nah-ah, ey-no-oh*. He chanted and intoned, really working himself up, and turned out to be pretty darned good at it. For his big finale, he held his hands in fists and shouted out over our heads, in his exaggerated Indian voice, "It's a good day to die! It's a good day to die, my sisters and my brothers!"

There was a long, rustling silence and he looked down at us from the lectern, waiting for a response. That was when Russell Binten, who everybody knew was the dumbest kid in school, dumber even than me, whispered to nobody in particular, "It ain't a good day for me!"

Oh, did we laugh. It took Principal Whipple a few smacks on the microphone to get us quiet. He then thanked Mr. DeLaine for coming and sharing his art with us and reminded us that there would be copies of Mr. DeLaine's books in the back available for purchase.

The doors in the back opened up, the bright day pouring in, and we all rushed to the exits like moths to a light.

Out on the parade grounds I searched for Cecil among the other kids splashing in the puddles, the girls and boys giddy with the chance to mix freely while the teachers and principal stayed inside to shake Vincent DeLaine's hand and tell him what a great Native American he was. I spied Cecil trying to look inconspicuous behind the bleachers and I started off toward him when I felt a hand on my neck and I was jerked off my feet, straight up in the air.

I was done for and I knew it. Somewhere along the line I had made a mistake—how could I have known that Nelson, locked in Principal Whipple's office, would be angry enough to throw himself against the door, splintering the jamb, and come out, like an angry bull busted out of his pen, to find me?

I turned to look at Nelson and what I saw terrified me: he wasn't smiling. His lips were turned down in rage and his eyes were like black cinders pressed into clay. He hit me so hard that I felt the wind rush past my ears as I hurtled backwards and landed in a puddle, icy water enveloping my face for a moment. I rolled over and lay in the mud, doomed. I thought about running, but my arms and legs felt dead to me, inert and useless as limbs of wax. My sole hope was that one of the teachers would come out of the auditorium and catch Nelson in the act of killing me.

"Hey-yah!" I heard somebody say as the other kids gathered around, their shoes sucking into the mud. "This is gonna be a good one!"

Nelson lifted me up by the belt, swung me around and slammed me to the ground, sending up a spray of brown water that made the girls squeal. I only had a second or two to recover before he began to pound me into the mud, his great fists landing on my head and back like heavy stones dropped from a great distance. I tried to curl up, to protect myself as best I could, but I felt paralyzed, disconnected from everything, and I began to suck in watery mud until I began to suffocate, unable to lift my head up enough to find air. I panicked and thrashed, the blows driving me deeper into the freezing muck, and then, little by little, I let myself ease into a warm soothing darkness that I wanted never to come back from.

SAVED AGAIN

BUT OF COURSE I came back—I always did. It was nearly two hours later, after Mr. Fitzsimmons dragged me out of the mud and into the infirmary, that I heard what had happened.

While Nelson was busy beating me into hamburger with the student body of Willie Sherman looking on, Cecil had just enough time to sprint over to the pile of tin where he had hidden his bow and arrows. He had planned to kill Nelson at a more appropriate time, without so many witnesses around, but decided, bless him, that he didn't have much of a choice.

The first arrow missed by five feet. Cecil moved closer and fired again, hitting Nelson in the side, just above the belt. They said he gave Edgar a couple of solid cracks to the back of the head before he noticed it sticking out of him. He looked around, annoyed as if somebody had shot him with a spitwad, and the next one speared through the inner portion of his thigh, hit him from behind with a wet, meaty sound that made some of the onlookers quail and gasp. The arrowhead exited on a downward angle just above his kneecap and blood dribbled off the end of it as if from a spigot.

I tryed to get him in the ass hole, Cecil wrote to me later, from the juvenile prison in Nevada. *Too bad.*

Nelson turned and saw Cecil standing on the fourth step of the bleachers, calmly nocking his last arrow. He was grinning, they told me, a perfect imitation of Nelson's grin, and didn't let up, even as Nelson left poor Edgar lying there, nothing more than a gray pile of clothes, shoes and hair. He lumbered toward Cecil with his skewered leg gone stiff and his flip-flops slinging droplets of mud all the way up his back.

Like the hunter that he was, Cecil waited. And grinned. Grinned like crazy, they told me later. Grinned like a kid about to blow out the candles on his birthday cake.

On came Nelson, gripping the arrow above his hip, working it around, finally wrenching it out, leaving a large piece of broken obsidian deep inside. Cecil waited until Nelson reached the bottom of the bleachers before he even bothered to pull back on the bowstring. Here Nelson hesitated. He was looking up, right along the shaft of an arrow at a boy who was grinning like crazy, the kind of grin he, Nelson, had been comfortable with all his life but could not manage to pull off now. Grimly, he hauled himself up onto the first step and Cecil let the arrow fly.

Hit him dead center, the easiest shot ever made. The six inches of arrow that stuck out of Nelson's abdomen vibrated, buzzed like a wasp, then quieted. Nelson gripped the arrow near the fletching, to test how solidly it had embedded itself, and then slowly pivoted and sat down, watched as the raspberry stain on his shirt spindled outward in a widening circle.

Cecil put down his bow, stepped past Nelson, walked over to me and lifted my head out of the water, poked his finger into my mouth, made sure I was breathing. He then stood, looked around and trotted across the parade grounds, slipped under the barbed-wire fence at the edge of the road and disappeared into the cedars on the other side.

He never made it to the Grand Canyon. They caught him two

days later trying to hitch a ride north of Payson, convicted him in the juvenile courts of aggravated assault and sent him up to the juvenile detention center in Nevada for thirty months. It was Nelson's fat that saved him from being sent away for much longer than that. It was all that blubber, the doctors said, that kept the final arrow from doing anything worse than lacerating his liver.

Vincent DeLaine, the Native American poet, emerged from the auditorium just in time to see me being carried off to the infirmary like a recently unearthed corpse, and Nelson laid out on the side of the road, two arrows still sticking out of him, attended to by Nurse DuCharme while the ambulance wailed toward us from Whiteriver. Vincent and his assistant practically dove into the Town Car before it fishtailed off, leaving a pile of unbought books that would eventually take up an entire shelf of the school library.

I came to on a cot in the infirmary, coughing up sludge water, saved once again. I was bruised and battered and crusted with mud, but would be as good as new in a week or so. For Edgar, once more, it wasn't a good day to die.

A VERY OLD MAN

TWO WEEKS LATER on a blustery March night out by the cattle guard Barry drove up in a green Volkswagen bus. I climbed in, slammed the door, and Barry, who was wearing yellow-tinted glasses and a suede jacket with fringes that moved like falling water, said "Hey, my man. What's the matter with you?"

I looked out the window at the few lights of Whiteriver gathered in the bowl of the valley below us. *What is wrong with me?* I thought. *Everything. Everything you could name.*

In these last weeks a pall had fallen over me: I wandered about aimlessly, barely eating, having to be dragged out of bed in the morning by Raymond or one of the other aides, spending all my free time at the jumping place, looking over the edge of the cliff, imagining what it would be like to leap off into some other place. Sitting on that lip of rock, my feet dangling out into nothing, I considered murdering somebody so I could be sent away to be with Cecil in Nevada, but they had expelled everyone I might have wanted to exterminate: Glen, Rotten Teeth and a few of the other bigger boys I had set up. Principal Whipple had found his beloved contraband stashed under their mattresses and it was more than he could bear— he sent away all six, made sure they were prosecuted by the courts, and promised that as long as he was principal they would never return.

As it turned out, he wasn't principal for much longer. Hearing that his wife had been doing nasty, unmentionable things with Nelson Norman was really the last straw. Like everybody else at Willie Sherman, he had heard the rumors, had even heard a firsthand account from me about Mr. Thomas and Mrs. Whipple making noises together in the Thomas home. Mr. Thomas—well, he could understand that, he said. Mr. Thomas was a big, strapping man, fairly good-looking. And there had been other rumors, about Joe Harris, the textbook salesman, and something about the math teacher, Mr. Card, who had stayed for only half a year. But Nelson, fat Nelson Norman, the worst of the delinquents, the same Nelson Norman who only a few days before tried to kill the little crossbreed? This was not something he could forget about, no he could not.

Practically the entire student body heard all of this come out one evening during an hour-long knock-down-drag-out from the back patio of the Whipple home. We all opened our windows to be able to hear everything clearly, and the Whipples' voices carried and echoed down the walls of the canyon, bringing them right to us. They shouted, then whispered fiercely for awhile, their voices rising until they were screaming at each other again, their words coming out sometimes like furious animal barks. Mrs. Whipple raged about living out here on the last outpost of hell with all these Indians, nothing to do but walk around in the mountains, do you expect me not to entertain thoughts? To enjoy spending time with somebody else while he was over there in his office with that little squaw-tramp and her red lipstick?

Everything ended when, in the midst of an incoherent crescendo of shouts, a slap rang out with a concussive report all the louder for the long silence that followed it. Then, crowded at the windows on the north side of the building, we watched Mrs. Whipple toss an overnight bag into the backseat of their Buick and motor away into the night. The next morning Principal Whipple resigned, packed up his things and, without a word to any of the students or teachers, got a ride out of town with the man who drove the bread truck and happened to be one of Mrs. Whipple's more regular suitors.

All of this because of me.

I began to realize then exactly how powerful I was. I could not be killed. You could beat me into a pulp, burn me with wires, kick my ribs in, run over my head with a jeep, but I wouldn't die on you. And wherever I went, it didn't matter where, ruin would follow, sooner or later. Things would be flung apart.

How could I explain any of this to Barry? I didn't even want to try. I laughed to myself and Barry looked over at me a little nervously. I fiddled with the broken knob on the glove box, said, "I'm all right."

"You don't look like you're all right." Barry squinted at me. "Is that a bruise on your head?"

I couldn't believe that he hadn't yet found out what had happened—he usually had his fingers into everything. He would find out about it sooner or later, I was sure, but in the meantime I was happy not to talk about it.

"I been sick," I said, sniffing a little. "Not feeling too good."

Barry put on his doctor-face—professionally concerned—and reached over to feel my forehead. "I know there's been a flu going

around. Schools, especially without properly trained medical person-
nel, spread the flu like nothing else."

Together we looked out the windshield at the road opening up
like a black tunnel in front of us. Barry told me we could go anywhere I wanted tonight—he could run his errands tomorrow—
maybe I'd like to go up to Show Low to see a midnight movie, or
over to Superior to eat at the all-night diner that served eleven different kinds of pie.

"I want to go see Art," I said, surprising myself. I looked at Barry,
who had his arms on the big steering wheel like a man hugging a
barrel. He stared straight ahead as if he hadn't heard me.

"Is he dead?" I said.

Barry sighed out of his nose. "No, he isn't dead, but I haven't
checked recently." The muscles of his face were pulled tight and his
cheekbones stuck out like big red knuckles.

"You know where he is?"

"I know."

"I want to see him."

"You want to see him? Art, a violent, shit-in-his-pants drunk?
You'd rather go see him than eat pie at Sister's?"

I nodded.

"All right then," Barry said, biting off his words. "We'll go see Art.
Just like good old times."

The van's small engine whined as Barry pushed down hard on the
gas. For forty-five minutes he kept his foot locked down on the
accelerator, taking it off only when a car ahead of us slowed him
down. He did not speak, did not seem to breathe, and his face held
itself in that same clenched expression. I was afraid, but tried not to
show it, tried not to grab my seat or brace myself against the dashboard when we swung around a curve so fast it felt like we were lifting off the road.

On a long stretch of highway that ribboned through the scrubland
plain, jackrabbits began showing up on the road, there seemed to be
at least one or two of them every mile, their eyes glowing red with

the headlights. Only a few had enough sense to get out of the way and the less alert ones would make a rather distinct *wa-wop* when the van drove over them. Barry continued to look straight ahead, his hands tightly gripping the wheel. It took thirteen rabbits going *wa-wop* before I got up the nerve to say anything: "What about these rabbits?"

Barry looked around, startled. He said, "Rabbits?"

We drove on to Globe and there was suddenly so much light it seemed we were swimming in it. Off to our left, I knew, on the other side of a hill, was St. Divine's, which Barry had told me was no longer a hospital, but a big garage where they parked trucks and stored machinery that dripped oil and smelled like diesel fuel.

I got nervous when Barry turned off the highway and made a series of turns, bottoming out in potholes and sliding over gravel when he touched the brakes. He cranked the wheel and we were in the parking lot of a run-down place called the Polar Bear Motel. On the neon sign in front was a bear in a black top hat with his butt stuck in the door of an igloo.

"Here we are," Barry said, not looking at me. "Number nine, straight ahead there. I'm guessing he's still here. I've come to check on him a few times, bring him what he needs. I'm not the type to hold grudges." Barry shook his head. "I hoped you'd forgotten about him by now, seen him for what he is."

At the end of the row of doors a lone figure, who had been leaning against the wall and smoking a cigarette, started walking our way. Barry poked his head out of the window and waved the man off. "You can stop right there. I don't got anything tonight. Conducting personal business here. A little privacy would be appreciated."

The man, who I could now see was wearing a shirt with an enormous red tongue on it, muttered something, stomped on his cigarette and disappeared into his room.

"Well?" Barry looked at me. "He's right in there. Looks like a light's on. I'll wait out here for you. Take as long as you'd like. Leave the door open, just in case. I'll keep an eye on you."

I climbed down out of the van and walked up to the scarred door. From where I stood, I could easily see through the large window, its glass crisscrossed with masking tape, into the room. Inside, the only illumination came from the TV, which was mounted on a wall bracket and showed nothing but snowy static, shining over the room like a fat, full moon. At first, everything seemed like a jumble of light and shadow but as my eyes adjusted I could make out a bed, piled with clothes and boxes and tin cans, a low table lined with empty bottles of all sizes and behind that, Art in a wheelchair.

I watched him for a long time and he did not move. He looked shrunken, his hands too big for his arms, his head covered with thinning hair that was now mostly white. Even in the strange flickering light of that room I could see the jaundiced hue of his skin, the calligraphy of burst capillaries written over his nose and cheeks, the milky gray of his eyes.

I put my hand on the doorknob, took it off. I looked back at Barry, who was only a shadow in the driver's seat of the van. I did not want Art to know that I was with Barry, that I had not, as I had promised, stuck him with the knife he had given me. Art stirred, mumbled something, and raised the bottle to his lips, his hand shaking so badly that the whiskey frothed out of the bottle and splashed down his chest.

"Sh-shit," I heard him say, in the weak, hollow voice of a very old man. A piece of me cracked loose and fell away.

I rubbed the urinal puck in my pocket until tiny granules of it began to come off. I took it out and turned it over: it had long since begun to fall apart, so I had resorted to wrapping it up with electrical tape. It now looked more like a badly shaped hockey puck than something you would find in a men's rest room.

I remembered the time at St. Divine's when Nurse George had caught me with it. I had been sitting under my covers, looking it over, when she pulled back my blankets and tried to snatch it away from me.

"My laws," she said, "what are you doing with that filthy thing?"

She had bright orange hair that seemed to catch fire when she was angry.

I gripped my puck with both hands. If she took it away I didn't know what I would do.

"Let him alone," Art said. "That little Chinaman orderly—Liu what's his name—gave it to him. Clean, from the supply closet. Ain't no dirtier than anything else in this place. He likes the odor it gives off."

Nurse George stuck out her chin. "I *hardly* think it's the type of thing—"

"You let that boy be," Art said. "Why don't you go stick a thermometer up somebody's wazoo?"

After the nurse had gone, huffing and banging the door shut on her way out, Art asked what in God's name I was doing with a urinal deodorizer.

"Ghosts," I told him.

"Ghosts?" he said.

"They bother me sometimes, at nights. This keeps 'em away."

Art nodded, ran his fingertips over his plaster arm cast like he was reading braille. "Well, I'm glad for you." He looked up and tried to manage a smile through a mouth that was capable only of a lopsided grimace. "I could probably use something like that myself."

Now, looking through the window at him, I felt as if my guts were full of ice, slowly melting. I hesitated only a moment before leaving the puck on the broken cement of his doorstep.

A WALK IN THE DARK

THE FIRST WEEK of April it rained almost without stopping, great vaporous clouds swarming around the mountains, mist and drizzle blown sideways and back up into the sky by sudden gusts. The sun, when it did show itself, cast a pale, greenish light over everything.

Edgar didn't much notice the rain. He walked across the parade grounds, sloshing through small ponds of unsettled water, through the halls of a Willie Sherman that now seemed strangely deserted. They were all gone: Rotten Teeth, Glen, Nelson, Sterling, Cecil, Principal Whipple and his wife. In the space of a few weeks Willie Sherman had been completely transformed, and I hated it more than ever. Even though I could go about my business unmolested, could take a shower without fear of being ambushed, could eat my lunch without keeping constantly alert for projectiles or attacks from behind, I couldn't stand it anymore: the guttering fluorescent lights, the creeping mildew smell of my own bunk, the raw loneliness that ate at me like a disease.

One entire Sunday I did nothing but sit in the boiler room and type: *cecilcecilcecilcecilcecilcecilcecilcecilcecilcecilcecilcecilcecilcecilcecilcecilcecilcecilcecil-cecilcecilcecilcecilcecilcecilcecilcecilcecilcecilcecilcecilcecilcecilcecilcecilcecilcecilcecil-cecilcecilcecilcecilcecilcecilcecilcecilcecilcecilcecilcecilcecilcecilcecilcecilcecilcecilcecilceci lcecilcecilcecilcecilcecilcecilcecilcecilcecilcecilcecilcecilcecilcecilcecilcecilcecilcecilcecil-cecilcecilcecilcecilcecilcecilcecilcecilcecilcecilcecilcecilcecilcecilcecilcecilcecilcecilcecil-cecilcecilcecilcecilcecilcecilcecilcecilcecil* until I ran out of ribbon and my hands cramped into claws.

And the ghosts came back. Now that I had given up my urinal puck they wouldn't leave me alone; I began to piss the bed again, woke up hollering in the night. Even in the day I saw visions, disturbances of air congealing into human forms, figures that moved only at the periphery of sight and spoke to me in faint, buzzing voices that crackled in my head like electricity.

Willie Sherman, I found out, was teeming with ghosts and the only way I could drive them off was by typing, sitting at my chair, the sound of the keys like the clattering of a chain. I would type myself into a trance, a small quiet place where nothing, not even my own thoughts, could find me. I tried other things to fend off the ghosts—the rock that had fallen out of my head, my bloody crucifix. I even tried a new deodorant cake from the bathroom urinals—this one square and ice blue—and carried it in my pocket, kept it under my pillow, but it had no magic in it. Like everything else at Willie Sherman, it wasn't worth a damn.

Nights, afraid to go to sleep, I would sit up waiting to see my mother. Sometimes I thought I felt her presence, imagined I heard her high, airy laugh. Now that she was dead I thought we could talk, that she could tell me why she had left me, gone away to California, and once she knew I was alive and okay, why she had never come to visit me.

But she never came; in death, as in life, she had better things to do. I had to settle for occasional dreams, short and abrupt—more like flashes in my sleep—of scenes, fragments of memory from my old life: my mother mashing beans in a pot or kneeling next to me at the side of the road, a hot, ticking car beside us, holding my tiny penis so I could pee into the weeds growing out of the cracks in the asphalt.

One day after class when the clouds had parted and the sky had opened wide like a mouth, I hiked off toward the flat-topped mesa to the west. I hit a game trail at the bottom of a gully and began to half-jog; I thought that if I could get far enough away from Willie Sherman this black depression that dragged at my insides might dissipate. Even when it got dark I didn't turn back; with Principal Whipple gone and no one yet to take over for him, the place had turned into a free-for-all. I would get in trouble only if I didn't make it back by Lights Out.

There was no moon and it wasn't long before I was lost, loping across rocky, uneven ground, thrashing through mesquite thickets, sometimes employing a swimmer's motion to claw my way out, stumbling down into arroyos where with each step I kicked up wet clumps of sand that fanned up and showered down the back of my shirt, filling my underwear and the pockets of my jeans. The sky, shot through with stars, turned slowly on some distant axis. Sliding down a crumbling bank, I blundered into a patch of prickly pear. The thin, barbed needles pinned my pants to my shins and knees, but I kept on until I tripped over something and skidded forward on my chest, driving the cactus spines deeper into the meat of my

legs. I lay flat, my cheek in the mud, my lungs heaving steam into
the thick air.

When I caught my breath, I noticed the smell. I had tripped over
the jutting corner of a board that had covered someone's home brew.
I could tell by the bitter, yeasty odor of it that it was fairly new,
recently tended, which meant I couldn't be too far from the school. I
pushed some mud away with my hands, pried back the board and
looked into the inky brew, which trembled and shifted like a miniature black sea, glittering with the stars overhead.

The sharp odor of it made me miss Cecil so much, so suddenly,
that it felt like my heart had been stung. I rolled over, put my face all
the way into the brew and sucked in as much as I could before my
throat constricted and streams foamed out of both nostrils. I gagged,
coughed, took a deep breath and although it felt like my insides were
melting and my head was full of fumes, almost immediately I felt
better. Before I stood up I took one more drink and had to gasp and
growl at the way it burned and soothed me at the same time.

I don't know how long I wandered through the brush, hardly feeling my feet touch the ground. A thin layer of clouds had covered up
the stars and I might as well have been blind the way I tripped and
careened between juniper and cedar trees that stabbed me in the eyes
with their needles. I came to a gravel road, veered off it, located it
again, and then found myself walking a game trail that felt familiar
even though I was more lost than I had ever been in my life. When I
stopped and heard the roar of the river it began to dawn on me. The
trail dipped, then rose at an incline for a quarter of a mile or so and I
glided heedlessly forward, knowing before they came each bend and
switchback, and when I stepped out onto that narrow platform of
rock I felt the hair on my arms stand up. After hours of stumbling
through the dark I had ended up here: the jumping place.

I stayed still for awhile, my whole body vibrating. There was a
buzzing at the back of my eyes and for a moment I thought I might
have a fit, but the feeling passed and I stood in the middle of that
perfect darkness, the river hissing below me, and felt no fear, no pain,

nothing. I held my hand on my crotch and was amazed at how much I wanted to jump and how difficult it was to come up with a reason not to.

Slowly I backed up along the trail that Sterling and I had worn smooth over these past few years with all our visits, twenty, thirty paces. I stopped and waited. I listened to the hissing river and to a single cricket peeping far away. I thought about the boys and girls of Willie Sherman, just a few hundred yards on the other side of the tree line, sleeping in their bunks. I thought about Art in his motel room drinking under the glare of a blank TV and Cecil in a place called Nevada where he shared a cell with three other young criminals. I thought about my father, some stranger who, I was sure, tried to forget every day that he had a child, and a mailman who tried to forget that he had killed one. I thought of my mother, up in heaven, and I hoped that there was music, like Raymond said, and that the beer never ran out. And I thought about Sterling, who I figured had become one of those angry ghosts who hung around Willie Sherman—he might even have pestered me a few times—and it made me feel good to believe that maybe he was here now, watching me.

I took one step forward, another, and then it was like my legs were no longer mine and I hurtled forward into nothing. I did not leap or dive, only ran until there was nothing under my feet and I realized I was falling only a second or so before I hit, before the hard shock of it jarred me to my bones.

At first I was aware of nothing but a red pain that covered everything. Then the cold began to seep through, a chaos in my ears, and I took in a mouthful of ice water when I tried to breathe, which brought me fully conscious. In ten terrifying seconds I learned to swim well enough to right myself and get my head above water. I flailed and kicked to keep from being dragged down and the same astonishing thought kept flashing through my mind: *I jumped into the river.*

The current yanked me along, slamming me into a submerged rock or tree, spinning me around and towing me under, until the river widened and grew shallow enough that the river bottom came up and hit me like a large, unyielding hand. I sank my fingers into the silt like grappling hooks, set my heels, and was finally able to lurch to my feet, the shallow flow knifing against the backs of my knees. Time and time again I was knocked down, the rug pulled out from under me, dragged ten or twenty feet before I managed to surge forward, slipping over the mossy river rocks, my joints stiffened with cold, and hug the soft, grass-covered bank. It took all the strength I had left to pull myself out of the water and lie down in the mud, which to me felt as warm as just-made pudding.

For awhile I did nothing but gasp and hack to get air into my waterlogged lungs. There was just enough light coming through the breaking canopy of clouds so that I could look across the river, which was swollen and angry, twice as wide as I had ever seen it. No, I realized, I hadn't jumped farther than anyone ever had before, hadn't flown past the red stones into the water. The river, gorged by rain and the snowmelt from the past couple of warm days had reached, in some places, all the way to the canyon walls. I had jumped—probably not very far at all—and the river had caught me.

Every part of me was either numb or alive with pain. It took me half an hour or so just to get up the nerve to use my left arm—the one that hurt the least—to cover myself with the warm, soupy mud. Before I fell asleep I was surprised to hear myself laugh, a hoarse, delirious hoot that echoed all the way down the canyon and into the dark sky.

THE ELDERS

I SHAMBLED ALONG the gravel road, limping stiffly and moaning like a sad, disoriented swamp monster risen from the muck. I was encased in a thick crust of dried mud and my left knee had swollen up so badly I had to tow my leg behind as if it was made of solid iron. Above everything else, the river had stolen both my shoes, one of my socks and one of the two pair of pants I owned. Thankfully, Edgar still had his underwear.

It was a sharp beautiful morning, birds singing and the sun warming everything like a blessing. Up ahead, I heard the rattling of bicycle chains before two people appeared on the rise ahead of me, coming along fast. I stepped off the road and tried to camouflage myself in the dirt and bushes; the last thing I wanted to do was give somebody a fright. I watched them out of the corner of my eye and they were easy to recognize: two young men, wearing white short-sleeved shirts and ties: the Elders.

When they saw me they both put on the brakes, their back tires chattering and hopping on the loose rock. One of them was thick-limbed with a wide, curved face, and the other, smaller and leaner, had a head of red-blond hair that shone in the sun like hammered copper.

"Hey," the big one said, "you okay?"

I looked down at my feet, which were bleeding from the gravel shards and broken beer bottles in the road. I thought if I stayed absolutely still and kept my head down they might give up on me and go on their way.

They got off their bikes, let them fall right in the middle of the road and came over to me. The blond one craned his neck and peered into my face as if I was something that had just fallen out of the sky. He said in nearly perfect Apache, "What happened to you?"

I glanced up at the big guy, who was looking a bit alarmed, and shrugged. I said in English, "I jumped off a cliff."

"What? You did what?" said the big one. His voice was much too high and sweet for such a large body. I saw from the black tag on his shirt that his name was Elder Turley.

"I jumped off a cliff. I don't feel real good."

The Elders looked at each other. "Have you been drinking?" asked the blond one, who, according to the tag on his shirt, was called Elder Spafford.

I shook my head, then nodded. "No," I said. "Yes."

The Elders quickly agreed that I should be gotten to a doctor as soon as possible. Elder Turley hoisted me onto his handlebars and began pumping at the pedals like a man possessed, his hot breath on the back of my neck. In the round mirror above his rubber hand-grips I could see my reflection. My eyes were startlingly white, like two boiled eggs embedded in a dirt clod. My hair was matted in such a way that it stuck up from both sides of my head like a pair of horns.

"Where do you live?" shouted Elder Spafford, pedaling furiously to pull up alongside. I told him and he asked me if they had a doctor there.

"A nurse!" I shouted back, the jouncing of the bike making it feel like every nerve in me was spitting sparks. "But she's not a very good one!"

Back at Willie Sherman, an AWOL operation was in full swing: there were two sheriff's cars in front of the main office and a few deputies, off in the distance, combing the bushes above the cavalry stables.

Raymond, who was talking to Mr. Hansen on the steps, was the first to see us. He took one look at me and said, "What in the name a God."

I was carried into the infirmary and Elder Spafford helped Raymond pour warm water on me to get the mud off while Elder Turley went to fetch the nurse.

"We found him on the side of the road," Elder Spafford said.

"He don't look so good," Raymond agreed. "Nossir, he don't."

When Nurse DuCharme appeared she took a long drag on her cigarette before stepping inside. She put her hands on her hips and in a puff of smoke said, "I guess we're going to have to name this place the Edgar Mint Memorial Hospital."

Eventually, they brought in a doctor from the Indian clinic, who pulled out a bunch of cactus thorns still embedded in my shins, cleaned the scratches and shallow lacerations that crisscrossed me from head to toe, set the small finger on my left hand which had been broken in two places, prodded and pulled on my badly twisted knee, and pronounced me the luckiest damn kid he had ever seen.

Once I was bandaged up and smelling of alcohol and salve, the Elders asked Raymond if they could say a prayer for me. Raymond patted me on the chest. "This boy, lemme tell you, he needs it." Elder Turley folded his big, hammy arms and offered up a short prayer, asking God to help me, to heal me, to look down on me in His love.

"You didn't save my life," I croaked at them from my bed before they left. I don't know what got into me to say such a thing. I only knew that I was sick to death of being saved.

TOUCHED BY GOD

THE WEEK I was in the infirmary the Elders stopped by twice. They brought comic books and peanut brittle and stayed awhile to keep me company. When Nurse DuCharme came in sucking on a cigarette, Elder Spafford told her straight out that it was neither ladylike nor healthy to be smoking in the presence of a sick child. Her face went red and she headed back across the road, mumbling something about know-it-all nincompoops.

Elder Turley shook his head. "People," he said.

The third time they came I had just got out of classes, my first day back. Except for my broken pinkie and my limp, which I exaggerated as much as I could, I was fine. Elder Spafford asked if we might go somewhere and talk about God a little bit. He said he had a special feeling about me, that I had been spared because I was a special person and was meant to do special things.

I sighed; I had heard all of this many times before.

The day was worn white with sunlight, and odd gusts of wind stirred up dust devils along the parade grounds. We sat down at the old picnic table just outside the cafeteria doors. Every inch of the table was covered with graffiti, but there was one message that dominated all others: someone had taken great care and consideration to gouge out the word BITCH in perfectly formed letters ten inches high. I watched the Elders closely but they didn't seem to notice.

We started with Elder Turley offering a prayer and then Elder Spafford asked me what I knew about God. I told them I didn't know anything about anything. Elder Spafford asked me if I knew why I was here on Earth, what the purpose of my existence might be.

"I think you're going to let me know," I said.

"I am," Elder Spafford nodded, his face full of conviction.

Over near the basketball courts, a group of kids had gathered and were taunting and cursing the Elders in four or five different tongues, none of them English. Normally, I would have been included, but it had become widely known not only that Edgar Mint was the one responsible for getting Nelson, Rotten Teeth and the rest shipped away, but that he had also leaped off the jumping place and survived. For the rest of his stay at Willie Sherman, no one would ever bother him again.

"Those kids are punks," Elder Turley said, glaring over his shoulder. "I really should go over and stomp on 'em some."

Elder Spafford continued on about God's great plan, about the gospel of Jesus Christ restored to the earth and how this had all been revealed to a boy about my age, the young prophet Joseph Smith. In a voice shot through with sincerity he told me of how young Joseph, confused by the many religions professing different truths, went off into the woods one day to pray, to ask God for guidance. I listened and idly scanned the table for any new graffiti that might have appeared since the last time I checked. When he got to the part about the boy Joseph kneeling in the grove to pray and seeing two figures outlined in light appearing in the air above him, I looked up, so excited that I blurted out, "Ghosts!"

"What?" said Elder Turley.

"Ghosts," I said. "I see ghosts sometimes too."

"You see ghosts?" Elder Spafford said.

Elder Turley leaned over to Elder Spafford and I heard him whisper behind his hand, "Evil spirits."

Elder Spafford swallowed. "Not ghosts, Edgar. The Father and the Son Jesus Christ themselves appeared to Joseph Smith. In person. One of the most wonderful events in human history. They told him that none of the religions were true and it would be his calling to bring that truth to light, to establish it once more upon the earth."

"Oh," I said.

Elder Spafford rummaged in his bag and came up with a book with a dark blue cover and gold lettering that said THE BOOK OF MORMON.

"Joseph Smith was responsible for bringing this book to us," Elder Spafford said, hefting it in his hand as if its worth lay in how much it weighed. "It is a book that will change the world."

"Did he type it?" I said.

Elder Turley started to laugh until Elder Spafford shot him a hard look.

"He didn't have a typewriter," Elder Spafford said, the little muscle in his jaw popping out. "But that really isn't important. What is important is that you read this book and find out if what it contains is true. If you do this, Edgar, I promise it will change your life. Do you know how to read?"

I nodded. "I just don't know how to write. That's why I have a typewriter."

Before they left, they asked if they could give me a blessing. This time, instead of folding their arms and praying, as they usually did before they left, they came behind me and put their hands on my head, their fingertips lightly touching my scalp. Across the road the kids had started yelling, laughing and pointing, and a sudden gust of wind blasted us with grit. In a near shout Elder Spafford called on the name of God and immediately I felt a warmth at the crown of my head, a light, liquid tingling that slowly moved down into my neck and chest.

"We ask Thee to bless this child," Elder Spafford called over the noise of the snickering children and the wind in the grass. "Free him from the evil spirits that torment him, give him peace, heal him, heal his body and his spirit." Elder Spafford paused for a moment and I began to feel like I was floating above the bench. "Allow Thy love to shower down upon him and let him know that he will never be abandoned, that he will always be protected, that he will always have Thy love. These blessings we ask Thee in the name of our Savior Jesus Christ, Amen."

Inexplicably, my eyes were spilling tears. The Elders lifted their hands off my head and I desperately ground a fistful of shirt into my face to wipe away the evidence. Before they rode away on their bikes, they each smiled and shook my hand.

In a daze, I headed out across the parade grounds toward the dormitory, feeling like the top of my head had been shot off. I started to climb the steps and it hit me right there, there was no doubt: Edgar had been touched by God.

EDGAR TAKES IT

FOR THE NEXT MONTH, the Elders came twice a week and taught me the gospel. They explained about heaven and hell and how to get to both places, they taught me how to pray. Instead of closing my eyes, folding my arms and praying out loud, like they showed me, I prayed with my typewriter.

My first prayer was something of an amateur effort:

God

   Is my mother up there? Please tell her hello. I am sorry about
everything I have done. I am getting better. Your friends the elders
are trying to help me.

                                              Thank you, Edgar

   When I showed my prayer to the Elders they nodded and said it was
pretty darn good, no doubt about it, I was really on my way. Together
we read verses from the Book of Mormon and the Bible, talked about
how Jesus died for our sins. Sometimes the Elders brought bottles of
orange soda or root beer, sometimes a box of crackers, and we would sit
at the table that said BITCH and discuss the matters of the Lord.

   Just because God had touched me, just because He filled me for a
moment with liquid light and had made the voices in my head and
the ghosts go away, did not mean that I had to accept Him. Elder
Spafford had explained this to me: I had free agency, the choice to
take God into my heart or reject Him out of hand. It was my
choice—a huge choice in a world that, for me, had no real choices at
all.

   The Elders taught me all they could and I tried my best to get it all
sorted out. I learned that my mother and I could be reunited and live
on together into eternity where nobody got old or sick or—Elder
Spafford promised me—bored. I learned that Jesus, God's only son,
had suffered for every one of my sins, for all the guilt and sorrow they
caused. This did not seem very fair to me, but I kept my mouth shut.
I learned that cigarettes, beer and coffee were all no-nos, and that
chastity, which I understood to mean keeping away from females
entirely, was a must. And most importantly, I learned about this God
who presided over this place called heaven where my mother was,
who had a plan for me, who loved me without qualification, who
watched over me. God, I learned, would never die, would never disappear without notice, would never beat anybody up, would never
grow sick or old or tired of living. He might become angry or disappointed, yes, but He would never abandon you.

Okay, I would accept Him, I decided. I'd have to be an idiot not to. So I typed Him a little prayer that said: *God. This is Edgar. I will take it.*

One morning, Elder Turley said they had done too much talking, they wanted to learn a little more about me. I told them all of the stories I had: my mother, the mailman, Grandma Paul, Dr. Pinkley pounding me back to life. I told them about St. Divine's and my mother's death, about Cecil saving me from Nelson and being sent away because of it.

Elder Spafford's eyes seemed to go by shades brighter as he listened, and when I was finished he put his hands on my shoulders.

"Edgar, God has spared you for some larger purpose," he said. "He has saved you from death to do a specific work, I am sure of it. I want you to pray and ask Him what it is. The spirit is telling me this. Can you feel it? God will let you know, all you have to do is ask."

That night I crept down to the boiler room, sat down at my typewriter and prayed. I listened to Uncle Julius wheezing for a few minutes before I began to type. I got only halfway down the page before I had my answer, before the blank half of the paper told me all I needed to know.

"I have it," I told them three days later when we sat down together in the thick light of a late spring morning. I ran my finger along a section of the table that said *I hate Mrs. Fielding* in shaky ballpoint lettering.

"Have what?" Elder Turley said.

"My purpose. What I'm supposed to do."

"Okay, shoot," Elder Turley said, yanking open a bag of pretzels from his backpack. "Lay it on us."

"It's the mailman," I said.

"What mailman?" said Elder Spafford.

"The one who ran over my head. He thinks he killed me, but he didn't. I'm going to find him and tell him I'm okay. That's what I'm supposed to do." I had been carrying around this answer with me for a long time—it just took God to confirm it.

The Elders looked at each other. "You're saying," Elder Spafford said, rubbing his hand over his head like he was trying to give it a quick polish, "that God spared you from being killed so that you could find the person who almost killed you and tell him you survived?"

I nodded—yes, that was it exactly. Elder Turley put his hand over his mouth, seemed to be trying to keep himself from grinning. I could tell they were both confused by this but it made perfect sense to me. My mother and father, Art and Grandma Paul and Cecil, they were all out of my control, they were all lost to me. But the mailman—I could do something for him. He was alive, I knew, suffering out there somewhere. I could relieve him of a burden he carried. I could do a little saving of my own.

That Sunday, the Elders took me to church with them, a small cinder-block building on the west edge of Whiteriver. I had expected the members to all be anglos, but the congregation was made up entirely of Indians except for a harried-looking white woman who sat in the front pew all by herself and cast uneasy glances at the dark-faced throng behind her. Most of the men wore ties and the women dresses and when they sang it echoed loud and beautiful in that small room.

Afterwards, we stood out in the raw heat and people came up to me, shook my hand and said welcome, we're glad to have you, let us know if there's something we can do. Some of them spoke to me in Apache, asked me if things up at Willie Sherman were as bad as they'd heard. I squinted and nodded and tried to forget that my hair was an unholy mess, that I was wearing my grease-stained jeans, a shirt that said *Budweiser Brewing Company* on the back, and tennis shoes so old they were held together with duct tape and hot glue. Everywhere I looked there were sons and daughters grab-assing on the dead lawn, fathers gathered around the open hood of somebody's Chevy pickup, mothers trying to round everyone up to get home for dinner. I had never seen anything like it.

On the way home I told the Elders I wanted to be baptized. They had brought up the subject with me a few times before but I had held them off, not because I was unsure, but because I thought that if I got baptized they would stop coming to see me.

I sat on Elder Turley's handlebars and told him when the road was bending right or left. "Help me!" he would yell. "Please help me, I can't see, somebody's head is right in my way!" Sometimes he veered off into the weeds, roaring that we were going down in flames, we were all going to die.

Normally, Elder Spafford would have given Elder Turley the evil eye, maybe said something about it being the Sabbath, but he pedaled alongside looking content.

"I know God is smiling right now," Elder Spafford said over the clanking of the chains, the crunch of tires on the dirt road. "He's happy with you. His angels are rejoicing."

Up ahead, on the last rise before Willie Sherman when we got off the bikes to walk, I asked the Elders about the possibility of going to live somewhere with an anglo family, where every kid had his own bicycle and you got to eat ice cream for dinner, a place where everyone had a mother and a father, maybe some brothers and sisters, possibly a dog.

Elder Spafford stopped in the middle of the road and took on a serious face. "Somebody told you about the placement program? Well. Usually we don't mention it until after baptism because we've had kids getting baptized just to get off the reservation. But, no, you're a different case altogether. I'll look into this. We need to get you away from that school, someplace where evil isn't staring you in the face everywhere you turn."

Behind us, a car came barreling up the road, lifting up a thick bank of dust. We moved off to the side and the car slowed, then skidded to a stop just ahead of us. It was a rust-eaten Oldsmobile with whitewall tires and a ragtop that had been shredded into the kind of thick netting you might find covering an air raid shelter.

Barry Pinkley stepped out of the driver's side, pushed his sunglasses down on his nose to have a look at us. He was wearing bell-bottom jeans and a yellow open-throated shirt with roses and tulips stitched around the collar. "Edgar?" he said. "Who are these people?"

Elder Turley let his bike drop and stepped in front of me. A woman, whose bleach-blond hair sparkled in the sun like cut crystal, appeared from the other side of the car, puffing delicately on a long cigarillo.

"How can we help you folks?" said Elder Spafford.

"Look," Barry said. "I'm a doctor, okay? I take care of this boy, Edgar, so if you'd just be on your merry way we're here to take him on a picnic." The woman reached in the backseat and, like a lawyer in a courtroom showing off evidence, held up a basket with a loaf of bread and a bag of Cheetos sticking out of it.

"A doctor?" said Elder Turley, taking a step closer to Barry.

"I . . . I'm not practicing right now, but I'm Edgar's guardian, technically speaking." Barry's ears were beginning to turn red. "This is ridiculous. Edgar, will you tell these jarheads who I am? Marlene and I came to take you on a picnic by the river. We've got Ding Dongs and Dr Pepper. I even bought a fishing pole."

For a moment everyone looked at me. In the quiet heat of the day the Oldsmobile stuttered and ticked. I stood in Elder Turley's shadow and kept my head down, watching a stinkbug that had climbed up onto my shoe and got itself stuck to a piece of duct tape.

Elder Spafford said, "Why don't you just tell us your name, where you live, and we'll check it out—"

Barry turned and got right in Elder Spafford's face. "My name? You want *my* name? And who the fuck are you, you inbred piece of dirt? And what do you think you're doing with this boy? Brainwashing him? Filling his head with holy-roller Jesus-on-the-cross bullshit? I saved this boy's life!"

Barry took a step toward me, as if to take me by the arm, but Elder Turley was on him and had him backed up and pinned to the side of the car before I knew what had happened. Marlene shrieked and giggled like this was all a fun game.

"Get in the car," Elder Turley grunted, his thick freckled forearm across Barry's chest. "Drive on out of here."

"You tell them, Edgar," Barry spit, looking at me over Elder Turley's shoulder. "Tell them who I *am*."

In one motion Elder Turley pulled open the car door and stuffed Barry inside. He told Barry to leave now before he really got angry. "My God, look how big he is!" Marlene squealed as she slipped into the passenger side.

Barry gave the car some gas and the rear tires spun, sending up twin geysers of dust. The Oldsmobile swung around in a wide arc like a speedboat doubling back, and lurched to a stop next to us again.

Barry now held a silver snub-nosed pistol and was leaning over Marlene to point it at Elder Turley's chest. A cloud of dust descended over us like a fine mist. Barry aimed the gun at Elder Spafford for a moment, then swung it back to Elder Turley.

Barry had taken his glasses off and his eyes looked like a pair of nails hammered into his face. He said, "If I ever see you two again I'll send you straight to the worst hell you could ever believe in."

LAST CONFESSION

BEFORE I COULD be baptized, first I had to confess. Confession is a vital part of repentance, the Elders told me, the only way to stand blameless before the Lord.

So one late May afternoon they brought another missionary along with them, a short, peanut-shaped guy who would hear all of my confessions and decide if I had enough of a broken spirit, if I was contrite and meek and repentant enough to make a personal, everlasting covenant with God Himself.

The day before, a man from the church who worked with the Indian Placement Program stopped by to talk to Uncle Julius, to have him sign some forms. He wore a shiny polyester blue suit and gave me a caramel to chew on while I answered his questions about my mother and father, where I had lived before Willie Sherman, why I thought it might be helpful to me to live with a Mormon family and go to school somewhere far away from here. When he headed out to his car I followed behind.

"Is there a family that will take me?" I asked him. "I don't even care what kind of family it is. Maybe just a mother and a brother, something like that."

"There just might be," he said, winking at me. "You never can tell what the Lord has in mind."

Now, here was this other missionary—Elder Doyle—asking me questions about Jesus and the prophets, wanting to know if my Elders had taught me everything I needed to know. For privacy we were down in the boiler room and Elder Doyle was perspiring so heavily drops of sweat were plopping off his nose onto his notepad like water out of a leaky faucet.

"Whew!" he said, grinning at me. He was squatting on Uncle Julius' cot and I sat across from him on a plastic five-gallon bucket. "Kinda toasty in here. Holy cow!"

After coming to the conclusion that I was well enough versed in the gospel to make my own good decision, he explained that we were going to have to discuss whether or not I had any outstanding sins that needed to be taken care of before I could enter the cleansing waters of baptism.

"You mean *all* my sins?" I said.

He nodded. "At least the big ones."

I fidgeted on my bucket for awhile, then let it fly:

I had lied too many times to count.

I had watched Mrs. Whipple doing the ficky-fick. Twice.

I had spied on Mrs. Whipple many times, hoping to see more ficky-fick.

I had hit Barry Pinkley with my typewriter.

I was responsible for Nelson and the others getting expelled, for Barry Pinkley getting fired, for the Whipples' divorce, for Grandma

Paul ending up in a crazy hospital, for Cecil being sent off to prison, for my mother drinking herself to death.

I had watched girls undressing through the bathroom window.

I had helped burn down the cavalry stables.

I had stolen urinal pucks, ballpoint pens, a crucifix, butterscotch candy, corn flakes, cans of gasoline, underwear, bottles of vanilla, rubber cement, shotgun shells, a Mr. Potato Head toy, bags of sugar and flour and yeast, syringes, comic books, a hacksaw, beer and whiskey, a deck of cards, money, a bag of contraband, typewriter ribbon, cigarettes, a clawhammer, nylon rope, a poster of a movie star in a bikini, cocoa powder, rubbing alcohol, firecrackers.

I had murdered Nelson Norman in my heart.

I had beat up Chester Holland and Walter Reed and punched Victor Ortiz when he wasn't expecting it.

I had tried to commit suicide.

Throughout it all, Elder Doyle did not blink. When I was done, he held up his finger as if to say something, then changed his mind. He scratched his head and pretended to write something on his wet notepad. "Hmmm," he said finally. "What about self-abuse?"

"I hit myself on the head with a brick," I confessed.

Elder Doyle went upstairs to talk to the other missionaries. Once he was gone, I nearly slumped right off my bucket; it was as if all the buckles and clasps inside of me had been unlatched, leaving me loose and free and able to breathe. Elder Spafford had told me not to be afraid, that confession was a wonderful thing, God's gift to me, and now I believed it.

After a few minutes the Elders called me upstairs. They were all beaming. I could be baptized next Saturday, they said, I had made it. Elder Turley picked me up and spun me around in the air until I was dizzy. I was twelve years old and I was going to become a member of God's own church, the Church of Jesus Christ of Latter-Day Saints. I had accepted God and He had accepted me. I had once been the miracle-boy and now I was going to be a saint.

BORN AGAIN

THE DAY OF my baptism clouds boiled up over the mountains,
grumbling and stirring the air, their edges as brilliant as white marble
against the blackening sky. I stood outside the church in a white
polyester jumpsuit two or three sizes too big for me, trying with all
my might not to grab my groin. Elder Spafford and Elder Turley
were running around grabbing hymnbooks, shaking hands with the
new arrivals, checking the galvanized tank out back that was filling
up with water from a garden hose attached to a little sputtering well
pump. Elder Spafford had told me they were trying to raise money
to build a proper baptismal font inside the building, but for now
we'd have to do it the old-fashioned way: in a cow tank.

I was glad when Elder Turley touched me on the shoulder and
told me to follow him inside to the bathroom. He began to change
from his regular missionary clothes into a white shirt, white pair of
pants and white tie with a little golden tie clip. He even had a white
belt. Tack on a couple of wings and you had yourself a burly, freckled
angel.

"Are you excited?" he said. "Are you nervous?"

I worked at rolling up my pant legs, which kept falling down and
were now covered with grass stains and dirt. "Little bit scared," I said.

"Scared?" said Elder Turley, pulling at the knot in his tie. "There's
nothing to be scared about. Come on, now! This is your big day.
Nothing to be worried about at all."

He didn't understand. I wasn't scared about becoming a new
person, about having my sins washed away forever—I was looking
forward to that. It was the cow tank, and the water in it, that made
me nervous. When the missionaries had explained baptism to me, I

had this idea of somebody pouring water over my head from a bucket; when they said *immersion* I thought they simply meant getting completely wet. But the cow tank was as big as a swimming pool and the water was getting pretty deep—I had checked a few times. I knew there was no way that hose water in a cow tank could do the kind of things to me the river water had, but I still wasn't comforted.

"Look," Elder Turley said, "I wasn't supposed to say anything until later, but maybe this will make you feel a little bit better. Brother Kalb from the placement program called to tell us they've got a family for you. He didn't tell me who they are, but he says they live up in Richland. That's only an hour from my hometown, can you believe it? It's a great place, Edgar, you're really going to love it." Elder Turley's grin had taken over his entire face. He gave me a playful chuck on the shoulder. "Go ahead and smile now. We're going to get you out of that school. You're going to have a real family. Real, God-fearing people. Your own kind."

In the chapel, they had a short prebaptismal service in which Elder Spafford and an Apache man named Brother Mendosa offered a few words about the meaning of baptism, how it was a symbol for death and resurrection: to be buried in the water and to rise again. A couple of hymns were sung. I sat in front, next to a straight-backed Elder Turley who couldn't hide his loopy grin, and hardly heard any of it. I was thinking about Richland, Utah, and this family that was going to take me in, imagining what kind of people could want somebody like me to come live with them in their home. While the congregation sang "There Is a Green Hill Far Away" I constructed in my mind a vast, panoramic picture: a little town with painted houses and the green lawns that Prissy had described to me—weedless and perfectly square—and children riding on bicycles down smooth blacktop streets, trailing a truck that played music and made ice cream available to anyone who wanted it. It all seemed impossible to me, right then—a dream—something I had absolutely no right to believe in or hope for.

In no time the service was over and we filed outside. Far off on the horizon the bottoms seemed to be dropping out of the clouds where a purple wall of rain had come down. A steady breeze carried the wet, clean smell of it. A flock of sparrows shot over our heads, tittering with alarm, and I heard a kid in the back ask his mother or father if he could someday have a karate suit like mine. Elder Spafford ushered me up near the tank and Elder Turley made a big show out of gingerly poking one finger in and yanking it out like somebody testing the water on a stove. Everybody laughed and an old man in a stained cowboy hat said, "Let's get that boy wet before we do."

Elder Turley knelt down in front of me. "You ready?" he said. "It's all right now, go ahead and breathe."

He clambered into the tank and lifted me over the edge, gently set me down into water so cold it burned. It hit him about waist-high, but was up around my shoulders and seemed to be making my heart miss every other beat.

"Well water," Elder Turley grinned at the congregation. "Maybe next time we'll do like headhunters and build a fire under this thing."

Elder Turley led me to the middle of the tank, where my feet sank down in a soft, spongy carpet of algae and moss. He had me grab hold of his forearm and took my right wrist tightly in his hand. "Okay," he whispered to me, "here we go." He lifted his right arm, palm outward, and waited for a clap of thunder to skip across the sky before he said the prayer: *Having been commissioned of Jesus Christ, I baptize you in the name of the Father, and of the Son, and of the Holy Ghost, Amen.*

Slowly, he eased me backwards. When the water closed over the top of me I did not shut my eyes, and in the instant he held me there I could see the world above me as if through a sheet of uneven glass—the gray rim of sky, the small brown faces crowded around, the warped, faraway form of Elder Turley. I lay back, suspended in that perfect moment before I was lifted up with one great rushing pull and I broke the surface, blinking and sputtering and weightless, made of nothing but air.

RICHLAND

I N HIS NEW BED, in his new home, Edgar dug his face into his soft down pillow, the darkness around him alive with animal sounds: the *scritch-scritch* of claws on glass, the chirrup of a guinea pig, the muffled squawking of parrots. He felt like he was caught in a dream, and the only way to come out of it was to fall into a deep, distant sleep.

Earlier that day, I had stood in front of the Alchesay Mercantile in Whiteriver with Raymond, waiting for the bus that would take me to Richland, Utah. I had my new steamer trunk, which contained a few clothes, my small collection of knickknacks, my knife, my Hermes Jubilee and the 11,789 pages that bore every last word and line of gibberish I had ever struck on paper (except for the letters I had sent to Cecil and Art)—all in all, more than a hundred pounds' worth of typewritten pages.

A couple of days before, I had caught a ride into Show Low with one of the cooks and spent an entire morning scouring the second-hand stores and pawnshops until I found the trunk under a stuffed antelope head at an establishment called the True Grit Trading Post.

"That there's an antique," said the grizzled proprietor, who was working on his own false teeth with a wire brush. He had carved himself a small alcove out of the avalanche of ancient farm implements, stuffed pheasants, railroad lanterns, milk bottles, high-button shoes, leather holsters, hatchets, lengths of collectible barbed wire, hand grenades, rusted bear traps and animal skulls, all attached to their own oval price tag on a string. High up on the far wall, presiding over everything with a sign that said NOT FOR SALE, was a mummified stingray.

For the life of him, Edgar couldn't figure out what somebody might want with a piece of barbed wire.

"A relic, that trunk," the proprietor said. "Seen more of the world than the whole ignurnt population of this town."

The tag on the trunk read *40$*. I took out the wad of cash Art had given me when I left St. Divine's—money I had not spent a single dollar of—and carefully laid two twenties on the counter.

The man set down his teeth on an old yellowed ledgerbook and eyed the money suspiciously. I watched the teeth carefully to make sure they didn't move. The guy looked like he was on the verge of sucking his entire face into his mouth. "Where's your folks?" he said.

"Don't got any," I said.

"Probably a couple a wild drunks, am I right? Too many drunk redskins running their pickups into trees around here. Far be it from me to say so, but they don't know how to manage their liquor."

He swiped the money off the counter and pointed a bent, tobacco-stained finger at me. "That trunk's not to be used for keeping comic books or smelly sneakers or goddamn empty whiskey bottles or other shenanigans. That thing has historical implications, you hear me? It deserves to be treated proper, with some dignity, not as if a little scalp-grabber like yourself would know about that."

I took hold of the trunk's cracked leather handle and hauled it out the door, knocking over an oil portrait of John Wayne on my way.

Two days later, when the bus pulled up in a punishing cloud of diesel smoke, Raymond and I began to attempt to wrestle the trunk into the luggage compartment, but the driver—a big black man with a hulking beer belly—waved us off. On the expanse of white shirt that covered his chest and belly his tie looked like nothing more than a small length of blue string.

"Back up now," he said. "You let me do my job here."

He positioned himself in front of the trunk like an Olympic weight lifter and grasped the handles on either side. He strained to heft it off the ground and let loose a thunderous, rippling fart which made the woman next to me flinch and backpedal as if one of the bus tires had blown.

The driver looked at Raymond and me, then up at the passengers, who were watching from their open windows. His smile was wide and full of pink gums. "No piece a luggage has ever done that to me before."

Raymond shook my hand and I climbed up the steps. His parting words to me were, "Don't let them white folks boss you around too much. It's their favorite thing to do."

I sat down next to a woman with a cat snuggled up under her sweater and almost immediately, despite my best efforts, fell asleep. It had taken nearly three months after my baptism for the necessary paperwork to find its way back and forth among the various church and government agencies, and during that time my insomnia had only intensified; my head was bursting with all the possibilities: *Would I have my own bed in my own room? Would there be a TV to watch? Would they allow me to type whenever I wanted? Would I be sent back if they didn't like me?*

During the days, I wandered the grounds, and on the weekends the Elders stopped by to study the scriptures and to assure me that the paperwork was going through, it would take a little time, there was nothing to worry about. In those three months I hardly spoke to anyone, ate my meals at the back of the cafeteria, and used all of my energy to turn myself invisible once again, to make sure I did nothing that would jeopardize my escape from Willie Sherman. The entire week before my bus trip, I didn't sleep more than an hour at a time.

On the bus, I slept so hard I was twice jounced out of my seat and into the aisleway. Both times I scrambled to my feet, wild-eyed, ready to fight or run, but the other passengers who weren't asleep themselves gave me dazed, half-lidded looks.

"Somebody tie that kid to his seat!" the bus driver boomed from up front.

The next time I woke up, the bus was empty and dark. I could hear crickets chirping and the sound of cars *shushing* by on a highway somewhere close by. Cool air drafted in through the window and I could hear the bus driver's voice below me.

"Never seen a kid sleep like that," he said. "Never, never. Five pit stops, dinner at the truck stop, one flat tire, and he never stirred. I'd call back, 'That boy dead or something?' and they say, 'Nope, still breathing, his chest is moving up and down.' People knocking him on the head with their bags on the way out and he's drooling all over hisself like a baby. I'm telling you, that boy can *sleep*."

"Is it all right if I wait here for him awhile?" This was another voice, a man's but lower and softer than the bus driver's. "If he's that tired maybe I should let him wake up on his own. I don't want to scare him."

"Suit yourself," said the bus driver. "Frank'll come in awhile to take her back to get gassed up and serviced, you can wait till then. But I'm telling you, you let that kid go and he'll sleep till Chinese Christmas. And watch yourself with his luggage. I think maybe he's got a couple of his brothers hid up in there."

I heard the bus driver walk off with a jangle of keys and I knelt up on my seat and put my head out the window. A man stood on the concrete platform by himself. A streetlamp shone down on him, obscuring his face in shadow, limning his hair and beard with a nimbus of yellow light. He was tall and lanky and had enormous hands that hung down at his sides like a couple of heavy rakes.

"Hello?" I said.

"Is that you, Edgar?"

"Yes," I said.

"You're awake?"

I nodded.

"My name's Clay," he said. "I'm here to pick you up and take you home."

"Okay," I said.

"You want to get off the bus and we'll get your things loaded up?"

"Okay," I said. "Where am I?"

"You're in Cedar City. Richland's not too far from here. You slept the whole way."

"I'm sorry."

"Don't be sorry. The bus took longer than it was supposed to. I'm glad you made it."

I got off the bus and showed Clay my trunk. He didn't comment on it, just clapped his big hands over the handles and hefted it up on his hip. He swayed for a moment, fighting for leverage, his knees quivering, then began a slow deliberate walk, each short step a contained struggle, out into the parking lot. With the muscles in his neck pulled so tight they looked like they might snap, he did his best to act casual, as if he was carrying nothing more than a sack of groceries home from the store. When he heaved the trunk into the bed of his red GMC, the truck's shocks *screeked* with alarm.

"It's heavy," I told him.

He nodded and gingerly stepped up into the cab. He worked to catch his breath and seemed to be having a hard time straightening out his back. He shook his head and smiled at me. He said, "I think I just about busted my spine on that one."

We drove for awhile through the dark desert and then came to the scattering of lights that was Richland. We passed houses lined up neatly along the road, big houses with new paint and two or three cars and almost always a pickup of one sort or another parked out front. We pulled up next to a large white house, its front so veiled in the foliage of two ancient weeping willows that I could see only the deep porch, a single window with a small balcony supported by ornate brackets, and the steep slanting roof, as dark and blank as an empty blackboard.

"What do you say we leave your trunk in the pickup for tonight," Clay said. "Tomorrow morning I'll round up a few neighbors and we'll haul it inside."

There was, indeed, a lawn of lush grass, sparkling with an early dew and perfectly square and green and level as a billiard table. I looked around for bicycles but in the darkness couldn't see any. Hanging on the eave over the porch was a small banner painted in thin blue letters: WELCOME HOME EDGAR!!

"Lana and the kids wanted to wait up to meet you," Clay said. "But it took you longer to get here than we expected. I'd guess they're asleep by now—school tomorrow, you know."

We climbed up on the wraparound porch and the first thing I noticed was that there were two front doors instead of one. The doors were identical, spaced about five feet apart. What did I know about houses? I figured one of them was for coming in and the other for going out. We entered through the door on the left and came into a large dim family room with overstuffed couches and shelves lined with books and plants, walls crowded with pictures: drooling babies, toddlers in plastic swimming pools, happy couples getting married, old people trussed up in suits and high-necked dresses, staring grimly into the camera. The house was glutted with knickknacks of every description: ceramic figurines and trinkets made of brass and a collection of tiny silver bells and crystal bowls and in the far corner a grandfather clock with a pendulum swinging smugly inside its glass belly.

God help me, but the first thing that went through little Edgar's mind was this: *So many things to steal.*

"You tired?" Clay whispered.

I shrugged. I felt like I might never sleep again.

"Are you hungry? Should I scare up something to eat?"

"I'm okay," I said. I hadn't eaten anything since yesterday and the mention of food made my throat fill up with saliva so that I had to swallow constantly.

Clay stood back and gave me an appraising look. "Bet you could use a sandwich. Come on in the kitchen and we'll get some grub."

After we ate—I had two turkey sandwiches and nearly finished a bag of potato chips by myself—Clay showed me around the house a little. Clay was made mostly of shoulder blades, kneecaps and ribs, and when he walked his boots clapped loudly on the wood floor. He told me the house was built by his great grandfather, a polygamist. "He had two wives, is what that means. Used to be common thing back in the old days, some had ten, even twenty wives, but they quit it a long time ago." Clay laughed. "Now we only get one, which is probably best for everybody."

I didn't say so, but it seemed that having an alternate wife or mother, a backup in case something happened to the first, wasn't such a bad idea.

Clay showed me how the house was almost two houses in one, separated by a wall down the middle, the two halves perfectly identical, each the mirror of the other, each with a downstairs and upstairs, a house with four chambers, he said, sort of like a heart. There was one small door at the base of the stairs that led from one side to the other, a door through which the polygamist husband used to pass back and forth from family to family, wife to wife. The two families didn't mix very much, Clay said, because the one wife didn't much care for the other.

The door, which had always been called "the portal," was narrow and low enough for Clay to have to duck, and when we passed through it was like we were passing from one world into another. On one side was a quiet, clean family room that smelled like lemon and incense, and on the other, a combination of smells and sounds that reminded me, in an odd way, of St. Divine's. The only illumination in the room came from two large aquariums, humming and gurgling and glowing with an amazing blue light, like pieces of a noonday sky caught in a box. Multicolored fish darted and dove, glinting in the water like tumbling coins. All around the room were cages and boxes and I could hear the shuffling of small bodies in sawdust, the squeaking of rodents, the rustling of wings. It smelled like wet newspaper, like alfalfa pellets, like urine, like feathers and fur. It smelled musty and rich and ammonial—it smelled *animal*.

"This part of the house we call 'the zoo,'" Clay said. Under our feet was an expansive oriental rug that glowed like a garden of exotic flowers.

"*Chingada puta!*" I heard somebody say.

I noticed Clay wince a little. He pointed to a large, dome-shaped cage, covered with a bedsheet. "That was Abelardo, one of the parrots. He only speaks Spanish."

"A bird said that?" I asked. This was getting stranger by the moment.

"We've got seven parrots in all," Clay said. "Some talk more than others. We also have some parakeets, a couple guinea pigs, I don't know how many dozen gerbils, some kangaroo mice and a rat named Keith. And that's just inside. We'll have Brayton introduce you to all the animals tomorrow. Right now, why don't we get you to bed."

I followed Clay to the top of the stairs, where he showed me how he had knocked out the wall to create another passageway, one more portal, to join the two upstairs sides of the house, creating one long hallway on the second floor. The doorway Clay had built was hung with a few strands of wooden beads and Clay brushed his hands along them so that they swung lazily, clicking together.

"Lana hung these things. For the life of me I still haven't figured out what the point of 'em is."

He quietly opened a door to our right and came out with a paper bag from which he took a new pair of pajamas, still in the plastic, and a whole package full of new underwear along with a toothbrush, my own bar of soap and bottle of shampoo. He explained that I would have to share a room with Brayton for awhile because the guest bedroom was being used by a woman named Trong, who needed a place to stay while she waited for the rest of her family to arrive from Cambodia.

I brushed my teeth, slipped into my new pajamas, and Clay helped me up onto the top bunk in the dark bedroom. Below me, a boy, my new roommate, my new brother, rolled over and grumbled in his sleep.

"That's Brayton," Clay said. "He moved to the bottom bunk because he thought you might want the top one. We've been working with him on being more charitable. That was his charitable act for the week."

Compared to the bunks at Willie Sherman, it was like heaven: the mattress was thick and soft and the sheets were fresh with the barest scent of soap. Clay put one of his big hands on my chest and gave me a light pat. "You okay?" he said.

I tried to tell him I felt fine but my throat caught and I bit down on the words because I knew if I opened my mouth again I might, for reasons I couldn't really understand, begin to weep.

Before he left he said, "Anything you need, you let us know. You sleep tight and we'll get you introduced to everybody tomorrow. We're real happy to have you, Edgar."

For a long time Edgar lay in the darkness, listening to the boy below him tossing and snorting in his sleep and the night-jungle sounds from downstairs. This was not at all what he had expected. But he would take it, yes he would.

THE MADSENS

I WOKE UP to find a little boy hovering over me, his face suspended in a white haze of early morning sunshine. I blinked to get everything in focus and the boy, who had thick brown hair smoothed down over his forehead, looked me over warily.

"You're Apache?" was the first thing he said to me. He was short, thick in the chest, and had a certain hangdog look to him that made you want to give him a hug, tell him to buck up, everything would be all right. He had a round face and a little nub of a chin like half of a rubber ball.

I nodded, propped myself up on my elbow. The room, I could see now, was painted yellow, which made it seem as bright as the sun itself. Glossy posters of classic cars and astronomical formations ricocheted light around the room. I hoped the kid wasn't here to tell me to get up because I didn't want to ever leave this soft and wonderful bed.

"Among Mexican slave owners the Apache were prized above all others," he said. "It didn't matter if they were beat up or starved or abused, they always cost the most because they could tolerate anything, could outlive anybody. Did you know that?"

"No," I said.

"General Crook—you ever heard of him?—called them the lions of the human race." He frowned a little. "You don't look very tough to me."

"I'm not," I said.

"These are all facts, you know. The Apaches disemboweled—that means to cut the stomach open so the guts spill out—their enemies, scalped them alive, poked out their eyeballs with sticks, cut off their, you know, private regions. They liked to bury people in anthills and smear their faces with honey. Sometimes marmalade, if they had it."

"I've only done some of that," I said, smiling. The color drained out of the boy's face, but he stood his ground.

"What's your name?" I said. I knew that Clay had told me the night before, but there was too much to take in at once. All I could remember was that somewhere in the house was a rat named Keith and a woman named Trong.

"Brain," said the boy.

"Brain?" I said.

"It's not my *real* name," he said. "But that's what everybody calls me."

"I'm Edgar," I said.

"I'm aware of that," said Brain.

"How old are you?"

"Seven. But I'm smart for my age. I read a lot. I go to the library every day. I have a set of *Britannica*s, which I prefer to read on the toilet." He walked to the far side of the room and pulled open a narrow door, which revealed a small bathroom with a commode and a sink. Right next to the toilet, there was indeed a row of shiny books on a shelf, their slick covers glistening red as wet blood.

"Please don't touch them," he said. "I'm sure you know about germs."

Brain informed me that breakfast was on the table, if I was interested. "Waffles with peaches and cream," he said. "That's what we have whenever we get a new guest."

Regretfully, I got out of bed and followed Brain down to the zoo, where the animals were putting up a real racket—the gerbils and mice spinning on their exercise wheels, the parrots chatting nonsense with one another—and through the narrow door to the other side. How can I explain the wondrousness of walking barefoot across carpet for the first time? Right then I didn't care about getting my own bicycle or free ice cream. Standing on that carpet in my new pajamas with the smell of waffles in the air—what else could I possibly need?

In the kitchen, I was introduced to my new mother, Lana, who gathered me into the folds of her terry cloth robe, hugging and kissing me on the forehead and telling me how long they had waited for this day, how pleased they were to have me. She locked her arms around me and delivered such a strong, heartfelt hug that it nearly took the air out of me.

At the table sat my new teenage sister, Sunny, a miniature version of Lana: they both had the same pale skin, so delicate it looked as if a pinch would crumble it, and long, ash-blond hair parted in the middle, like the two panels of a curtain. Sunny slumped in her chair, her eyes showing a half-lidded look of disdain. She glared at me flatly for a second and then turned her gaze toward the large bay window, where hummingbirds hovered and dove around a feeder. Suddenly I felt ridiculous in my new red pajamas, with my wild bed hair and my I'm-so-happy-I-could-die grin. I made a grab for my crotch but was able to stop my hand at the last minute.

"Sunny," said Lana, "the least you can do is say hello."

Without looking at me or even turning my way, Sunny said, "*Hello*. Nice to meet you."

Lana sighed, stacked my plate high with waffles and scrambled eggs. She said, "Brain, are you being nice to Edgar?"

"Not really," Brain said.

I began to eat, shoveling the food in, my fork gripped in my hand like a weapon. I could not seem to stop myself, even with Brain and Sunny watching me, hardly touching their own food. Lana flitted around me, pouring orange juice and milk, replacing waffles as they disappeared, ignoring her own children completely. She told me that Clay had brought my trunk in, that he would help me get it up the stairs after he got home from work.

While she talked, I ate like a hog at a trough—not only because I was famished but because it gave me something to do. I didn't know what to say or how to act, so I ate until I could not force another forkful down my throat.

"We'll have to introduce you to Trong before too long," Lana said. "She's around here somewhere."

"She doesn't speak English," Brain said. "And all she eats is rice and some fish paste that makes the house stink. I've never once seen her take a shower."

"Brain," Lana said.

"I take showers," I said.

"Of course you do," Lana said. "I guess Brain isn't old enough to understand that different people of different cultures do things differently. We're all different."

"Only most of us don't eat fish paste and forget to wash up after ourselves," Brain said. "Plus, she has a mustache."

Sunny sighed through her teeth. "I've got to get to school." She put on a green windbreaker, picked up a stack of books, swung her hair in a wide, slicing arc and marched out the front door. As she went, I couldn't help but notice how her tight jeans gripped her behind like two hands.

Lana gave me another quick hug. "I've got to get going, too. I'm sorry this is so rushed, Edgar, but tonight we'll get properly acquainted. I told Brain he could stay home from school today and show you around, help get you settled. He says he isn't learning anything at school anyway."

Brain shook his head in disgust. He said, "The second grade."

Later, after I'd dug some clothes out of my trunk and Brain had spent a half an hour or so on the toilet reading his *Britannica*s (he was currently becoming versed in West Indian trade routes and the internal combustion process) he took me out into the backyard, which was enormous: two and a half acres fenced with barbed wire. There was a small barn, a split-rail corral, a large, elaborate chicken coop filled with chickens of all colors, an old yellow train car and rows and rows of what looked like rabbit hutches. A shaggy patch pony stood with its chest against the fence, asleep on its feet, and next to it a blue-gray cat stretched out in an empty tin water trough.

The Madsens lived on the outskirts of town, where the ostentatious polygamist houses with deep, Midwestern porches and filigreed balconets were interspersed with newer, single-level ranchers of clapboard or brick. All of the houses hedged up close to the dirt road with their acreages stretching out behind. To the north the neighbors kept an immaculate flower and herb garden with a greenhouse and a fishpond, and to the south a labyrinthine puzzle of galvanized stock tanks, pickup shells, brush hogs, PVC pipe, pallets of cement block and gooseneck hay trailers clustered around a couple of homemade Quonset huts. Beyond each fenced-in property was raw, untouched scrubland: mesquite and cedar and occasional outcroppings of Navajo sandstone.

I followed Brain out around the barn and there was a small brown woman sitting in the sun, her back against the bright red planks, so thin that she looked like she had been carved out of a shadow.

"There's Trong," Brain said. "She'll probably give you the willies."

Trong smiled at us—a flash of white—and went back to some kind of sewing, her small hands moving secretly in her lap.

"Why's she here?" I said, trying to hold off the neighbor's spotted cow dog, who had run up and was nosing me vigorously between the legs.

Brain shrugged. "She needed somewhere to stay for awhile. We'll take in just about anybody." He looked up at me, then back at the anthill he was kicking apart with the toe of his tennis shoe. "It's my mother that finds all these people. Before Trong there was an exchange student from Syria, his name was Ibrahim. All he wanted to do was play Ping-Pong. He smelled funny too. For a month and a half we had a whole wetback family living with us. They took over the whole upstairs and I had to sleep downstairs with the parrots yelling in Spanish all night."

"Can I ask you something?" I said.

"You *may*," he said.

"I don't smell, do I?"

He gave me a sniff. "You don't smell bad," he said, "but you don't smell good, either."

With the bored air of a tour guide, he showed me the backyard and all the animals in it. He explained that his mother worked down at the State Wildlife Office, had a doctorate in zoology and took in any animal that any stranger wanted to dump off on them. So, along with the chickens, a dried-up milk cow, a couple of goats and a whole population of farm cats, there was a three-legged armadillo named Otis, a deaf mule named Dorothy and a turkey buzzard by the name of Doug. The one species of animal the Madsens didn't have was a dog.

"My dad hates all these animals," Brain said. "So do our neighbors. That's why we name the animals after them. Every time we get a new animal, we name it after somebody on this street. Mostly, they're just old people who complain a lot."

Across the way, Dorothy let loose an earsplitting honk as if to affirm what had just been said. We stood in front of Doug's pen, watching the big vulture preen on his perch, slump-shouldered and solemn, and Brain explained that Doug had some kind of ear infection that had permanently disrupted his equilibrium, making it impossible for him to fly. Somebody had found him flopping around out by the cement plant and brought him in because everybody knew that Lana Madsen would take any animal of any kind, even a spraddle-legged old vulture.

"He eats dog food," Brain said. "Alpo. Anything else he turns up his nose."

I told Brain about Cecil, my friend, who used to play tricks on the vultures down in Arizona, play dead and then scare the daylights out of them when they swooped in close.

Brain eyed me skeptically. "Just because they eat dead things doesn't mean they're stupid. They're smarter than you think."

"Not *that* smart," I said, with the tone of someone who knows what they're talking about. I looked back at the house. "Hey, this house has two back doors, just like in front."

"So what?" Brain said. "Anyway, I was going to tell you about the worst pet we ever had, a monkey named Omar. He belonged to the wetback family, and when they disappeared without even saying thank you to anybody, they left their monkey. A spider monkey, if you know what that is."

"You had a monkey?" I said. The last time I had ever seen a monkey was King Kong night at Willie Sherman, the same night I slipped through the window of the Thomas household with my pockets full of marbles. After the uproar over the movie that night, Mrs. Theodore decided she'd had enough with all the laughing and shenanigans and threw the film reels onto the trash heap the next day. So I had only gotten to see the first fifteen minutes of it—I never found out what had happened to the big monkey.

"He was a bully, that monkey," Brain said. "My mom stretched a wire between those two big trees there and put him on a pulley leash so he could roam all over the place. He'd sit up in one of the trees all day long, in the same spot, waiting for one of the neighbor's dogs to forget and wander underneath. Then he'd drop out of the sky like a kamikaze and land right on top of the dog, biting him on the neck and riding him around. My mom said Omar was just playing, that's what monkeys do. Well tell that to the dog."

Brain kicked at an old bale of hay, exasperated.

"I was afraid of him too, this was a couple of years ago when I was pretty little, so I decided to make friends with him. I took some Smarties and put some on the ground for him. He ate them up really fast and then sat there holding his little wrinkled hand out, like he was waiting for his change at the grocery store."

"What are Smarties?" I said.

"Candy?" Brain said. "You know what that is?"

"I know what Dum Dums are."

Brain squinted at me. "Is that supposed to be a joke?"

He continued, "I gave him some more *Smarties* and the next thing I knew he crawled up on me and was hugging me around the neck, giving me these little kisses. His breath smelled like garbage but I gave him the candy until it was all gone. When I tried to set him down, he bit me on the forehead"—Brain pointed to a faint puckered scar above his left eye—"and then he crawled back into my lap like we were best friends again, giving me more hugs and sticking his fingers into my pockets. I sat there for an *hour,* yelling for my mom, my dad, anybody, but our neighbor over there, Sister Brindle—that's who the donkey's named after—came out of her house and told me to keep it down, she was trying to watch *The Price Is Right*. Well I got mad and gave Omar a slap on the head and made a break for it. He bit me pretty good on my behind, but I got away. My mom was in Seattle at some conference and my dad said it was my decision about what to do about Omar. 'Put him to sleep,' I said. He was just going to keep biting people and dogs. I had to go get three shots at the doctor's office, which was worse than getting bit. The doctor says, 'So what happened to you?' and I say 'Got bit by a monkey' and everybody laughs."

"So you killed the monkey?" I said.

"*I* didn't kill him. My dad called up Marvin Johnson, some kid in our ward who likes to shoot things. He came by in his pickup and took Omar out to the desert. I heard Marvin tell somebody that he gave Omar a ten-second head start. Omar didn't deserve it, though. He was a bad monkey."

Brain smiled. "We told my mom that we took him up to the zoo in Salt Lake. Don't tell her or she'd shoot us all."

Brain showed me how to feed and water each animal—he said I was going to have to learn to "earn my keep"—and then went and sprayed the chickens with a hose while I transferred fifty-pound bags of alfalfa pellets from the back of an old horse trailer to the shed where the hay and oats were stacked. I heaved the last bag onto the pile and collapsed on it. There had been only fifteen bags but it felt as if my arms had been yanked out of their sockets.

Brain continued to spray the chickens, who squawked and flapped their wings in great goggle-eyed alarm.

"Why are you doing that?" I called out to him.

Brain yelled back, "Because chickens hate water!"

He eventually turned off the hose and came to stand in the doorway. "I wish I could have helped you here, but that's what I get for being small." He sat down next to me and folded his hands in his lap in a studied, formal way. "I can tell you a couple of things that will make it easier on you here. First of all, don't touch any of my things. Second, don't pay any attention to my sister. She's on medication for some kind of condition she has, her brain has problems. Third, don't worry if it seems like my parents don't talk to each other much. They say they're working things out. About what, I don't know. Fourth, when you eat, hold your fork like a regular person."

"Are other Mormons like your family?" I said.

"Oh no, no," Brain shook his head. "They're a lot worse."

He waved his hand at the dust motes that dove and circled in the light coming through the gaps between the wood slats. He edged closer to me and whispered, "Do you know anything about sexual intercourse?"

"No," I said.

"Dang," said Brain.

I stepped outside the barn and tried to steer Brain in the direction of the house; I wanted to get back in there, take off my shoes and walk around on the carpet some more.

"There's one other thing you should know," Brain said when we got to the back door. "Three years ago my little brother Dean died. He was two when it happened. He's the reason all these animals are here. He's why Trong's here, he's why you're here. He's the reason for everything."

SETTLING IN

A MOTHER, A FATHER, a sister, a brother, a soft bed, ten new pairs of new underwear, three square meals a day with snacks in between—Edgar, for once in his life, had everything he needed. And more. The Madsens bought me two new pairs of Keds, a whole wardrobe full of flashy polyester shirts and tight-fitting pants, a Sunday outfit with a white shirt, tie and platform shoes, even a wristwatch that had a picture of a flaming race car on its face. About two weeks after I arrived from Willie Sherman, I asked Brain if he had a bicycle; I hadn't seen one around the house. The next day Clay brought home a chopper-style two-wheeler with a banana seat and multicolored tassels on the handgrips. The bike was painted a speckled, metallic gold and I believed, for awhile, that it *was* gold—only a metal of great worth could have sparkled with such brilliance.

"Saw this at a garage sale the Willards are having," Clay said. "Thought maybe Edgar could put it to some use."

With everybody out on the porch watching, I wobbled down the hill, lost control, veered off into an irrigation ditch and ended up tangled in the Christensens' barbed-wire fence. I unhooked my shirt, quickly looked the bicycle over to make sure that it hadn't been

scratched or marred, and came up grinning like a wild man: Edgar
had his bike.

And the food. Who could have imagined such food? Aside from
the late night omelets and pancakes at truck stops with Barry, I had
no memory of ever eating a meal that was not cooked by some
underpaid worker and served on a tray. Lana liked to make
casseroles—tuna casserole, hamburger casserole, broccoli and potato
casserole—and every time I could, all by myself, eat half the pan.
Sometimes when no one else was around, I would pick through the
cupboards and pantry and refrigerator and sample whatever I might
come across: a hard-boiled egg or two, a handful of chocolate chips
from a plastic bag in the pantry, a sleeve of soda crackers, a family-
sized tub of Dream Whip, maybe a cold piece of Shake 'n Bake
chicken. Once I'd had enough I'd wash it all down with a stiff swig
of pickle water.

And ice cream! Who needed an ice cream truck when there was
all the ice cream you could ever eat, right there in the freezer?

I loved the long days when everyone was at school or work and it
was just Trong, me and the animals haunting the house. It was very
hard for me not to steal anything; the house was so full of *stuff*: a ham
radio in the basement, stacks of magazines, records and church
books, a chess set made of ivory and obsidian, trophies, tools of all
kinds, jewelry, old toys and sports equipment and board games. Like
an archaeologist at the site of a lost civilization, I discovered things I
never knew existed: wheat grinders and hair dryers and douche bags,
castanets and BB guns, life-size dummies of biblical figures, tampons
and soldering irons, doodads and thingamajigs without name or
apparent purpose, all of it out in the open, waiting to be taken. I
searched every nook and cranny, every drawer and closet and cubby-
hole. In the attic I rifled through the boxes of photos and keepsakes
and Christmas decorations. I took the lacy, satiny things out of
Sunny's drawers and piled them on top of me while I lay on her bed,
pressing her pastel-colored underthings to my face. Like a dog, I
sniffed around that house for days. How good everything smelled! I

had come from an olfactory hell—the ammoniac smell of urine, the stench of the shithouses rising up like deadly fog on hot summer days, the odor of sweaty towels and disinfectant and moldy mattresses and floor wax, and the dusty smell of history blowing out of the heater vents—and had managed to fall into a fragrant paradise: clean laundry appearing in my drawers as if by magic, fresh bread in the kitchen, a bathroom that breathed a fine mist of lavender and lemon and perfume, comforters and pillows that smelled like a sharp winter morning.

Those carefree days of eating and snooping didn't last long, however. After two weeks Lana decided that I had "acclimated" myself well enough, it was time for me to go to school. I told her I would be more than happy to stay home and feed the animals and watch the soap operas on TV and make sure Trong stayed away from the chicken coop (she had once, as a favor to the family, butchered two of the chickens, none of whom were ever to be eaten, and cooked them up with ginger and hot pepper sauce). But Lana insisted that I start school—she was most concerned, she said, about my becoming a contributing member of the community. Lana was a political activist of sorts, she belonged to various clubs and societies—Audubon and the Sierra Club—and worked for the John Swavely for Congress campaign. John Swavely was a Democrat, which meant he didn't have a shadow of a chance in Richland or anywhere else in Utah, but Lana faithfully attended the campaign meetings and kept *John Swavely for Congress* paraphernalia all over the house.

"School is not about figures and conjugating verbs," she told me. "It's learning how to get along with your fellow man, it's all about becoming a social animal. Too bad Brain hasn't figured that out yet."

After walking the halls and enduring the stares of the boys and girls I passed, I understood right away that Richland High would be no different from Willie Sherman. It was much nicer: there was a football field with grass so green it looked artificial; an asphalt parking lot full of pickup trucks and Volkswagen Bugs and old muscle cars painted with threatening colors; a rubber jogging track, one of only three, it was proclaimed loudly and often, in the entire state of Utah; a large concrete classroom building with an enormous buck-toothed beaver painted on the outside wall of the gymnasium. The beaver was about fifteen feet tall, smiling goofily and wielding a large ax. Underneath the beaver's feet large cartoon letters proclaimed: BEAVERS ALL THE WAY!!!

On my very first day at Richland High I found myself sitting alone at an empty table in the cafeteria, staring at my tray of food: corn dog, corn, purple Jell-O, milk. I had tried to make things go differently, to alter my destiny: my tray held formally in front of me, I boldly sat down next to a trio of rather homely girls who were hunched over their food in such a secretive way they might have been hatching a murder plot. They all looked over at me and one of them, who wore makeup in a way that made me think of a clown, turned and said, "That seat is saved." I had never heard this expression before, but it seemed to carry the weight of law. My seat was saved! What choice did I have but to find an empty table where—I hoped—none of the seats had been saved. All alone with my corn dog, I watched everything around me very carefully: the cafeteria looked and smelled and sounded just like the cafeteria at Willie Sherman. There was no difference except that the kids, in general, were better dressed, and the graffiti scratched into the tables was not nearly as interesting.

I tried very hard not to feel sorry for myself. I had a bike and a family and no one had tried to hurt me yet. I decided then and there, amid the roar of that lunchroom, that when the time came for somebody to try and hurt me, I would be ready.

It took four days, much longer than I had expected. In the locker room before gym class a kid named Clint began to harass me, calling me "chief" and "Nancy" and yanking on my hair, asking why I did-n't get a regular haircut, was I really some kind of Indian? Did I live in *tee*-pee? I smiled and did my best to ignore Clint but it was clear he wasn't going to give up. Eventually he recruited another boy to help him and they pulled me down to the cold tiled floor and Clint straddled my chest while the other boy held my arms behind my head.

"Don't hurt me, please," I said. I figured it couldn't hurt to ask.

"We're not going to hurt you, Nancy!" Clint said. Clint was covered with pink freckles, had the squat build of a wrestler, and wore braces. Braces, now this was a novelty. I had seen other anglo kids walking around with metal in their mouths, some of them even had straps and wires wrapped around their heads, but this was the first time I was able to get a close look at this mess of crisscrossing metal full of food bits and tooth-scum all strung together with rubber bands. Clint's mouth scared me much more than he himself ever could.

Resting all his weight on my chest, Clint struck a thoughtful pose. "Hmm. I guess we'll give you the typewriter. Do you know what the typewriter is, Geronimo?"

I tried to explain that I had a typewriter of my very own, a Hermes Jubilee 2000, in fact, but Clint didn't seem interested. He grabbed both my ears and twisted them, making a ratcheting mechanical noise deep in his throat. "See?" he said. "I'm feeding in the paper. Get it? Typewriter?"

He commenced tapping on my chest with the ends of his blunt fingers, doing a pretty good imitation of typewriter keys being struck: *tik-tik-tak-tak-tik-tik-tak-tak* with his tongue. Every once in awhile, he would call out *ding!*—the sound of the carriage reaching its end—and would give me a solid slap on the face as if to return the carriage to its proper position. It did seem that Clint knew his way around a typewriter.

It was excruciating, this tapping on my chest, a very painful kind of tickling, and I squirmed and kicked, but Clint was a big boy and Clint's accomplice, who I didn't get a good look at, held my wrists with a solid grip. Clint began to type harder, his fingers bruising my chest like little ball-peen hammers, and the slaps he was giving me got harder as well, so that I could feel my left eye begin to swell. I looked up at Clint's homely face and knew, despite the terrifying aspect of his mouth, that he could not really hurt me. Immediately, I relaxed, stopped fighting it, which made Clint type and slap all that much harder.

He began to narrate the letter he was typing. It was a love letter, he said, to my mother. "Dear Squaw," he typed, his fingers drilling into my chest with each word. "Thank you for the top-notch blow job you gave me behind the dumpster last night. I appreciate it very much." The boy holding my wrists began to cackle and I felt his grip loosen. Clint continued, "I know I am hung like a mule, which can make it difficult for some people, but you did your best."

The kid behind me choked with laughter and I yanked both wrists free at the same time, bringing the heel of my hand up against Clint's snubby nose with all the force I could muster. He fell straight backwards like a tipped-over statue and I was on top of him, just as he had been on top of me a second before. I delivered five or six punches to his face, aiming for those braces with each shot, his head ringing out each time with a hollow *tup* against the tile floor. Every time I hit him he made a surprised, high-pitched squeaking noise— *heek! heek! heek!*—which sounded very much like the sound Keith the Rat would make whenever he got agitated or hungry. By now there were a dozen boys standing around, but none of them came after me as I might have expected. Clint lay there quiet for a moment, both hands pressed over his bloody face, and then said, with an air of almost cheerful resignation, "Would you take a look at this!"

Somebody went to get Coach Miller, who wore a tight green T-shirt and very small gym shorts which were barely capable of containing his genitals.

"Well," Clint gargled, "I think my fucking nose is busted."

"No swearing," Coach Miller said.

Coach Miller took a look at Clint's nose, which was now bleeding freely down the sides of his face, and decided that it wasn't broken, but sprained. "People don't think there could be such a thing as a sprained nose, but that's where they're wrong," Coach Miller paused in his ministrations to inform us. Once he had Clint on his feet with

a towel pressed against his face, he asked what had happened. I knew
things looked bad: Clint lying on the floor all bloody, his lips turned
to hamburger on those braces, me standing over him. I didn't even
try to explain myself, I knew it would do no good, but in the end I
was saved by a tattletale. Some chubby kid with an out-of-control
cowlick and the complexion of a salami piped up with the entire
story, how Clint had harassed me, then had given me the typewriter
with the help of Paul Halloway—he pointed at Paul Halloway with a
dramatic flair, like a lawyer in a courtroom—and how Clint made
some dirty comments about my mother, which made me go wild
and punch Clint out, even while he was down I kept punching,
which was understandable after the things he had said about my
mother, things having to do with oral intercourse. The kid went on
and on until Coach Miller said, "Do me a favor, Jeremy, and shut
your piehole?"

There was one difference, I would come to learn, between white
kids and Indians. Among white kids there are tattletales everywhere.
Indians? An Indian wouldn't tattle to save his own mother. Indians,
over the years, have learned the value of keeping their mouths shut.

Coach Miller had heard enough from the tattletale and decided
that Clint had got what he deserved. "You mess with somebody"—
he looked around at all the boys, staring each of them in the eye,
keeping his gaze on Paul Halloway for the longest time—"and you
might just get messed with yourself. You think somebody's easy
pickin's, maybe they're scrawny or slow in the head or what have
you"—here he put his hand on my shoulder—"but they might just
have it in 'em to whip your butt. Remember that next time you
want to pick on somebody."

We all looked at Clint. I felt sorry for him standing there with his
sprained nose and hamburger lips and the bloody towel jammed into
his face. He didn't seem to want to hold a grudge. He came over to
me and gave me a slap on the back. "I shoudda nebber said anything
about your buther," he said. "Dat's where I went wrong."

"My mother's dead," I told him.

He waggled his chin sadly. "Dat's edzactly what I'm togging about."

Something like justice seemed to have occurred and I was confused by it. Just to be safe, for the rest of PE I hung as close to Coach Miller as I could, but nobody came after me, there was no attempt at retribution. Clint even played volleyball on my team, able to use only one arm because his other one was occupied with pressing an ice pack against his face.

Later that day, back in class, everyone turned to stare at me. This was when I was still in special ed; it took them six weeks to discover that I could actually read and do a little math and write with the aid of a typewriter, which eventually landed me in the regular class with everybody else. There were eight other students in special ed, all of them boys, and a teacher, Mrs. Cuthbert, who spent twenty minutes of each hour having coffee and gossiping with the assistant principal in the teachers' lounge.

Directly in front of me sat Pendleton Rittenhouse, a fat kid who continually dug wax out of his ear and smelled it before depositing it on the hem of his shirt. I had been called retarded a few times—I knew it had to do with my damaged brain—but I was pretty certain that Pendleton, brain-damaged or not, was about as retarded as a person could get.

"You broke Clint Crosby's nose?" Pendleton said.

"Sprained it."

"What's your name?" said another kid, Kyle, who sat up front.

"Edgar."

"Somebody said you were in prison before you came here. A prison for Indians."

I shrugged. They were all looking at me. Mrs. Cuthbert was nowhere to be seen. I said, "I'm Apache. Apaches kill people sometimes."

In front of me, Pendleton Rittenhouse's eyes gleamed. He put his hand up to his mouth and did the Indian war whoop, the kind you see them do on television: *ooo-ooo-ooo-ooo-ooo*. Then everybody in the class joined in, all of them whooping it up and looking at me.

Apparently, I was a hero.

When I got home that afternoon, Sunny was sitting at the kitchen table, checking on her eye makeup with a compact mirror, which she seemed to do every two minutes or so. She looked up at me. "I heard you whipped Clint Crosby's butt."

In the month I'd lived in the same house with her, it was only the second time she'd said a word to me.

EDGAR COUNTS HIS BLESSINGS

SO BRAIN AND EDGAR struck a bargain: I would do most of his chores and he, in return, would allow me to type in his room between the hours of four-thirty and seven o'clock. I would rush through the chores—Brain would usually hang around and toss hay to Dorothy or clean the newspaper out of the parrot cages, just to make it look good—and then I would sprint back up to the room where I had my Hermes Jubilee situated on top of my trunk and try to get as much typing in as I could before dinner. Lana had offered to get me a desk (Brain had refused to let me use his, he said it would interrupt his "processes") but I came to enjoy kneeling at that trunk—the carpet was soft and easy on my knees, and whether I was typing letters to Art or Cecil or to God Himself, it always felt a little like prayer.

While I typed Brain would sit on his toilet reading his *Britannica*s and thinking his thoughts. Sometimes I would hear him give a strange little laugh, a soft *coo-hoo-hoo*—it sounded like a couple of doves had been trapped in the bathroom. Even though Brain had expressly forbidden me to touch his *Britannica*s, I had browsed through them on occasion, scanning the pictures of various species of penguins or reading up on the Corn Belt. Never once had I come across anything remotely funny.

Each week I would send a letter to both Art and Cecil, usually four or five pages of unimaginably boring descriptions of the life I led. In the letters to Cecil, especially, I included every detail of my new life, the chairs and the carpets and the lawns. I told him about the savory casseroles, the pies, the hamburgers cooked on a grill, the ice cream in big vats in a freezer out in the garage; I described for him the thickness and softness of my mattress, the fluffiness of my pillows (two pillows!), the underwear and tube socks, all bleached white, in such numbers that I could not wear all of them in two weeks' time; I described for him every piece of clothing I owned, their color and cut, and the 22-inch TV and the big stereo and the pool table in the basement. I told him all about the grand-father clock and the animals. I wrote to him about the hall bath-room, which to me seemed like an attempt to create an earthly version of the Celestial Kingdom, the Mormon version of heaven:

> The hall bathroom is the best one. It has pink carpet all over the floor and little soaps like roses and naked babies on the wallpaper. Smells like flowers, but better. There is carpet ON TOP of the toi-let, right on the lid, and the seat is padded like you're sitting on a couch! I stay in there as long as I want until somebody tells me it's time to come out.
>
> Also, it's very CLEAN here.

Sometimes I went overboard. I told Cecil that, along with a bike, I had my very own Appaloosa stallion, and a go-cart that shot fire out of its tailpipe. I told him I had a girlfriend named Cynthia who made me cupcakes and wrote love notes to me on perfumed paper. I explained that, in Cecil's absence, I had become quite a basketball player and the high school coach wanted me to try out for the team because of my deadly outside shot.

There is also this girl I live with, I wrote to Cecil. *I see her nipples almost every day.*

They were small lies, but they filled me with shame: I wanted to do the right thing, to keep the commandments, and most of all, I didn't want God to find any good reason to send me back to Willie Sherman.

"You lie, you steal, you take the Lord's name in vain," Brother Hughes, our Sunday school teacher, had explained to us one Sabbath morning, "and you might as well be stabbing Jesus right in the heart." I didn't like the idea that God might not continue to look favorably on me, that he might allow the ghosts to start plaguing me again. And I didn't want to stab anyone in the heart, much less Jesus, the savior of the world.

One of the things I did to help me feel a little less guilty was sending, in every letter to Cecil, a five or a ten from the wad Art had given me; I knew his uncle never gave him any money and I figured he could use it to stock up on Dum Dums.

Brain, who I annoyed to no end, could not understand my typing at all.

"It's a waste of time," he said. "You're not *learning* anything."

"I'm writing letters to my friends."

"Good friends!" he scoffed. "They never write back, do they?" He was right; I'd been in Utah for over six months and hadn't heard from Art or Cecil. I never really expected anything from Art; he'd only ever written me that one postcard, after all, but I wondered about Cecil. He'd written me twice when I was at Willie Sherman: a couple of brief notes in his blocky handwriting telling me that the Nevada Juvenile Detention Center was not a very good place, but anything was better than Willie Sherman.

"How many friends do *you* have?" I asked Brain, and he immediately fell silent. We were in bed, in the dark. It was a frosty February night, the baseboard heaters ticking and shuddering like little mechanical beasts settling into sleep. Brain rarely spoke to me outside the bedroom, but there were nights when he was feeling generous or restless and we would talk. Sometimes we talked for hours; I asked a lot of questions and Brain usually had answers. If he didn't he would wake up the next morning and go to his *Britannica*s to find the answers. On those rare occasions when I would give him a few

details about my life at St. Divine's and Willie Sherman he would listen in skeptical silence.

"I have one friend," Brain said. "Gordon Dickey."

"Dickey!" I said.

"He's my best friend."

"How come he never comes over here?"

I could hear Brain turn over and conduct a small wrestling match
with his blanket; he sometimes fought with his bedcovers as if they
had betrayed him in a fundamental way.

"You want to know why he doesn't come over here? He's afraid
of Trong, that's why. One day he was over here and she creeped him
out with that look she gives you out of the side of her eyes. Sunny
has all kinds of friends, but how come you hardly ever see any of
them over here? Weird people and animals all over the place, that's
why. There you are in the backyard playing with your friend and a
vulture's watching you. It's impossible!"

The beam of headlights lit up the frost on the window, throwing rippling permutations of light on the far wall. We listened to Clay's truck
move slowly over the crackling gravel of the driveway, idle for a
moment, and then rattle into silence. Clay never seemed to get home
before it was dark, and often, like tonight, he would get home well after
everyone had gone to bed. I saw him so rarely that he hardly seemed
part of the household. Whenever he saw me he would shake my hand
as if we were perfect strangers and ask me how things were going.

Edgar always answered with the old standby: "Fine."

"And anyway, back to our original subject, most of that typing
you do is just typing to nobody in particular, don't think I don't read
it all, you leave it lying around and this *is* my room. And then there's
this stuff you're typing to God. You think God is going to read it?
Give me a break."

"Those are my prayers," I said. "We're supposed to pray every day."

"Yes," Brain said. "But a prayer is something you *say,* not write. You're
supposed to *talk* to God. What, you think you can just lay out those
pages and God's going to look down and read them? Good luck!"

In fact, that's exactly what I had done—it never occurred to me that God might be able to hear prayers but would not be able to read them (maybe, I wondered, he couldn't see through the roof of the house?). Usually, my prayers did not go more than one page and I would simply set down that page next to my Hermes Jubilee so God could have a good look at it if He wanted. In church, we had been taught that before we started asking for favors, we should first list all the things we were thankful for—they called it counting your blessings. They even had a song:

> *Count your many blessings*
> *Name them one by one*
> *Count your many blessings*
> *See what God has done*

So every day I whipped out a new prayer and left it next to the typewriter for God to read.

Dear God,

Thank you for getting me out of Willie Sherman. Thank you for the Madsens and for my bed and this house and for the carpet and all my clothes. Thank you for the televisions and the cop shows. Thank you for peach pie. Thank you for keeping Dr. Pinkley and the ghosts away. Thank you for potato chip casserole. Thank you for the new toothpaste which tastes better than the blue kind. Thank you for my bike it has a loose chain and a tire that keeps getting flat. What else? I'm thinking about it. Thank you for the model spaceship I got for Christmas. Brain put it together.

Please bless Art. And bless Cecil in Nevada until he gets out of the detention center and I can see him. Bless Uncle Julius who might be dead already. Bless Maria and Raymond and the Elders. I hope you'll help me find the mailman. Please bless my mother who should be up there. Maybe Grandma Paul too but I doubt it.

Bless the animals especially the gerbils who won't stop dying. I'm sorry for stealing and the violence on Clint Crosby and for bad thoughts. I'm working on it please believe me.

IN THE NAME OF OUR SAVIOR
AND LORD JESUS CHRIST, AMEN.
From Edgar P. Mint

Beneath me, Brain sighed. "It probably doesn't matter. Prayers don't really do anything anyway. We can say prayers all day long and nothing important will ever happen. Don't tell anybody I said that though."

"I think maybe you're wrong," I said.

"If you knew anything at all, then maybe I would take your opinion into consideration," Brain said. "Do you have anything you want to ask me? I think I'm about ready to go to sleep."

I was silent for a moment. "I'd like you to tell me where Nevada is."

"You want me to tell you where Nevada is?" Brain said, his voice rising ominously. "You really want me to tell you the location of Nevada?"

I didn't answer him; I knew it was best to wait out Brain and his moments of aggravation.

"Have you ever heard of a map, Edgar? What do you do in school?"

Edgar bided his time: an answer would be forthcoming sooner or later.

The bunk bed shifted as Brain threw off his blankets. He got up, eased the bedroom door shut and flipped on the light. He stalked into the little bathroom and removed one of his *Britannica*s from the shelf. He placed it ceremoniously on his desk and opened it, carefully shuffling through its pages. His dark blue pajamas showed chubby astronauts cartwheeling through the outer reaches of space. Without looking up, he said, "Are you coming down here or not?"

There in the book was a picture of Nevada: a state shaped like something out of my geometry book in school. Brain had his stubby little finger digging right into the middle of it.

"I'm looking for Ely," I said. "Ely, Nevada."

"Right there," Brain said. "All you have to do is look. You've got rods and cones like the rest of us."

"Is it far away?" I said, shielding my eyes like somebody gazing out to sea on a sunny day.

"Look, that's Utah, right there, right on the border. We live in Richland. You see this thing? This means an inch equals fifty miles." He pulled a ruler off the shelf. "It's three and a half inches away. Do a little math, and you get approximately a hundred and seventy-five miles. It's all right here, I really shouldn't have to show you this. You're in *high school*."

"You told me never to touch your *Britannica*s."

"Have you ever tried the library? Have you ever thought of getting some reference material of your own?"

"I was wondering if I could get a bus to Ely."

"You can get a bus to pretty much anywhere you want, excluding overseas travel."

"How much will it cost?"

Brain looked like he was becoming nauseous. He slapped the book shut and covered his face with his hands. "Call the bus company," he said through his fingers. "Sunny can show you how to use the phone, she's the expert."

Down the hall we heard voices. Brain jumped from his chair and opened our door a crack. It was Lana and Clay talking, their voices suddenly rising, but muffled and indistinct through their closed door. Clay and Lana hardly talked during the regular hours of the day; even on the weekends, they always seemed to be zooming past each other as if they were afraid of being caught in the same place at the same time, but very often, at night, they would talk, sometimes shout, and even if Brain and I were in the middle of a very interesting conversation he would suddenly go dead quiet and I would look over the edge of my bed at him listening with his entire body, his eyes wide and searching.

Of these late night conversations I could only catch bits and pieces that I would type out on my Hermes Jubilee the next day:

> *. . . can't talk about this anymore, not one more minute . . .*
> *Will you look at me?*
> *Why? Why don't you just—why?*
> *. . . these damn animals, the smell . . .*
> *. . . listening to what I'm saying?*
> *. . . don't talk, don't talk, don't say another word . . .*

I would look over my notes, trying to divine some sense from these fragments, but it was all a mystery to me. The one time I asked Brain what they were talking about, he snapped at me in a queer, altered voice, "Why don't you mind your own lousy business."

Tonight, Brain stood on the other side of the doorframe, his ear placed directly in the opening. I got down on one knee and, just like Brain, hung my ear in the space between the door and the frame; once and for all, I wanted to figure out what all the fuss was about.

In no time at all my neck began to ache and stiffen. There was half a minute of silence before Clay said something unintelligible and then Lana said, her higher voice cutting through the closed door at the far end of the long hallway, "I've had it! What do you think this is?"

The parrots downstairs, inspired by the commotion, began a round of yapping and squawking at each other, sending the entire zoo into a frenzy of scratching and squeaking and cage-rattling.

"Touchdown!" shouted Blondie, a yellow-headed parrot who bullied the other parrots and liked to kick sunflower seeds all over the floor. "It's overtime! Overtime!"

Brain's face twisted into a frightening grimace. "One of these days I'm going to murder every one of those parrots."

Just then the door opened, the corner of it catching me on the side of the head. I howled out of surprise more than anything and fell backwards, rolling. I looked up to see Sunny standing in the doorway. She wore a striped T-shirt under which, it was clear, she was braless. Her pointed breasts swung only slightly but with a freedom that was illuminating. Her hair was pulled back into a single braid and from my vantage point on the floor I could see the hem of her panties, just an inch or so of pink, silky fabric that covered a mysterious curve of flesh.

She glared at Brain, who had taken a few steps back. Her eyes were green and luminous. She said, "What do you think you're doing, you little jerk?"

"Don't call me a jerk. And how about putting some pants on."

Sunny's nostrils flared. "I'll call you a lot worse you little piece of—" She started toward Brain as if to grab him but we heard Clay and Lana's door open, and we all froze.

"*What* is going on down there," Lana called.

Sunny stepped back into the hall. "These two are talking, keeping me awake, and look, they've got the light on!"

"All right you boys, come on out," Clay said.

Brain and I glanced at each other, waited for a moment, then stepped into the hall at the same time. Down at the far end, Clay and Lana were framed by their doorway, a soft yellow light behind them. Clay was still dressed and Lana had on her terry cloth robe. Sunny had already passed through the beads, which swung and clicked, and was standing in front of her bedroom door.

"Brain," Lana said, "explain to me this instant what you two are doing up at this hour."

"Edgar wanted me to show him where Nevada is."

"Ha!" Sunny said. "You see what I'm saying?"

"You keep your voice down, young lady," Clay warned.

"She hit Edgar with the door!" yelled Brain.

"You little shithead!" said Sunny.

Suddenly everyone was hollering at once, including the parrots, and in the midst of it all, Blondie shouted "Touchdown!" a little more jubilantly than usual. Trong had come out of her room at the other end of the hall and smiled her enigmatic smile. As suddenly as the tumult began, it quieted. We all stood outside our respective rooms, looking at each other from a distance like beasts who had just been freed from their cages and didn't know exactly what to do with themselves.

So this is what it's like, Edgar thought. *This is what it's like to be a family.*

FOR YOUNG MEN ONLY

A BRIGHT SUNDAY morning and we were all packed into a cramped, unventilated room listening to Brother Hughes reciting Book of Mormon stories. Brother Hughes had long, drooping ears that seemed to be in the process of melting off his head and stray hairs that curled out from his temples like guitar-string ends. While he spoke of great, bloody battles waged in the name of God, Edgar sat in the back near the radiator, locked in mortal battle with his own pecker.

I knew it was a serious transgression to have a hard-on in church—it was one of those sins that needed no explanation. Even worse was the procession of bad thoughts through my head—I couldn't stop them. In front of me sat Brenda Hollander, whose bra strap lay exposed on her smooth, tanned shoulder and that, by itself, was enough to keep my stubborn erection in a constant struggle to shoulder its way out from between my thighs.

I shifted in my seat, crossed my legs, yanked at my pants, quietly hummed "How Great Thou Art," anything to find a little relief. The tie I was wearing—Lana had knotted it for me—felt like a length of baling wire cinched snug around my neck. I was going on fourteen and had only now found myself subjected to the peculiar assaults of puberty; like everything else, puberty had come slow to Edgar. The wet dreams, the odd tenderness in my nipples, the sprouting hair, the numbing haze in my brain when I encountered a member of the opposite sex, the hard-ons ambushing me at all hours of the day. An innocent word like "nudist" could keep me in a state of rabid horniness for hours. Suddenly I was remembering all those dime-store novels I read in the Dungeon, the phrases that pulsed in my mind like neon signs in a dark window: *the wet, palpitating flower of her sex* and *her warm woman's cocoon* and *he plunged his thick heat into her pulsing cleft* and a longer one that intrigued me with the sheer dizziness of its mystery: *his tongue flicked across her nub and into her very center, bringing her closer to the brink of bliss she felt herself climbing toward, as though she were on a ladder, taking one rung at a time, and each of the rungs was made of roses, lifting her higher and higher into a churning thundercloud of pure ecstasy.*

Even though I had a pretty good notion of what it was all about, it was Brain who, in cold hard language, actually explained the mechanics and ultimate purpose of sex to me. One evening after chores he asked me if I might have picked up any new scuttlebutt about sexual intercourse at school, and I told him that I hadn't learned much of anything, but that when I lived in Arizona I had seen it taking place not once, but twice.

"You mean you saw two people . . . ?"

I nodded. "A man and a lady."

He said, "I've seen gerbils do it, they do it all the time, but it's hard to tell what's going on, exactly. I once saw Brother Harper's cows, but never humans."

"Humans have to take their clothes off," I told him. "Then they press together, rubbing, and then they make sounds."

I made the sounds for Brain. He narrowed his eyes.

With an exaggerated nonchalance he wandered into the bathroom and came out with one of his *Britannica*s. He opened it up to a bookmarked page, took a couple of deep breaths and read, "Human reproduction begins with sexual intercourse, in which the male sexual organ, the penis, is inserted into the female vagina. If the reproductive act comes to fruition, sperm cells are passed from the male body into the female, in the process fertilizing the female egg and forming a new organism."

Brain looked up at me, blinking. "Does this sound like correct information to you?"

I shrugged, scratched my neck.

"I don't like the term 'penis' very much," Brain sighed. "But my mother calls it a tally-whacker."

I nodded at his *Britannica*. "That thing probably doesn't say anything about oral intercourse."

Brain's eyebrows shot up. He said, "Oral?"

When he couldn't find anything about it in the Oligarchy–Pontoon encyclopedia, I explained oral intercourse to him, as far as I could understand it, and watched him go deadly pale. He staggered backwards a little, allowing his *Britannica* to flop shut. "Why?" he said, his voice pleading. "Why would anybody?"

I had once shared Brain's incredulity—what could a person ever want with something like oral intercourse?—but that was before puberty had swamped me like a rushtide. Now the very words themselves, independently of what they described, seduced me, I could not keep them out of my mind, even in church, where I kept vigil on Brenda Hollander's bra strap and thought about, along with oral intercourse, nipples and pink panties and the giant, balloon-bosomed woman on the highway billboard who wore a halter top and straddled a Goodyear tire.

"When we are at our most prideful, or most haughty, that is when God strikes us down, let me be the first to tell you," Brother Hughes said. Brother Hughes was the kind of teacher who had to bear his testimony to us every Sunday and cry a little to let us know he was serious about it. He was just revving up, starting to get emotional, building up for a big finish. Nobody was paying any attention to him.

For weeks we had been talking about the two main groups in the Book of Mormon: the Nephites and the Lamanites. They both lived on the American continent hundreds of years ago and fought all the time, fought like cats and dogs—this is what the whole Book of

Mormon seemed to be about: the Nephites butchering the Lamanites and vice versa. It was not as exciting as it might sound, but anything was better than the Bible. Brother Hughes made much of the fact that the Lamanites had not followed the will of God and had therefore been marked with a curse: dark skin.

"The darkness in their hearts was matched only by the darkness of their skin," Brother Hughes said. "Eventually they became so evil, so wild and bloodthirsty, that they completely eradicated the Nephites, wiped them off the face of the earth. Those Lamanites are the ancestors of the people today known as the American Indians. Edgar, will you come stand up here next to me?"

I stared down at my shirt as if I was counting its buttons.

He asked again, I ignored him, and he finally came and took my arm and led me up to the front.

"Edgar here, in his own way, is a relic of those Book of Mormon times," Brother Hughes said, gripping my elbow, holding me in place. My face felt hot enough to ignite paper. "Out in the world they might call him an American Indian, but we know better. In truth he is as much a Lamanite as the prophet Samuel or King Lamoni."

There I stood, a Lamanite with a hard-on. I crossed my legs, blinked my eyes rapidly, made clicking noises with my tongue, desperate to divert attention from my groin.

Meanwhile, Brother Hughes bore his testimony, told us how much he loved the Book of Mormon, that he knew that it was a true book and that Joseph Smith was a prophet of God and that Jesus Christ was his personal savior, had suffered and died on the cross for his many, well, let's face it, countless sins. His eyes got misty, then rimmed with water, and then the tears started to flow freely, plowing down his smooth cheeks in orderly lines. This man had crying down to a science. I felt like crying with him. None of this, the extreme embarrassment, the invocation of the name of God, the sincere Christian emotion of our teacher, did anything to discourage my boner; it felt like it was trying to tear a hole in my pants.

After I was allowed to sit down, I heard Scotty Webster whisper loudly, "Hey! Edgar is the Lamanites and we'll be the Nephites and we'll have us a war!" I looked around, feeling very vulnerable, but nobody was taking up Scotty's call to arms.

That night, after being persecuted all Sabbath long by an unyielding erection, I knew the time had come. There was no way I could let this go on any longer. I had been fighting it for weeks and I knew, despite the grave consequences, I was going to do the unthinkable: I was going to jack off. It was a sin, yes, and a big one; our church leaders had spent a lot of time and effort to explain this to us. At first, when they talked about masturbation, they used cryptic, indecipherable language that sounded like a secret code. In our weekly priesthood meeting they handed out a pamphlet to everyone called "For Young Men Only." Inside it had pictures of an assembly line, a large gear works and a couple of smokestacks putting up clouds of steam, and it explained that a young man's body is like a factory, a factory which produces a certain substance. Sometimes, it said, this factory overproduces this certain substance, and occasionally has to expel it, usually in the middle of the night. These "night emissions" are perfectly natural, it explained, nothing to be ashamed of, but for the boy to manipulate his own factory so that the substance is expelled according to his whims, now this is certainly a sin. Our bodies are temples, the pamphlet concluded, and are not to be tampered with.

I read the pamphlet four times, beginning to end, and was left completely mystified.

Later, after church, I was leaning against the back wall, still trying to decipher it, when Vince Brown, a kid who had large fleshy lips and got so excited he spit when he talked, sidled up to me.

"You know what that thing's about!?" he nearly shrieked. Right away, I had to move out of range: spit was flying everywhere. "I didn't know either until my brother told me! It's about jacking off!" Vince hooted and got right in my face, practically had me pinned against the wall.

"You know?" he said. "Wanking?"

Apparently the pamphlet was not as effective as the leaders had hoped because two weeks later the bishopric held a special meeting after Boy Scouts on Wednesday night. Bishop Newhauser, a man with stark white dentures and eerie light blue eyes, explained that the bishopric was becoming alarmed at the amount of "unchaste thoughts and deeds" going on among the youth of the ward.

"We've decided to take some action," Bishop Newhauser said, standing up in front of the portable blackboard. The meeting was held on the auditorium stage, and the hot lights were trained in one spot at the front while the rest of us were left in the darkness, sur-rounded by velveteen curtains that smelled of dust. "We can't sit idly by while Satan is sowing his tares in our midst.

"The ability to procreate is a sacred thing," the bishop said. Already the stage lights were having their effect; droplets of sweat were popping out all over his forehead like blisters. "And when you fiddle with it"—he stopped suddenly and cleared his throat—"what I'm saying here is when you *abuse* it, this power we all have, you are desecrating not only yourself, but your family, your God, and His church upon the earth."

Bishop Newhauser told us there were some things we could do to combat this evil among us. With great care he wrote up on the board:

1. Spend no more than one minute in the bathroom.
2. When in bed, always keep hands on top of blanket and above waist level.
3. Avoid solitary pursuits.
4. In case of immoral thoughts, sing a hymn.
5. Wear two pair of underwear.
6. Pray. Pray. Pray.

Before he let us go, he held up his hands as if to quiet us down, even though no one had made the slightest noise through the entire ordeal. By now he was so thoroughly soaked with sweat that his tie hung from his neck like a dishrag.

"Just so there is no confusion," he said, knotting his hands into fists, "what we are talking about, what we are talking about here is . . . *masturbation*." He let the clinical nastiness of the word sink in. "What we are talking about here, young men, is *keeping your hands to yourselves*."

I had done my best, I had tried praying and singing hymns, I had even curbed my time in the pink bathroom. But there was no way around it now, I had reached a breaking point: I was going to let my hands have their way.

Even in that hormone-frenzied state, I felt a bitter sense of helplessness. In this world of right and wrong, good and evil, there were rules, laws created for my own well-being, and I knew with a certainty it was simply not possible for me to keep them.

That night I lay in bed until I could hear Brain making his little *harrumph*ing sleep noises beneath me. When I heard the grandfather clock chime eleven times I slipped out of bed. I made sure that there was no light showing underneath any of the other bedroom doors, crept down the stairs, careful not to upset the parrots, and followed my hard-on into the backyard.

In church I had learned that the home was a sacred place, a haven for the family unit, a temple, as much a temple as the one in Salt Lake City. In the front room next to the grandfather clock hung a large proclamation in needlepoint that Clay's mother, Grandma LaRue, had made: *This House Is a Temple—Let None Defile It.* To Mormons, just about everything was sacred in one way or another. I would defile my own body, my own temple, and hope God gave me a little credit for leaving the Madsen house out of it.

So I crept outside. I had it out of my pants before I reached the water tank and it took only three or four teeth-clenching tugs before a rushing orgasm drew all the strength out of my legs and brought me to my knees. I knelt there, my body as rigid as a fence post, trying to live in that moment forever, and then I felt it, the flash of a short circuit somewhere deep inside my damaged brain, the electric flutter of an oncoming fit rising up my legs, and I toppled forward into that familiar darkness.

I woke up facedown in the dirt. I rolled over and watched my breath rise as steam into a night sky scattered with stars. Faraway houses on a distant hill gave off a soft, buttery light, as if immersed in water. My heart beat slow and strong in my ears and I felt a peaceful clarity, not what I would have expected after desecrating my own sacred temple and topping it off with an epileptic fit. I turned my head to my left and could see Adelle, one of the goats, peering at me, her face stuck between the slats of the fence, her black nose glistening like a piece of coal. She didn't seem alarmed to see me like this, which made me feel oddly comfortable, lying in the dirt as I was with my pecker in my fist, my pajama bottoms bunched around my thighs. I realized that I was already hard again, and this time it took about thirty seconds of inexpert mashing and squeezing to reach that shuddering state of bliss. I felt the same hot prickle in my nerves, but this time I did not black out. I sank into such a feeling of utter contentment that I eventually fell asleep. I woke up sometime in the early morning, soaked with dew, my hair full of sticks and chicken feathers, my arms and neck peppered with dirt and gravel and bits of straw, and I climbed up the stairs and into my soft bed a filthy, happy boy.

NIGHT AND DAY

AFTER THAT NIGHT, Edgar went on a masturbation binge: behind the water tank, in the old boxcar, on the far side of the horse corrals, in the bathroom at school, once in the backseat of the school bus when he couldn't wait to get home. But never in the house and never in the barn; the dry dustiness of that barn, its smell and shadowy feel, reminded me of the cavalry stables at Willie Sherman and the frayed rope swinging above Sterling's wheelchair. I couldn't have jacked off in that barn if I wanted to.

I felt wicked, but that wasn't enough to stop me. And adding this new dimension to my lifestyle was not easy; Brain knew something was up. He peered at me over his cereal at the breakfast table, his eyes sharp with suspicion. He had been dubious of me ever since I had explained oral intercourse to him. He read every page of typing I did during the day, spied on me through the big keyhole of the bathroom door, but I was too much of a sneak and a thief to get caught by such a square little guy as Brain.

For that first month or so I jacked off so much that I threw my arm out. One morning I woke up with a hot tingling in my elbow and my whole arm seized up like a burned-out piston. I could barely move it; it twitched and shuddered on its own like something in the last throes. It took me five minutes just to get my pants on.

Lana, who had the uncanny ability to detect physical or emotional distress in anybody, human or animal, who seemed forever on the lookout for those who needed healing or consolation, who bore a ready sympathy that could be tapped like a vat, noticed my problem right away. She asked what had happened and I told her that I wasn't sure, maybe I had slept on it funny.

"We should take you to the doctor, just in case," she said. She was already dressed for work and smelled like the sandalwood oil she dabbed on her wrists every morning.

"No doctor," I said. "Please."

Lana pursed her lips. "Doctors are the good guys," she said. "They're there to *help*."

So we went to the doctor. Dr. Wand, a high priest in our ward, was a cheerful old man who hummed "Yankee Doodle Dandy" while he scribbled things down on a thick pad of paper and occasionally scratched his butt with his fancy silver pen. I was relieved when he didn't ask me how I was feeling or offer me his stethoscope to play with. He poked my arm, thumped it, gave it a yank as if he was trying to start a lawn mower. I stared straight ahead, trying not to grimace or flinch.

"Will you touch your ear for me?" he said.

I tried to swing my arm up to the side of my head, but all the connections were wrong, the blood vessels pinched, the nerves crossed up; it seemed that the arm hanging from my shoulder belonged to someone else entirely. I tried it again and managed to poke myself in the eye.

He held the arm up in front of my face, where it hung limp as an empty bread sack. "Tell me, young sir, how did you get this limb of yours into such a state?" I looked over at Lana, who sat on a chair next to the examination table with a copy of *The Disabled American* in her lap.

"Slept on it funny?" I said.

Dr. Wand stepped back in shock as if I'd told him I'd hurt my arm tossing a spear at a charging rhino on the wild plains of Africa. "Sister Wand?" he called out. "Would you step in here a moment?"

Sister Wand, who doubled as the receptionist and nurse, looked like a frazzled owl. She had a round face, close-together eyes and fly-away kinky white hair.

"Sister Wand, this young man says he got his arm in this state by sleeping on it—how did you put it?—*funny*," Dr. Wand said, giving my arm a shake so it flopped and bounced with its own dead weight. "Have you ever seen such a case as this?"

"He must have slept on it *really* funny," said Sister Wand.

"Are there any other possibilities?" Dr. Wand said to me.

"Basketball?" I said.

"You play basketball, do you?"

"No," I admitted.

"He doesn't play basketball, Sister Wand," Dr. Wand said. "Any other kind of physical activity, something with repetitive movements? Maybe you're a shot-putter on the track team, maybe you sand a lot of furniture?"

"I type," I offered. "I type every day."

"He types, Sister Wand."

"It's a skill not many boys have anymore," Sister Wand said.

Dr. Wand shoved his hands into the pockets of his lab coat and scrutinized me under those bristling eyebrows. I felt the heat rising to my face. Dr. Wand looked like he was about to bust out with a laugh. He composed himself, glanced at Lana, who seemed completely confused by all of this, and stood right next to me and whispered, as if he didn't want Lana and Sister Wand to hear what he would say next.

"What we are going to do, my young typing friend, is fit you with a sling, which you are to wear for three weeks, night and day, in bed, in the bathroom, behind the woodshed, wherever you may roam. You won't take it off except to bathe, and even then you must keep this limb of yours perfectly stationary, no repetitive movements. Three weeks, night and day, you hear me?"

"Night and day," I said, nodding.

"I'll make sure," Lana said. "Night and day."

"You've got to give that arm a break," Dr. Wand said, patting me on the leg. "Many productive years ahead of you yet. It's a good idea to pace yourself."

"Slow down, son," said Sister Wand.

"Night and day," I said, hopping off the table and heading for the door. "Okay."

I took it for granted that God had done this to my right arm as a punishment for my sins, but He had made one mistake: He had spared my left.

So there was Edgar one night, over by the windmill, in his sling and green flannel pajamas, wanking awkwardly with his left, concentrating so hard that he wasn't sure if he heard the noise behind him. Maybe it was one of the cats; they were always coming up looking for a scratch behind the ears or a scrap of food.

Then there was a distinctly human sound, so out of place here in this land of animals: somebody cleared their throat. I froze. I did not look back, did not move at all, but sat motionless in the weeds hoping in vain that my bright plaid pajamas might find a way to camouflage themselves among the drab colors of dirt and fence and cloudy midnight sky.

"Edgar," came the voice, a harsh whisper.

It was Sunny. She was wearing a sweater and a down vest, her blond hair giving off a dim glow. She stood with her arms cradled against her, her elbows in her palms.

"I'm out here checking on the animals," I said.

Sunny stepped closer. "Aren't you cold? You should at least put some shoes on."

As casually as if I was folding a pair of tube socks, I arranged my genitals back into my underwear. "I'm not cold," I said. "I get hot in the house."

We both peered into the small space of dark air that separated us. "I've seen you out here a bunch of times," she said. "But don't worry, I'm not going to tell on you."

"Okay," I said. My voice sounded thin, childlike. I was having a hard time catching my breath. I squeaked, "I won't tell on you either."

Even when she was not catching me abusing myself in the barnyard in the middle of the night, Sunny made me nervous. It was not only that she was a girl in close proximity, sleeping in her underthings in the room right next to mine, using the same bathroom I did, sometimes stepping out of a cloud of steam in nothing but a towel wrapped snugly around her body, water dripping off the ends of her hair. It was her quiet, self-assured ferocity, her dead-eye glare, her long, blood-colored nails. All of her friends had that same menacing air. Once I came in one afternoon from doing my chores to find Sunny and two of her friends sitting on the couch with a magazine, their butts jammed together. I stood in the doorway to the kitchen and they all looked up at me at the same time. The chubby one acted like she was puking, her finger in her mouth, and the tall one with blue eyeliner and frizzy hair that had been bleached into an impossible hue of green rolled her eyes and said, "Oh, *God*."

I did not turn around, just stepped backwards, walking in a slow reverse, and stood on the other side of the refrigerator in the empty kitchen, stayed there without moving until they left a half hour later.

Now, Sunny sat on an overturned plastic feed bucket and swung her hair around. It seemed to me that if you ever got in the way of that swinging hair it could take your head right off. "I don't feel like going inside yet. I've been going out every weekend and they don't even know about it."

I squatted on a hardened bag of cement and Sunny slipped a can of Budweiser out of the pocket of her vest. She popped it open, took a couple of sips, offered it to me.

I wanted to take it, I would have taken just about anything she offered me, but something made me shake my head.

"You take all that church stuff pretty seriously, don't you?" she said.

I shrugged, picked up a few pebbles with my toes. I said, "I don't like beer."

"I don't like it either," Sunny said. "But then again I like it quite a lot. So do you like living here? It's horrible, isn't it?"

"It's pretty good."

"Wherever you were before must have been a dump."

I smiled.

"Is it true you got your head squashed by a car?"

"Mail jeep," I said. "The mailman who ran over me thinks he killed me, but he didn't. I'm going to find him and tell him I'm okay—it's my purpose in life."

Sunny regarded me for awhile; maybe I had said too much.

"Would you mind if I touched it?" she said.

"Touched what?"

"Your head, Romeo. I want to know what it feels like."

She set her beer next to me and rested the fingertips of both her hands on my scalp. I felt an electric tingle at each point of contact, a vibration of heat. She moved her nails lightly over the side of my head, which made me convulse in a full-body shiver.

"Brain said you are on medication," I said, panting a little.

Sunny's fingers suddenly pressed into my head almost to the point of hurting. She said, "That little fag."

"I used to be on medication when I lived in a hospital," I said. "Everybody in there was on medication. I was in a coma. Had to ride around in a wheelchair a lot of the time."

"It's none of your business," she said.

Out on the humped ridge of sandstone to the south the low, gray form of a coyote moved slowly through the sagebrush and cedar trees, appearing and disappearing like a ghost.

The pressure from Sunny's fingers eased but she kept her hands in my hair. "You probably thought you were going to come to this great place and live with a big happy family and everything would be perfect. I know that's what you thought. That's what they all think. I don't know why my mom keeps bringing people to live here. All these animals, jeez. She thinks it will fix something. But it never does. Nothing will fix it."

"Fix what?"

"Come on. You hear them yelling at night, don't you? Do you ever see them talking to each other? They're married you know, husband and wife? They used to love each other, I remember them kissing all the time, totally in love, I remember it. They used to check on us every night. Then little Dean, and there it all goes. They still can't handle it. I think they hate each other."

She picked up her beer and, instead of a polite sip this time, took a long swallow, the gurgling rush of liquid loud in her throat. She was quiet for a long time, then poured the rest of the beer onto the ground. Droplets of mud spattered my feet. She bent down a little, looking me in the face. In her eyes glowed the miniature lights of the far-off houses. "You don't know about any of this, do you? Nobody talks about it in this house, we act like it never happened."

"Brain told me," I said.

"Don't listen to him. That little jerk doesn't have any idea because nobody has told him squat. He thinks he's the next Einstein and he doesn't know what's going on in his own family. He doesn't know a thing."

"I don't know anything either," I said.

"Then I'll tell you," she said, and sat down next to me on my bag of cement. Our thighs touched. My sprained right arm, cradled in its sling, touched hers. She was stepping on my foot and didn't seem to know it. "I'll tell you everything."

LITTLE DEAN

LITTLE DEAN WAS an angel. Everybody said so. He had his mother's blond hair, but his was as curly as hers was straight, and his eyes were the deepest blue, almost violet. Folks were always telling Clay and Lana that they should take him to Hollywood, put him in commercials, they could make a mint off a baby that cute. A happy baby, never colicky, he chirped and cooed and sang, his face taken up with that famous, gap-toothed grin. By the time he was one he was already speaking, his voice high-pitched and a little raspy. He would walk around in wide-eyed wonder, pointing at things with a pudgy finger, naming them: "Floor! Light! Kitty! Cup! Ball! Chair!" When he didn't know what something was he would hold out his hands, palms up, a look of earnest puzzlement on his face and ask "Wazzat? Wazzat?" until somebody came up with the necessary information.

Neighbors would stop by just to visit him, people from the ward would call to ask if they could baby-sit him for the day. At church, there was always a pack of women, young and old, milling around him like groupies. They would fawn over him, whisper and squeal and chatter at him, ask to hold him, and he would always oblige: he'd flirt and make peekaboo faces and give out kisses to anyone who asked.

Look at him, everybody said, he really is an angel, a baby of light.

Nobody, not even the old grandmothers who were the daughters of old-time polygamists, had ever seen such a beautiful, good-spirited baby boy. Straight from heaven! they would say. An angel straight from God!

It was a Saturday afternoon, three days before his second birthday, and he was asleep in his crib while Clay worked at the desk downstairs, preparing for his Sunday school class. Dean's crib was an antique, an heirloom, built by Clay's great-grandfather only a few months after his family had crossed the plains, all the way from Ohio to settle in this small valley in the middle of a desert. Countless Madsen babies had slept in that crib through the years, including Clay's grandfather, Clay's father and Clay himself, and eventually Sunny and Brain. The crib was sturdy and beautifully fashioned out of the oak planks of the same covered wagon that had brought the family so far, but it had one small flaw, a flaw that had never shown itself over the course of a hundred years and those dozens and dozens of babies: the vertical slats were a little too far apart, wide enough for a baby, if it really wanted, to get its head through. In his sleep little Dean managed to push his head between the bars and when he had tried to pull himself out, became wedged securely there, his face caught in a mound of bedding.

While his father read the Sermon on the Mount downstairs, no more than thirty feet away, Little Dean quietly suffocated and died.

He was buried in the town cemetery in the huge family plot shaded by a couple of elm trees. In the three years since the day of the funeral, Lana had never been back to the cemetery, but Clay went every week to tend the grave, to water the flowers he had planted there, to spray and polish the smooth granite headstone with glass cleaner. Every time he would stop by the house to ask Lana to come with him, and every time she would refuse.

After the graveside service, when the family and a large portion of the town retired to the house for a luncheon, Clay pushed through the throng of mourners and friends, climbed the stairs to Dean's room, and smashed the crib to kindling with his bare hands.

A MISSIONARY VISIT

OUT IN THE OLD railroad car, behind the peat moss bags and stacked rolls of barbed wire, Edgar counted coins. It was a hot summer day, the still air full of dust and fat, ponderous flies that orbited my head like tiny black planets. Here in this shadowy hidden place I kept my crucifix and the rock that had fallen out of my head and other secret belongings, the notes that I wrote to Sunny but never gave to her, the letters I had written to my mailman, the prayers I typed asking forgiveness for all of my bad thoughts and self-desecrations. And now I had one more sin to repent of, one more apology to make. God had saved me from death, had taken me into His bosom, had washed away my sins with baptism, had banished the ghosts that tormented me, had rescued me from Willie Sherman and given me everything I could have wanted, and here I was letting him down. Edgar was, once again, a thief.

Over the past few weeks I had stolen thirty-five dollars' worth of small change, one coin at a time, from Clay's bedroom dresser or from the purse that Lana left hanging over the back of a chair in the kitchen. Each quarter, nickel and dime: one more stab in Jesus' tender heart.

You're a good boy, Art had told me the day I left St. Divine's. I knew that it wasn't true.

I now had enough to buy a round-trip bus ticket to Nevada. In two days, while Clay and Lana were gone to a wedding in Ogden, I planned to take a trip and visit Cecil. It had been well over a year since I had last seen him, since he had saved me from Nelson and got shipped off to prison because of it, and only now had I decided to do something more than send him boring letters, many of them full of lies, with a few dollars tucked in the envelope. There was something that I had finally been able to admit to myself: I had done all I could to forget Cecil. It made me burn with shame to think of it. I had abandoned him for casseroles and a soft bed and cartoons on Saturday morning. I thought I would be able to lose myself completely in the comforts of a new family, I thought I could distract myself with the root beer floats and the Christmas presents and the lush pinkness of the heavenly bathroom, but it was still there, like a cold piece of metal lodged somewhere in the soft tissues of my gut: I missed Cecil. I was lonely for him.

But I had to keep my visit a secret from Lana and Clay. I wanted them to believe that I had left my old life entirely, that I had forgotten about it, that I had no place or past to go back to. I wanted to give them no choice but to keep me.

Brain was the only one I told about my trip. He had showed me where Nevada was, after all, and even though I hadn't asked him to, he'd ended up calling the bus station for me to get price quotes and a schedule. He wrote it all down for me on a slip of paper and left it on top of my typewriter. Underneath all the pertinent information he had written: *P.S. Sometimes you aggravate me.*

I shoveled the coins from the *Irish Eddie's Potato Flakes* can into the pockets of my jeans. This morning I had filched the last fifty cents I needed from Lana's purse. I was going to pedal down to the KUM-n-GO Mart and transfer all that change into dollar bills. I didn't want any foul-ups. Early Saturday morning I would go up to the window at the bus station, pay the lady with paper money, take the bus to see Cecil and be back before Clay and Lana got home from their wedding late that night.

I was walking around the barn toward the garage when Clay opened the back door.

"Edgar," he said. He had come home for lunch and was powdered head to toe with drywall dust. He looked like a sugar donut. "Come on in a minute. Somebody here to see you."

I turned my body to try to hide the bulges in my jean pockets. I said, "Right now?"

"Right now. They're waiting on you."

I walked in slow motion, doing my damnedest not to jingle. Clay held the door open and I passed through the kitchen into the living room. What I saw was like a hand clapping against my chest. Sunny slumped on one of the couches in shorts and a T-shirt. On the other couch sat Dr. Pinkley and Jeffrey. They were both dressed up as missionaries: white short-sleeved shirts with black name tags, dark slacks and shoes buffed to a high acrylic finish. Jeffrey's hair was so short you could see the white of his scalp. The way they were smiling you couldn't help but believe they had the Lord on their side.

I might have saved myself right then, might have kept it all from coming apart. I should have done whatever was necessary to drive them out of that house; maybe I could have stomped my feet, raised a ruckus, hollered bloody murder, exposed those two men for what they were: interlopers, criminals, frauds of the first degree. But I did nothing. I stood there like a prisoner caught in the guard-tower spotlight, trembling so that the coins in my pockets made a low metallic buzzing.

I felt Clay's hand on my back. He pushed me gently forward. Jeffrey and Dr. Pinkley stood at the same time and both held their hands out to me. They seemed to be doing everything in sync.

"This must be Edgar," Dr. Pinkley said.

"Be polite now," Clay said. "Go ahead and shake their hands."

I had a hard time hearing anything because a siren wailed from somewhere deep inside my head. I held out my hand to them over the coffee table and they both gave it a vigorous shake.

"I was just telling Brother Madsen and—Sunny, is it?—that we're in the area checking on some of the placement families, to gauge how the program is working out."

"I mentioned that they look a little old for missionaries," Clay said.

"Lots of people tell us that," Jeffrey said. He had a Bible and Book of Mormon in his lap and his name tag said ELDER WILTBANK. It was the first time I had ever seen him looking anything except wretched. "We are older than most, that's why we've been given this assignment. You don't give this kind of assignment to any kid off the farm. We receive our directions straight from the men in Salt Lake."

"*Ppfft,*" I said.

Everybody looked at me and then at each other. Jeffrey sighed. "Yup, those men in Salt Lake."

I sat down next to Sunny. The coins in my pocket shifted and tinkled. Barry sat on the edge of the couch cushion and looked me right in the eyes, no more than six feet away. All I could think about was the shiny gun he had waved around the last time I'd seen him. If it was possible, he looked more gaunt and angular than before, but his short hair, brilliant with some kind of styling oil, his plain blue tie, his name tag that said ELDER RIVERS, all gave him an air of righteous authority that was hard to deny. "Brother Madsen has told us that you've been a wonderful addition to their family, Edgar, nothing but good to report. That's the kind of thing we like to hear."

Jeffrey kept his head bobbing up and down in affirmation. "Praise the Lord," he said. "Praise Jesus."

"Have you enjoyed having Edgar in your family?" Barry asked Sunny.

"He's all right," she shrugged. "We've had a lot worse."

Jeffrey giggled like a cartoon mouse. "A lot worse!" he said. "Amen."

Barry stood and pulled Jeffrey up from the couch by the arm. "We should really let you get on with your day. We'd like to talk with Edgar in private for a moment if you don't mind."

Clay stood to leave and Barry suggested they might take me for a drive, have a little chat, maybe get an ice cream cone.

"Not to worry," Barry said, showing off his missionary smile. "We'll have him back here in a jiffy."

We all stood and Jeffrey told Clay it would be an honor if he could leave a blessing on this household on their way out. Barry glared at Jeffrey, who folded his arms, bowed his head, squinched his eyes shut, drew in a long, dramatic breath and prayed, "Our loving Father who art in heaven . . ." He paused, as if concentrating all of his humble desire toward the heavens. "We thank thee for one more beautiful day on this Thy green earth, for the opportunity we have to find ourselves here in the house of this good family, Thy servants every one. We ask Thee, O Lord, by the Melchizedek priesthood which we hold, to bless this house and its occupants with all the bounty of Thy kindness, with the hearty abundance of Thy spirit, bless them with safety and peace and comfort and joyousness, bless them in their work and play, in all their sleeping and waking hours, in their comings and goings and everything in between."

Jeffrey's voice had taken on a kind of exalted Southern twang. Right in the middle of the prayer he looked up and gave me a big wink.

"May Thy spirit dwell in this house, Heavenly Father, let no evil enter herewith, allow the milk of human kindness to be in evidence at all times . . . yes, and the blood of the Lamb, let us never forget that, may we always remember. Give us the strength to carry on in our travails, great Jehovah, be in our hearts every moment, we pray in the name of our Savior and Lord Jesus Christ, Amen."

Once we were safely outside Jeffrey said, "Who ever heard such a ring-a-ding kickass prayer?"

Barry put his hands on my shoulders. "Look how big he is now. Do you see this?"

He tried to hug me but I took a step back.

"Okay, all right," he said. "Let's go somewhere we can talk."

I felt dazed, blinded by the stark afternoon light. I walked with them into the shade of the willow trees and out again.

"Did you see little blondie in there, Elder Rivers?" Jeffrey said. "Perky little hooters! Yea, I sayeth unto you, behold!"

Barry grabbed Jeffrey's tie and gave it a yank as if it were the leash of a disobedient dog. "Would you keep your voice down? You're high, aren't you? I told you we have to watch it around here. They were looking at us funny in there. They were suspicious."

Jeffrey wrestled his tie from Barry's grasp, situated it around his neck again. "I'm not *high*. Jesus! I'm merely relaxed. I had them eating out of my hand. Nobody suspected anything, nobody ever suspects anything. I am a man of God, a humble servant of the Word. You worry too much."

We were standing in front of their car, a white Buick sedan. Barry opened the front passenger door for me and I stopped in my tracks; I was not about to get into that car.

"Come on, let's go," Barry said. "We can't keep you away too long."

I shook my head, turned away, looked down at my own shadow.

"You see this?" Barry looked at Jeffrey. "You see what they've done to him?"

Barry slammed the door, came over to me. "We're your friends, Edgar, we are, not these people. I think you've forgotten about this at some point. They'll do anything to keep you in their clutches, they don't care about you. Only as long as you live by their rules, sure, they'll be nice to you, give you what you want, but the minute you start to go your own way, they'll throw you right out on your ear, take my word for it."

I looked up at him. He had his face very close to mine and I could smell his metallic breath. His hair gleamed like a freshly washed blackboard.

Jeffrey said, "These people are buggy, is what they are. Did you see their house? Two front doors. What kind of place is this."

"Why are you wearing missionary clothes?" I said.

"It's good for business." Jeffrey clapped his Bible and Book of Mormon together. "Your big goofy friends are the ones who gave us the idea. We can do our thing and the cops watch us go right on by. Everybody trusts a missionary!"

"Mormons don't say 'Praise the Lord,'" I said. "And they don't say 'Praise Jesus' either."

Jeffrey sniffed. "Great, now we have an expert."

"It's the only way we could see you," Barry said. "Do you know it took us this long just to get this address from these people? I don't know what it is with these Mormons. They won't take a bribe, I've never seen anything like it. They're demented. I tried everything, but they wouldn't give me the information. Finally I had to pay somebody to break into the church offices and steal your file. This is the kind of thing I'm talking about."

Timothy Boyd, a little kid who lived four houses up, pedaled by on his bike. Jeffrey yelled at him, "Howdy-ho, there little tyke!"

Timothy rubbernecked and nearly skidded off the road into an irrigation ditch.

Jeffrey said, "These people are nuts."

"Look," Barry said. "Forget about the car. We can take a little walk along the road here. I just want to talk to you for awhile, find out how you're doing, it's been a long time. You don't have any reason to be afraid of us."

I looked down at Barry's spit-shined shoes, which were liquid and black, like the pupil of an eye.

"Harmless," Jeffrey said. "Harmless as baby kittens."

"You stay here," Barry said to Jeffrey. "I'm going to take a walk with Edgar. Don't talk to anybody. And no smoking."

Jeffrey wagged his finger at Barry. "You know the rules, Elder. Companions are supposed to stick together at all times. It's the first rule of missionary life. Only to shit, shower or shave shall we part company. Thus sayeth the Lord."

Barry wiped his mouth. "You can tag along behind. But don't yell at any more kids and try not to swear."

We set off down the hill and I felt better the farther we got away from the house. I looked back to see if anybody was watching us, but the afternoon was still and empty, full of white light that glinted off bottle caps and bits of glass in the road. The crackling buzz of locusts rose and died in an incessant rhythm.

"I want you to know one thing," Barry said to me. "There are no hard feelings about you taking up with the Mormons and coming out here. I won't even hold it against you that you didn't tell me about it. I understand that school was not an easy place to be in, and I'll take full responsibility for not getting you out of there sooner. I was going through some difficult times."

"What about Art?" I said.

"Art? What about him?"

"Is he dead?"

Barry stopped suddenly, and Jeffrey, who was walking dutifully a few steps behind, ran right into him.

"Look, Edgar," Barry said, his teeth clenched. He grabbed my arm, his fingers pressing all the way to the bone. "You need to forget about Art, I'm telling you this for your own good. I don't know what's become of him, he's a lost cause. Has he ever done anything to help you? Who has taken the effort to be here for you, to look out for you? Think about it for a minute."

We crossed the road and walked next to an overflowing irrigation ditch, the water full of leaves and twigs and clumps of dirty foam. Barry asked me about life with the Madsens. He wanted to know how they were treating me, what the school was like, what kind of things they were teaching me in church.

Behind us, Jeffrey said, "Coma-boy, what do you have in your pants?"

"Money," I said.

"Money!" Jeffrey said. "It looks like you might be getting the hang of things."

We stopped for a moment in the shade of a locust tree that hung out over the road from the Sutherlands' yard. On the far side of the house, Mrs. Sutherland and her son Roger, a thirty-five-year-old mongoloid, were irrigating their garden: perfect rows of chard, carrots, spinach, peppers and young corn. Near the road were two or three arbors of grapes and just beyond them was a bed of flowers artfully planted around a few granite boulders. While they irrigated, Roger and Mrs. Sutherland sang "Abide with Me." They sang beautifully together, Roger's voice, high and sweet, alternating between harmony and melody with each verse. Chuckers, their miniature schnauzer, would occasionally join in with a thin, undulating howl.

"This place is freaked," Jeffrey said.

Roger saw us. "Aieeee!" he called, waving with the enthusiasm of the dim-witted.

Jeffrey waved back. "Aieeee!"

"Son of a bitch," Barry growled, grabbing Jeffrey by the arm. We walked the way we had come, moving faster than before, struggling in the heat to get up the long hill. When we got back to the car, Barry's cheeks were a bright pink and Jeffrey was sucking air as if through a straw.

"We've got to get going," Barry said. "But I've got a couple of things for you first." He took out a business card and wrote on the back of it. "If you ever need anything, any kind of favor at all, this is the number you can call, don't you hesitate. I'll be here for you, Edgar. We don't want to act in a rash manner, you know, we want to take it slow and easy, not rush things, but everything is going to work out for us this time, I can feel it. I'm dedicated, Edgar, I have the means to do what has to be done."

"I know one thing," I said.

"Name it," he said.

"Could you find the mailman for me, find out where he is?"

"The mailman?"

"The one who ran over me. I want to find him. I want to tell him I'm okay."

Barry sighed. "That guy disappeared off the face of the earth—what—six years ago? I'll see what I can do, Edgar. I'll poke around a little."

"Are you going home now?" I said.

"Not really sure where home is anymore, but yes, we've got to get going. One other thing, though. You like baseball?"

"Yes," I lied.

"I think maybe we should go find some lepers to cure," Jeffrey said, looking around, hitching up his pants. "Maybe cast out a few demons, who knows."

Barry opened the car's trunk, took out a baseball mitt and handed it to me. He was beaming. "This was my first mitt. You might be a little big for it now, but I think it will work for you."

"Oh Jesus Christ," Jeffrey said. He tossed his scriptures into the front seat and got into the car.

It was an outfielder's mitt, the leather worn smooth and shiny with age. In the webbing there was a baseball with writing on it. *Barry Terrence Pinkley. First Home Run. Little League, 1952.*

I acted as if I liked the mitt, and Barry and I shook hands.

"I don't want you to worry," he said. "You're not alone, Edgar. We'll be around. You can count on it."

Barry got into the Buick and started the engine. I looked at the business card Barry had given me.

Elder Rivers & Elder Wiltbank

The Church of Jesus Christ of Latter-Day Saints

"Called to Serve"

Barry turned the car around and sped off down the hill. Dust rose up behind the car in one dense column. Jeffrey put his head out the window and waved back at me. I could barely see him through the billowing grit.

"Praise Jesus!" he yelled. "Praise the Lord! *Aieeeeeee!*"

THE KUM-N-GO

FOR A LONG TIME I stood at the front gate. I wanted to open that gate, go back inside the house, but I was having trouble doing it. After a while I went over to the irrigation ditch, said a little prayer and dipped my right hand into the cold water. It was the hand that Barry had touched and I was baptizing it, washing away all the impurities. Immediately I felt better.

Then I dropped the mitt and baseball into the flowing ditch. The mitt quickly absorbed water and disappeared, but the ball bobbed and rolled in the fast current, all the way past the Sutherlands'. It shrank into a tiny white dot moving across the landscape until it was sucked into a culvert and didn't emerge on the other side.

I went up to my room and typed nonsense on my Hermes Jubilee for awhile, really gave that typewriter a good pounding. It was not between the hours of four-thirty and seven, but Brain was nowhere to be seen. He was probably at the library, learning. I typed the same page over and over again until it was almost completely black and moist with ink, and I felt myself calming down. I thought the house was empty, but Clay was downstairs in the kitchen, looking at blueprints spread out over the counter. I walked by as quietly as I could, heading for the door that led into the garage, but he saw me. He said, "You all have a good conversation?"

My pockets were still packed with coins. I nodded, tried to situate my hands over the bulges in my pants as naturally as possible.

"Something I wanted to talk to you about. Brain told me you were planning on going to visit your friend in Nevada. He said you were going to take a bus. I'll be happy to take you on my day off. I checked the map and it's only three hours from here. I talked with

Lana about it. We didn't think it was very safe for you to be going that far alone."

"Oh," Edgar said, gripping the coins in his pockets so his pants were pulled up to expose his socks.

"We'll go then, in the next week or so. Don't be afraid to tell us these things, Edgar, we're more than happy to help you out. All you have to do is ask."

Now I wasn't sure what to do with all this money: it seemed to be burning into my thighs. I went to the garage, got out my bike, which had a partially flat rear tire, and rode the mile and a half to the KUM-n-GO market. On my way, I passed the Sutherlands'. Roger yelled "Aieee!" at me. I ignored him.

The whole way there, I thought about Cecil and tried to push Dr. Pinkley out of my mind. Now, not only was I going to visit Cecil, but I had enough money to buy him a bagful of Dum Dums, no, a whole wheelbarrow full of Dum Dums.

The KUM-n-GO market sat by itself at the far west end of town. It had a gasoline pump outside which no longer worked and an old sign that said *Coke 15¢* that made people mad when they went in only to find out that a Coke was actually going to cost them thirty-five cents. The cashier, a fat blond woman who wore lipstick the color of bubble gum, was talking on the phone. I sidled down the candy aisle and stood in front of the Dum Dums. I could buy that entire bin of them if I wanted to. I imagined walking into that prison with a whole armful of suckers as colorful and sweet-smelling as a bouquet of flowers, imagined the look of grateful astonishment on Cecil's face.

I reached deep into the Dum Dums and pulled out two handfuls. I looked at the cashier, who still had the phone receiver pressed between her fleshy shoulder and head while she went at her nails with an emery board. Instead of taking the Dum Dums up to the counter and paying for them with my stolen money, I began stuffing the candy into my front pockets, already occupied by thirty-five dollars in coins but still big enough to hold a handful each. Still the cashier didn't turn around and I crammed more Dum Dums into my back pockets, into my socks. It was all too easy. With one hand I stretched out the front of my T-shirt and with the other scooped as many as I could into the pouch the loose fabric made. I stood in front of the counter, daring the cashier to turn around, but she went right on filing her nails, saying, "Mm-hmm. Huh. Wha—? No way. Who? No way, Linda."

Edgar pushed open the door and stepped out into the hot afternoon light, bristling with Dum Dums. He mounted his golden bike and pedaled homeward, a clear and sudden feeling in him that everything was a circle and he was at its center. It was all spinning in toward him: his old self, his old life, spiraling closer and closer, it was all coming back.

FORGIVENESS

WE DROVE THROUGH the open desert, the flat plain spreading out on either side of the road until it fell away into the gray, drizzling sky. There was nothing but dirt and split-rail fences crisscrossing like badly made sutures and clumps of sagebrush and mesquite that looked like scattered puffs of black smoke in the distance. Occasionally we would pass an old windmill or run-down picket house or a solitary trailer connected to the world by a single sagging wire.

Clay drove with talk radio on and I sat on the far edge of the pickup seat, hunched against the door, trying to work up some courage. In my lap I had my school backpack and in the backpack were two bags, one filled with Dum Dums for Cecil, the other with the wages of sin: thirty-five dollars in stolen coins. I put my hand in the backpack, took it out again. I had been doing this for an hour now, ever since we'd left Richland.

A few days before, Lana had called the detention center to find out about visiting hours and had made an appointment for us to see Cecil today at five o'clock. We had a special dinner for him, a box full of chicken lasagna, garlic bread and lemon cake. And I had brought my own little secret: Art's knife, tucked into my sock. I didn't know what things were like at the detention center, but I figured a knife like mine could be of some use there.

"You don't see this kind of weather very often around here," Clay said. It would spit for awhile, tiny droplets building up on the windshield until Clay had to turn on the wipers, which would take only a few seconds to dry up and begin streaking and stuttering against the glass. "This is real uncommon. Around these parts, either it's raining or it's not. This is less like rain and more like indecision."

I had the bag of coins in my hand. I held my breath, counted to ten and pulled it out of the backpack. It was actually three brown paper bags, one inside the other inside the other, strong enough to keep from tearing under all that weight. I set it on the seat between us.

"What you got there?" Clay said.

I said, "It's money."

"What's it for?"

"It's for you."

"Why are you giving it to me?"

"Because it's yours. I stole it."

Clay seemed not to have heard me. I always had a hard time reading Clay's expressions because his beard almost completely obscured his mouth; if he was smiling you could only tell by the way the skin around his eyes wrinkled. Clay's beard was a favorite subject of gossip in the ward. Some said it was against church guidelines, some said it was a bad example to the youth, some said it was just plain unnecessary. I heard one old high priest, Brother Retchler, say, "What a good man like Clay Madsen wants with looking like one a them bumble-minded hippies, well I don't got the foggiest."

Clay pulled the bag open, looked inside. He said, "You stole this money?"

I told Clay everything. I said I was sorry, that I would never do it again.

I had learned in church there were five steps to repentance: (1) Feel remorse, (2) Confess, (3) Ask forgiveness, (4) Make amends, (5) Never sin again. Clearly, number 5 was the real bugger. Once you had repented, or so I was told, God would forget about the sin as if it had never happened, it would be erased right out of the record books. There were angels in heaven, apparently, keeping track of everything. I knew I had a lot of sins logged in my record book and it was nice to think that I might get rid of at least one of them. I tried to forget about the fact that there was another bag in my back-pack crammed full of stolen merchandise; I would have to take my transgressions one at a time.

"You did right in telling me," he said. "But why didn't you just ask us? You're part of our family, Edgar, you can ask us for anything and we'll do our best to help you."

Asking: now that was something that had never occurred to Edgar. For his entire life he had lived in a world where asking was a waste of time, a notion to laugh at; you took what you could get.

"I have one question for you and I want you to answer me as truthfully as you can," Clay said. "Do you like living with us, being a part of our family?"

I nodded with such enthusiasm I bit my tongue. "Yes, I like it a lot. Very much. Yes I do. I really like it. A lot."

"That's good, then," Clay said. Somewhere under that beard he seemed to be grinning. "Because we like having you. All of us, even Brain and Sunny, though they'd never admit to it."

Edgar decided right then there was nothing better in this world than confessing your sins, asking forgiveness, unloading the burden of guilt. I leaned against the door, which vibrated pleasantly against the back of my head. In no time at all I was asleep.

I woke up to the sound of the engine shutting off. We were in the middle of a large parking lot full of cars. The sky was still a wash of gray and the small trees jutting up at intervals among the cars bowed in the wind, their few leaves rattling. The building was modern, made of red brick with a glass front that said *State of Nevada Juvenile Detention and Rehabilitation* in gold letters. There were no guard towers or razor wire, just a ten-foot-high chain-link fence that surrounded the entire property. All in all, it seemed like a pretty nice place to me.

We went inside, where a short, barrel-shaped woman in a uniform waited behind a counter. Clay, holding the cardboard box that contained Cecil's dinner, told her that we had come for visiting hours.

"Name?" she said.

"Cecil Jimenez," I said. I had my bag of Dum Dums. I thought about offering the lady one of them. She wore false eyelashes and maroon lipstick and something about the tired lines of her face reminded me of the nurses at St. Divine's.

She told us to wait, picked up the phone and talked into it with her hand cupped over her mouth. She put the phone down, sighed, fidgeted, looked through some papers.

"Look," she said. "I can't seem to locate my boss, you'll need to talk to him about this."

"We made an appointment," Clay said. "My wife called last week. This is visiting day, isn't it? We just drove three hours."

The woman looked around, as if for somebody who might help her, but the office was empty except for us.

"What's your relation?" she said.

Clay said, "My relation?"

"To the inmate."

"We're his friends, ma'am, and we're here to visit with him. I don't see what the problem is."

The woman picked up the phone again, slammed it back down, mumbled something under her breath. "All right," she said. "Sir, if you'd step over here with me I'd like to have a word with you."

Clay walked around behind the counter and the woman met him next to the far wall under a poster that read, in orange fiery letters, *POT is NOT so HOT.* She whispered, her voice no more than a rustle, but in that quiet office I heard every word: "I'm sorry to tell you this, sir, but you can't visit the inmate because he's, ah, deceived."

"Deceived," Clay said, as if he was trying to get his tongue around a word he had never heard before.

"Oh shoot," the woman said, stomping her feet. "I meant deceased. This makes me nervous. De*ceased*."

"De*ceased*," Clay said.

The woman was breathing fast. "As of Thursday morning. That's when they found him. Looks like he tried to escape through the heating system and fell down one of the old incinerator shafts from the original building. They should have grated those things off a long time ago but nobody got around to it. It's been in the paper. Family's been notified but nobody's come to claim the body. There might be lawsuits in the offing, you see. That's where everybody is right now, at a meeting with the Board of Corrections."

Clay put the box of food on the counter and his big hands fell to his sides, dangling as if from loose ropes. Clay and the woman stood very close to each other, almost touching. I could tell neither of them wanted to look at me. He backed away from her, turned quickly and told me we needed to go, but I already had my arm locked around the push-handle of the glass door.

"No visits today," Clay said, his face pale. "We'll talk about it in the truck."

"I want to see him," I said.

Clay tried to put his hand on my shoulder but I reared back. I kept one arm around the door handle. I wasn't going anywhere.

"You think he heard us?" said the woman.

"I'm sorry, but we can't see him today," Clay said. "There was an accident."

"He heard us, oh Jesus," the woman said. She sounded like she was going to cry. "Just take a look at him. No doubt about it."

Clay knelt down at my side. He put his arm around my waist and pulled me close until I could feel his whiskers on my cheek. His breath smelled like Big Red gum and his voice was so hoarse and

low that it crackled in my ear. "I'm sorry, Edgar. He's—there's nothing we can do."

"I want to see him," I said. I was not going to leave this place
without seeing him, without giving him these Dum Dums I had
stolen for him.

Clay asked the woman where Cecil was and she wrote the directions for the hospital on a blue slip of paper. We rode in the truck for
a few minutes and stopped in front of a brick building almost identical to the one we had just left. A warm mist fell in slow waves, making no noise at all. We walked down long white hallways, our wet
shoes squeaking on the tile floor, and passed into a room where a
young, chocolate-skinned man sat at a desk eating beef jerky. He
wore a light blue hospital uniform and a name tag that said NARCISCO.

"You the funeral home?" he said to Clay. "They's supposed to send
somebody this morning."

"We're here to see Cecil Jimenez," Clay said. "The people from
the detention center told us this is where he is."

"The boy in the papers? He's here. You the family?"

"We're friends."

Narcisco shook his head. His cheeks were spongy with acne scars
and his slicked hair shone in the electric light like a puddle of the
blackest oil. "If you ain't the family or the funeral people then I ain't
got no business with you. You want, I can call my supervisor down
here but she'll tell you the same thing."

"This boy was his best friend," Clay said. "He just wants to see
him one last time."

Narcisco shrugged, went back to gnawing on his jerky. He said,
"Can't do nothing for you."

Clay took out his wallet and pulled out all the bills inside, dropped
them on the desk. Narcisco stared at the money for a long time, not
blinking or moving. "*Carajo,*" he said. "I'll give you one minute. If I
pound on the door, that means you get your asses out of there. I
don't feel like getting fired today."

He got up and pulled the lever on a wide stainless steel door.

"They was going to do an autopsy on him, then decided not to. Autopsies ain't free, you know."

Narcisco pulled the door open and waved us in. "He's the one on the left, I think, and don't touch."

Clay went in first and I followed. The room was small and cold and there were only two gurneys there, shoved against opposite walls, both covered with the same light blue cloth of Narcisco's uniform. The door clicked shut behind us. Clay went to the gurney on the left, lifted the cloth, his hand shaking, and let it back down. "Ah, damn," he said. I stared at the shiny brass drain in the middle of the floor that seemed to gather all the light in the room.

"Edgar, I don't know ..." Clay said. His eyes were red and wet and his jaw hung slack. I watched my hand reach out to pull away the cloth. Clay made no move to stop me.

Cecil lay on his back, his face tilted toward us. His skin was yellow-white and his eyes, both ringed with dark purpling bruises, were closed. His left hand, crusted black with blood, hung slightly off the edge of the gurney, and his hair, always so carefully combed down over his forehead, was matted and pressed in odd, swirling configurations against his scalp like a wheat field after a hailstorm. From inside the darkness of his slightly opened mouth I could see the tooth he had chipped on a toilet bowl struggling with Nelson and his tribe.

I held my shirt in my fists and tried without luck to tear it in half. Since the moment we had left the office, I had not stopped praying, mumbling *please please please,* begging God to wipe away everything the woman had told Clay. In the cab of the truck and walking down the long corridors of that hospital, I made bargains, promising God that I would never sin again if He would make it all a mistake, a lie, a misunderstanding. I longed for my typewriter, wanting to put my promises down in ink, wanting to make them last. The words I whispered into my hands disappeared the moment they came out of my mouth, but I said them anyway, and with all the faith I had: *Please, I will do anything, I will give anything, it will be okay, please.*

But here he was, death written all over him in stark light and shadow. Against every reasonable explanation, here was this *thing* that had once been my friend Cecil, stiff and pale and empty, something to be shoved against a wall and draped with a cloth. I tried to cry or laugh or yell, to make some noise of protest, but every bone and muscle in me was locked tight and I stood there trembling with fury, the paper bag of Dum Dums rattling in my hand.

In an instant the tiny flames of faith and hope I had borne into that room flared into oblivion, leaving a single black desire, hard and cold as a cinder at the center of my chest: I wanted to kill the God who had done this to Cecil, who had done this to me. He might have been able to forgive me for stealing, for all my other sins, but I knew I would never forgive Him for this. Right then, if only it were possible, I would have taken Art's knife from my sock and with all the strength of my child's body, driven it into His heart. Forget about forgiveness and repentance, I would have murdered God the Father, I would have slashed and stabbed and gutted Him for what had been done to Cecil and to Art's wife and daughters, to my mother, to little Dean, to Ismore, to Sterling, to all the dead people in the world and to all the people who had to go on with their lives, remembering.

The heavy door opened behind us and Narcisco told us to get a move on, it was time. He drummed a pen on the tiled wall, the sound of it echoing wildly in that small space, and then he walked over to me and tugged on my shirt sleeve. "Get your asses on out of here, come on."

Clay turned and gave Narcisco a sudden, fierce shove, sent him reeling backwards into the thick steel door, which boomed and shook on its hinges.

"You stay away," Clay whispered, his voice cracking like ice.

Narcisco picked himself up, checked to see that his uniform was still situated properly. "You, *pendejo,* you're lucky I don't beat you all to shit right now, fucking Ichabod Crane, fucking Abraham fucking Lincoln."

Clay asked me if I was ready to go. I nodded and he pulled the cloth back over Cecil's face and that was all.

We left in a hurry, Narcisco yelling down the hall that he was going to call the cops if we didn't get the hell on out. Outside, we sat together in the cab of the pickup for a long time, staring out the windshield at a sky that was beginning to clear, the low sun pouring itself under the edge of a vault of dark clouds.

Clay mumbled, shook his head. He was pale behind his dark beard and he kept his eyes closed. "It's not . . ." he said, his voice a falling whisper. His hands, covered with hairs glowing bronze in the slanting light, gripped the steering wheel and let go again. "It's not fair."

Eventually we drove, the sun at our backs, the desert full of elongated shadows, all pointing us in the same direction. On one side was a range of low mountains, mute in the distance and on the other sandstone buttes that blazed in the dusk like red coals. I opened up the bag I still held and took out a Dum Dum. It was pineapple flavored and instead of sucking on it, as Cecil used to do with such care and love, I crushed it between my molars, the violent *crack* it made loud and satisfying. The highway hummed, the world grew dark around us and one by one I ate them all, gnashed them into a thick, crunching syrup—cherry, root beer, watermelon, mystery flavor, cream soda, lemon-lime, all mixed together—their sticks littering the floor under my feet like tiny bones, their gritty sweetness a poison on my tongue.

THE FINAL RESURRECTION

FOR THE REST of that summer I lived in a daze, a sense of desolation trailing me like a swarm of flies. All my desires had dried up, my pastimes gone sour; I no longer had any interest in eating or watching television or jacking off—I felt hollow and ungainly, like a jerry-rigged mannequin constructed of wood and scrap metal and rope. During those long empty summer days that replaced each other without variation, I would sleep most of the morning, making my rounds with the animals, feeding and watering them, cleaning out the pens and cages, and then spend a good part of the afternoon typing, which Brain was wise enough never to bother me about.

Mostly I typed jibberish, descending into a kind of trance where there was nothing but the clicking of the keys and the hammers striking paper, the rhythm getting the best of me, speeding into a heedless, breakneck pace that often ended with the hammers jamming together like too many fingers reaching for the last piece of pie. Sometimes the rhythm would slow—I can't say I had much control over any of this—stretching out until each hammer stroke was the ticking of a clock or the beating of a worn-out heart. I could type for two or three hours at a time, my fingers pounding out words and phrases without sense or meaning except to express the blackness inside me.

One day Lana found me typing in my room and asked me to stop for awhile so she could talk to me. It was late afternoon and strips of light from the window shade fell across her face like the bars of a cage. She looked at the stacks of sheets I had typed, each nearly blacked out with a storm of letters, and asked me to sit next to her on Brain's bed. In kind, whispered words she explained the concept of resurrection to me, how at the time of Christ's Second Coming all mankind would be resurrected, we would all rise up out of our graves, our bodies youthful and without blemish, never to die again. She held her hand on my arm and her eyes grew damp and soft as she talked. I knew that she was thinking of little Dean and looking forward to the day when she would be able to pick him up and hug him close again. But in my state I found no comfort in anything she told me. I imagined the entire population of the world, everyone who had ever lived, clawing themselves out of the ground all at once, disoriented and groggy after the long sleep, clods of dirt falling from their hair and clothes, dust rising off them like smoke, and the teeming confusion of millions of people trying to find their lost loved ones at the same time. Those lucky enough to die or be buried

together would have it easy—but what about the rest of us? How
would we ever find each other? For weeks I had dreams of wandering dirty and lost through milling crowds, searching the blighted
earth for my mother, for Cecil, calling out their names until I was
hoarse. In the worst of the nightmares these millions of frustrated,
worn-out people, grimy and abject as refugees, would become agitated, tripping over each other, pushing through the tangle of limbs
and faces, shouting for their fathers and mothers and children and
grandparents, getting so fed up and angry that somebody would end
up bumping somebody else and a fight would start, punches thrown
and faces scratched and the next thing you know there would be a
worldwide brawl, millions of dirty, resurrected people gone berserk,
grappling and yelling and biting, throwing rocks and yanking at each
other's rotten clothes, and Jesus looking down sadly from His golden
throne wondering how it had ever come to this.

During those days that yawned into weeks I tried very hard to
convince myself that God and Jesus and the resurrection were just a
bunch of lies told by some well-meaning anglos, but it was no use.
God was out there. He had touched me and I had felt His presence,
which was more than I could say about my own father.

I believed in Him in the same simple and dogged way Grandma
Paul had believed in Him. But because I believed He existed did not
mean that I had to trust Him, or even like Him. Just as much as I
knew He lived, I also knew that He wasn't the kind, benevolent guy
everyone had made him out to be, and I vowed never to be caught
begging anything from Him again. From all that I had witnessed and
been a part of in my short life, I could come to only one of two con-
clusions: either God was a crazed lunatic or He was just plain mean.

The only comfort I could find during that time was in my dreams
and fantasies about the mailman. I didn't have any idea where he
was, but every day I drafted a different letter to him, telling him that
I was alive and well. These letters, like my letters to Cecil, were often
full of lies: I told him that I was living the carefree life of a child who
had everything he needed. I told him that I was happy.

I had begun to feel some kind of kinship with this man I didn't
know, a connection: I understood what it meant to be responsible, by
accident or fate, for the death of another human being. More than
anything, I became obsessed with the idea that I could relieve him of
that burden—I could track him down and knock on his door and
say, *Look! It's me! I'm alive!* How thrilled he would be, this child he
had killed years ago suddenly appearing at his door, in his own way
resurrected, grown and whole and healthy, once dead but now alive
and full of good news, nothing less than a miracle. I fantasized about
such a moment endlessly, shamelessly; it was the only way I could
relieve myself of the steady hurt, the guilt that burned in my throat
like bile. I imagined him with his white skin, his orange hair and
blue uniform, the pants of which he had wrapped around my head
to stop the bleeding that summer day long ago. He would invite me
into his house and I would tell him my miraculous story. He would
listen in awe and he would hug me, weeping, *Thank you, Edgar, thank
you, I am so happy,* transformed in an instant from a man twisted
inside out with guilt and grief to someone struck with the realiza-
tion that our worst mistakes can be retrieved, that death can be traded in for life, that what has been destroyed can be made whole again.

STRANGER

ONE BRIGHT SEPTEMBER morning I came out of a deep, troubled
sleep to find my sheets soaked: that familiar clinging chill. I jumped
up, threw the blanket off and pulled at the sheets, hand over hand,
like an islander hauling in a net full of fish. How could I have ever
wet them this badly? It was as if Edgar's bed had been run through a
car wash.

Brain rolled out of the bottom bunk, his hair in a tangled commotion, and watched me strip off my wet pajamas, the elastic waistband snapping against my legs. "What happened?" he said.

"Nothing," I said. "Don't worry about it, go back to sleep."

Brain walked out of the room and I yelled after him to come back. He returned with Lana, who immediately began trying to pull the sheets away from me, saying it was okay, nothing to worry about, Edgar, it happens to the best of us. Soon we were engaged in a tug-of-war, Lana full of soft, soothing words while she heaved and yanked, Edgar apologizing with everything he had, digging his heels into the mattress and twisting the ends of the sheets around his fore- arms. It was a struggle, but eventually Lana was able to break my grip and wrest the sheets away, which she dropped on the floor next to my wet pajamas. "One more thing and it will be all over," she said, and with the no-nonsense attitude of a nurse went to work peeling my underwear down to my ankles. Now I didn't complain or resist; I had reached the dregs of humiliation and could go no lower.

After Lana left to throw the wet sheets in the washer, I sat naked and heedless on my damp, stripped-down mattress. Brain stepped to the left and to the right, craned his neck, squinted.

"Hey," he said. "You have hairs on your tally-whacker."

He nodded slyly as if he had just obtained a very important clue, as if suddenly everything made sense. "I was wondering," he said, "when you were going to move out of my room."

I knew this was coming, I just didn't expect it this soon. The night before, during Family Home Evening, Lana had made two announcements, the first of which was that Trong, who had gone to visit her cousin in Kansas City, had decided to stay there and would not be returning. Now that her room was free, I could move in any time I wanted. Of course, I didn't want to move in, I wanted nothing to do with a room where a beautiful baby had strangled to death in his own crib. I knew little Dean's ghost was in that room and I knew if I moved in he would haunt me to no end.

But I didn't say anything, made no objection. Family Home

Evenings were about harmony and positive feelings, not about con-
flict, this is something our church leaders had made clear to all of us.
Every Monday night we were to come together, sing hymns, discuss
the gospel essentials, play a game or two and have some refreshments,
always refreshments. We were supposed to find joy and comfort in each
other's company. We were supposed to learn how to love each other.

Lana would round us up and we would sit together in the overstuffed, sweet-smelling family room, facing off warily, Clay and
Lana's grim pioneer ancestors watching us from their places on the
wall. Sunny would sigh and bite her nails, Brain would mumble
under his breath whenever somebody said "who" when they should
have said "whom," Edgar would sit perfectly still and do his best not
to utter a word, Clay would sink into his recliner until he drifted off,
and Lana would talk herself frantic, trying to fill the silence, reading
out of the Family Home Evening manual, which had on its cover a
picture of a toothy, ecstatic family paddling a canoe.

Last night, though, was a little different. First was the Trong
announcement and then Lana got really serious, her voice taking on
an unusual amount of gravity. Instead of lounging in his La-Z-Boy,
Clay sat next to her on the couch. Brain and Sunny gave each other
questioning looks. Clay and Lana were almost touching.

"Your father and I have been discussing this over the past couple
of months and we decided to bring it up with you tonight. It's something that affects all of us and something we should decide together.
It's something we'll all have to agree on, and even then there are no
guarantees that we can make it happen. We were wondering what
you would think about Edgar becoming a permanent member of
our family."

There was a stretched-out moment in which I heard the grandfather clock tick six times.

"You mean forever?" Brain said.

Lana nodded. "Of course. But that's only if it's something Edgar
wants and something you and Sunny would accept. It also depends on
Edgar's uncle, who is his legal guardian, and the government will have

a say in it, adoption is something that's complicated and can take a lot of time, so we don't want to rush into it. I want you all to think about it, pray about it. It's something we'll have to decide on together."

The only word I heard in all of that was "adoption." I looked at Brain, who glared darkly back at me. Even Sunny, whose face never seemed to deviate from its look of disaffected boredom, wore an expression of mild shock.

Adoption, Edgar said to himself over and over. It was a word that sounded too much like hope.

And that was it for Family Home Evening. There was no lesson from the manual, no opening or closing hymn, not even a prayer. Lana said, "Well, refreshments in the kitchen!" and we sat around the dining room table, eyeing each other nervously and stuffing ourselves with warm peach cobbler topped with ice cream.

Now, only twelve hours later and Brain was already trying to boot me out of his room. I got off my bed and pulled on a pair of cutoffs.

"You're not going to take a shower?" Brain said. "You just got done peeing all over yourself, like in the old days."

I had forgotten that during one of our late night conversations, I confessed to Brain that I had once been a bed-wetter. I promised myself right then I would never tell him another secret again.

"I'll shower in awhile," I said. "Right now I'll be going downstairs."

Brain followed me. He wasn't about to let me off the hook. Down in the zoo I pretended to feed the fish.

"I'll help you move out today after school," Brain said. "You don't even have to ask me."

"I'm not moving," I said.

"Oh yes you are. That's your room now. That's where all the guests are supposed to stay. That's the *guest* room."

"I don't want to stay there."

"It doesn't matter what you want. Do you think this is your house now or something? Do you think because you've been sleeping in my room you're in charge?"

"I don't think that."

"Good, because you're not. I tried to be nice and let you take my bed. Then you pee all over it. That's what charity will get you. Now Trong is gone and you won't even get out of my room. What's the point!"

I walked over to where Keith the Rat was spinning furiously on his wheel. I tapped the cage, dropped a couple of feed pellets next to him. He went on without pausing, a manic glint in his beady eyes. I was trying to keep as much distance between me and Brain as possible; if he got too close to me I was afraid I might throttle him. He stayed right at my heels, but I made a point of keeping him at my back. He stepped up next to me and said in a low voice, as if he didn't want the parrots to hear, "The only reason my parents want to adopt you is because they feel sorry for you. It's because you've got no father and a dead mother and a dead best friend and nowhere else to go."

I turned and grabbed him by the shoulder, gouging my thumb into the tender flesh just below his clavicle—something Rotten Teeth often did to me when he wanted to cause pain without putting out a whole lot of effort. I wanted to tell Brain that he should be careful too, he might end up dead like my mother and Cecil, death is what seemed to happen to the people who were close to me, but I had my teeth clenched in such a blind, flashing anger that I couldn't get the words out. Instead, I delivered the message as best I could by driving my thumb into his shoulder like a railroad spike.

He wrenched himself out of my grip and backed slowly up the stairs, his left hand on his right shoulder, his face flushed so red it looked like it had been turned inside out. "You don't ever touch me again," he growled. He had not cried out when I'd grabbed him, but now his eyes were filled with tears and he moved stiffly, still in pain. The scar on his forehead where Omar the monkey bit him had turned a dark, pulsing purple.

"I'm sorry," I called from the bottom of the stairs, but even to my ears it sounded like a hollow apology, made more out of habit than anything else.

Brain shook his head. He went all the way to the top of the stairs. He looked down on me from that great height and made a pronouncement that seemed to carry the difficult weight of truth.

"You will never be my brother," he said, his voice grating and full of tears. "You're a *stranger*. I don't know who you think you're kidding."

EDGAR AND SUNNY

ON A BREEZY, moonless night I waited for Sunny. Earlier I'd listened from the top bunk as she creaked open her bedroom door, passed through the clicking beads of the upper portal, went down the stairs on the zoo side and out the back way. It was a Friday night, and I'd learned over these past few months that Friday night was her preferred night for sneaking out into the mysterious world of sandwash beer parties and cruising Main until the early hours of the morning.

Restless, I lay in bed for an hour or so, and then put on jeans and a sweatshirt over my pajamas. I crept out into the backyard and waited for Sunny to come back. Since the first time I talked to her months ago we'd had a few late night conversations sitting next to the water tank. In the light of day she ignored me, hardly looked at me, but late at night in the secret confines of the backyard she tolerated me, even seemed to like me a little. Maybe the fact that she was usually drunk had something to do with it.

On one of those nights she had found me next to Doug the vulture's pen, digging a hole with a gardening shovel. That night, unlike most of the others, I was not in the backyard waiting for her to come home, hoping to talk to her. I was there to bury my crucifix. It had always spooked me a little, but now I couldn't stand to look at it, couldn't bear having it anywhere near me. It reminded me too much of Cecil: the bloody, half-naked Jesus, his head lolling to one side, his mouth open as if in the middle of one last agonized groan. Along with everything else, Mormons were against crucifixes and crosses of any sort. We should remember Jesus as He was in life, they said, not in gory, gruesome death.

As if it were that easy.

What kind of father, Edgar typed, *could do this to his own son?*

It didn't seem right to throw the crucifix away, so with my doctor's penlight poking from my mouth, I dug a hole as deep as my arm could reach, hacking through a network of tree roots, and dropped the crucifix inside. While she watched me fill the hole back up with dirt, Sunny launched into a breathless monologue about how she and her friends had almost rolled their car into a culvert on their way home from a party in the cedars south of town. She didn't bother to ask what I was doing. She had long since accepted that in the early hours of the morning Edgar could often be found in the backyard jacking off or talking to animals or burying crucifixes.

Sunny and I had begun to share secrets. She told me about her late night escapades and the boys she was in love with and what was going on between Lana and Clay. She rambled and flipped her hair around wildly, sometimes seeming to forget that I was even there. I found out Lana was seeing a psychologist for depression and that ever since little Dean's death she had been trying to convince Clay that they should move, get as far as they could from this small-minded town and this house haunted by Dean's presence. She'd had several job offers in other states, but Clay refused to go; he could not abandon his son's grave.

In return, I told Sunny bits and pieces about my life at St. Divine's and Willie Sherman, steering clear of any story that included my mother, Cecil or Dr. Pinkley. Sunny laughed in horror at the shit-eating episode but squinted suspiciously when I told her I had jumped off a cliff and not suffered any damage to speak of. Because she had shown interest in my head, and the way it had become broken and put back together, I told her about the mailman and about how he had run over me.

"They should have thrown that mailman in jail," Sunny had said.

I shook my head. "No. It wasn't his fault. He didn't know I was under there. He tried to save me afterwards."

"He should have looked. It's in the mailman code of conduct or something. Any moron knows that. Mailmen are supposed to look under their jeeps before they drive away. It's part of their job."

"They couldn't throw him in jail because he ran away," I said. "He thinks he killed me, but he didn't. He hurt himself because he thought he killed me. I'm going to find him and tell him I'm all right."

I went into the boxcar and dug out one of the more simple drafts of the letter I planned to send to the mailman. I held my penlight for her while she read it.

Dear Sir,

My name is Edgar Mint. A long time ago when you were a mailman in Arizona you ran over my head. I know you felt bad about it. I wanted to tell you that I'm not dead. I'm not even damaged too much. I get seizures and my skull is lumpy but that's it. Also, I was in a coma. Now I live with a nice family in Utah. I don't know where you are, but I hope to find you some day. Don't worry about me, I am fine, I am not dead. I hope you don't feel bad any more. Everything is all right.

                                    Your friend, Edgar P. Mint

p.s. I can not sign my name because my brain has one other small problem. I can't write. Don't worry about that either, I have a typewriter.

I was hoping Sunny would be impressed with my noble intentions, but she handed the letter back to me, sighed, picked up a pebble and plinked it into the water tank. She said, "How are you going to find him anyway? You don't even know his name. Come on, Edgar. Be real."

That crushed me. *Be real*. Even the slightest indication of disapproval from Sunny could keep me moping for days. But the most offhanded compliment or show of interest could keep me floating in a warm, happy fog for a week. I was an orphan and, like orphans everywhere, wanted little more than to be loved.

Tonight I was prepared to captivate her with a few more of my stories. In my fist I had the rock that had fallen out of my head, and I planned to show it to her, maybe even offer it to her as a token of my feelings. I couldn't imagine how she could fail to be impressed with it; it had fallen out of my head, after all, and there were still bits of crusted blood on it.

I was also considering making up a few episodes which might make me come off as a little more gallant and dashing; I didn't think jumping off a cliff in despair or being made to eat shit cast me in a particularly heroic light. But it seemed to be taking forever for her to come home. For more than an hour I walked around in the dark among the pens and corrals, trying to stay warm, scratching the goats between their horns, watching Otis the insomniac armadillo bang around in his cage like a little gray tank, talking to Dorothy the mule who was my favorite conversation partner because she would keep one big round eye on me and nod in resigned agreement at everything I said. Eventually, I lay down on a bale of fiberglass insulation and fell asleep.

When I woke up, Sunny was already there, sitting on the back steps. She had her face in her hands and she was sobbing. The breeze of earlier tonight had turned into a stiff wind which made the trees creak and groan, their bare branches clattering together like the legs of enormous horror-movie insects. I stood next to her for awhile, wringing my hands, trying to think of the best thing to say or do, the wind lifting my hair up off my head and setting it back down again.

The insulation had gotten into my pants and under my shirt, making me gyrate in an ecstasy of itching. Sunny's face was wet with tears, her eyes bleeding mascara.

"What," she said, "are you just going to stand there forever?" She choked on another sob, gagging and coughing until strings of mucus-thickened saliva stretched out of her mouth onto her shoes.

I sat down next to her and said, "Are you all right?"

"Ha!" she shouted into the wind and cried some more. I put my hand on her puffy nylon jacket, so lightly that she didn't notice me touching her. She cried for a long time. Each time I thought she was finished, she started again. My arm was beginning to ache and my butt itched unmercifully. When it seemed like she was finally settling down I said, "I have this rock here—"

"You know Mark Jacobsen?" Sunny said suddenly, looking up at me. I nodded. Mark Jacobsen was one of the boys she liked, maybe *the* boy. I had seen him a few times at school. He was tanned and loose-limbed and wore a puka shell necklace. He walked the halls with a slouched confidence, pointing slyly at everyone he knew. I hated him.

"Mark Jacobsen is such a *bastard*," Sunny said, swiping her mouth with the back of her hand. She started crying again, but not with as much conviction as before. In gradual, infinitesimal progressions I felt myself sliding closer to her until our thighs touched. I held my breath and then let it out as slowly as I could, my muscles rigid and slightly trembling. Sunny's hair kept blowing into my face, the ends whipping my eyes and tickling my ears.

"I'll bet you've never kissed anybody, have you," she said.

"Well," I breathed. "No."

For some reason, this made her laugh. "Would you like to?" she said.

"Like to what?"

She gave me a slap on the shoulder. "To kiss someone, aren't you listening?"

"Kiss who?"

"Who do you think? Do you see anyone else around here?"

My blood ran like water in my veins. "I don't know," I said. "I could probably think about it."

She laughed again, and as she did she leaned into me and I felt her slick face touching mine and I turned just enough that our mouths were lined up and she kissed me, a soft wet movement of flesh that sent a tingling all the way to my toes. Her fingertips moved like raindrops over the peaks and valleys and plains of my puzzled-together head. The wind lifted her hair up on each side of our faces, leaving us, for a moment, in a small contained space, the only sound the moist friction of our lips.

She pulled away and scooted a few inches away from me on the steps. I felt as if I had no strength in me at all and I wanted to let myself fall into her, like an exhausted man falling into a feather bed, but somehow I managed to keep myself upright. For awhile, neither of us said anything. We looked out into the blue darkness and listened to the wind.

Sunny made a funny, hiccuping laugh and stood up. Before she went inside she said, "Well, at least I kissed somebody tonight."

A DRIVE IN THE SNOW

I'll be waiting for you tonight at 12:00 at the stop sign at the bottom of the hill. I have somebody special I want you to meet! Don't be late!

Love, Barry

I found the note before classes started, resting on top of my book in my locker at school. I looked around, seized suddenly by the feeling that I was being watched, the blood boiling in my ears. But it was just the same students cruising the halls, shouting at each other and guffawing and bumping shoulders, not giving me a thought.

The last time I'd seen Dr. Pinkley was the day after Thanksgiving; I was with Lana and Brain at Shearer's department store and I looked out the window and there he was at the gas station across the street, talking on the pay phone. It was the first time I'd seen him since he showed up at the house dressed as a missionary. He was wearing his mirrored sunglasses and gray overcoat and he began shouting into the phone with such a ferocity that it looked like he was going to take a bite out of the receiver. I tried to read his lips but his mouth was moving too fast. The only words I could make out were "rip-off" and "Mexico." He then jumped into his car, a blue Torino, and disappeared going down Hamilton Street.

When we got home from our day of shopping, I expected to see that blue Torino in front of the house and Dr. Pinkley on the couch sipping a hot chocolate and chatting with Sunny. For at least a couple of weeks afterwards I existed in a state of low-grade paranoia: all day long I listened for his knock on one of the front doors or a tapping on my bedroom window. I watched for him at basketball games and church services. But he never showed up. He had come all the way to Richland and had not tried to contact me. This both disappointed me and gave me hope: maybe he had given up on me completely.

I knew, deep inside, that this was a false hope, a simple self-delusion. Barry was the only consistent thing in my life, he was as imminent as the weather. Every time I thought of him a panic would swell in the space behind my heart and lungs, like a tremor rattling up from deep underground. I felt helpless against the very idea of him; I could not hide from him, could not outrun him, could not find a way to slip out from under his shadow. Many times I had considered calling the police, or telling Lana and Clay everything. But I knew Barry Pinkley too well. Nobody—not the police, not the Mormons—could keep him away from me as long as he wanted to be a part of my life.

One thing I was sure of: if I did not show up at the appointed hour he would come and get me. I imagined him jimmying one of the windows and creeping through the quiet halls of that house, his dim presence like an infection.

That afternoon it began to snow. It was late February and we'd had a week of warm, blustery weather. Today, though, the sky had gone gray and flat and by the time I snuck out of the house that night there was nearly a foot of powdery snow on the ground. It continued to come down, the black, deadened air filled with tiny crystals of ice that fell with such a deliberate slowness that the houses and the humped forms of cars and shrubs and the glittering, skeletal trees seemed to rise up gently into the night sky.

I practically skied down the hill, *shooshing* through the powder, which swirled up in curtains of sparkling dust. I was wearing only jeans, a sweatshirt and my tennies—digging my winter boots and coat from the hall closet would have made too much noise—but I did not feel cold at all. The car, a maroon Crown Victoria, waited for me at the corner, its brake lights making two pink pools in the snow.

The door opened for me and I slid into the hot, smoke-filled interior. Barry was at the wheel and next to him sat a brunette who wore a jacket stitched together from the pelts of what must have been at least a dozen different creatures. Jeffrey slouched in the backseat, the ember of his cigarette glowing like a lit fuse.

Barry introduced the woman to me as Roberta, his fiancée. He reached over Roberta to pat my knee. "You ready to have a little fun tonight?"

"Okay," I said, and he stepped on the accelerator. The engine revved, the tires spun and whirred and Barry waited patiently, whistling a little tune and pressing the gas down all the way, until the car lurched once and inched haltingly forward, like a wagon pulled by a team of oxen. By the time we made it to the highway we were plowing forward into the dark night with a smooth momentum, throwing up billowing arcs of white on either side.

We drove for forty-five minutes, clumps of snow obscuring all the windows, Barry concentrating on the road through the narrow swath the wipers made and pushing Roberta's hand away when she tried to rub his leg.

"You get out of that house all right?" Barry shouted over the squall of the heater. "Nobody saw you leave?"

"I'm pretty quiet!" I shouted back.

Roberta smiled at me and patted my head as if I were a dog. She had beautifully feathered hair and I kept getting strong whiffs of her musky perfume. She yelled at Barry, "You didn't tell me he was a little Tonto!" By the time we stopped I realized something of a miracle had occurred; we'd been in that car for most of an hour and Jeffrey had not uttered a single word.

When Barry opened the door, I caught a glimpse of a split-level ranch house with icicles hanging off the gutter in rows like the teeth of fish, and in the distance some kind of electrical plant glowing with a yellow phosphorescent light and putting up billows of steam. Barry and Roberta got out and Barry told me to stay in the car for a few minutes, Jeffrey would keep me company, they had to arrange a few things and then they would come and get me. Once the door had shut Jeffrey said, "That man, coma-boy, is beginning to get on my nerves."

"Why are we here?" I said.

Jeffrey snorted with gusto. "You think I have any notion whatsoever? You think he tells me anything? He's losing it. He used to have it together, but now that the Mexicans moved in and took away our clientele, he decided he could find himself a market up this way. A bold plan, coma-boy, I'll grant you. Who would have ever thought the drug trade might be plied hereabouts? Not I. There are dope fiends everywhere, I'm telling you, even here in La-La-ville. Down south every fifth man, woman or child is a pothead or pill-popper in some form or another. Up here, maybe it's one in twenty-five, very hard to say. And even worse, around here they know how to camouflage themselves to look like the rest of the population. Where I come from a dope fiend *looks* like a dope fiend, it's in his interest to

appear as such." Through his nose he whistled a wistful little tune. "It
was a much simpler place."

Already snow had blanketed the windshield, leaving us with nothing but the murky light from the instrument panel. The idling car
rumbled and shook.

"So now what happens?" Jeffrey said. "The good doctor is distressed,
he is dismayed by this bad turn of fortune, by the apparent failure of his
new venture, and he is getting high more often than yours truly. He
sometimes gets so whacked out I have to pilot the ship, I know you
must shudder to think of it. Believe me, I was not cut out for leadership
or decision making. Do you mind if I light up a J back here?"

I heard a rustling of fabric and then Jeffrey's lighter gave off a flash
that made colored paisleys swim across my vision. The lighter
snapped shut and I heard deep sucking noises, and then the smoke
curled around the back of my head, making my eyes burn.

"I feel like I am in the presence of a kindred soul here," Jeffrey
said. "Why do you put up with him? You don't like him, do you?"

I hesitated. "No."

"Of course not. But here you are. He can be very persuasive. And
yet the irony is he can't get what he wants, which is to live the
dream, you know, the white clapboard house on Maple Street with
the wife baking cookies and Edgar the coma-boy sitting at the
kitchen table doing his homework, preparing himself for a medical
career. Problem is no woman will put up with him for more than
two weeks and he's hooked on morphine and little Edgar is big
Edgar and getting bigger all the time. The dream is dying, and I fear
things might get ugly. You know that mitt he gave you? I was with
him when he bought it at a pawnshop. He's never thrown a baseball
in his life. He's a warped son of a bitch."

I breathed in the smoke and immediately I felt as if my eyes were
floating, suspended in a warm, bubbling liquid. A question dislodged
itself from somewhere deep inside my head: "Did he kill my mother?"

Jeffrey laughed—*haw-haw-haw!*—as if I had told a particularly fine
joke. "He just gave her what she wanted, that's all! Hmm, yes. Same

for me, same for that old shithead Art, same for all of us. That's his talent. He knows what people want and he gives it to them, and there's really nothing in the world worse than that."

Another volley of smoke hit me in the back of the head. Jeffrey said, "I'm sorry about your mother, by the way. For some, death comes as a blessing."

"And Art? Is he dead too?"

"He should be so lucky. Still plugging away as far as I know. I sort of miss those good old days of convalescence, don't you? There's something worthwhile in reclining in bed and taking your meals on a tray. If only the nurses had been the tiniest bit sexy."

The driver's-side door opened and there was Barry, wearing a wide smile which lasted for only a couple of seconds. Snow lay on his hair like a cap of white lace. He peered into the backseat. "Are you . . . It's like the inside of a bong in here!" Swearing and spitting, he opened the back door, grabbed a fistful of Jeffrey's long hair and hauled him, trailing tendrils of smoke, out into the yard where they swung around in a tight circle like a couple of square dancers. When Barry released his grip Jeffrey staggered wildly backwards, arms going in circles, finally losing his footing and skidding into the deep snow. Barry bent over, his hands on his knees, catching his breath, and Jeffrey lay still on his back, buried except for his suede shoes pointing at the sky.

"Alas," came his muffled voice from out of the snow. "The bloom is off the rose."

EDGAR THE FABULOUS

IT WAS A SURPRISE party. Barry opened the front door and we stepped into a dark room which flared suddenly with light and the scattered shouts of "Surprise!!" Edgar was not surprised at all. His eyesight had become exceptionally clear and his bones felt as if they were filled with slow-moving sap. He wanted to laugh but seemed to have forgotten how.

Besides Barry and Roberta, there were five or six other adults gathered around a wooden table which supported a gargantuan, five-tiered white cake. The only one missing was Jeffrey, who had stayed prostrate in the snow despite Barry's efforts to get him to come in with us. Some wrapped presents lay next to the cake and a few red balloons were getting kicked around on the floor. The room smelled of marijuana and lemony air deodorizer.

"Roberta's the one who arranged for that cake," Barry said. "Have you ever seen anything like it?"

"A midget could live in that cake," said a short bald man in over-alls. "A whole family of midgets."

"It's not my birthday," I said.

"I know that," Barry said. "This is a get-to-know-you party, in your honor. These are some of my friends and I wanted you to meet them. I've told them all about you."

One by one he introduced them. The tiny bald guy was named Donovan. Ned the Man, flabby and pale and wearing a blue bathrobe, sat quietly at the table contemplating the cake. The dark-haired woman in the tube top was Annie. The middle-aged man in the sports jacket who came over and gave me a friendly chuck on the shoulder was named Dr. Cuevas. "My house!" Dr. Cuevas said in a strong accent. "You are bery bery welcome to be here." Trisha and Robin, who looked like sisters, gossiped with Roberta in a corner.

Soon a cry went up for Ned the Man to play one of his famous songs on the baby grand in the living room. Ned the Man shook his head shyly and tried to hide behind the cake.

"Ned the Man can flat-out play," Donovan told me. "And he doesn't do the old standards, like you'd think. Every song he does, he makes it up on the spot. The only difference between him and Elton John is Elton John isn't afraid to leave his own bedroom during day-light hours."

There was more urging, the women giving Ned the Man little shoves toward the piano. Ned the Man glanced around coyly. He was so pale he looked like he had been soaking for months in a barrel of vinegar. "Shall I?" he said, and everybody shouted "Yes!" He nodded with an air of resignation. "In honor of Edgar, then."

He sat at the piano, looked the keys over and began to play, his fingers moving expertly up and down the board. Suddenly he began to sing in a loud Broadway voice, *"Oh Ed-gar . . . he is so fab . . . u . . . lous, he is so mar . . . ve . . . lous, he makes my heart sing Love! Love! . . . Lo-OOOOOOOOOVE!!!"* He ended with a pounding flourish of chords and we applauded. Ned the Man sat with his head lowered, his hands in his lap, humble in his genius.

Next I opened the presents: a red sweater from Roberta, a packet of a dozen combs in all the colors of the rainbow from Annie, a bottle of Jovan Musk cologne from someone who wanted to remain anonymous. The last present was from Barry. He placed it in my hands gently, delicately, as if he was handing me a lit stick of dynamite. I knew what it was before I ripped the paper away: a stethoscope. His stethoscope.

"I bought that the day I got my acceptance letter from Johns Hopkins," Barry said. Roberta gave him a comforting pat. "It's hardly been out of my sight since."

Dr. Cuevas came over and gave it a close inspection. "Oooo," he said. "A Benderman! The Cadillac of the stethoscopes!" He took it from me, and instead of placing it around my neck the regular way, by pulling apart the earpieces, he solemnly slipped it over the top of my head as if he was conferring on me a medal of great honor.

One of the sisters came up to me, swiveling her hips and talking in a Southern belle voice, "Hello there, Doctor, are you ready to give me my physical now?" All the women shrieked with laughter and Barry told them to cut it out.

Until then, I'd been having a good time in spite of myself, but the stethoscope had ruined everything. It felt like an anchor chain around my neck. While I ate cake and drank Coke and watched the adults dance around the piano while Ned the Man played *chink-a-chink-a-chink-a* rockabilly tunes, I tried to get up the nerve to take it off. I thought about my empty bed in the darkness of the Madsen house. I wondered what they would do if they found me missing. Would they call the police? Would they cry and carry on? I imagined a SWAT team, like those on television, crashing into the house through all the windows, rescuing me and hauling Barry and Ned the Man and everybody else away in handcuffs. It was a fantasy that pleased me to no end.

By the time we left it had quit snowing and turned deadly cold. The place where Jeffrey had fallen was now an empty, human-shaped indentation and his footprints traced a wandering path out into the road and disappeared among the tire tracks. Behind us, the power plant glimmered in the darkness like a city of gold. I asked Barry where Jeffrey was, my breath sliding from the corners of my mouth in ribbons of steam.

"He went off to sulk somewhere," Barry said. "Don't worry, he'll be back. He has to turn everything into a drama."

Roberta had fallen asleep on the couch with an empty bottle of beer tucked between her breasts, so it was only Barry and me. Barry drove now with a contented heedlessness, the big car sliding all over the freshly plowed road.

"I want you to know that I'll be around a lot more these days," he said. "I hope we can spend more time together, you know, get used to each other. You had fun tonight, didn't you?"

I nodded. "That was a big cake."

"A beauty, no doubt about it. You liked Roberta, didn't you? She's a great woman, a real find."

"Nice," I said. "She's nice."

"Those are good friends, too, good people, the best. Nothing more important in this world than your friends. Remember that."

I asked Barry if he'd had any luck in finding my mailman.

"Well," he said. "I made a couple of calls, you know, cashed in a few chips, and I found out something that I didn't know about before, I don't know how I missed it. The Postal Service doesn't deliver to the reservation, Edgar, that mailman had no business being anywhere near San Carlos. What was he doing there? It's a mystery. You can bet I'm on the case."

For awhile we drove in silence, the only sounds the whirring heater fan and the crackling of tires on the icy road. I put the stethoscope in my ears—I had not taken it off at the party—and listened to my own heart. The hissing, watery *glug-glug glug-glug* I heard was the kind of noise you'd expect to hear bubbling up from the darkest depths of the sea.

I don't know what made me say it. I don't know if it was the marijuana smoke I'd inhaled or how tired I was, but I blurted it out suddenly, as if it wanted to come out of its own accord: "The Madsens want to adopt me." I still had the stethoscope on my chest and the words sounded rumbling and fathomless in my ears, like the voice of God.

Barry turned off the heater and looked at me. "What? Say that again?"

"The Madsens. They want to adopt me."

Without looking back at the road, Barry put his foot on the brake, not hard, but hard enough to make the car fishtail and slide onto the shoulder, where it ground to a stop. He never took his eyes off me. "Did they tell you this?"

I nodded.

"I should have guessed!" Barry slapped his palms on the dashboard. "These people will do anything to keep their grip on you. I know firsthand how they work, their methods of persuasion, they're masters at it. I mean, just with those missionary clothes we practically converted three different people, and we weren't even trying! They took one look at us and pretty much dropped to their knees, 'Baptize me! Baptize me, please!' It's spooky. I'm telling you, if somebody doesn't stop them, these people are going to end up ruling the world."

I took the stethoscope out of my ears. I said, "The Madsens are nice."

"Then this is what you want?" Barry said. "You want them to adopt you?"

Yes, I thought. *Yes yes yes.* As much as I knew, deep down, that it would never happen, that theirs was a world in which I didn't belong, I still wanted it, of course I did, I wanted it with all my heart.

"Well?" Barry said.

I shrugged.

Barry gave the ignition a vicious crank. "We'll see what happens," he said. "Let's just see what happens."

THE LONG WALK

HERE WAS EDGAR, for the seventh time in six months, waking up in a cold, soggy bed. It was not yet dawn and a bar of light lay under the closed door of Brain's bathroom. From the other side of the door came the soft, queer sound of his laughter: *coo-hoo coo-hoo-hoo-hoo.* Something wasn't right: though I was wringing wet from the waist up, my underwear and pajama bottoms were entirely dry, as if somebody had held me by the ankles and dunked me into a pool halfway. Even the back of my head was wet. I was pulling at the sheets, confounded, when Brain came out of the bathroom carrying a tall glass of water.

He switched off the light and I could see he was blinking as he crept up to the bunk beds, trying to get his eyes to adjust to the darkness. He climbed the first two rungs of the ladder, still making that little laugh of his. Just as he held the glass out over me, I grabbed his wrist, which caused him to jerk, sloshing some of the water in the glass right back into his face. He fell off the ladder, went down hard on the carpet and sat up sputtering and rubbing his eyes like a toddler in a bathtub.

"You!" I said.

"What?"

"You did it!"

"What? Edgar, it wasn't . . ." Water dripped from his eyelashes and nose. He clambered to his feet and backed up toward the bathroom until all I could see clearly were the whites of his eyes. "Are you going to hurt me?"

I was seriously considering it. Over the past few months he had been telling everyone who would listen that Edgar was a bed-wetter. The last time it had happened he stood next to me while Lana stripped off the bedding and said with a resigned sigh, "I hate to say it but it looks like it's about time for rubber sheets!" He had even used my Hermes Jubilee to write a letter to Dr. Pete, a retired physician who had his own newspaper column and dispensed medical advice to people who wrote in with their questions. In his letter, Brain told Dr. Pete that an "acquaintance of the family" was having trouble holding his bladder during the night. Dr. Pete had responded by saying that bed-wetting was normally the result of some sort of psychological upset, and if it continued after the age of six or seven should be treated by a trained therapist. Brain had cut the article out of the paper and pinned it to the bulletin board in the kitchen, where it stayed for most of the day before Lana saw it and took it down.

"It was you," I said. "This whole time."

In the darkness, I thought I saw Brain smile. "You don't belong here," he said. "I don't know why you can't figure it out. And I don't know how you could go this long without figuring out that your pee didn't smell like pee. Give me a break."

Brain had been doing everything he could think of to make life difficult for me. He had pretty much stopped talking to me, had reduced my typing time to an hour and a half a night, had made me confine all of my belongings to a six-by-six space around my steamer trunk, which he had marked off with masking tape. At first I thought he just wanted me out of his room, but it didn't take long for me to see that he wanted me out of the house altogether.

When I had told Lana and Clay that I didn't want to move to Dean's room, they seemed perplexed, maybe even a little miffed. They told me I could stay where I wanted, but every once in awhile they would politely inquire if I hadn't changed my mind. What a shame to let a nice room like that go to waste, they said, where I could type at my leisure and have all the elbow room I needed. I came to understand that for the Madsens, little Dean's room was more than a room: it was a space that needed to be filled.

So I gave in. I didn't want to seem ungrateful, I wanted only to please. Two days after I caught Brain trying to pour a glass of water on my crotch, Clay helped me move my trunk, my typewriter, my ever-growing wardrobe and collection of accessories. The room had two windows and wallpaper with dancing bears and ducks wearing galoshes. Even though a succession of exotic strangers had lived in it over the past three years, the room seemed to breathe the sweet, powdery smell of baby.

For the first time in my life I had a room all to myself. I was terrified. I lay awake, listening to the unsettled rasp of my own breathing, expecting at any moment to hear the strange echo of a baby's laughter or the desperate snuffling sound of a little boy suffocating to death in his own blanket. I would stare at the ducks on the wallpaper, who often seemed to shift around in their galoshes ever so slightly, and I would wonder if my bed was situated in the same part of the room as Dean's crib, if he had died right here, in the very spot where I now lay. The buzzing silence would get to be too much and I would have to get out of bed to creep around the house, checking on the animals, eating whatever was available in the refrigerator, trying to put my mind on other things.

And I always listened for Sunny. Over the winter she went out infrequently and it was too cold for me to wait in the back for her, so since that windy night we kissed on the back steps we had hardly talked. It was one of the reasons I had wanted to stay in Brain's room: to be close to Sunny. I liked to imagine her sleeping on the other side of the wall, her smooth skin bathed in moonlight, her small hands clasped on top of the pink flowers of her comforter. Now I felt like an outcast, all the way down at the end of the hall. The weather was getting warmer and I might not be able to hear her sneaking out.

So on those sleepless nights I would often get up and look out into the hall, which was always kept lit, on the off chance that I might catch her tiptoeing down the stairs. One night I did see Clay and Lana's bedroom door open and Clay step out. I jumped back in bed, pulled the covers up to my chin and listened to his creaking footsteps coming closer, past Sunny's room, through the beads and past Brain's room and then he was in my doorway, skinny as a nail in nothing but his temple garments, the light behind him eroding the thin cutout of his frame into almost nothing. I watched him through the blur of my eyelashes. He stood there for a minute or so, taking deep, shuddering breaths through his nose, and then he was gone.

Every three or four nights I would hear the beads of the upstairs portal swing and click and the same creaking as he padded down that long hallway. And then one night the arguing started, Clay and Lana's voices traveling like surging electrical currents through the walls. Even down here, all the way at the other end, I could pick out an occasional word. *So?* I heard Lana say, her voice high and sharp. *Is that all?* I pictured Sunny in her bed, straining to hear, and Brain in his, listening with his entire body, his eyes wide, and even Keith the Rat and the guinea pigs and the dozens of nameless gerbils and all the parrots, suddenly awake, the entire house poised around the disturbance at its center.

After twenty minutes the shouting was over and it was quiet again. The grandfather clock chimed and one of the parrots hummed part of a TV commercial in its sleep. I knew he would come and I waited. When he filled up my doorway with his shadow it felt as if the room became bigger, expanding all around me. He stayed much longer this time, sucking air through his nose, holding, blowing it out through his mouth. Then he stepped into the room, quietly, and stood over me. I closed my eyes all the way and lay rigid under my blanket, light flickering under my eyelids. I felt the pressure in the mattress when he knelt, placing both hands on the bed for support, and lowered his face to kiss me on the side of the forehead, a gentle father's kiss. With his fingers he touched my hair and then he got up, his knees popping, and stumbled out into the light to make the long walk back.

THE GOOD SAMARITAN

"I'VE GOT SOMETHING very important to show you!" Alan Lovejoy shouted over the tearing wind and the *brup-brup-brup-brup* of his dirt bike. "You won't believe this, you're going to flip out!"

Alan Lovejoy and I had become friends over a Sunday school lesson. Sister Dill, who was the new Sunday school teacher for the fourteen-to-fifteen-year-olds, had presented a lesson on the importance of being kind to the lowly, the powerless, the unpopular, the weak, the abused. She inflicted the parable of the Good Samaritan on us once again (our teachers had a way of sneaking it into just about every lesson) and showed us a picture of Jesus with His arms around three of the kind of undesirables she was talking about: a cowled leper, a chubby prostitute with tears running down her cheeks, and a disheveled publican, who peered over his shoulder as if he was worried about getting beaned with a rock. Sister Dill challenged us all, in the upcoming week, to become more Christ-like, to seek out the downtrodden and lowly, and to offer them our friendship and love. Three seconds hadn't passed after the closing prayer before Alan Lovejoy was at my side.

"Hey Edgar, I was wondering if you'd like to go take a ride on my new dirt bike some time." He whacked me on the back like we were

old pals. "I've got my permit and now I can drive on-road." For a
moment Alan and I eyed each other. This was the first time he had
ever said a word to me. We both knew what was going on, but I
decided I'd play along as long as I got a ride on a dirt bike out of it.

"Okay," I said. "You can come pick me up after school. Wednesday
would be fine."

Alan was tall and handsome in a sort of prissy way, with his pointed nose and thin, pale neck and blue eyes as shiny as new paint. Alan
was the kind of kid who was popular and well liked and managed
not to have any real friends—he was just too righteous. He organ-
ized service projects, had been the president of both the deacons and
teachers quorums, became an Eagle Scout before he turned fourteen. He was one of those kids who made a point of praying over his
food in the lunchroom. When he was asked to talk in sacrament
meeting—which seemed to be every other month or so—he did not
read from prepared notes but quoted scriptures from memory and
told Book of Mormon stories in a way that made even the children
in the congregation sit up and listen. When he bore his testimony, it
was like poetry, each word singular and carefully placed, his hushed
voice an instrument of beauty and conviction.

The only thing that Alan Lovejoy and I had in common was that
we were both converts. Alan's family, Ohio Catholics who had never
met a Mormon until coming to Utah, had moved to Richland when
Alan was eleven. Within a year, Alan had been converted and baptized, but his parents and little sister were still holding out. In
Richland, as in pretty much all of Utah, if you were not a Mormon
you were a "nonmember," and if you were a "nonmember" you had
to be constantly on the ready for the barrage of pamphlets, missionary visits and invitations to sacrament meetings, firesides, ward parties, dances and potluck dinners. A few years ago at Christmastime,
in a foolhardy show of defiance, Alan's father had erected not one
but three fifteen-foot-high crosses on his front lawn and strung them
with Christmas lights. For two days a group of neighbors and members of the ward, including Alan himself, kept a vigil in front of the

Lovejoy home, softly humming hymns and Christmas carols until Mr. Lovejoy came out in his Notre Dame T-shirt and yelled "Good Lord, enough already!" and took the crosses down.

For several weeks Alan had come by every Wednesday to pick me up on his motorcycle. Sometimes we would go out on the trails south of town, sometimes back to Alan's house, where we would sit in his basement and play foosball or throw darts and drink the lemonade his mother made. Alan believed this kind of thing was bringing joy and fulfillment to my pitiful existence. Often he would have me quiz him on his scriptures; he had been the seminary scripture-chase champion three years running and was not about to relinquish the title. But today it was a Friday, and Alan had shown up unannounced in front of the house, revving his engine until I came out onto the porch.

Now I held on tight as he leaned expertly into the curves of an old railroad access road. I shouted, "Where are we going!"

"You'll see!" he shouted back. "It's right up here."

He pulled over and parked the bike behind a thicket of wild oak. Off to our left was a gravel pit dug into the side of a small butte. It was the time of year when spring was giving way to summer and the afternoon light was so flat and bright it was like brass against your teeth. Far off to the west a storm was coming over the horizon, turning the air the color of a bruise. Alan said, "We have to walk in the rest of the way. And try to be quiet."

I followed him up the road a ways before he cut out through some cedar trees and crept down a gradual slope that descended toward a small, swift-running creek choked in places with young cattails and willows. He positioned himself behind a low, stickery bush and peered down at something by the creek. "They're here," he said. "I knew it."

I squatted next to him and looked through an open space in the bush. What I saw gave me an instant, muscle-locking chill, like ice water at the roots of my hair. Down next to the creek, about seventy-five yards away, Lana and Dr. Pinkley sat together on the hood of

Lana's Country Squire station wagon. I closed my eyes for a moment, felt my innards heaping themselves up behind my ribs. When I opened my eyes they were still there. Their backs were to us and they were sitting about six inches apart. The sun made eerie, rippling reflections between them on the hood of the car.

I studied them, trying with all my might to turn them into two strangers I had never before laid eyes on.

"You know who that is?" Alan whispered.

"Who?" I said, my voice nothing more than a hollow scratch.

"That's Sister Madsen, can you see? I don't know who the guy is, but I saw them together at the Swavely meetings. My mother caters those things, you know, and I help with the layout and cleanup. I noticed this guy getting really friendly with Sister Madsen, sitting next to her and getting her punch and all that. Then one day they sat outside by his car and drove away together. I knew something was funny so I followed them. This is the third time I've seen them out here."

Alan's blue eyes smoldered with a pure, virtuous heat. "This has really been eating at me, Edgar, I don't know what's the appropriate thing to do here. I've prayed about it but haven't received a clear answer. I felt prompted to bring you out so you could help me make the right decision. This isn't right, it just isn't. Sister Madsen is a married woman, and this guy, I don't think he's even a member. He smokes, and look at that hair."

"Have you told anybody?" I said.

"I thought about telling Bishop Newhauser, but I wanted to bring you out here first. Do you know who that guy is?"

I shook my head, tried to make out their voices, which seemed to dissolve instantly into the sun-scalded air. Slowly, Barry reached behind Lana and moved his hand up her back. She went stiff for a moment, then seemed, ever so slightly, to move toward him.

"Oh no," Alan said.

Barry Pinkley made circles with his fingers on the back of Lana's pink blouse, running his hand up into her hair. The first time they

kissed I hardly saw it was so quick, then they kissed again, which
they held for a few seconds.

"Ah no, no way," Alan said, his voice taking on a tone of lordly
pain. "This is all new. They've never done this before."

Bone by muscle by joint, I could feel myself slowly coming apart.
Watching Lana and Barry touch each other in ways I had never seen
Lana and Clay come close to, I felt it, that cold, creeping thing—the
ruin that I brought with me wherever I went, that had been trailing
me my entire life, like a shadow or an infection or a curse, gathering
itself together and catching up with me once again. I had believed
that I could outrun it, that I could escape into another, better world.
I had even made myself believe that God, in His goodness and
mercy, had cleansed me of it in the waters of baptism, that I had
become a new and improved Edgar, transformed and glorified by the
spirit. But then last summer I had walked into the Madsens' living
room to discover Barry, more real than any ghost, sitting on the
couch and grinning like a fallen angel, and I knew I had been fool-
ing myself. Then in that cold morgue I had lifted up a sheet to find
the dead body of my friend Cecil, just one more person hapless
enough to fall under the shadow of Edgar's life, and I had come to
understand that nothing had really changed, that I would never be
good or strong enough to escape what, in the end, was part of me, as
much a part of me as my heart and guts and lungs.

In an effort to keep my balance I grabbed at the bush we were
hiding behind and the stickers speared into my palms, making them
bleed. Over the horizon lightning branched out of the sky like a
crack on a windshield. Lana and Barry did not sit together much
longer. Lana stood, put her face in her hands, turning toward us, and
shook her head in what looked like disbelief. Before she got in her
car and drove away, she smiled at Barry, and kissed him quickly once
more on the mouth.

Barry watched her go, then immediately went to his car, which
was partially hidden behind an embankment covered with long
grass. It was a blue El Camino with a yellow stripe down the side, the

same car Barry had been driving the last time I saw him, about six weeks before.

On that day he had called me at home during breakfast, presenting himself to Clay as Elder Rivers, and told me he was going to pick me up after school. He had asked me to bring the mitt and ball he had given me; he wanted to take me to the park to play a little catch. I spent an hour digging around the garage until I found an old softball mitt of Clay's and a few scuffed, gray baseballs. Barry didn't notice that I didn't have the mitt or ball he'd given me—he brought a big, floppy glove of his own and threw the baseball like a person who was left-handed but didn't know it. He looked like a wreck: his face wrung out and pasty, his checkered shirt and denim pants as wrinkled as any two items of clothing could ever hope to be. I asked him if he had found my mailman yet.

"I don't know what it is with you and the mailman," he said. "But I've got a guy looking into it, says he's got some leads." Every time he threw the ball his sunglasses slid all the way down to the tip of his nose and nearly fell off. "Those people you're with say anything more about that adoption?"

I shrugged, tried my best to act like I didn't care. "They're working on it, I guess. People have come over to the house a few times with forms and papers. They said they've hit some roadblocks. Clay drove down to Phoenix last week to talk to the government."

I slung the ball with everything I had. Barry stuck out his glove and the ball sailed by and hit him in the sternum with a sharp crack.

"Good one," he coughed. "Right on the money."

A pronounced jitteriness came over him: he bounced on his toes like a boxer, slapped his hand into the glove and called "*Hey-batta hey-batta hey-batta-batta-batta*" even though nobody was doing any batting. It was a cool windy day, but he was already sweating through his shirt and he dropped every ball I tossed to him. Finally, I rainbowed the ball over his head, just to make him go after it, and he ran it down like his life was at stake, pumping his knees, his feet pounding hard on the turf, his oily hair flapping forward into his eyes.

When he came back he was wheezing and pressing the palm of his hand into the center of his chest, like he was trying to kick-start his own heart. "One second," he gasped, holding up a finger. "I'll be right back."

He went to the car and got inside. I could only see his head, which rested against the back of the seat. Behind the silver sunglasses that blanked out his eyes his face was completely slack. When he came back, he walked with a loose-jointed shuffle, a big smile on his face. A light, weird and cold as a glacier, came off his skin. "I forgot my glove," he said, looking all around. "And the ball too!" It didn't seem to matter to him. We sat down on a picnic table and he smoked a cigarette without saying anything. He smelled like sweat and chemicals. I glanced around to make sure no one I knew was watching us. The park was deserted except for an old guy trying to get a kite up into the air. I asked Barry where Jeffrey was.

"Disappeared," Barry said, waving his cigarette in a circle. "That night in the snow is the last I saw of him. He was getting to be a drag anyway. I have the feeling he'll show up again when he needs something. You can do all the favors in the world for somebody, you can offer them friendship and loyalty, and they'll abandon you every time when things get rough."

He took off his sunglasses and looked at me under heavy lids. His eyes were bloodshot and watery and without focus.

"Are you sick?" I said.

He jammed the sunglasses back against his face. "Look, you don't worry about me. You worry about yourself. You worry about these Mormons turning your brain into egg salad."

I scanned the table. The only interesting bit of graffiti was a message scrawled in magic marker: *Jim Jr. Has Large Balls.*

For a time Barry kept perfectly still. I tried to see past his mirrored sunglasses but was unable to tell what his eyes were doing. Slowly, like a sinking ship easing into the great deep, he leaned forward, slumping until his head rested on his folded arms. Within seconds he was lightly snoring. He slept like that for nearly half an hour. I finally had to shake him awake so I could make it home in time for dinner.

Now, Alan and I watched as Barry rummaged around in the El Camino and came out with his black doctor's bag. He faced us and I could see that he was in much better shape than the last time I'd seen him; he was neatly shaved, with his shaggy hair parted on the side and combed back over his ears. He put on his sunglasses and rolled up the left sleeve of his shirt. He took a few things out of his bag, looked them over closely.

"Oh no," Alan said.

"What?" I said. I was having a hard time getting a good view through all the leaves, and had to pull back a branch to get a better line of sight. He'd already wrapped a piece of surgical tubing around his biceps and was pushing the needle of a syringe into his forearm.

"Please, please no. This is too much," Alan said. "This is drug abuse if I ever saw it."

Gone suddenly limp, Barry dropped the syringe and tubing into the bag and lay back on the hood of the car with his arms outspread. He slid off the hood in a slow, leisurely way, took a few stumbling steps and splayed himself out on a sandbar next to the creek.

"We're going to have to call the cops, that's all there is to it," Alan said. "Oh man, this is unseemly. This is about as serious as it gets. He gives himself a little too much of that stuff and it's an overdose. He could *die*. I know all about this."

I felt like wringing Alan Lovejoy's skinny neck. I said, "Let's go. I need to go home."

Back at the house, Lana's car was in the driveway as if everything was normal, as if everything in the world was still in its rightful place. Alan turned off his dirt bike. "We're going to have to go to the authorities about this," he said. His breathing was heavy and labored, his face lit with a fevered righteousness. "Sister Madsen is being corrupted by some kind of drug addict. We have to do the right thing here."

"Come inside for a second," I said. "I want to show you something."

We entered the door on the right, the one that opened into the zoo, and Alan followed me up the stairs. I got into my trunk, moved some papers around and took out the knife Art had given me. I opened the blade while Alan watched, and put the point of it into his belly.

"Hey!" Alan said. "Ouch!"

He tried to back up, but I stayed right with him, keeping the knife pressed into his belly button until I had him pinned against the wall.

"Promise you won't tell anybody what you saw," I said.

"Edgar, we have to do the right thing . . ."

I pushed the knife in a little harder. "Swear to God," I said.

"What?"

"Swear to God that you'll never tell anybody about seeing Sister Madsen and that man."

Alan tried to yell for help, but his voice had deserted him.

"Swear," I said.

"I swear," he croaked.

"To God."

"I swear to God."

"And Jesus."

"I swear to God and Jesus."

With my free hand I picked up a Book of Mormon off my desk. "Kiss this and then swear to God and Jesus."

I held it up so he could kiss it. Some dark part of me was enjoying this. He swore to God and Jesus and then made a whimpering sound when I eased the knife away.

"I don't know why you're doing this, but you need to think about—"

"If you ever tell anybody, I will sneak into your house at night and cut your throat," I told him. "Your mom and dad and little sister too. And that dog you have. Poochie."

Alan slid away from me along the wall and practically dove out the door. I followed him down the stairs to make sure he didn't talk to anybody on his way out. Down in the zoo he tripped over a bag of feed pellets and went down in a full knees-and-elbows sprawl. He didn't bother getting to his feet, just scrambled forward like an infantryman under heavy fire until he made it to the door.

He hauled himself up, pushed open the screen door and turned to me. He had regained a little of his composure, though his skin was still as pale as milk and his chest heaved. His expression was sad, Christ-like.

"God bless you, Edgar," he said.

Edgar laughed right in his face.

FAMILIES ARE FOREVER

IN THE DARK, sleeping house Edgar lay awake in his bed, listening. There was nothing unusual, only the regular night sounds: the queer mewling voices of the parrots, Keith the Rat doing laps on his wheel, the grandfather clock and its chimes, the old bones of the house settling and creaking, pipes ticking behind walls, and occasionally, from out of nowhere, a strange little hiccuping noise that I assumed was the ghost of little Dean making itself known in the black of night. No Sunny creeping down the stairs, no late night arguments between Lana and Clay. There was, though, something new in the air of that house, a pressure, a nearly undetectable change in atmosphere that I could taste on my tongue. Sometimes, when I listened very closely, I thought I could hear the pioneer ancestors mumbling and whispering restlessly from their places on the wall.

It was three weeks ago that I had seen Lana and Barry down by the creek, and during that time I had done nothing but wait and watch and listen, sick in my guts with dread. I scrutinized every move Lana made, her dress and habits and posture. I rifled her purse, combed every inch of her car, looked under her bed and in her closet, but found nothing out of the ordinary. The only change I discovered was her perfume. She no longer wore the sandalwood oil she had used since I had lived here. Her new perfume was flowery and sweet, and each morning, when she came into the kitchen smelling strongly of it, it made me feel so queasy I couldn't finish my Eggo waffles or bowl of Wheaties.

Even though I knew better, I tried hard to believe that what I had seen out by the creek was an isolated occurrence, that Lana and Barry's relationship was not a relationship at all, but something without past or future, a singular event. All I knew was that every Friday Lana left for the Swavely campaign meetings and usually didn't come back until well into the evening. I considered doing all kinds of things, from calling Barry and threatening to expose him, to telling Lana that her new friend was an off-of-center drug-addicted former doctor who had once tried to kidnap me. But in the end I decided to sit tight, wait, see how things turned out. To take some kind of action now, I was sure, would only make things worse.

In the meantime I couldn't sleep. I'd stay up half the night, listening for something—I wasn't even sure what—and the next day in class I'd end up snoozing with my head propped in my hand. Tonight I threw off my sheets and went downstairs. I checked on the animals—Keith the Rat was sleeping peacefully for once—and passed through the portal into the living room. Unlike the zoo, which was always lit up by the aquariums, this room was dark and shadowed, the only light slanting in from a streetlamp outside. I walked in a circle, the carpet thick between my toes, and looked at the pictures on the walls, which I had to peer at to see clearly. There was Sunny, four or five years old with ribbons in her hair, glowering furiously from Santa's lap; Clay and Lana on their wedding day in front of the St. George temple, holding hands next to a pine tree, Clay looking ridiculous in a crew cut and Lana so young and beautiful and shining I could hardly take my eyes off her; a school picture of Brain, refusing to smile, as somber and constipated as all of the ancestors put together, probably angry that his valuable time was being taken up with picture taking when he could be back in the classroom reading up on the Revolutionary War or doing long division; the four of them standing together next to a churning fountain with the Salt Lake temple in the background and a caption underneath that read FAMILIES ARE FOREVER. Nowhere, on any wall in the entire house, was there a picture of little Dean.

In the dark cave of the kitchen the old refrigerator hummed to itself, then quieted. For a time I did nothing but listen, the only sound the insistent ticking of the grandfather clock. I opened its glass door, stopped the swinging pendulum with my hand, and a dead silence filled the room like water rising in a tank. The old house was still, the animals asleep. And then I snapped alert: I could hear something, a faint rumble, not much more than a vibration underneath the layer of silence, a sound which at first I took to be nothing more than the coursing of my own blood, the soft stirring of every wet thing inside of me, but then realized it was coming from outside. I went to the window. On the other side of the fence, in the gravel under the dangling branches of the willow tree, was a car I had never seen before, a green Pierce-Arrow with its engine idling. Its headlights were off and there was nothing but pure black behind the windows. I knew without a doubt that it was Barry Pinkley in that car, watching.

It was too dark for him to see me, for me to see him. Then his face flared out of the void in bold orange, lit by the flame of a match. The light was gone in an instant, leaving only the tip of his cigarette pulsing and twitching like an ailing firefly. Barry was a mystery to me, even a threat, forever lurking beyond the edge of sight, and yet I was not scared of him, not really. I knew that he loved me, in his own way, more than anyone in my life ever had. And I knew that if I looked hard enough, I could find some small part of me that loved him back.

We are fools for those who'd have us. At a family reunion I'd heard Clay's uncle Bart say this while clutching his fat wife Sharon in one hairy arm. I'd typed it on my Hermes Jubilee the minute we got home. *We are fools for those who'd have us,* he'd said, grinning like somebody who didn't know any better. *And I'm the biggest fool of all.*

I knew I could walk out the front door right now, get in that car, and tell Barry to take me away. Off we would go, never to be heard from again, and the Madsens would be safe. They could go on, trying to figure out how to be a forever family, just as they had before Edgar and his damaged head had shown up in their lives. With me gone, the animals would still get fed, the chores would get done. There would still be waffles with peaches and cream and Family Home Evening and church on Sunday. Tomorrow morning, somebody would find the clock stopped and set the pendulum swinging again. There would be no pictures of me on the wall for anyone to take down.

But I didn't move. I stayed where I was, my feet planted in that carpet that was as soft and plush as a bed of moss. The ember of Barry's cigarette retreated slowly toward his face, sometimes casting just enough light that I could see the faint image of his lips and nostrils. Then the cigarette went out and he sat again in the blank darkness of his car like a fish in an aquarium filled with ink. I stared out that window through the ghost of my own reflection and nothing happened but the beat of my heart. I didn't move until the car pulled out into the road, gravel snapping under the tires, and glided slowly away, headlights off, past the quiet, shadowed homes of the good, the righteous, the unsuspecting.

WHAT EDGAR WANTED

I EMERGED OUT of the clamor and crush of school, walked right past the yellow bus and headed east toward the center of town. The Orson Niehart Community Center, where the John Swavely for

Congress meetings were held every week, was near the old depot on the opposite side of Richland, which meant I had a long way to go.

After a mile or so I was wishing for my golden bike, even with its perpetually flat rear tire. It was already May—school would be out in only two weeks—and the hot sun poured down like molten metal on top of my head. I walked along Canal Street, with its traffic lights and tourist shops that sold Indian jewelry and clocks made of petrified wood, and took a shortcut through Pioneer Park, where a statue of Brigham Young, looking paunchy and irate and wearing a cap of white bird droppings, presided over the wrought-iron benches and the dry grass and a couple of Mexican guys sleeping under their hats. By the time I made it to the community center, soaked with sweat and nursing a stitch in my side, Lana's car was already in the parking lot.

For awhile I hung back behind the old brick depot, its high windows and arched front entrance boarded over, and watched a few more people drive up and go inside. There were maybe two dozen cars in the parking lot, none of which I recognized as Barry's. After fifteen minutes or so, a banana-colored Monte Carlo with bad shocks barreled into the lot and pulled cockeyed into one of the handicapped spaces. Barry slipped off his sunglasses and stood in front of one of the windows for a moment, parting his hair with a big green comb, before he went inside.

I stepped out onto the sidewalk into open view. I tried to call out to him, but it felt as if my lungs were two sacks of sand, and what rose out of them was more of a hoarse whistle than any word you might be able to look up in the dictionary.

Barry swiveled his head around, looked up into the sky. I came across the street and he peered at me through the falling afternoon light. He put his sunglasses back on as if to see me better.

"Edgar," he said. "Holy sh—what are you doing here?"

I stopped about ten feet away from him. I said, "I want to talk to you."

Barry looked around. "How did you know I was here?"

"I saw you with Lana," I said. "I saw you."

"What did you see?"

"I saw you kiss her." It made me shudder to say it. "She's a married woman."

Barry turned his head slightly and the low sun flashed off the mirrored lenses on his face, making everything in my vision go red.

"Come here," he ordered. "We can't stand out in the open like this." He shepherded me around to the side of the building where a squat green air-conditioning unit sat at the end of a squared-off hedge rife with orange berries.

"Look," he said. He shook his head and looked down at his shoes. "I know you probably don't understand . . ."

I had to unclench my jaw to speak, and what came out was nearly a growl: "You stay away from her."

Barry raised his head in surprise. He wore a clean striped shirt and jeans. The sharp alcohol scent of aftershave wafted off of him. "You need to calm down a little here. Okay? You need to listen to me for a second. Jesus."

I carried my backpack in front of me against my chest, and had my right hand slipped inside it, clutching my knife. For the last few weeks I had been packing the knife in my sock in hopes of encountering Alan under the right circumstances so I might reiterate my threats, but he avoided me like I was sin itself. Even in church, he sat on the other side of the Sunday school class and refused to look at me. Once, when I approached him after sacrament meeting, he saw me and sidled up next to Bishop Newhauser, praying, I suppose, that the bishop might emanate some kind of righteous force field that would repel me and my kind.

Barry kept his gaze leveled at me. In the shade at the side of the community center, his pupils had dilated, flooding his eyes with darkness. The knife felt heavy and smooth in my hand and it alone gave me the confidence to hold my ground.

"Stay away from her," I said. "Don't ever come to that house again."

"Hold on, Edgar—"

"I don't want to see you anymore."

Barry jerked still, as if he had been seized suddenly from within, and his face shriveled in anger. He was standing against the hedge and with one hand he grabbed a handful of leaves and gave a stiff yank, causing a shower of berries to spring into the air as bright as gumballs. When he tried to pull away, the cuff of his shirt snagged on a twig and in an attempt to extricate himself he pivoted and writhed, his ears turning pink, his face pulsing. All at once he gave up trying to escape and attacked that hedge. With a sudden crazed energy, he punched it, kicked it, tore at its leaves and branches with his hands, trying to rip it out of the ground, a hail of berries sling-shotting and ricocheting every which way, bouncing and finally settling in the grass around his feet.

When he was done, he stood with his back to me, breathing hard. "Hah ... I'm sorry," he said. In an instant, his skin had become clammy and slick. "I'm really sorry about that. I haven't been feeling all that great."

He walked around in a tight circle, stopped, put his hand on my shoulder. When he tried to pull me closer to him I yanked my arm away and stepped back, still gripping the knife inside my backpack.

Barry stared at me for a moment, his palms upturned, before his whole body slumped and he sat down heavily on the wire grille that covered the air conditioner. His sleeve was torn all the way up to the elbow. He mashed his forearm against his mouth and started to weep, a low, hoarse keening. He wiped his nose with his sleeve and didn't look up.

"I don't know," he said, his words wet and thick. "I don't fucking know."

He bent so far over that his head was nearly between his knees. "I've tried, everything I've done, it's for you," he said. "When they brought you in that day on that stretcher, you were a lost cause, but I saw hope in you, I knew there was something there." Barry snuffled and made a hawking sound in his throat. "When nobody else wanted you I tried to get you out of that hospital. I've wanted so much to make you a good home, find a way that we wouldn't have to be on the run all the time, you know? It hasn't been easy. I searched you out, followed you all the way up here. What do you think I'm doing here? Getting my kicks? I'm doing this for you. I'm trying to help *you*."

"Please," I said, my voice a pitiful, ragged thing.

Barry made a few more hiccuping sobs. "Now Jeffrey is gone and Roberta won't return my calls and my health is falling apart. Everything is going to shit. Except for you. You're my ray of hope. Do you see? And then you look at me like you're scared of me, like I'm the goddamned bogeyman."

The hot coal of anger in my chest had crumbled to ash, leaving an empty, burned-out hole. The muscles in my arms and neck went loose and I let go of my knife. It was all I could do to keep myself from telling him I was sorry.

The air conditioner switched on, blowing up warm air that made Barry's shirt billow and flap like a sail. He looked up at me, his cheeks shiny with tears. Over the whirring of the fan he said, "Do you hear me, Edgar? Can you understand what I'm telling you?"

I hung my head, defeated. Barry wiped his face with the hem of his shirt, gulped a few deep breaths. He laughed and dabbed at his eyes. When he looked up he was already smiling again.

He jumped up from the air conditioner and put his hand on my shoulder and held it there, testing me. He said, "You know enough to keep your mouth shut about this, don't you?"

I stared at my feet, gripped with shame.

He let out a shuddering sigh. He said, "Do you need a ride home? How'd you get here anyway?"

"I like to walk," I whispered.

"Well, all right then, you get on home and I better get into that meeting, it must be half over by now. We've got to put up the good fight for John Swavely, you know."

I walked with him to the front of the building. Before he went inside he turned to me. "I almost forgot. It looks like my guy came through. We found your mailman. I had to pay extra for all the trouble it took, but you got your wish. Don't have it on me now, but I'll give you the address next time I see you."

Barry laughed and took off his sunglasses. A single orange berry was still caught in his hair. "Come on, Edgar, smile a little bit, show some life! This is what you wanted, isn't it? I got you exactly what you wanted."

A DANGEROUS PLACE

TWO WEEKS LATER I came home after the last day of school to find Brain in the zoo hugging a thirty-pound bag of birdseed. He told me that Lana was moving out of the master bedroom into the storage room downstairs.

"Moving?" I said.

"We're going to take all this stuff down to the basement and put a bed in here, okay?" Brain said, his face blank with shock. "It's *temporary*."

The storage room, not much bigger than a closet, was where all the bags of feed and sawdust and birdseed and old cages and aquariums were kept. It had no windows, smelled like a chicken coop and hardly seemed big enough to accommodate a bed, much less a dresser or anything else. Lana came down the stairs with a box full of clothes. She wore an old sweatshirt and shorts. Her legs, which I had never seen out in the open like this before, were smooth and so pale that a complex road map of thin blue veins showed through the skin.

"I'm going to stay down here for a bit," Lana said to me. She forced a smile and brushed her fingers across my hair, which made something in my chest knot up tight. "I already explained it to Brain and Sunny. Clay and I need a little time alone. Getting on each

other's nerves, I guess. It's nothing for anybody to worry about. A little breather is all."

"A breather," Brain said, nodding. "A short-term situation."

Lana took the clothes from the box and set them on a chair. She
hummed and went *bah-bah-bah* with her lips, like someone who didn't
have a care in the world.

That day at the community center, I had not walked home right
away, but hung around behind the old depot waiting for the meeting
to end. Barry was one of the first to come out. He sat in his car,
drumming the steering wheel with his fingers and checking himself
out in the rearview mirror. People walked in bunches out of the glass
doors, and Barry saluted them as they went by, nodding and saying
"Hey" and "Bye-bye now" and "Have a good one." Lana was the last
one out. Her arms full of papers and campaign leaflets, she locked
the doors behind her. She walked casually over to Barry's car and
they chatted through the driver's window like two people comment-
ing on the lack of rain or the sorry excuse for a football team the
Beavers had fielded last year, her blond hair reflecting the light like a
sheet of falling water. Barry took her by the wrist and kissed each
knuckle of her hand, carefully, one by one. When he pulled out of
the parking lot and turned left on Pratt Street, Lana, in her station
wagon, was following right behind.

Now she was filling the empty box with bottles and tubes of medicine: salves and dewormers and iodine. *On a long and lonesome highway,* she sang under her breath, *east of Abilene.* From just outside the
door, Brain watched her with a kind of sick wonder.

"You can have my room," I offered. Brain gave me the evil eye.
The bag of birdseed was beginning to put a real strain on him.

"We're not about to kick you out of your room," Lana said.
"Anyway, I'm kind of looking forward to being down here with the
animals. I've been ignoring them these past few months. It'll be nice
to have a change."

For the rest of that week I hardly saw Lana or Clay, and never
once together. Lana now used the door on the right, the one that led

into the zoo, and she would pass through to the other side only to make dinner and breakfast and clean the kitchen at night. Clay would come home late from work as usual and Lana would already be in her temporary room, reading or listening to records on a small turntable. Having her in that room was like living with a stranger: none of us knew how to act. If we spoke at all it was in whispers; when we watched TV we kept the volume so low you could barely hear it; when we ate dinner there was nothing but the scraping of chairs and the clink of silverware. When I passed Brain or Sunny in the house, we only looked at each other and went on, like prisoners under the watchful gaze of a guard. I assumed, like me, that they were wishing for the good old days when Lana and Clay cared enough to bicker and shout at each other into the deep hours of the night.

One muggy midnight found me sitting up in bed, the quiet of the house pressed on my eardrums like a weight. The strain was getting to be too much, the silence too heavy; I wasn't strong enough to lug this secret around on my own anymore. I put on some jeans and a T-shirt and stole down the hall, passing through the beads so slowly, with such care, they made no noise at all. I stood in front of Sunny's door for a good five minutes, shifting from one foot to the other like somebody waiting for a bus.

Lightly, I tapped my knuckles against the door so that it sounded like nothing more than the timbers of the house popping, expanding with the new heat of summer. I knocked again, waited, then turned the knob and stepped inside. Sunny's room, which in no way reflected her personality, was crammed with puffy quilts and pillows and stuffed animals and Raggedy Ann dolls, a room so soft you felt, even in the dark, like you were stepping into a dense, downy cloud.

I let the door whine shut behind me. I whispered her name and she groaned in her sleep. I could just make her out, lying on her side with her back to me.

I took a few steps closer. "Sunny, it's me, Edgar."

She rolled over and blinked furiously. "Who?" she said. "What?"

"It's Edgar," I said. "I'm in your room."

She sat up and kneaded her face with her palms. She was wearing white panties and a tight sleeveless T-shirt with three stars embroidered in the space just above her breasts.

"I can't believe you're in here," she said, her voice cobwebbed with sleep.

"I was wondering if you could come outside with me."

"You can ask me right here," she said. "You can even sit down on my bed if you want." She peeled the comforter back so that I could see her legs all the way down to her ankles, on which she wore a pair of anklets hung with the tiniest silver bells. She patted the mattress. I wanted so much to sink into that mattress, to press my nose into her T-shirt, into her hair, into her skin, and breathe it all in until I could breathe no longer.

I said, "I don't think your mom and dad would want me in here."

"Who cares what they want."

"Just for a minute," I said. "Please."

Sunny sighed and flung the comforter to the side. I opened the door and descended the stairs with those silver bells tinkling behind me.

She sat next to me on the back steps. It was warm and still, and somewhere far off a cow bawled and was quiet. I glanced sideways at her and could see she hadn't put anything on; her smooth bare legs reflected the moon, and her painted toenails shone like jewels. On her chest, just above the line of her shirt, swirled a small galaxy of freckles.

"I haven't heard you sneaking out in a long time," I said.

Sunny looked up into the vast spill of stars and shrugged.

"Did you know that I'm going to find out where that mailman is?" I said. "You didn't think I could do it."

"That's what you brought me out here to say?"

"No, I just haven't talked to you in awhile. You don't go out like before."

Sunny tucked her knees under her chin. "I'm not into it anymore, not with those people. You think you have friends and then they're saying all kinds of crap behind your back. I had enough."

I sucked in a mouthful of air, let it out. "I wanted to ask you about something."

"Look," she said. "If you're wondering about this whole adoption business, I'll tell you the truth about it right now. It's just one more thing Mom and Dad cooked up to keep themselves distracted. They've never mentioned adoption with any of the others before, so you should probably feel flattered about that, but it won't happen, I can see it already. You notice how they were all gung-ho about it in the beginning, filling out the forms and making the phone calls, and now they hardly mention it anymore? I just think you should know what's going on."

"I know," I whispered.

"And now Mom moving into that little room, it's pathetic, as if that's going to solve anything, as if it's going to help them love each other again." Her voice broke and she leaned her forehead against her knee for awhile, breathing hard. The chickens, roosting in their coop, murmured and groused in their sleep.

Sunny lifted her head. "I guess you probably want to kiss me?"

She turned to me, her mouth a tight gleaming circle, her chin a little cup, and something in the way she looked at me made me feel such a deep, tugging sadness at the root of my stomach that I could have wept. I turned away from her and stared at my hands.

"Well?" she said.

There was this image I couldn't get out of my mind: Barry kissing Lana, the way he touched her, his fingers snagging like hooks on the shiny fabric of her blouse. I felt myself sliding ever so slightly away from Sunny.

She stood right up and crossed her arms over her breasts. "All right, then," she said. "Forget it."

"No." I clambered after her, but she was already pulling open the screen door, the one on the left. I entered through the door on the right. The portal downstairs was closed, but I could hear her on the

other side, at the bottom step, and we started up our respective stair-
cases. I went slowly, my ear close to the wall, and followed her meas-
ured, deliberate creaking, the muffled tinkling of bells. I kept my
hand pressed against the wall as I went, as if I might feel her through
it, and it seemed that in my fingertips I could detect a certain rippling heat. As much as I was confused and angry at Lana for giving
into Barry, for letting a person such as him infiltrate her life and put
her family at risk, I understood right then, and all too well, the desire
to touch and be touched, even when it was wrong, especially when
it was wrong.

We made it to the top of the stairs at the same time and looked at
each other through the hanging beads. After a pause, she walked
through them and they slithered across her body like snakes and fell
away. We sat on the top step together, and when our hands touched
the first time a blue spark of static electricity snapped between us,
making me jump. Sunny held her hand over her mouth, trying to hold
in a laugh, and pressed her shoulder into mine. She put her face into
my neck and I could feel her mouth, cold and so soft, moving down
the length of my collarbone as she pulled the collar of my shirt away.
I could smell talcum powder and the herbal conditioner she used on
her hair and her own musky scent that seemed to breathe out of her
pores in a dense mist. I had forgotten all about Lana and Barry and
wanting to talk to Sunny about it, my mind was a whistling void. I felt
so weak and without weight or substance that I could not make myself
move away or toward her. She worked her way back up my neck to
my chin and mouth and kissed me with such an insistence that I felt
myself leaning back a little, like a man in a stiff wind, not strong
enough to hold myself up straight. Her hand began creeping up my
leg at an excruciating pace, and then she was undoing the button of
my jeans and pulling down the zipper, so slowly that the zipper teeth
released one at a time: *pop . . . pop . . . pop . . . pop . . . pop.* She reached
inside my pants and pressed her hand against me and I could feel the
heat of her skin through my underwear, her fingertips tracking small
circles, moving just enough to bring on an orgasm that brimmed in

me with such an overwhelming rush that I didn't notice the fit rising up along with it, didn't notice the surging pulse along the net of my nerves, didn't notice anything but that warm whirlpool of pleasure that sucked me in until I felt only the abrupt sensation of pitching forward, of dropping away into space. And then I was lying on my back at the bottom of the stairs, coming to with the echo of Sunny's scream ringing off the walls of the house.

Even then, at the bottom of the stairs with my legs rolled back over my head and my butt straight in the air, I was still not sure what had happened. I heard Clay yelling down the hall, wanting to know what was going on, and Sunny jabbering something about how she had heard a noise and come out of her room to find me exactly as I was at the bottom of the stairs. All around me the zoo was in an uproar, the gerbils squeaking, the guinea pigs hooting and scrabbling, the parrots rattling their cages.

"Look," I heard Brain say from the top of the stairs, "he fell down so hard it knocked his pants off!"

It was true: in the course of my descent my jeans had been pulled down around my knees. I felt fortunate that my underwear was still in place.

Clay bounded down the stairs and looked at me through the V of my legs.

"Can you move?" he said, his voice warbling with panic.

I groaned and managed to roll over into a more natural position. Then Lana was there, helping me pull up my pants while Clay checked me for broken bones or other injury. Do I even have to say it? Except for a sore neck, Edgar was fine, perfect: not a scratch, not a bruise, not a bump on the head.

"What happened?" Lana said. "Can you talk?"

"I don't know," I said. "I woke up like this."

"But you have your clothes on," Lana said.

Brain slapped the banister. "Sleepwalking," he said. "I knew it!"

"That's probably what it was," Sunny said. I looked up at her and her eyes were still wide with shock.

"I'll bet, in his sleep, he didn't pull his pants on all the way and that's what caused him to trip and fall down the stairs," Brain said. He was so excited he could hardly stand still. "That's my initial theory."

I gingerly got to my feet and made sure that my pants were buttoned. My shorts were full of a sticky mess. Clay and Lana both helped me up and then they stood together, eyeing me quizzically. In his panic, it appeared, Clay had forgotten himself and had his arm around Lana's waist. They stayed that way for a couple of seconds before Lana pulled away from him to pat me on the cheek.

"You've got to watch yourself, honey," she said. "I guess this world is just a dangerous place for you."

We were quiet for a moment and then Brain said, "How about we all go and have some hot chocolate?"

We looked at each other and Clay shook his head. "Let's get back to bed. Come on. Morning comes early." And we all went back to our separate rooms, Clay in one distant corner of the house, Lana in the other.

LETTING LOOSE THE BEASTS

BRAIN'S TENTH BIRTHDAY, and we all sat around the dining room table waiting for Clay so the party could begin. Gordon Dickey was there, as were a couple of sad sacks from Brain's Sunday school class who moped around like they'd rather be at the dentist's office waiting to get a tooth pulled. And there was one unexpected guest: Uncle Larry. Uncle Larry was a big lug of a man with a silver flattop and a bolo tie in the shape of a dollar sign. He had stopped by on his way home from a horse auction in Flagstaff to say hello, and when he'd found out it was Brain's birthday he'd run off to the nearest store—Kreckinger's Hardware—and bought Brain a framing hammer, which he'd wrapped up in a sheet from the Sunday funny pages.

It was a warm summer evening and twilight drifted into the house like a shimmering cloud of powdered crystal. Crepe streamers hung from the ceiling and the cake on the table said *The Big Ten!!!* in blocky candy letters. Wearing his Sunday shirt and a green clip-on tie, Brain sat in the place of honor looking sour. Lana had parted his hair down the middle and plastered it to his head with water, which made him look like an angry muskrat.

Uncle Larry, who was Clay's uncle and lived in Reno, was providing the preparty entertainment. "Okay, you honyocks," he said. "Who can tell me what kind of animal it is that says 'moof'?"

"A dog?" said Gordon Dickey.

"That was a pretty mediocre guess," said Uncle Larry. "Anybody else want to take a pop at it?"

"A bear?" I said.

Uncle Larry shook his head sadly. "Humor doesn't come easy to you boys, I guess. I ought to have started off with some easier jokes. The answer is a buck-toothed cow. Moof!"

Gordon Dickey said, "You have hair in your ears, Uncle Larry."

Lana, who was in the kitchen with Sunny, came out with a pitcher of Kool-Aid. "Your dad'll be here any minute, honey," she said to Brain. "I'm sure he just had to finish up a job or something."

"It's one thing to work hard," Uncle Larry said, holding out his paper cup, which had fat little rocket ships on it, "and it's a whole 'nother thing to know when to stop."

We drank Kool-Aid and ate chips with onion dip. The presents stayed where they were on the table. Uncle Larry told us about how, for his tenth birthday, he had received nothing but a four-foot length of rope. "We was poor and I was happy to have that rope. I had an active mind, is what I'm trying to relate to you here. I made it into whatever I wanted, a pet rattlesnake and a bullwhip and a Winchester lever-action rifle and all kinds of other things I can't remember at this point in time. When you get old like me you lose your imagination. I know I tied my sister up with that rope. Tied her up so good I couldn't get the knot undone and left her in the milking barn till Grandma Madsen found her a couple hours later. Oh you should have been there for the butt-whippin' on that day. It was a time to remember."

Lana clattered some plates and silverware onto the table. "Why don't we go ahead with the piñata. Maybe Clay will make it in time for the cake."

The piñata, a multicolored bull, hung from a plant hook out on the porch. The bull had stubby horns and bulging white eyeballs that stared off in different directions. Uncle Larry manned the rope and yanked on it like a monk in a belfry, the bull bobbing up and down crazily, nearly impossible to hit. One of the sad sacks, now in a blindfold, swung wildly with a yellow Wiffle ball bat that didn't once make contact.

"Come on, Uncle Larry!" Gordon Dickey said. "Let him hit the bull."

"Looks more like a steer to me," Uncle Larry said, pausing for a moment to peer between the piñata's hind legs. "Anyhow, you keep your undies on straight, you'll get your chance."

When it was Brain's turn he waited calm and blindfolded, holding the bat out in front of him like a samurai master, his ear cocked for any sound of movement. He had hardly said a word to anybody since the party started and now his mouth was set in a determined grimace. Grinning with mischief, Uncle Larry slowly lowered the bull so it was right in front of Brain, who lashed out with a sudden, vicious whack across its spine. Brain missed a couple of times before he connected solidly again, the sound of it like a gunshot echoing out over the neighborhood, and then he went berserk, swinging in a wild, all-out frenzy and yelling *yah! yah! yah!* The blindfold slipped down around his neck and he zeroed in, the bat a yellow blur. A horn broke off, bits of crepe paper flung up into the air like parade

confetti, but still the bull would not break. One of the sad sacks started to cry and Lana yelled at Brain to stop, but he kept it up, his
cheeks pink and his eyes on fire, until his arms gave out. The bull was
now hornless and badly dented and missing all of its shaggy crepe-
paper fur, but hadn't given up a single piece of candy.

Uncle Larry, who'd stopped pulling on the rope altogether and let
Brain clobber it nearly to a pulp, said, "I'll tell you what, this young
fella might have a future in the mafia."

He went back in the house and came back unwrapping the hammer he'd bought earlier. "That flyswatter don't got enough weight
behind it. Give this a whirl. If it don't work then I'm going to buy
my own piñata to keep my personal valuables in."

Brain swallowed hard, his face screwed up into a desperate scowl,
his lips wet and shiny with spit. He grabbed the hammer and with
one sweeping blow took half the bull's head off. "Olé!" Uncle Larry
said. The piñata tipped forward and all the candy came out in one
crackling gush, fanning out over the wooden deck at our feet.

After we dutifully scooped up the candy and stuffed our pockets
with it, we went back inside, where the birthday song was sung, the
presents opened, the cake and ice cream eaten. Light drained from
the windows like water from a sink. Still Clay did not show up.
Brain's friends went home and Uncle Larry, who had taken Lana
into the kitchen and, in a voice loud enough for everybody to hear,
told her that she should lay her husband upside the head with that
hammer for not showing up for his own son's birthday party, left so
he could get back to Reno before his own wife decided to commit
similar violence upon him. Lana made calls to three of Clay's crew,
who said they'd left him at the job site at six o'clock. Just when Lana
was on her way out the door to look for him, we heard Clay's truck
pull up in the driveway.

Brain and I were laid out on the rug in the living room; I watched
"Hawaii Five-O" while Brain created elaborate contraptions with
the Erector set he'd gotten from Gordon Dickey. We immediately

got up and looked out the window. Clay was still sitting in the cab of his pickup, not moving. Lana had started to walk out toward the pickup, but stopped halfway there; something, it was clear, had frightened her. The truck door creaked open and Clay stepped out, speckled head to toe with wall plaster. It was caught in his hair and beard and spattered across his blue jeans in spiraling constellations, and in his hand he held a piece of paper. He stood next to the truck for a moment without speaking. It was full dark now and in the light spilling out from the porch his face looked hard and blank, like something made out of varnished wood.

He held out the paper to Lana. "I want you to read this and I want you to tell me if it's the truth."

Lana took a step back as if she'd run into a cobweb. "Clay," she said, a thin wire of pleading in her voice.

"I want you to read it right now," he said.

She retreated up onto the porch, her car keys jangling in her hand. "Whatever it is, we should talk about it upstairs."

She came inside and he followed her up the stairs, neither of them looking at us, moving forward blindly, like two people passing by in a dream. They shut the bedroom door behind them and there was silence. Sunny came out of her room and said, "What? What is it?" Brain and I climbed the stairs and we stared down the hall, waiting. We heard the sound of Lana's voice and then something struck the door with such force that the jamb splintered and the wall shook. There was shouting and crying and a muffled commotion and it seemed that all the strife and grief that room had contained for so long was trying to break out, rattling the door like a hard wind. Clay's voice rose above everything else and I only heard one word, clear and loud, like a spade hitting wet dirt. *Slut.*

Eventually Clay came out, his sad eyes now lit with some internal voltage, the piece of paper crumpled in his fist. The knuckles of his other hand were scraped a bright red. Lana clutched at his shirt and tried to pull him back. "Listen to me," she said. "Please listen." He grabbed her wrist and yanked at it forcefully, trying to free himself, wrenching her arm side to side, and they struggled like that, locked together in a desperate clinch, until Sunny, crying *no no no no no,* rushed in and pushed them apart.

Clay stalked past us, went downstairs into the zoo and began to wreck it: he pushed over the aquariums, swept the mice and gerbil cages to the floor, flushed the parrots out of their cages and into the living room, where they went squawking and flapping, searching for an escape, swooping into the kitchen and up the stairs, their wings going *thup-thup-thup-thup* against the ceiling. Lana screamed at him to stop but he kept going, his face grim and contorted, knocking over the feed cans and bags of sawdust and the box where Tom and Marcus, the two guinea pigs, cowered and shrieked.

Next to me, Brain, still in his birthday tie, trembled as if he'd been struck.

Clay propped open the door and stumbled into the back, where he moved with a methodical fury, opening every pen and hutch and corral. Out came the blattering goats and Dorothy the mule and Mimi the milk cow, and in no time the dogs in the neighborhood had put up a great howl, roused by the sudden ruckus. Clay charged into the chicken coop and stomped around in circles, sending the chickens out the door in a blur of thumping wings. By now some of the mice and parrots had made it outside, and the barn cats zig-zagged around, unsure of who or what to chase, and then, one by one, half a dozen neighbor dogs showed up and began a crazed, incessant barking, pausing only to chase the cats and snap at the goats and the flapping, terrified chickens.

Dorothy, in a fit of panic, had run right into the barbed-wire fence and had become tangled there, honking like an air horn, her legs splayed out under her. One of the big spotted tomcats darted into the house and came out with an angelfish quivering in its teeth. All around, chicken feathers floated slowly down, swirling suddenly with some turbulence of air, and gerbils whizzed underfoot and parrots flew low overhead, flashing green and yellow in the dark, and above everything, in the lowest branch of the cottonwood tree, sat Doug the vulture, calmly watching the chaos below, solemn and quiet as a shadow.

A CONCERNED BROTHER

AFTER THE ANIMALS were captured and put back in their rightful places and the neighbors had gone home and Clay had driven away to stay the night with his brother, Edgar sat on the wet carpet of the zoo, comforting Keith the Rat, who was hunched in the back of his cage, shivering and burying his head in the sawdust. Everything had been put back in its place, more or less, but there was still turquoise aquarium gravel strewn across the floor, and bits of wet shredded newspaper and clumps of sawdust stuck to the walls and tables; the zoo smelled even worse than it usually did. Even though Keith the Rat's cage had been knocked over like most of the others, he was one of the few who did not make a break for it. When I came back inside I found him hiding behind the bookshelf, his tail twitching in plain sight as pink and hairless as an earthworm.

Neighbors from up and down the street helped us round up all the animals. Within three minutes of the time the commotion began, they were out in force, chasing chickens and rabbits, extracting Dorothy from the barbed-wire fence, casting about in the bushes and poking under piles of lumber, searching for mice and gerbils. Bobo Boyd, Timothy Boyd's big brother, got out his new lariat and ran down the goats who had gotten into the Christensens' alfalfa field. None of the fish could be saved, but all but two of the parrots had been retrieved and Doug the vulture made it easy on everybody by having a dizzy spell and falling off his branch. Our neighbor four houses up, an old guy named Brother Shields, came by holding Marcus the guinea pig out in front of him and said, "I don't know what the hell this is, but I found it runnin' for its life down the middle of the road."

All of this had taken place in a matter of forty-five minutes, and now the house was quiet again. Sunny and Brain were in their rooms and Lana was in the upstairs bedroom, talking to her mother on the telephone. Clay had disappeared almost immediately, but had called home and talked to Sunny, told her he was sorry for what he had done, to ask forgiveness from all of us. He said he would stay at Uncle Richard's place for the night so he could think things through.

Just after I had returned Keith the Rat to his cage, I found the paper that Clay had come home with on the floor of the zoo. It was crumpled and wet, but still legible:

Dear Brother Madsen,

I have agonized over writing this letter for weeks, and in the end have decided to do it because I believe your family and marriage could be at stake. On several occasions over the last two months I have seen your wife, Sister Madsen, with another man. I don't know this man's name or occupation, and I can't say that their relationship goes beyond the kissing and touching I witnessed, but I decided, for the sake of your eternal marriage, that it is something you should know about, before it is too late. I have no doubt that Sister Madsen is a good, upstanding daughter of God, but I also know that God created us in the flesh, and that the flesh is weak.

I have kept this knowledge in all confidentiality, and now I leave it in your hands.

Sincerely,
A Concerned Brother

I guess I had underestimated him; Alan Lovejoy *was* so righteous, so filled with the power and spirit of God that he couldn't be intimidated for too long by the likes of me. I considered going to his house and delivering on the promise I had made to him a few weeks ago but decided instead to do what I should have done in the first place, what might have saved this family from coming apart as it had tonight.

I went into the kitchen, my feet squishing in the wet carpet, and picked up the phone. Lana was off now and a dial tone blared from the receiver, which felt as heavy as a brick in my hand. I swallowed and dialed the number from the card Barry had given me. The man who answered told me Barry wasn't living there anymore and gave me another number. The phone rang two dozen times before Barry picked it up.

"What?" he said.

"It's Edgar," I said, once I had freed my tongue, which felt like it had rusted to the roof of my mouth.

"Who? Who is it?"

"Edgar," I said. "Edgar Mint."

"Edgar! My God, what's going on, are you okay?"

For a moment I listened to his shallow breathing, which came across the phone line as dense static.

"Hello?" he said.

I coughed and cleared my throat, and somewhere inside, found the words. "I want you to come pick me up."

THE NEEDLE

OUT UNDER THE black sky, invisible in the darkness, Edgar waited like the phantom he was. A hot breeze pushing up out of the south rustled the leaves and bushes and seemed to blow right through him. Watching for Barry's car, he paced in the gravel by the irrigation ditch and could not hear his own footsteps. It was as if he was already gone, all his substantial parts—his bones and guts and sinews—disappeared, leaving behind a creature made only of air.

I had felt it the moment I hung up the phone: my self vanishing, my atoms scattering away into some other place. I walked up the stairs and it was like I was floating. I knelt down in my room, the door shut behind me, and typed a short letter. I filled my trunk with all my papers and the millions of words I'd typed on them, and on top of those stacks and bundles I put my knife and Barry's stethoscope and my Hermes Jubilee. Everything else I left: my closet full of clothes, my stacks of clean underwear, my designer jeans, my Sunday ties, my flaming-car wristwatch, the turntable and old Isley Brothers records Lana had given to me for my birthday, my personalized leather-bound set of scriptures.

I made one last circuit of the house. I walked the long upstairs hallway, passing through the beads, and paused at Sunny's door, where I could hear intermittent sobs. I rested my hand on the doorknob, took it away. Brain was quiet in his room and I heard nothing from Lana's. There was no longer light coming from under the door and I imagined her in there, staring into the dark, alone on the white expanse of that bed.

For awhile I sat on the carpeted toilet lid in the pink bathroom, taking in the smell of soap and clean towels and perfume. I looked in the mirror and saw nothing but a shadow of myself. Down in the living room I turned on the television for a moment, just to hear the low murmur of voices, and in the dark kitchen I opened the refrigerator. The light that shone out of it was radiant and golden, nearly blinding, like the light that might pour out of heaven itself, and I closed it without taking anything.

I went outside to wait. When Barry pulled up with his headlights off I stepped out from the night shadows of the willow tree to meet him. He jumped out and ran up to hug me, the embodiment of concern. I hugged him back with as much conviction as I could muster.

"What's wrong?" he said. "What's going on?"

I told him that I wanted him to take me now, I was ready, I wanted to go away with him and never come back. "I need some help with my trunk," I said. "Then we can get going."

"What happened?" he said. I hadn't told him much of anything on the phone, only that he needed to come and get me right away, it was an emergency.

"There was a big fight," I said. "I can't live here anymore, I don't want to. I want to go with you."

"Edgar, this is all a little sudden—"

"I'm leaving them a note," I said. "They'll think I ran away. Nobody will know anything."

Barry wore a crumpled felt jacket and an expression of bewilderment. He raked his fingers through the lopsided bramble of his hair and followed me into the house. At the top of the stairs he stopped and looked around intently, his eyes glinting in the low light. He whispered, "Where is she?"

"Who?"

"Lana."

"She's not here," I lied. "She went to stay with a friend."

He looked down the hall. "Her bedroom's that one, at the end, isn't it?"

For a moment it seemed he leaned as if to turn that way but he made an abrupt swivel and came with me into the guest room.

After we slid the trunk along the carpet and guided it carefully down the stairs to keep it from thumping, we had trouble. The floor of the zoo was wet, which made the sliding more difficult and noisy. Fortunately, the animals, dazed and exhausted from their brief dash for freedom, kept still in their cages. By the time we had pushed, dragged, coaxed, nudged the trunk outside, down from the porch and onto the cement walkway, Barry was heaving and making a rattling noise deep in his lungs. "What the hell you got in here, Edgar?"

"Words," I said, shaking my head. "Too many words."

We scraped the trunk along the walkway, across the gravel and up to the car, where it took both of us to lift one end into the backseat. One of the neighbor's dogs, a drooling Lab named Gringo still hopped up over all the excitement earlier this evening, came up to us, wagging his tail and making friendly woofing noises, and stuck his nose in Barry's butt. Barry slung a handful of gravel at Gringo and chased him down the street, hissing through his teeth, "You better run you fucking dog!" When Barry came back we situated ourselves on the other end of the trunk and with one last heave managed to slide it in, the shocks groaning, the back end settling so low that the wheel wells nearly rested on the tires.

Barry slammed the door shut and slumped against it. "Unbelievable," he gasped. "It's really happening, hoo-boy. Good thing I brought the Victoria."

I told Barry to wait a second and ran into the house, where I left the note I had typed on the coffee table in the living room.

Dear Madsens (Clay, Lana, Sunny, Brain),
     I am going away. Don't worry, I'll be fine. I was happy living with you and I'm sorry I have to go.
     You were kind to me. Thank you.
                                        Your friend, Edgar P. Mint

For a few seconds I stood in the silence of that house, a numbness spreading over me like thick oil. Somewhere out in the dark Gringo yowled a sad canine tune. When I ran out to the car Barry was already at the wheel, sucking on a cigarette with unabashed desperation.

He looked over at me, as if waiting for me to speak. I asked him the only question left in my head: "Do you have the mailman's address?"

He slipped a yellow piece of paper out of his shirt pocket, then tucked it back in. "Got it right here," he said. Curling ropes of smoke snaked out of his nostrils. "I have it on very good authority that this is our man. But we can talk about that later. Right now we've got to figure out what we're going to do with you."

He left the headlights off until we got to the highway, quizzing me like a detective. He wanted to know exactly what had happened in the Madsen house, what the fight was about, where Lana had gone. I

stared out my window, at the dark world falling away, and said as little as I could. When he pressed harder, I turned to him. "It doesn't
matter anymore, right? Now we can go away somewhere. We don't
even have to stay around here. Maybe we could go back to Arizona.
I'll bet that's where Jeffrey is."

Barry laughed. "We'll put you up tonight at my place until we figure out our plan of action. But I can't just up and leave like that. My
business investments are starting to pay off, and Lana, she needs a little support right now, it sounds like things might have reached a
head tonight."

"No," I said. "You're not going back there."

Barry sighed, gave the steering wheel a little shake. "You need to
understand something, Edgar. I'll admit that I struck up a relationship with Lana as a way to gather information, to assess the situation. It was for your own good. I wanted to know what kind of
people you were living with, what kind of things they were trying
to put in your head. And you know what? I found Lana to be not
the person I expected at all. She's smart and funny, and the greatest
thing about her is her desire to help people. Look at what she's
done for you. And I share that desire. That's why we hit it off. And
now I can see she needs support. She's in a bad marriage, she's
unhappy at home—I mean, this guy she's married to, come on. She
needs help."

His face glistened with sweat and his eyes gave off a strange, otherworldly glow. He patted me on the leg. "You know me. You know I
wouldn't abandon somebody in their hour of need. I'm not that type
of person."

I felt my chest constrict, as if caught by a slowly winding chain,
and I covered my head in my arms. The hot night air swirled in from
the window and the car door hummed against my head. Eventually I
fell into something very much like the coma I had lived through all
those years before: I sank so deeply into myself, became so disconnected, that everything outside my body seemed to exist on some
other, distant plane.

"Edgar?" Barry said, and it was like he was shouting at me through a windstorm. I made no answer, no movement; I'm not sure I could have had I wanted to.

I don't know how long we drove. Barry called my name again, put his hand on my back. "Are you sleeping?" he said. When he got no response, he slowed the car and pulled over. With the engine off, the sudden, heavy silence was almost painful. I heard movement, paper rattling and the clink of glass. I turned my head just enough so that I could see him through the slits of my eyelids. He already had the rubber tubing around his arm and was pushing the needle in with a desperate, shaking hand. Once he had injected himself, he went instantly loose and a low moan of pleasure eased out of him like a few notes of a lullaby. His head lolled to the side and the hand that held the syringe fell to his lap, leaving it dangling, still in his arm.

I sat up. Barry did not move, did not seem to breathe; his body had gone so slack it was as if he had melted into the seat. In slow motion I reached across and eased the syringe out of his arm. In that moment, when I held the empty needle in my hand, it came to me, a thought that rose up from someplace cold and deep: *It would be so easy.* I rummaged through his open doctor's bag, came up with one of the small glass vials—there were eight or nine of them, all the same—and drew out as much of the amber liquid as the syringe would hold. At St. Divine's I had seen it done hundreds of times and the whole procedure felt natural to me, like a ritual I had performed every day of my life. The rubber tubing was still wrapped snug at the base of his biceps and his veins stood out against the bruised and pitted flesh of his inner arm. On one of those veins quivered a tiny jewel of blood and that is where I placed the end of the needle. His face caught in an expression of serene rapture, Barry kept utterly still. His chest did not move and even in the quiet bubble of that car I could not hear the push and pull of his lungs. *So easy,* I thought, and this time I did not falter, I did not give in to fear or doubt or weakness. I slipped in the needle and pushed the plunger down.

EDGAR AT THE WHEEL

IN THE LIGHT of a low half-moon the road shone like the bottom of a greased skillet. I kept the speedometer on thirty and even though this section of desert highway was nothing but straightaway, my back and arms strained with tension; this was the first time I had ever driven a car.

A few minutes earlier I had pushed Barry to the far side of the seat and now he lay slumped in the corner, his chin resting on his chest. I didn't know if he was dead or not. Two or three seconds after I had given him the injection he had stiffened and made a childlike whimper of surprise, but since then hadn't stirred. With my heart tapping hard against my sternum, I had watched him: his jaw clenching and unclenching, his eyes fluttering under their lids, his arms making tiny jerking movements as if pulled by wires. When he was still I got his stethoscope out of my trunk and placed the bell on his chest. All I could hear was a cosmic hiss, like the sound of solar storms brought to earth on radio waves. I held my breath, straining, and thought I could detect a certain drumbeat of blood, but I couldn't tell if it was coming from his chest or my own ears.

The big car was an automatic, so now all I had to do was keep a steady pressure on the gas pedal, but it seemed that it wanted to speed up, to hurtle down that road with the whole rumbling enterprise of its engine. Working the accelerator with my right, I tapped the brakes with my left, which made the car halt and lurch. Every time I hit a bump Barry's head wavered like the needle on a compass. A cold sweat had broken out at my hairline and my eyes burned from the effort of trying to keep inside the lines. I hugged the enormous steering wheel like it was a life preserver.

Up ahead, at the side of the road, a man materialized suddenly as if he had stepped out of a fold in the air. He straddled the white line and held out his thumb. I swung out into the other lane and then something made me lay on the brake so hard that I cracked my nose against the steering wheel and Barry slid to the floor. I looked back and the man was jogging up to the car, still a couple of hundred feet away, red as a demon in the glow of the brake lights. I grabbed Barry under the armpits and pulled him onto the seat next to me, propped him up as well as I could. The man slipped into the front seat without saying anything. He was an Indian, with matted, shoulder-length hair and a heavy brow that stuck out over his face like an eroded riverbank. He gave off the odor of bus seats and cigarettes and wine. He looked straight out the windshield, waiting patiently for us to be on our way.

"I'm trying to get to Globe," I said. "It's in Arizona."

His words were quiet and clipped. "Okay by me."

"Is this the right way?"

For the first time the man looked at me. "Might want to take 270. Few miles back. Maybe put on your lights."

I pushed and pulled on all the buttons I could find until the headlights came on. I was startled to see the way the road lit up in front of me. With the hazards clicking and wipers flapping, I swung the car around, scraped over a few clumps of sagebrush and spun out in the soft dirt on the shoulder before I got us headed in the opposite direction. A jackrabbit dashed into the glare of the headlights and I gave the wheel a yank, which made the car fishtail and swing out into the other lane, the tires screaming sideways over the asphalt, before I could get everything straightened out.

"I don't know how to drive," I told the Indian.

For the next few miles I slowed down to a crawl, wandered all over the road, hit the brakes occasionally, just to illustrate my point. Finally, I asked the man if he didn't want to take the wheel for awhile.

"Looking for a ride," he said.

So I went out into the other lane of the deserted road and stayed there, inching along. I pushed on the gas and watched the Indian out of the corner of my eye as we sped up to forty, then fifty miles an hour. Implacable as a mannequin, he didn't even seem to blink. I stopped the car in the middle of the road and fished around in Barry's front pockets until I came up with a large wad of crumpled bills.

"You can have this," I said, "if you'll drive us down to Globe."

"Don't want your money," he said.

I opened Barry's doctor bag and showed him the contents of it. "What about this?"

He didn't bother to look in the bag. "Don't got a license. Cops stop us, they'll haul me back to jail. Maybe I should try my luck with somebody else."

I rested my head against the back of the seat and closed my eyes. My skull was filled with a dense and heavy fog and I wanted nothing more than to go to sleep.

"You Indi'n?" the Indian said.

"No," I said. "Yes."

I looked over at him and he smiled, which made it clear that he was not in possession of all of his teeth. He pushed open the passenger door and stepped out. I thought he was going to walk away, but he came around the back of the car and stood next to my open window.

"I'll drive," he said. "But if the cops stop us, I'm making a break for it."

We changed places and the Indian adjusted his mirrors, checked his gauges and laid on the gas as if it was something he was born to. The wheels squealed and we were off, hurtling south, our headlights cutting a wedge into the darkness that lay like dense smoke over the broken desert terrain. We drove for hours, stopping once to get gas at an all-night station in Flagstaff. The Indian didn't say a word the whole time, even when Barry, gradually slumping to the side, came to rest his head on his shoulder. The Indian kept his hands perfectly positioned on the wheel and never once took his eyes off the road.

Only when we hit the northern outskirts of Globe did he speak. "Where you want to go?"

To the east the sky was beginning to pale just a bit, but night hadn't yet lifted. I looked out the window at the medical supply store we were now passing, a gray cinder-block building whose display window sported several flesh-colored dummies dressed up in leg braces and hernia trusses. As much as I wanted to, I had not been able to sleep the whole way down, and in a carsick stupor did nothing more than stare out at the wide mouth of the car sucking in the illuminated road. I glanced over at Barry and the Indian, nestled together on the far side of the seat like lovers. At one point I had worked up enough courage to reach out and touch Barry's hand and found that it was neither warm nor cold.

I said, "Polar Bear Motel."

We searched the winding streets for awhile before the Indian stopped at a Circle K to ask for directions. We looped around a particularly tight corner and Barry lurched across the seat and slid down until his head was next to my hip. I heard what I thought was a low groan of air escape from his mouth. The Indian drove on, unperturbed.

I felt an odd sense of déjà vu navigating these avenues that snaked among the old sandstone storefronts and darkened cowboy bars, streets that felt entirely familiar but were not known to me at all. Eventually the sign for the Polar Bear Motel rose up over the top of a small hill like a neon beacon. The Indian swung the big car into the parking lot and I got out before we came to a stop.

Only the office, with its burnt-out NO VACANCY sign, had a light on. I found the door with the number 9 on it and knocked. When no answer came, I peered through the cracked window and could see that the room was bare, the bed made up. I went to the office and rang the buzzer by the door. A couple of minutes passed before a thin woman in a long T-shirt opened the door a crack and blinked at me, light pouring through the snarl of her hair like sunshine out of a storm cloud.

"I'm looking for Art Crozier," I said.

She said, "Do you know how late it is, buster?"

"He used to live in room number nine. Maybe two or three years ago."

Her hand on her brow, she sighed with a deep, uncomplicated weariness. "He moved, honey. Right up the hill here. God, my head hurts. He pays Lucinda to clean up around his place every week. Take this road till you can't go no more. That's his place. The one on the right."

I directed the Indian up the hill according to the woman's directions until we came to a small beige duplex surrounded by a chain-link fence. I looked at the Indian and he said, "I'll wait for you. Don't got much on my schedule."

I stood in front of the door on the right and gave it a solid knock. I heard a series of unidentifiable noises, then what sounded like an angry, muttering voice. I knocked again. Someone came thumping closer to the door and a voice boomed out like thunder, "WHO THE HELL IS IT?"

"Man," said the Indian from the open window of the car. "That guy's got a set of pipes on him, hey?"

I yelled, "It's Edgar! Edgar Mint!"

The door swung inward and there was Art on the other side of the screen, haggard and loose-skinned, leaning on an aluminum walker. The yellow glow from inside lit up his white hair, which was as fine as the fluff of a dandelion and looked like it might lift off his head if you were to breathe too hard.

"Is it . . . ?" he said.

I pulled open the screen door. "It's me," I said. Despite everything, I must have been smiling. "It's Edgar."

Art could have been smiling or scowling, there really was no way to tell. I realized that I was now nearly as tall as him. He wore a pair of baggy painter pants and a sleeveless undershirt. He reached out and put his hand on the back of my neck, his fingers as cold and heavy as granite on my skin. He gave me a good shake. "Look at you," he said. "I'll be damned."

I stepped into a small room which was dominated by an old, dec-
imated leather recliner. The plank floor under my feet was pitted
with cigarette burns. To the left was a galley kitchen, its tiny counter
space cluttered with bottles of pills and liquor bottles of all sorts. The
paneled walls were bare except for an old calendar that showed a
big-breasted blonde brandishing a chain saw.

"Well God bless you," Art said, shaking his head. "Here you are."

I sat on a folding chair next to the massive television with a small
green screen and Art leaned against the arm of the recliner. He
looked a little better than the last time I'd seen him through the window of the motel room. His eyes were clearer, his face less swollen
and red. The mass of scar tissue on his jaw had gone from pink to a
milky gray and his forehead and arms were peppered with liver
spots, though he could have been no more than sixty years old.

In less than a minute, I told him everything that had happened,
everything I had done. The words rolled right out of me and I kept
my eyes closed against the bright overhead light. And then I had
nothing left to say and it was quiet.

For a time Art stared blankly at the floor and then with great
effort he pushed himself away from the recliner and shuffled the
short distance over to me without his walker. He put his hand on my
shoulder and I could feel him lean into me, steadying himself. He
put his face close to mine and I got a whiff of hair oil and wallet
leather and sweat. I could detect no trace of his infamous cologne.
"You done the right thing," he said, looking me level in the eye.
"Don't you worry about it now. We'll get it took care of."

He hobbled into the back room and returned wearing a faded
denim jacket and a pair of scuffed brogues. Instead of his walker, he
now employed two canes, one that had four little rubber-tipped legs
for extra support. Outside, the Indian sat on the hood smoking a cigarette.

"Borrowed a butt from the ashtray," he said.

Art peered through the windshield for a moment before opening the passenger door and putting his fingers against Barry's neck. His bones creaked and popped when he bent down to place his ear next to Barry's face.

"He's dead?" I whispered.

Art nodded. He was wheezing and already a layer of sweat glistened on his forehead. "If he ain't, he's at the very door."

"I didn't use the knife, like you told me to," I said.

Art gave his head a rueful shake. He said, "I guess it's the thought that counts."

He slammed the door. "This ain't as big a problem as it looks. Just going to have to apply ourselves, nothing some elbow grease won't fix." He pointed his wooden cane at the Indian, who was floating smoke rings into the shadowy reaches of an ironwood tree. "What about him?"

With a conviction that surprised me, I said, "He won't tell anybody."

Art took a billfold from his jacket and offered the Indian a couple of twenties.

"Everybody wanting to give me money," the Indian said.

"This is neither bribe nor charity," Art said gruffly. The hand that held the money shook as if another invisible hand was trying to wrestle the bills from its grip. "This is for your trouble. This is for looking after this boy when he needed help."

The Indian looked at both of us, his eyes bright in the darkness, and laughed. He took the money, shoved it into his sack, and tossed his cigarette, which arced like a meteor into the weeds. He slung the sack over his shoulder and ambled away down the hill, laughing the whole way.

Art watched the Indian go. "I can't see to save my life," he said. "So you're going to have to do the driving."

Art showed me how to pull the seat up, adjust the steering wheel and mirrors, and signal when I turned. "Steady now, steady, that's the way," he said as I braked at the bottom of the hill. First, we stopped by his old house, where he had lived with his family before the accident. It was an avocado-colored rancher with a brick facade and a sign out front that said *Dirk Fondley Realtors.* The lawn was a tangle of dead weeds, and a huge elaborate spiderweb full of sticks and the empty carapaces of insects encased the front doorway.

Art chuckled. "I'd never give a thought to selling that house, but I can't live in it neither. Put it on the market to keep the neighbors from howling, city codes and all that. Guess what it's listed at? Quarter of a million bucks. I guess there won't be a *Sold* sign going up anytime soon."

He took out a key ring from his pocket, his hand shaking so the keys jangled with a steady tambourine rhythm, located one in particular and instructed me to go into the garage and get a pair of bolt cutters that were hanging on the wall next to the pickax. "Yellow handles," he said. "Can't miss 'em."

I entered the garage through a door at the side of the house. The door's hinges gave a series of rusty squeaks and then I was standing in the dark garage, inhaling the smell of old motor oil and gasoline and dust. I flipped the light switch and nothing happened. It took a few seconds for my eyes to adjust to the murky, predawn light and I could see that the garage was still crammed with the entire range of out-of-doors family paraphernalia: roller skates and sleeping bags and rosebush fertilizer and two old tricycles and a Big Wheel hanging from hooks in the ceiling. In the far corner hunched an orange barbecue grill tangled helplessly in a volleyball net.

The silence had a texture to it, a heft, and I could sense the uneasy presence of ghosts in that place, could feel them watching me. I located the bolt cutters as quickly as I could, holding my breath as if I had entered a room full of poisonous gas. Outside, pulling the door shut, I saw at my feet two small handprints pressed into the cement walkway. *Emily 6 yrs,* it said under one of them, and under the other, *Sally Sue 9 yrs.*

I got into the car and Art was still staring out the window at the house. He turned to me, surprised as if he hadn't heard me get in.

"Everything okay in there?" he said, his eyes moist and unblinking.

"Fine," I said, trying to suppress a shudder. "No problem."

"Nobody's been in there? Nothing disturbed?"

I shook my head. "A little dusty."

He looked out at the house again. He was seeing years and days I had no way of knowing. He let out a breath that was almost a gasp and then he slapped his leg. "Okay. All right then. Let's go get this done before there's too much light."

Art had me circle back around the Polar Bear Motel and then we were on a dirt road that passed a brick factory, a gravel pit and a wrecking yard before things opened up and we hit a two-track that looped through a scrub-dotted plain hemmed in on one side by the Ildicott mines and slag piles and smelter, and on the other by the rambling sandstone edifice up on a hill that had once been St. Divine's. We rumbled over a cattle guard with a posted sign that said PRIVATE PROPERTY KEEP OUT.

"See that little circle of fence over there?" Art said. "That's Bob's Drop. An old mine shaft, I think I might of pointed it out to you once upon a time. It don't look like there's a road that goes out there anymore. We'll have to take it cross-country."

I pointed the Crown Victoria in the direction of Bob's Drop and gritted my teeth as we lurched and thumped over mounds of sage-brush and mesquite that raked at the underside of the car with a screeching sound like the metal hull of a submarine coming apart.

Bob's Drop was not much more than a large hole in the ground surrounded by a six-foot-high chain-link fence placarded with more KEEP OUT signs and a few that said DANGER and PELIGRO, the indi-vidual letters spitting lightning bolts for effect. I remembered the night, long ago, when Art showed me this place through his spyglass. We sat up on the hospital roof, waiting for a fireworks show that never came.

I helped Art out of the car and he surveyed the scene. Though the sun was not yet up, the eastern rim of the world was a burning violet wire beneath the bright little dot of a rising Venus. Overhead, thousands of flashing stars hung down like ornaments from a sky that was deep-sea blue. Pieces of broken concrete and half-buried rusted couplings and lengths of track littered the ground around our feet. Twenty yards away a decrepit ore car lay tipped over next to a huge flowering yucca.

Art navigated around the desert vegetation and took a good long look at the gate that was padlocked with a chain. "I was thinking we could snap the lock, do it easy, but that might be too obvious. I think I got a better idea." With painful care he circumnavigated the fence and found a portion that was overgrown with sagebrush. I fetched the cutters for him, and while struggling to hold back the sagebrush with his leg, he snipped about two feet worth of the fence wire from the ground up.

"We'll slide him under right here and nobody'll be the wiser. We'll get this done right quick, then we can put it out of our minds."

He coached me how to slip my arms under Barry's armpits and drag him the twenty feet from the car to the fence. Barry was heavier than I ever could have imagined. I strained just to pull him from the seat onto the ground, his zip-up boots thumping against the glove box and floor. I hugged him close to my chest, put my chin in his hair and pulled with everything I had. Twice I tripped over clumps of sagebrush, sprawling backwards with Barry's full weight on top of me. Both times I lay back in the dirt, the smell of cigarettes and sweat rising from his hair, and squeezed him with such a force that he wheezed as if alive. By the time I'd made it to the breach in the fence, my lungs were boiling in my chest, my legs gone wooden with exhaustion.

"Heck, that was the easy part," Art said with a forced cheerfulness. "Now we got to drag his sorry ass under this fence."

With great difficulty he bent down and lifted part of the fence like the flap of a tent. I crawled through and, as quickly as possible, turned around and grabbed Barry's wrists. I gave a solid yank, but now with his entire body laid out in the soft dirt and only his arms to pull him by, friction and inertia and gravity and all kinds of other scientific concepts I didn't care to understand were conspiring against me.

Art struggled mightily to hold his piece of the fence up. His arms shook and the muscles of his neck were pulling the skin of his face into a taut, mottled mask. Through his teeth he said, "You got to get a little leverage. Brace your foot against that post and try it thataway."

I did as I was told and was able to negotiate Barry through an inch or two at a time. Once we had him halfway under, Art had to lean against the fence and take a rest. We both wiped the sweat from our faces and gulped like winded hound dogs at the cool morning air. I sat down with Barry's needle-marked arms in my lap and looked up at St. Divine's, where it perched up on that hill with its darkened windows and boarded-over doors like a horror-movie haunted house. Art turned to look at it too.

"Seems like a dream, don't it?" he said, idly unhooking Barry's shirt from the sharp, snipped-off ends of the fence wire. "Hell, maybe this here is a dream, what we're doing right now. Maybe it's all a dream, every minute, start to finish. Tell you the truth, I sure do hope so."

We caught our breaths and went at it again. The tip of the sun came over the horizon, throwing long columns of dusty light that shot out for miles a few feet above the ground. I got Barry's legs all the way through and Art let the fence down with a grateful groan. I found one last reserve of energy and reared back, hauling Barry the last six feet until my heel hit one of the creosoted timbers at the lip of the shaft, and I tottered there, Barry's weight the only thing holding me back. "DON'T FALL IN THE HOLE!" Art shouted. I caught my balance and let go of Barry all at once so that his arms flopped out over the black void. His mouth was open now, his tongue and teeth caked with dust. With his eyes creased shut, he seemed to have been caught in the middle of a hearty laugh.

I stared blankly at my shadow stretched out thirty feet in front of me, trying to hold myself steady, the yawning hole breathing its moist subterranean air up into my face. Every bit of my strength was gone and I wavered at the edge, as hollow as an echo. I felt so weak I could not make myself move. I closed my eyes and did my best to keep down the sob that was trying to rise out of my throat.

"Just a little push, son," Art said. "Then it's over."

I could feel the dawning sun on the back of my neck and it seemed that it might be a good idea to stand there and do nothing for at least an entire day, if not forever. Then, like a jolt in my brain, I remembered the mailman's address. I bent down to take the yellow paper out of Barry's shirt pocket and slipped it into my jeans. It was that folded square of paper, like a piece of warmth against my thigh, that gave me the strength I needed to pick Barry up by the ankles and roll him into the dark tunnel of air. There was a single, ringing thud a second after he went in and then nothing. Art and I held still, our heads cocked, listening, but there was no sound at all, and Barry was simply gone, vanished in a single breath, as if he had never existed, as if he had never walked this earth, never tasted this air or been touched by this brilliant morning light.

THE YELLOW PAPER

BACK AT ART'S house, I fell into his narrow twin bed and slept all that day and the entire night. When I woke up it was morning again and Art had breakfast going full swing in the kitchen. "I'll run a bath for you," he said. "Have to apologize for no shower. Never could work them nozzles anyhow."

He took my filthy clothes and told me he'd have Lucinda give them a good washing. I soaked in the tub for half an hour, not a thought in my head, and got out to find some of Art's clean clothes on the chair by the door. The shirt was a starched white button-up, only a size or two too big, and I cinched up the green twill pants with a belt whose copper buckle read *Isringhousen Industries Employee of the Year.*

When I came out into the front room he turned from where he was forking slabs of bacon onto a paper towel. "Lookit here," he said. "Slick as an otter."

My trunk sat in the front room, wedged between the recliner and the produce crate that served as a coffee table.

"I had someone come get rid of that car for us," he said from the kitchen. "I took a peek inside to make sure that trunk was yours. Looks like you've run that old typewriter through its paces."

We sat down together at the rickety card table by the window and ate huevos rancheros, bacon, hash browns and deep-fried scones with honey. It looked like enough food to feed six people, but by the time we were done the plates and serving dishes held only crumbs.

"More where that came from," Art said. "I'll whip up another batch before you can blink twice. Living alone like this, a man's got to learn his way around the kitchen."

I held my gut and forced a smile to show him that I couldn't take any more. He cleared the dishes, leaning on his four-legged cane, each step a wearisome enterprise, but would not let me help. Once he had everything cleaned up he settled back into his chair, his lungs rasping. He took out a handkerchief and wiped his brow, then dabbed at a line of spittle on his chin. "Already hot as billy heck in here, ain't it?" He folded the handkerchief with the formality of ritual, put it back in his pocket, and placed both hands on the table, his fingers meshed together like the teeth of gears. He said, "You know you're welcome to stay here as long as you'd like."

I gazed out the window where a barefoot little girl walked at the edge of the road, making a trail in the dirt with the broken-off end of a TV antenna.

"I think maybe I got somewhere to go," I said.

Art nodded, looking away, and got up to limp across the front room, his bad leg clumping on the wood floor. He opened a curio cabinet where there was a stack of sheet paper a couple of inches thick. My old urinal puck, still swathed in black tape, sat on top like a paperweight.

"Got something I wanted to say to you," he said. He rested his cane against the recliner and carefully took the sheaf of papers down. "After that one time, I never wrote back to you because I figured you'd come to forget about me and that hospital and everybody in it and that it would be the best thing for you. But you never stopped writing, you never did."

Something caught in his voice and he swallowed, his hands shaking so that the urinal puck skittered and jumped across the smooth surface of the paper. He turned so that he was talking to the wall. "These letters . . . " he sniffed and hawked, rubbed his hand roughly against the scruff of his face. "You can't know how much they helped me. They were all I had, is what I'm saying. They kept me going when I didn't have nothing left. You can't know."

For a time he didn't move. He looked down at the stack of paper, gave it a couple of taps with the ends of his fingers, then set it back in its place inside the cabinet. He took up his cane and negotiated around my trunk and without looking at me, went into the kitchen, where he began to wash the dishes. Plates and bowls jangled in the metal sink and steam curled up over his head. I heard him say "Oh hell," and he came to me and took my head in his wet hands and pulled my cheek against the cold steel of his belt buckle.

Then he went right back to the dishes. With a black wad of steel wool he scoured the griddle, two frying pans and a chipped ceramic coffeepot. I sat in my chair feeling blasted, unsteady, parched. Even after my long bath and three glasses of orange juice, my tongue was like paper, my veins full of nothing but dust and salt.

Over the splash of the dishwater Art said, "So where is it you're off to?"

I gripped the table, pulled myself up, and went back into the bedroom, where my dirty clothes lay at the bottom of a hamper. I took the yellow paper from the pocket of my jeans. In a blocky, masculine script it said,

> B—
>
> This looks solid. If there's a problem, you let me know—
>> Nicholas Petenko
>> 107 Washington St.
>> Stony Run, Pennsylvania
>
>> > > > —TC

In the kitchen Art was still obscured in a cloud of steam. He swabbed off the stovetop, put a Yuban coffee can full of bacon grease under the sink. When he turned to look at me, water dripped from the ends of his fingers onto his shoes.

I said, "Do you know where Pennsylvania is?"

STONY

RUN

EDGAR ON THE ROAD

IN THE HEAT of a July afternoon, Edgar stepped out of the taxi
and peered down the row of houses through the shadows of the
trees. Everything was green: thick lawns and hedges and lilac
bushes and creeping vines that smothered fences and birdbaths and
swallowed chimneys whole. The trees' roots had wreaked havoc on
the sidewalk, grinding it into crumbs in some places and in others
heaving it into large broken sections like slabs of arctic ice.

"Here we go," said the cabdriver. "One-oh-seven. Bing bang
boing. Okay then. Yessiree."

The cabdriver was a small Italian man who had not stopped talking since he picked me up at the bus station. He had been called in
special because his taxi—a sky-blue station wagon with mag rims—
was the only one in town big enough to handle my trunk. Now he
was standing behind the car with the back door open, looking rue-
fully at the piece of luggage it had taken him five minutes and a borrowed dolly to load up. We were parked on a steep incline and it
seemed that the trunk, at any second, might slide right out the back
of the car and go skidding down the hill like a runaway sled.

The cabdriver took a shiny steel comb from his shirt pocket and
smoothed his thinning hair in artful waves across the top of his head.
He wore a white T-shirt and metallic pants. Without a hint of anger
or irritation he said, "I'm telling you right now I have handled a lot

of luggage in my life but never have I handled luggage such as this luggage. I'm telling you right now."

He set his feet and pulled on the broken straps of the trunk and, aided by gravity, eased it slowly out of the car. From where I was standing it looked like the car was giving birth to a boxy, smaller version of itself and the cabdriver was the attending doctor, coaxing things along. I tried to offer my assistance, but he held up his hand. "Dangerous," he said. "We got dangerous luggage here."

When the trunk finally clapped down hard onto the pavement, the cabdriver stared at it as if he didn't know what to do next. He took the comb out of his pocket and made a couple more passes across his scalp. I helped him push the trunk to the side of the curb and told him I would take care of it from there.

"What your problem is," he said, "is you got to learn to throw things out. You's a pack rat, am I right? You keep everything, can't toss nothing out. I've seen it before. My own son, Michael Vincent, he had this very problem. Kept everything. Gum wrappers, for chrissakes. A whole drawer full of 'em. What is a person going to do with a drawer full of gum wrappers? See? I don't understand it." He gave me a friendly chuck on the back and took the money I offered him. "Throw something away once in awhile. That's my advice. You'll be a happier individual."

He drove away and I hunkered down on my battle-scarred trunk to try and get my bearings. I felt frayed at the edges, close to coming clean apart. Over the last four days I had been riding a series of Greyhound buses and in my legs and ass I could still feel the constant jar and rumble of the road. A small blue flame of nausea, fed by motion sickness and the greasy road food I had eaten, guttered fitfully in the pit of my gut.

I had spent my last day in Globe with Art, and early the next morning he went with me to the bus station, bought my tickets, and slipped a roll of cash into my pocket that turned out to be three hundred dollars in fifties and twenties.

"You need more of that, give me the word," he said. For the first time since I had been with him, his breath smelled vaguely of whiskey. "I'll find a way to get it to you."

He had also bought me several new pairs of pants and some plaid shirts with metal snap-buttons. I asked if he wouldn't mind if I took the clothes he had lent me after my bath. In those baggy, tattered clothes fragrant with soap and the woody tang of cedar and Art's own particular smells I felt comforted, even protected. They were all I wore over those four long days riding the bus and I had them on even now, stiff with grime despite the few perfunctory washings in rest-stop bathroom sinks.

For an hour Art and I sat together in the bus station, saying very little and having donuts and hot chocolate he bought for us at the snack shop. When the call came over the loudspeakers we stood up together and he reached out and gave my hand a thorough shaking, just as he had on that windy April day nearly half my lifetime ago, and stood by while I climbed the bus steps. And just as he had on that long-ago day, he turned and limped slowly away. He swung his hips to get his bad leg moving, the rubber tips of his canes squeaking on the tile floor, and hobbled down the concourse, not wanting, I suppose, to watch me be carried off once again into some other, faraway life.

The bus pulled out, groaning and shuddering like an animal waking from sleep, and so Edgar was off, loosed again into the world, fearful and alone. In less than an hour we were already passing through Whiteriver, and I crawled across the aisle so that I could see, far off on the other side of the canyon and just above the tops of the trees that lined the parade grounds, the roofs of the dormitories of Willie Sherman, haunted on this very day, no doubt, by a few permanent savages who had been abandoned for the summer. Principal Whipple's observation tower jutted over the canopy of leaves and beyond that, up on a shallow rise, the white silo and the shadow of black earth where the cavalry stables once stood.

Then it was up through the piney White Mountains and into New Mexico, a land of narrow, zigzagging sandwashes and chaparral and thin buttes rising out of the piles of red rock scree. And on across the desert plain, flat and empty as the palm of a hand, which rolled away on both sides in an endless expanse. Somewhere in Kansas the green started in earnest, fields of wheat and corn and oats in every shade, so shocking in its depth against the black road and the fallow fields and the pale cloudless sky, and then we were in Missouri, where the countryside closed in, the road crowded mercilessly by a mass of vegetation that filled the air with its wet, rotting breath. As long as we were moving I was okay, the small vent overhead blowing a miniature recycled breeze over the top of my head, but when the bus would stop to pick up new passengers or make some repair, the thick air would settle around me in a cloud of hot vapor and I would struggle to breathe, sometimes working myself into a huffing, bug-eyed panic, like a fish drowning on the deck of a boat.

I hardly slept at all. I don't know if it was the humidity keeping me awake, or the wild confusion of thoughts in my head, or the constant stop and start, the exchange of passengers and luggage, but in those four days I did not sleep more than an hour at a stretch. I leaned my forehead into the window and watched the towns and fields and billboards slide past, struck with wonder that the United States of America could be so appallingly huge.

The people who sat next to me either ignored me or wanted to pass the time talking. With the talkers I affected my expression of blank disregard, the one I had so painstakingly developed in my days at Willie Sherman. It was somewhere in Indiana, I believe, that I finally managed to fall into a deep early-morning sleep, when I felt the man sitting next to me rest his hand firmly on my crotch. He was a thick-necked guy who smelled like hair spray. When I looked up at him he flashed me a broad, friendly smile that reminded me instantly of Nelson Norman. I did not shout or make a scene, I merely slipped out Art's knife from its place in my sock, pulled open the blade and jabbed the tip firmly into the back of his hand. For a second his mouth went wide in a frozen scream, his silver fillings glinting, and then he was dancing down the aisle, shaking his hand as if it were on fire, saying "Owee, ouch, shit!" He spent the rest of his trip up front, near the bus driver, peering back at me from time to time, trying to find in himself the wherewithal to come and retrieve the bag he had abandoned under his seat.

After all the unrelenting green, passing through the brick and asphalt of cities like Cleveland and Pittsburgh was a relief. I put my head out the window and gawked like a wolf boy at the billowing steelworks and rusting bridges and square towers of glass. The closer to Stony Run, Pennsylvania, I got, the harder it was to shake the sensation that I was disappearing, dissolving into the wet air like cigarette smoke. For almost two straight days nobody looked at me or bothered me and I rode with my head against the window, lost in an exhausted trance, until I changed buses one last time in a town called Dirksville and headed for Stony Run on a ribbon of shattered country blacktop.

And now, feeling as if I had been dropped out of the sky by a passing plane, here I was in front of what I hoped was the house of the man who, by his absentmindedness or negligence or pure bad luck, had started me on this journey eight years ago. More than ever I felt like a phantom, invisible and powerless in the world of the living, a feeling reinforced by the people who passed by: a woman dragging a cart of groceries, two little girls dressed in identical pink outfits and a man walking a miniature black wiener dog at the end of a chain, none of whom gave me a second look, as if a filthy half-breed Apache teenager in old man's clothes sitting on a battered steamer trunk at the side of the road was a sight they came across on a regular basis hereabouts.

I watched the house for some sign of movement or habitation. Two stories of brick the color of dried blood, beset on all sides by ivy and other creeping plants, it was not the house I had envisioned in my fantasies. The house in my dreams was clean and white and dignified, something with green shutters and new paint at the edge of a golden field of wheat. With its rusted rain gutters and broken porch swing and wooden shingles edged with moss, this house seemed just this side of shabby. I took out the yellow paper, now smudged and fuzzy with overhandling, to make sure I was at the right address.

I stood up and tested my faintly prickling legs. I didn't know how long I had been sitting on that trunk; riding the bus for so long had rattled my senses and warped my perception of time. The sky was shrouded in a flat gray haze, as it had been for the last couple of days, and I tried to imagine how hot it might be if the sun was out. I took a deep breath, which felt like trying to swallow a damp flannel rag.

I left my trunk where it was, stepped over the buckling sidewalk and stood at the low iron gate, which had been left hanging open. I waited there for awhile, not yet ready to walk up that narrow cement path, climb those steps, and knock on that heavy wooden door.

Above me, all the leaves in the trees began to shake and clatter. A few seconds later it was pouring rain. There was no stirring of air, no distant thunder or flash of lightning, no warning of any kind. One moment it was calm and the next there was a hail of raindrops tearing through the leaves overhead and hitting me on the neck and back as hard as pennies.

In no time I was soaked. I let the warm, battering rain wash the sheen of grime and grease from my hair and skin and clothes. It coursed down the center of my back like a waterfall, poured out of the crack of my butt and overflowed in my shoes. It felt wonderful, and only when it began to ease up a little did I climb up onto the porch and give the door three solid knocks.

No answer came right away and I knocked again. I thought I could hear a wooden creaking somewhere on the second level and then someone was thunking down the stairs. The door opened to reveal a short, dark woman in a brightly flowered dress, her black hair pulled back from her face and threaded with gray. My throat swelled hot with disappointment.

"Hello?" she said, her face caught in a smile that faded a little as she got a good look at me. Her eyes settled somewhere around my belt and I realized with a start that I had my crotch in a stranglehold.

I dug into my pockets and came up with the dripping yellow paper, the words on it now smeared beyond recognition.

I swallowed. "Does Nicholas Petenko live here?"

The syllables of the name felt odd in my mouth; this was the first time I had spoken them out loud. The woman opened the door a little wider, her eyes narrowing. Her words shaped and flattened by some accent I couldn't place, she said, "Who are you?"

When I told her she froze, her eyes trained on my face. The rain drummed on the awning over our heads and splashed from the clogged gutters. She braced her arm against the doorjamb.

"Your name, please," she said. "Say it again."

"I'm Edgar Mint. I'm trying to find a man named Nicholas Petenko. He was a mailman in Arizona." I dangled the limp piece of paper in front of her as evidence of my claims.

She stared past me then, into the torrent of rain that had already made a lake out of the front yard. She seemed to be looking at something that I couldn't see. A car *shished* by in the street. I murmured something about my trunk getting wet out there and she looked at me again.

"You are Edgar," she said, as if to reassure herself, and when I nodded her face unlocked itself from that blank expression and brimmed over with a tide of such strong emotion it seemed to pain her. She faltered a little, falling against the door, her eyebrows creasing together, her mouth curling open to reveal a set of straight, white teeth, her bright eyes, like two little lights, suddenly dribbling tears. She moaned, crossed herself, gripped my wrist in her shaking hand, and knelt at my feet. "God?" she said, "God?" as if she was calling a child in for supper, and then in a language I didn't understand, began to pray.

A PICTURE

BEWILDERED, A PUDDLE spreading around his feet, Edgar sat on a corduroy love seat in a corner of the large front room, with its tatted and doilied armchairs, its dressers and china cabinets whose every knob sported red and blue tassels, its every wall hung with pictures of saints and icons, its oaken floor worn smooth as brown glass.

The woman brought a large glass of limeade from the kitchen and insisted I drink it before we talked. The limeade was sweet and freshly squeezed and swimming with bits of pulp, and even though I had not been thirsty a second before, I could not help but drink it down in a few gulps.

This seemed to please her. She nodded, unable to take her eyes off me, as if she was afraid I might vanish if she looked away. Her face was dark and plump with little bulldog jowls, and the fine wrinkles that radiated from the corners of her eyes and mouth deepened into grooves when she smiled. She held a string of black prayer beads which she absently wove between her fingers and around her wrist.

I wiped at my forehead with my wet sleeve and listened for a moment, hoping to hear the creak of a floorboard or the thump of a footstep overhead, but we were alone. "I'm trying to find this man," I said. "Nicholas Petenko."

"I'm Rosa Petenko, see?" she said. "Nicholas is my husband."

I sat forward in my chair and nearly fell off it. "Is he here?" I said. "Where is he?"

She tried to smile at me but couldn't quite manage it. She tapped the beads against her chest. "Lord above took him," she said, making a little shrug. "One year and five months."

I went still for a moment, not breathing or thinking, and then my shoulders collapsed and I shrank in on myself like someone who has come to realize, at long last, that he has been the butt of an elaborate practical joke. I eased back into the chair and nodded and swallowed down the bitter taste in my throat. I closed my eyes, wondering how I ever had the gall to believe that things might come out any different than this. I almost laughed out loud.

"Edgar?" Rosa said, but I didn't open my eyes. I felt her hand on my arm for a moment and then I heard her open one of the drawers of a cabinet behind me. When I looked up she was sitting across from me again, now wearing wire-rimmed reading glasses and holding a picture framed in brass.

"A picture, see?" she said.

I took the picture from her. It showed three people standing next to a bush in the heavy glare of an early afternoon. In the background a billboard said *Drink Ovaltine!!* A younger Rosa, her hair black and long, squinted into the camera, and next to her was a balding man in a white T-shirt who was looking down at the boy standing between them. A brown barefoot boy with a few freckles scattered over his nose, clutching a half-eaten candy bar.

"You don't know all this, do you?" she said. "No? You don't remember. Nobody told it to you."

For a moment I could not remember who I was or where I was supposed to be. I shook my head and she seemed almost delighted by the confounded look on my face.

I pointed at the man in the picture. "This is Nicholas? Your husband?"

Rosa nodded. "I'll tell it to you, everything, but first I want you to tell me this miracle." She tapped the glass above little Edgar's face with her fingernail. "How you came from there"—and now she patted my knee—"all the way to here."

I opened my mouth to find that nothing would come out. I couldn't keep my eyes off the picture; I was trying to determine if little Edgar was smiling or frowning. The sun was hard on his face and he had that candy bar in a death grip. The man was looking down at him, his nose wrinkled as if he had just smelled something funny. From his mouth dangled an unlit cigarette.

I told Rosa about my bus trip from Arizona. Then I backed up and told her the bare bones of what I knew about the accident and my miraculous survival and my mother's death, about my stay at St. Divine's and Willie Sherman and the Madsen home. I had to speak slowly; my mind was a dark and empty cave in which I groped for words. I did not look up from that picture the whole time and when I did, Rosa was crying again.

"Edgar," she said. She pressed her beads against her lips and sighed. "Let me tell you all the things you don't know about. I guess we both got some learning to do."

ROSA AND NICHOLAS

EIGHT YEARS AGO, on a Saturday morning in May, Rosa and Nicholas walked out of the Safeway in downtown Globe to find a dirty Indian boy standing next to their car, eyeballing the package of Moon Pies on the front seat. They asked him where his mother was and he shrugged. The boy's clothes were stained and threadbare, his hair was full of dust and the hole in the seat of his jeans made it clear he wasn't wearing any underwear. Rosa took him by the hand back into the store, where they presented him to the manager, who sighed and made a few desultory announcements over the intercom about a lost Indian kid by the name of Edgar Mint.

"I wouldn't worry too much about it," the manager said. "These Indians, they let their kids run wild, it's cultural. His mama'll turn up sooner or later."

They waited twenty minutes, and when no one showed to claim the boy they circled the parking lot, then the entire store itself. The only Indian they could see was an old guy sitting on the steps of the bank across the street. They took Edgar over to him and asked if he knew who the boy belonged to.

"Wish I could help you," he said. "All I got to say about it is somebody oughta clean that kid up."

So that's what they did. In ten minutes they had him home, in the bathtub covered in suds, and Rosa in the kitchen cooking up hash cakes and grilled cheese sandwiches. After showing the boy his collection of Marine Corps tattoos, Nicholas emptied out the utensil drawer and he and Edgar splashed each other and performed dive-bomber and submarine maneuvers with an assortment of spatulas, ladles and potato mashers. Once the boy was thoroughly clean, Nicholas lifted him out of the tub and dried him off with exquisite care, rubbing down every inch of him as if waxing and buffing an expensive vintage automobile.

They had no toys for Edgar to play with, no spare clean clothes for him to wear; theirs was not a house of children. They had spent most of the eleven years of their marriage trying to make a family, but it never did take. They had consulted doctors as far away as Seattle and Minneapolis, had even traveled to Denver to receive a special bless-ing at the hands of Bishop Chekanov, but still their two extra bed-rooms remained empty.

Rosa and Nicholas had met in the Philippines, where Nicholas had spent three years fighting the Japanese. Ten years after the war he went back with a group of veterans from the II Corps, for whom Rosa, a grammar school English teacher from Manila, had been hired as an interpreter. They were both single, over thirty, and full of a hopeful loneliness that verged on desperation. On the second night of the tour Nicholas walked Rosa back to her hotel room and they ending up kissing and groping in the elevator. Nicholas left the tour and Rosa called in sick and they spent the rest of the week get-ting to know each other. Nicholas flew home and before the year was out had saved up enough money to bring Rosa to Pennsylvania and buy her a band of gold so they could get married in the Joy of All Who Sorrow Orthodox Church in Nicholas' hometown of Stony Run.

Nicholas had come home from the war with a mysterious jungle virus or amoebic bacteria the American doctors could not diagnose: cycles of diarrhea, exhaustion, dizziness, night sweats and fluid in the lungs. Now it seemed only to be getting worse and the doctors came up with a last-ditch suggestion: move to the desert and the dry air. So they packed up their Ford and moved to Globe, where Nicholas got a job with the post office. His symptoms gradually began to vanish and they bought an old stucco house at the mouth of Copper Canyon, but even with Nicholas at full health they could not make a family. Eventually they gave up on the doctors and put their faith in God. Every day they prayed, and often in the evenings they would sit in the backyard in their spring-back chairs talking about their future children as if it was just a matter of time before there were three or four of them scribbling on the walls, clamoring for snacks and keeping them up all hours of the night.

This went on for five or six years until all at once, it seemed, they had exhausted their hope. By some silent mutual accord they agreed that they would no longer talk about it, no longer pray to God to bless them with the desire of their hearts. They came to believe that God, in His own way, had already given them their answer.

And now, after so many years of quiet evenings and languid afternoons, there was something strangely discomfiting to Rosa about the sudden commotion this Indian boy was causing. She didn't like the way Nicholas carried on so easily with him, spinning him around in the air and tickling him until he squealed for mercy. She was out back, hanging up Edgar's newly washed clothes, and she could hear Nicholas at the table, trying to teach him how to sing "The Battle Hymn of the Republic" in Ukrainian. She stepped inside and leaned against the doorway to watch them. Sitting at the far end of the table in nothing but a towel, the boy had stuffed an entire sandwich into his mouth, which wasn't helping his Ukrainian any. Nicholas began to laugh so hard he slid halfway off his chair, and Edgar, wide-eyed, started giggling until he had to struggle to keep the sandwich in his mouth. Rosa couldn't help herself: she began to laugh too.

Eventually they drove Edgar out to the reservation. They'd questioned him thoroughly and all they'd found out was that he was seven years old, his mother was named Gloria and he lived in a house with a beer-tree out front. It didn't take them long to find the beer-tree house and when Gloria came out to retrieve Edgar, stumbling into the afternoon light with the glazed expression of someone who had been shaken out of a deep sleep, she made no attempt to explain

where she had been or why her son had been left alone in the parking lot of the Safeway.

Before they went home, Nicholas wrote down their address and
phone number and told her they'd be more than happy to baby-sit
Edgar anytime, all she needed to do was give them a call. The next
Saturday, at ten in the morning, Gloria called from the pay phone at
the Circle K and asked if Nicholas and Rosa could look after Edgar
for the day while she went out with friends. And so it became a
weekly ritual: Nicholas and Rosa would get up early so they could
fetch Edgar, feed him a big breakfast, and have the rest of the day to
take him to the river or the dog track or the municipal swimming
pool, where he would splash around in the baby pool with toddlers
half his age. Often he would stay the night and after he was sleeping
soundly in the G.I. Joe pajamas they had bought for him, they would
bring chairs in from the kitchen, sit outside his door, and watch him
sleep. Nicholas would balance an ashtray in his lap and they would
smoke and drink chilled vodka out of a jelly jar. At first, they both
felt a little ridiculous, but how could they ever have known, in all
their imaginings, what a sweet and blessed thing it might be to have
a child sleeping in their house?

During the week, the house seemed vacant, full of echoes. Rosa
and Nicholas went about their lives as always, but at night in the dark
of their bedroom they talked about the boy. He was a quiet, poker-
faced little guy, but he was smart, they didn't doubt that one bit.
Even though he had not spent a day in school he could pick out certain words on billboards and street signs and was a whiz at checkers.
He had a pretty good arm on him and Nicholas thought he might
make a good ballplayer one day. They weren't sure if it was funny or
disturbing how he would sit on the couch to watch cartoons and
immediately begin to bounce his head against the cushion, back and
forth in steady rhythm, like a peg on a metronome. They couldn't
help but laugh at his habit of walking around with a hand locked
securely on his crotch.

Then one afternoon Gloria showed up at the house in badly

applied makeup and a pair of alligator pumps. Rosa had her sit at the
dining room table and offered coffee. In a slur of words, Gloria
explained why she had come: she wanted Nicholas and Rosa to take
Edgar. She knew they were fond of him, and it was clear that he
liked being with them. She knew she wasn't a good mother and
wanted him to have a better life. All she asked in return was enough
money to settle her debts and buy a bus ticket to Los Angeles.

It felt to Rosa as if all the light in the room had gathered into her
chest. "Anything you want, we'll give it to you," she said. "First thing
to do is get a lawyer to make some adoption papers—"

"No," Gloria said, slamming her china cup on the table. "No
adoption, nothing like that. You say adoption and here come the
government people, sniffing around like dogs. They almost took
Edgar one time before, put him in some foster home. I know about
it. They got papers and it's waiting around for this and that and
they're stopping by your house every other day, snooping and poking around like they know better than God." She was shaking her
head now, swirling the coffee around in her cup until it spilled on
her hand. "I'm leaving for L.A. in two weeks. I'll find the money I
need one way or the other. You don't want Edgar, I'll take him with
me."

That night Nicholas called up one of his old war buddies, a jolly
Greek who had started his own law practice in Baltimore. "It's
dicey!" the Greek roared over the phone. "Suddenly the mama
changes her mind and the whole game is up, kiss all your time and
money good-bye. Take my advice, go down to Mexico and bribe a
priest at an orphanage if you're really dying for a baby right quick.
There's no faster or cheaper way to do it. They'll doctor you up all
the necessary paperwork and—zoom!—you're on your way."

For three straight nights Nicholas and Rosa talked about it until
the light came up over the hills, going over every possible scenario,
trying to convince each other of what was already a foregone conclusion. There was no decision at all to make, and both of them
knew it. God, on his own terms and in his own time, had brought

them their child. They would take Edgar back to the place where they had begun, and start all over again.

The next day they put their house on the market for such a low price the realtor laughed with great hilarity until he realized they were serious. Nicholas took two weeks of sick leave from the post office and flew out to Stony Run to prepare their new home. It was the one Nicholas had grown up in, and it had sat vacant since his mother's death. Rosa stayed behind to pack up their things and show prospective buyers around the house, which sold in ten days.

On the day before they were to meet Gloria at the bus station so they could make their transaction and go their separate ways, Nicholas drove out to San Carlos to talk to Gloria and to drop off some of the money they'd agreed on as an offering of good faith. It was his last day on the job and he was too nervous to wait any longer, so he abandoned his route and, with a jeep full of mail sacks, headed for the reservation.

Gloria was inside the house at the kitchen table with four cans of beer set out in front of her and a bowl of melting ice cubes. Edgar was nowhere to be seen and the whole house ticked like a heating oven. Gloria was so drunk Nicholas had to yell at her to get her to respond. Finally, he put a hundred-dollar bill on the table and told her he and Rosa would be back that evening.

When Nicholas stepped out into the hot white light, he wondered where Edgar might be. Probably in the back, he decided, digging holes or destroying anthills or spying on the neighbors. He wanted to tell the little guy good-bye, but knew he would be seeing him again soon enough. On his way out of the yard he ran his hands through the hanging beer cans. He sat on the hot vinyl seat of his jeep for a moment and listened to the strangely soothing music of the beer-tree. Then he cranked the ignition, started forward and crushed the life out of the boy he had come to love as his own son.

Rosa was in the basement and did not hear her husband drive up and go into the garage. She was pouring out a bucket of water when she heard someone coming down the stairs. She turned and there was a man, naked except for his shoes and underwear, covered in blood and holding an ice pick.

At first she didn't recognize Nicholas and gathered herself to scream. Even when she saw who it was, her husband, this shy and courteous man who, after eleven years of marriage still asked permission to kiss her, the fear that had clutched at her throat did not fall away. It was not the blood that frightened her, smeared over his mouth and arms and dabbed across his chest in dark rosettes. And it was not the ice pick, so obviously the cause of the small hole to the left of his Adam's apple that leaked a single thick rivulet of blood. It was the look on his face, the lost and ravaged look of a man whose heart had been ripped right out of him.

With the hem of her wet skirt she wiped the blood from his mouth and neck. She begged him to speak but he could only shake his head and whine like a child who wanted something but didn't know how to ask.

In an examination room at the hospital, after the doctor had given him a tranquilizer shot and put a couple of sutures in his neck, Nicholas explained to Rosa what had happened. He told her all of it in three or four sentences, short and to the point: He had gone out to San Carlos. He left some money with Gloria and told her they would come back later. He didn't know how it happened, but somehow he had run over Edgar. *I killed him,* he said. *I killed our boy.*

Rosa asked him if he was sure that Edgar was dead and Nicholas nodded, shuddering, his eyes gone dark. *He wasn't breathing and his head was crushed,* he told her. *I put my hands on it and I could feel it give.*

Even in her panic and grief, Rosa knew what had to be done. She led her husband out of the hospital, where the sun was a fierce white ball overhead, and took him home. While he sat slumped in the front seat, his face glazed with shock, she loaded up the suitcases she had already packed for their trip. They drove down to Phoenix, got a room in an airport motel and flew out the next morning, the empty seat next to them a silent accusation.

For six years they lived in the old family house in Stony Run and hardly mentioned Edgar again. It wasn't long before Nicholas' jungle sickness returned, reinvigorated by the wet heat of the Pennsylvania summers. Their life became one long series of doctor visits, a never-ending regimen of pills and drops and tonics and powders and experimental diets. Still, every morning, six times a week Nicholas would pull himself out of bed and go to work at the packing plant where he'd been hired on as a freight manager. He worked long hours, came home in the evenings and sat in his plaid easy chair in the TV room where he took his dinners and watched game shows until he lost himself to a droning sleep.

Sometimes Rosa wanted to sit down with him and talk it all out; she thought, if nothing else, it might ease his nervousness, might help the ulcers that were burning holes in his stomach. But whenever Rosa brought up the subject, Nicholas closed his eyes, grimacing a little as if waiting out a cramp in his bowels, until she left him alone. An uneasiness had come between them and she felt close to him only when he'd drink his vodka on Friday nights, which usually turned him childlike, even a little impish. He would talk to her then, and wasn't afraid to touch her. Sometimes he'd even pull out his dusty accordion and play polka music that would make the dishes rattle in the cupboards.

Mostly it was a sad life they led, full of hard silences and the cycle of Nicholas' ailments. Many of their old friends did not know what to make of these two strangely morose and withdrawn people who used to host Hawaiian pig roasts in their backyard and had once taken second place in the Kiwanis Harvest Talent Show for their piano duet of "Be My Showboat," which they played with their elbows. Worse than anything, they could no longer go to each other for solace. Rosa simply accepted this as their fate, as their just reward for wanting too much, for reaching beyond their bounds, for trying to take what was not rightfully theirs.

Then one winter Nicholas came down with viral pneumonia and for three weeks lay in his hospital bed, grinding out each breath, until finally he gave up, tired of fighting his own worn-out

and contaminated body, and one morning let himself drown in the
fluid that had swamped his lungs. The family doctor, a World War II
vet himself, claimed that it was the war that had killed Nicholas, it
just took thirty years to do it. Rosa knew better.

Since his death she had made the half-mile walk to the Joy of All
Who Sorrow every Wednesday, Saturday and Sunday to attend services, to pray and ask for direction; she wanted to know what the
Lord had in mind for her. For a year and a half she waited for an
answer, until Edgar Mint, like Lazarus from the tomb, walked out of
a rainstorm and into her life a second time.

EDGAR'S ROOM

MY HANDS HELD on to each other in my lap and I felt hard and brittle, as if I might fall apart at the slightest touch. I had kept my head
down and eyes closed the whole time Rosa talked, her words washing into my mind like the images of a dream. When I looked up I
was struck by the strangeness of the light coming through the windows, where water ran down the glass as thick as oil.

Rosa watched me over her reading glasses. Her face was fixed in
lines, rapt and unmoving, the dark skin of her cheeks tracked with
tears. She went to a mahogany cabinet on the far side of the room
and took a small stack of pictures from one of the drawers.

"Nicky wanted me to throw these away," she said. Her voice was
pitted and rough and her accent clipped her words around the edges.
"But I kept them down under the stairs. I like to look at them, see?"

They were mostly pictures of little Edgar: little Edgar at the carni-
val trying to heft a rubber sledgehammer over his head, little Edgar
posing with a clown, little Edgar in a buckaroo getup sighting down
the barrel of a cap gun six-shooter, little Edgar sweaty and asleep in

the backseat of a car, little Edgar doing a Superman impression in his underwear, a beach towel clothespinned around his neck. There were a few others with Rosa and Nicholas and then I came to one of me with my mother. We were standing in front of a plain brick wall. She had her hand draped over my chest and I held tightly to one of her silver-ringed fingers. She was smiling.

A pressure built in my chest, expanding against my ribs. Rosa had gone into the kitchen and come back with a hand towel. "Look at this!" she said, suddenly flustered, dabbing the towel at my hair. "I let you sit there all wet and cold."

"How much," I said.

"How much?"

"How much money were you going to pay for me?"

She stepped back, looked down at her hands mechanically folding the towel into a tight square. "Oh Edgar, please—"

I said, "I'd like to know, I guess."

She hesitated. She tucked the towel up under her chin. She said, "Nine hundred dollars."

I asked if I could use the bathroom. My feet had gone numb and I could not feel them make contact with the floor. I stood at the bottom of the stairs to check my balance and grabbed the banister with both hands, going up fist over fist, like a mountaineer scaling the face of a cliff.

A claw-foot tub and a chipped sink filled most of the small bathroom. The faded, rose-colored wallpaper was peppered with scorch marks and black speckles of mold. A bunch of empty shower curtain hooks hung scattered along the length of the circular steel bar suspended above the tub like a halo.

I closed the door behind me and sat on the tub's curved lip. I began to choke up and I didn't know if I was going to vomit or suffocate. I put my hand on the toilet lid, but it was something else coming up, a wind gathering deep in the hollows of me and pushing into my chest and throat. I tried to hold it in but it blew through the cracks of my teeth and out my nose with a sharp hissing whine.

I could hear Rosa on the other side of the door and though I knew she was listening I couldn't stop. There were so many things I had never cried for. But I cried for them now. My body slacked and I sobbed. I coughed and gagged. I pulled my shirt over my face and cried so hard that I could feel my once-broken skull strain at its seams.

Through the door Rosa called my name. "It's not your fault," she said. "None of it."

After a time she came in and took a towel from the rack. I cried and she dried my face and hair. She helped me off with my wet shirt and draped the towel around my shoulders. It wasn't long before I had settled into hiccuping and sniffling and rubbing at my eyes with the heels of my hands. Rosa ran her fingers through my hair and along the top of my head, pressing on it, testing its strength.

"It's lumpy," I told her, and we laughed.

"Come on with me," she said, giving my wrist a little shake. "I got one more thing for you to see."

She took a ring of skeleton keys from the top of the banister post and led me down to the end of the upstairs hallway. She tried five or six keys before she found the one that fit. She twisted and rattled the glass knob until the door opened, scraping unwillingly across the floor.

Along the edges of the room were stacked boxes and great, rolled-up bolts of fabric and different-sized spools of vinyl and leather. Under one window squatted an industrial sewing machine with a polished metal ring like a steering wheel. Everything was covered in a furry layer of dust and a few cobwebs swayed from the blades of the ceiling fan.

"Mess, mess, mess!" Rosa cried, slapping the dust from a pillow which was leaking cotton batting from an open seam. "My arthritis got too bad and we had to move it all up here."

She pushed aside a moldering slab of foam rubber to reveal a small child's bed and, behind that, shoved into a corner, a three-quarter-size desk with a matching chair. Cowboys tossed lariats and herded galloping mustangs across the bedspread. The headboard and desk and chair had also been designed with a Western theme; they were trimmed with rope and showed boots and spurs and crossed pistols in bas-relief.

"This room was for you, see?" Rosa said. "Nicholas got it all ready for you when he came back here. He did it himself."

The room smelled of leather and machine oil and must. On the wall above the bed was thumbtacked a laminated map of the world, one corner of which had curled down so that only Australia and a few South Pacific islands were visible. On top of the desk was a stack of *Big Chief* notebooks and an unopened box of pencils.

"This is my bed?" I said.

"Only yours," she said.

"Did I like cowboys?"

Rosa shrugged. "I don't know. Nicholas liked cowboys. Why do all men want to be a cowboy? Only God knows."

Feeling suddenly peculiar in my own body, I sat down on the creaking bed and leaned back. The rain had stopped and the leaves of the oak outside tapped delicately against the windowpane. Rosa stood next to the bed and shyly put her hand on my chest. In a voice so low I almost didn't hear it she said, "Every day I missed you."

That night, after I had a bath and Rosa enlisted a bunch of neighbor boys to help bring my wet trunk inside, we sat down to dinner under the glass chandelier in the dining room. The table was crammed with Ukrainian and Filipino dishes: spring rolls and sinigang soup and cabbage dumplings. I ate with a sweating, careless abandon; I was fond of casseroles, but no casserole I had ever eaten could compare to these pan-fried sausages and crunchy noodles laced with bits of onion and egg. Rosa wore a long dress full of crocuses and her hair was pulled back into a tight bun which shone from the back of her head like a spotlight. I helped her with the dishes and then we sat in the TV room and watched "The Rockford Files" and "Police Woman" while outside the green dark rolled down.

"We got a guest room upstairs with a foldout bed and bathroom," Rosa said. "Okay for you?"

She sat in a plush velour lounge chair and I was sunk down in the loose springs of Nicholas' old recliner, which smelled of Brylcreem and pipe smoke. I told her that I'd rather sleep in the room with the cowboy bed.

"Oh no, dusty!" she said. "Too much stuff everywhere!"

She looked at me, the blue glow from the television flickering against the side of her face, and she smiled. She went into the kitchen and brought back a half pint of butter brickle ice cream. "Okay. You eat this and I fix up your room."

For a half hour I stared at the television in a trance and listened to the thumping and scraping overhead, the clatter of Rosa's shoes on the wooden floor. When I had finished off the ice cream I looked out the window into the backyard. In the blue-green dark I could make out a small lawn bordered by whitewashed stones and the rusted skeleton of an old swing set from which hung four empty chains. All around, glowing yellow lights circled and hovered. For a time I stared out the window, spellbound, and then went out the back door and stepped into the unmowed grass. The air was dewy and thick and I walked toward the center of the lawn, brushing spider silk from my lips and eyelashes. The yellow lights seemed to orbit me, moving with a slow, underwater languor, flickering and blinking out and flaring suddenly in the dark grass. I heard the screen door creak open and then Rosa was at my side.

"I've never seen this before," I said.

"Fireflies?" she said. "Nicholas told me the lonely ones, they're the brightest. Every one looks bright to me."

Back inside, I opened my trunk, which had done a fairly good job of protecting my belongings from the rain; the paper bundles at the bottom were soaked around the edges but my Hermes Jubilee had stayed high and dry. I took the typewriter and followed Rosa upstairs to my room, which she had swept and dusted and sprayed and polished. In the deep glow of the lamp it looked like a different room altogether, though the massive sewing machine still crouched in its place next to the window and there were bolts of fabric stacked against the far wall. The cowboy bedspread was gone, replaced by a sunflower quilt. The map of the world had been spread out flat against the wall, showing the continents and seas, and the newly waxed floor shone like the still waters of a pond.

Rosa helped me into bed and switched off the lamp. I thought I might type a little before I went to sleep but I didn't want to be impolite. "We'll get these other things out of here tomorrow. Anything else for you? Anything I can get?"

I shook my head. "I'm doing all right."

"Nothing? Some water maybe?"

"Water," I said. "Okay."

Rosa got me a tall glass of water and I drank down the whole thing. "I used to wet the bed," I told her.

"I know," she said.

She took the glass and kissed my forehead and told me she'd see me in the morning. After she closed the door behind her I lay under those clean sheets and listened to the branches against the window and the shouts of children in the faraway night and the strange electrical buzz of cicadas. I couldn't help myself; I got up and went to my desk. In the thick darkness, I found one of the *Big Chief* notebooks and ripped out a page. I rolled the sheet of paper into my Hermes Jubilee and typed a paragraph or two of happy nonsense before I slipped back under the covers and, for the first time I could remember, went to sleep in a bed that felt like my own.

ROSA AND EDGAR

AROUND ME THE events and dreams of my life have settled like layers of sediment. Stacks of paper line the walls, spill out of the closet and crowd the desk. Like a geologist studying the strata of metamorphic rock I can read the epochs of Edgar's short existence: from St. Divine's, the light blue paper of old ECG readouts the nurses let him use; from Willie Sherman, the brown, gritty theme paper he stole in bulk from the supply room interspersed with the thick, cream-colored school stationery he lifted from Maria's office when he felt like treating himself; from the Madsens', the reams of recycled mimeograph paper, often smeared with violet ink, that Lana brought home from her office. Showing themselves occasionally within the larger formations are smaller deposits of black, ink-soaked paper from those times of difficulty and sadness when pounding the keys, blotting out one page after the other, was Edgar's only comfort.

On one side of my desk, water-stained, crumpled and dog-eared and bound with twine and rubber bands and kite string and electrical wire, is the record of my life before I came to Pennsylvania. On the other side, typed exclusively on twenty-pound bond the color of alabaster and arranged in rows as orderly and white as the columns of a Greek temple, is the humdrum daily narrative of my last thirteen years.

Thirteen years. That is how long I have slept in this child's bed and typed at this child's desk. That is the span over which Rosa begged me to move into the guest room, where my feet wouldn't jut off the end of the mattress and my knees wouldn't thump the underside of the desk when I sat down to my typing. But I could never bring myself to move out. It was simple: this was my room, these were my things, and I wasn't about to give them up.

For the first year or so, when I actually still fit in my bed, I did not leave the house much. It was as if I was in recovery from a sustained illness or a near mortal wound suffered in combat: I took my breakfast in bed, napped several times a day, mowed the lawn in my pajamas, showered only when the mood took me (not very often), watched TV until I felt like I was going blind. Every week I went with Rosa to the city library and checked out the limit of half a dozen books, which would usually take me no more than three or four days to finish.

Eventually, I began to venture out more. On Monday nights I

would accompany Rosa to Bingo Night at the Community Fellowship Hall, a moss-green Quonset hut that sits off the old state highway in a stand of towering elms. We would take Garland Street, walking side by side under the blue globes of the streetlamps, past the elementary school and the abandoned Burnside Girls' Academy, and then on to the crumbling highway flanked on both sides by piles of glittering coal slag from which have grown countless stunted birches, their trunks slender and bone white. From Youngstown Bridge the fellowship hall would slowly rise into view, lit up at both ends like a spaceship taking off into the night.

For Rosa, Bingo was no pastime, it was business; she would spread out five tickets in front of her, a bingo stamp in each knobbed hand, her face set with concentration, a tiny bulldog Filipino woman ready to win come hell or high water. When she won, which was more often than not, her piercing little girl's voice would ring out, the call of "Bingo!" rebounding off the ribbed ceiling of the hall like the cry of a wild wetland bird, and the whole room would deflate, you could almost hear it in the mumbling and sighing and the crumpling of tickets: *Not her again.*

Afterwards, walking home in the dark, Rosa would count her money and snap her purse shut with a final click. "Those people in there, they think it's luck," she would say, shaking her head. "It's not luck, no no no. It's *prayer.*"

At least three times a day Rosa would kneel in her icon corner, the place in the living room where icons of saints and prophets and martyrs were clustered on the wall above the radiator in their stiff, awkward poses, gazing steadily into the middle distance with eyes a thousand years old, their heads encased in halos of tarnished gold. She would light a vigil candle and chant and read from the prayer book, sometimes prostrating herself, talking to God insistently and a little loudly, as if He was in the other room trying to read the newspaper.

It took her more than a year to convince me to attend liturgy with her. The Joy of All Who Sorrow is situated in the very center of downtown Stony Run, on the corner next to the post office, and it was built at the turn of the century by Slavic immigrants who came in droves to mine the beds of anthracite upon which the town had been built. Before she and Nicholas were married there, Rosa converted from Roman Catholicism and, until I began to attend church on a regular basis, was the only dark face in a congregation of white-skinned, fair-haired Slavs (upon my arrival in Stony Run, Rosa told anyone who asked that I was the son of a distant relative, come to stay indefinitely. Even though she and I looked nothing alike and had accents that marked us as coming from different corners of the world, everyone assumed that I was of Filipino descent—to the people of Stony Run a dark face is a dark face).

My first day at church I hardly knew what to make of the dim, candlelit room swirling with wreaths of incense, the acolytes and priests in their brocade vestments brandishing gold crosses and swinging censers, the choir chanting in some Byzantine minor key. It was otherworldly, nothing like the simple, spare Mormon chapels I had been in, and as alien to me—a native of sand and crag and oven-heated air—as these swelling Pennsylvania hills, more lush and green and overgrown than the Garden of Eden itself.

Midway through the liturgy came the "kiss of peace" and suddenly everyone was kissing everyone else, me included. I had never been a part of so much kissing in my life. These people kissed the priest's robe, his hand, the jeweled Gospel book as it was carried by in procession, and then without warning they were kissing each other, pressing in from all sides, reaching out to me with a kind of cheerful indifference, seeming not to notice that I was a stranger in that place, grabbing my hand and pulling me in for a peck on the cheek or neck. Those first few Sundays I would duck and bob and weave like a boxer trying to slip a jab, but they would get me anyhow—there were too many to try and fend off all at once—and eventually I gave in and began to return the hugs and handshakes, to kiss back. I kissed babies and mothers and men with lumberjack beards and teenage girls in short skirts and whiskery old ladies—I kissed them all.

To me, this is the beauty of it: there isn't all that much to tell about these last thirteen years. I mowed the lawn. I played Bingo. I went to church and kissed perfect strangers. I shoveled snow, shopped for groceries, cleaned the gutters, locked myself out of the house. There has been very little in the way of epic event; no bloody accidents, no bedlam or treachery, no fires or beatings or fistfights, no suicides or untimely deaths. Nothing but the balance of days, the ten o'clock news, the light hanging in the trees like cobwebs, the frost-coated grass, the Sunday paper thumping on the porch before dawn, the dishes in the sink.

This is not to say there weren't milestones. At eighteen Edgar got his driver's license so he could prowl the hilly byways of town in a jacked-up orange Chevette he bought from Father Grinev's son-in-law; at twenty he went on his first date; at twenty-three he lost his virginity to a woman he met in a bowling alley and never saw again; at twenty-four he smoked his first joint and came to believe he understood with perfect clarity the purpose and configuration of the universe and his place in it until he woke up the next morning with somebody else's shoes on.

In the last thirteen years I haven't become any wiser or better or stronger. In many ways, it occurs to me now, I have lived my life in reverse. In the first half of my life I had to make all the hard choices and ride out the consequences, while in the second half I have lived the sheltered and uncluttered life of a child. Every night I have been tucked into my child's bed, every day I have sat at my child's desk to read and type. I have had my hair cut in the kitchen with an old sheet tucked around my neck and Mentholatum rubbed into my chest during cold season. I have eaten a lot of cookies and milk.

I have not been able to live completely free of the adult world. At nineteen I got a job working with Mr. Oselskiy, a member of our congregation and the owner/editor of the only local newspaper in the valley, *The Blind Canary*. At first I made minimum wage filing records, emptying ashtrays and badgering lapsed subscribers over the phone, but Mr. Oselskiy began to see hints of my talent when he let

me write filler pieces about the Association of Firefighters awards
banquet or the rash of lawn-ornament thefts in Cutler Township (a
few years back Mr. Oselskiy confessed to me that as far as he was
concerned, *everything* in *The Blind Canary* is filler, besides the ads). It
quickly became apparent that I had what it took to become a capable newsman: I am a stickler for detail, people feel comfortable talking to me, and I can type like a son of a bitch. Now I do sports,
crime, the municipal beat and anything that smacks of "human interest." I write profiles of bottle-cap collectors and one-armed war
heroes and spelling-bee champs, I cover UFO sightings and the public outcry over seminude dancers at a local tavern. Occasionally, I
provide our readership with home improvement tips or recipes or
high-handed movie reviews, and every other week I write a shame-
less gossip column under the pseudonym "Bianca Walters."

There's nothing to it, really. I go out with my notepad and people
spill their guts to me. I show up on their doorsteps and they offer
their life stories, their small triumphs, their secret angers and regrets.
I usually put away my notepad, which is just for show anyway, and
listen patiently until they've said all they have to say. After that is the
easy part. I go home, sit down in front of my Hermes Jubilee, and do
what I've been doing every day for the past twenty years: I type up
all the gritty details.

While I have found some fulfillment in my professional life, I can
claim nothing of the sort when it comes to matters of the spirit.
Though I have gone to church every week with Rosa, prayed with
her over meals and before bedtime, stood with her through countless
vespers and liturgies, and faithfully fasted with her the forty days of
Lent, God and I have come to no real understanding. Unlike Rosa, I
can see no divine purpose behind the tangle of this existence, no
ordering hand. It is all a mystery, or more accurately, a mess. There
are no heroes or villains, no saviors or demons or angels. Only those
who have died and those of us who, for whatever reason, have survived. None of this will keep me from believing in God. I believe in
Him, I just don't know that I will ever have faith in Him.

So you might say God and I are at something of a standstill. I haven't forgiven Him and I have no reason to expect that He will do the same for me. We are both accountable for our own abominations and that, I have come to believe, is the way it should be. There have been many times, walking down the dark wooden corridors of the church, that I've considered stopping by Father Grinev's office to make the necessary confessions, to unburden myself of what I carry. I've wondered: could it free me of the nightmares I have of Barry tumbling through a dark void, never hitting bottom? Could it relieve the guilt I feel not only for Barry's death but also for everything else, for my mother, for Cecil, for Nicholas, all of whom, it seems clear to me even now, gave up their lives on my behalf? Maybe, but something holds me back. I will keep my sins to myself, I have learned to accept them as my own, and there is some small comfort in that.

And still there is happiness. In many ways, all I have been typing over the past thirteen years is one page of happy nonsense after another. I won't say there isn't the minor daily heartbreak of memory and what-might-have-been. The bad dreams and late night regrets. And the humidity around here is a torture. But I am not too jaded or proud to thank God for small favors, to count my blessings.

Every week I type a long letter to Art and sometimes we talk on the phone. I have to hold the receiver at least half a foot from my head so as not to risk permanent damage to my eardrums; the older Art gets the louder he becomes. For two years I have been seeing a woman named Mitzi Harrison. Mitzi has two small boys from a previous marriage and Art has become something of a surrogate grandpa to them. He sends presents and candy on holidays and makes sure I keep him informed about any major breakthroughs in motor skills or potty training. Despite a white-knuckle fear of flying and being confined to a wheelchair and needing a twenty-four-hour nurse, he makes periodical rumblings about coming out to visit.

I keep in intermittent touch with Sunny. After all these years we still share secrets; besides Art, she is the only one from my old life who knows the truth of my disappearance from the Madsen house. A couple of years after I left, the Madsens moved from Richland to Olympia, Washington, where Lana works with the park service and Clay runs a new construction company. Brain returned from a church mission to Bolivia awhile back and is about to enter graduate school at Syracuse as, of all things, a drama student. Sunny, married and divorced, lives in Denver and makes good money writing marketing copy for the Coors Brewing Company.

A few months ago she sent me a letter full of details about Lana and Clay's thirtieth wedding anniversary party. They celebrated it back in Richland, in the old community center packed with neighbors and family and friends and nine different kinds of Jell-O salad. *You should have seen it,* Sunny wrote. *Food and streamers everywhere and my folks dancing out there in the middle of all these old people, my dad swinging his hips and yelling to the music, "That's the way, uh-huh, uh-huh, I like it, uh-huh, uh-huh . . ." I could have sworn they were all drunk.*

I read that letter out on the porch, bright autumn leaves drifting around my feet, and nearly bawled with joy.

But there has been no greater blessing than Rosa. For thirteen years she and I did one simple thing: we were good to each other. We got each other drinks. We said *please* and *thank you* and *doesn't that shirt look nice.* We bought cards for each other on Valentine's Day and found inordinate pleasure in watching reruns of "The Benny Hill Show." We took turns cleaning the toilet. We talked bad about the neighbors and made fun of the persnickety old widows who liked to stand up front during liturgy and show off their new permanents. We played Scrabble and Yahtzee and let each other get away with murder.

After her first stroke, I was able to care for Rosa almost without help. I have grown into a large man (I have my father's bull neck and long arms) and it wasn't difficult at all to carry her up and down the stairs a dozen times a day, to transfer her from couch to wheelchair to bed and back again. The home care nurse came a few times a week to help with her rehabilitation and Mrs. McPherson from down the street would stop by every once in awhile to make dinner or keep Rosa company while I went out with Mitzi on weekends. I drove Rosa to church and to the hospital, I bathed her and helped her in the bathroom until she learned again to do it herself, I fixed meals and positioned her wheelchair at the icon corner so she could say her prayers morning and night, I came to know what she needed before she ever had to ask.

By seven months she had progressed so well that she could make do with a cane and got fed up with me and my solicitous ways. I'd try to help her out of her chair or take her dishes from the table and she'd give me a good swat on the shoulder and say in that funny, childish voice of hers, "Go way! Get out of here!" The doctors had told us that for her there was a high risk of another stroke, but it was something that never crossed my mind until I woke up last Monday morning to a quiet house. Rosa had always gotten up before me without fail, even in those first days home from the hospital when she would sit up in bed and hum to herself or flip through a magazine with her good arm until I decided to climb out of bed so we could start the day.

By the time I stood in her bedroom doorway I already knew. I pulled the covers back and touched her face. I did not have to check her pulse to know she was gone. I had seen it before; I knew what it looked like. I pulled up a chair and sat next to her bed to wait. I didn't want any overeager paramedics crashing in to try and revive her. For an hour I sat with her and looked at the window where frost grew like the pale imprints of fossilized ferns.

The next night I spent at the church for Rosa's funeral vigil; she lay in her casket in the flickering candle-glow and Father Grinev led us through the psalms and songs and prayers.

> *What earthly sweetness remains unmixed with grief?*
> *What glory stands immutable on the earth?*
> *All things are but feeble shadows, all things are*
> *most deluding dreams, yet one moment only,*
> *and death shall supplant them all.*

When it was over, when we had all passed by to give our final kiss, Father Grinev, a big, bearded man who makes me think of Attila the Hun, stopped me in the vestibule. He had just spent an entire night leading dire chants of the deepest gravity and gloom and he was smiling. He clapped a thick hand on my back and said, "I hope this doesn't mean you're going to stop coming to church!" Then he wrestled me into a bear hug that nearly cracked my spine. A day later, in the middle of a snowstorm, under two barren birch trees, we put Rosa into the ground next to her husband.

For three days I have been knocking around this suddenly too-large house, trying to get everything cleaned and ready before I go. I'm moving in with Mitzi and her two boys, who live in Bloomsburg, a couple of towns over. Our plan is to eventually get married, and it is only hitting me now that I am going to be, by all accounts, a father. A father to two little boys whose typical morning consists of tearing a phone book into confetti and flushing various household items down the toilet until it clogs. Their names are Dale and Ronny, ages three and five. I am not too embarrassed to say I am mortally afraid.

I have swept and mopped and waxed all the floors, covered the furniture, scrubbed the bathroom, emptied and defrosted the refrigerator, turned the mattresses, carefully packed up Rosa's things for storage, drained the pipes, shut off the power, tossed out garbage bags full of food and medicines and vitamins and old bills and statements and receipts. Mitzi stopped to help a couple of nights after her shift at the county courthouse and Mrs. McPherson has been strong-arming the neighbors and church ladies into bringing casseroles, of which there are seventeen, stacked into mini-pyramids on the kitchen counter.

Now that I have pulled down all the shades and switched off the furnace, the house is dim and cool and quiet as a tomb. Outside it's a clear day, a bleached winter sun glittering on the hard crust of snow and burning inside each icicle like a flame. I am sitting at my desk in the dark, wondering what to do with all of these pages, bundled and stacked and useless, my zigzag life accumulated on paper. I have considered lugging it all with me wherever I go, every misspelled word and throwaway moment, every detail and passing observation, every line of senseless finger-talk, but it has long since outgrown my steamer trunk and would take a rental truck and a dolly and a couple of strapping men to haul it the twenty miles to Mitzi's apartment, where there would be no place to put it. I have even entertained dramatic thoughts of dragging it out back and torching it with lighter fluid, making a bonfire that would raise a flood of melted snow, or waiting for a blustery day to release it into the wind, page after page, like a flock of pigeons. But I think I will leave it where it is. For me it will be a comfort to know that it is all here, written down, just in case.

I'm supposed to meet Mitzi at Klutsner's Deli for lunch to celebrate this new stage in our relationship, and I have a little time, so I roll a clean sheet into my typewriter and let my fingers have their way. In awhile, after I have added a few more inconsequential words and pages to this sprawling pile, I will put on my coat, pick up my Hermes Jubilee, lock the doors behind me, and emerge from the shadows of this house into the bright day, blinking and holding my hand to the sky, amazed at the light, like a man raised from the dead.